Remember Me, Cowboy

RACHAEL JOHNS
ALISSA CALLEN
MELISSA MCCLONE
MEGAN CRANE

TULE
PUBLISHING

CONTENTS

Tease Me, Cowboy   1

Cherish Me, Cowboy   115

Kiss Me, Cowboy   255

Please Me, Cowboy   397

Tease Me, Cowboy

A Montana Born Rodeo Novella

Rachael Johns

DEDICATION

For Jane Porter—a truly inspirational woman and writer, thanks for inviting me to be part of Montana Born Books. And to Alissa, Megan and Melissa, who were such fun and so easy to work with on the 76th Copper Mountain Rodeo novellas. Love you all!

READERS LETTER

When Jane Porter emailed and asked if I'd like to write a rodeo story for Montana Born Books, I was so excited. I read the first rodeo series (75th Copper Mountain Rodeo) last year when it first came out and fell in love with small-town Marietta. Since then I've devoured as many of the novellas set in Marietta as I can, many written by authors I've admired for years. So it's a privilege to find my own home in Marietta and bring you my first Montana Born story—TEASE ME, COWBOY.

As with most stories, the seeds of this one have been germinating in my mind for a while now, waiting for the perfect moment. It mostly started with a conversation on Twitter where one author said she would like to tell her younger self to enjoy herself more and experiment with more men. As I'm a sucker for first-love stories, I thought about giving my heroine this regret also. And thus, Selah Davis, the "good" daughter of the church minister in Marietta, was born.

I had such fun writing this novella (in which Selah and her first-love cowboy, Levi Monroe, return to Marietta for the rodeo, and Selah's best friends dare her to proposition him), and I hope you'll enjoy reading it just as much! Do let me know what you think on Twitter or Facebook.

Happy reading,
Rach!

Chapter One

A S MUCH AS Selah Davis loved her life in Seattle, she got an all-over buzz every time she came home to Old Town Marietta. No one could say it was the cocktail of dirt, dung and dust that perpetually lingered in the air, but there was just something about the place.

And, although this would be a fleeting visit—four days in town to cover the 76th Annual Copper Mountain Rodeo for the magazine she wrote for—there were certain things Selah would make the time for. A visit to her folks—obligatory and, thankfully, already ticked off the list. A burger at the Main St. Diner—they were like none other in the whole of the United States—and a drink at Grey's Saloon with her gal pals.

That was the one bad thing about moving away. Although she came back for engagements, weddings, babies and the like, not always in that order, mind you, she missed having her best friends around on a day-to-day basis. The friends she'd made in Seattle were mostly through the magazine, and yes, they did hang out outside of work, but if she were honest, they were really only acquaintances. Not people she'd share her deepest, darkest and occasionally dirty secrets with. Not friends with whom she could belly laugh or ugly cry, like Sage, Chelsea and Jenny.

It had been over eight months since she'd last seen them,

which was why Selah was like a child counting down to Santa as she hung at the bar in Grey's Saloon waiting for her friends to arrive.

"Hey, long time no see."

Selah smiled at Reese Kendrick, one of the bartenders at Grey's and an old acquaintance. "Hi, Reese. How you doing?"

"You know…same old, same old. Can I get you a drink?"

She shook her head and glanced back toward the entrance. "I think I'll wait for the girls."

Reese shrugged. "Suit yourself." He then turned to attend to the cowboys lined up along the other end of the bar.

Due to the influx of outsiders to Marietta for the rodeo, Grey's was busier than usual. Selah had already been approached by half a dozen, quite good-looking—but also quite tipsy—men, so she kept her head down now, hoping to fly under the radar until her friends arrived. Cowboys had a reputation, and one-night stands were not her thing. Besides, her priorities for the next few days were catching up with her friends and writing her story. Her interest in hot cowboys was purely professional.

Chelsea showed first, looking almost like another person as she waltzed up to the bar to join Selah. She no longer looked like the high school history teacher she was—gone were the conservative clothes she'd always worn, replaced by a flirty skirt, funky knee-high boots and a figure-hugging shirt.

"You look awesome," Selah told her friend, smiling in approval as she gave her the once-over.

Chelsea beamed in reply, her whole face glowing, and Selah guessed her guy, Jasper Flint, could take responsibility for this new woman. She'd met him briefly at Colton and Jenny's wedding last Christmas, but couldn't wait to get to know him better. "You don't look so bad yourself," Chelsea said. "It's so good to see you."

They were in the middle of a crazy reunion hug when Selah

felt a tap on her shoulder and turned to see Sage and Jenny standing behind them. Girly shrieks ensued as the four of them danced around in a group hug, uncaring about what anyone thought. When they broke away, Selah took a moment to scrutinize Jenny, who'd recently announced she and Colton were expecting their first baby.

"Oh, my, we're all growing up," she said, beaming at her friend. "It's true what they say about the pregnancy glow."

In reply, Jenny placed a hand on her barely visible bump, but she didn't say anything. She didn't need to. Her grin looked too big for her face, and she radiated bliss from her sparkling eyes. Selah felt her own eyes prickling. Last year, when Jenny's longtime boyfriend and boss, Charles Monmouth, had called off their wedding, they'd all been devastated for her, but Colton was so much better for Jenny, so everything had worked out well in the end.

"I'm so happy for you," Selah said, as she wrapped her friend in an extra hug. "I want to hear all the news. From all of you."

All agreed this was a delightful plan, so they ordered a round of Cosmos (a mocktail for Jenny) from grumpy Grey himself and took their drinks to a table in the far corner of the establishment, where they hopefully wouldn't be bothered by amorous cowboys.

In unison, all four women took a sip of their bright pink cocktails and sighed their contentment.

"So, when do we start bridesmaid-dress shopping?" Selah asked.

Her friends looked at her curiously.

"Well"—she shrugged with a smile—"won't Jasper be popping the question soon?"

Chelsea's face turned a sweet red as she took a quick sip of her Cosmo, then said, "He may have dropped a couple of hints."

Excited discussion ensued about other upcoming nuptials and babies in Marietta. Selah could be forgiven for thinking there was something in the water, for it seemed every second person she knew had either recently fallen in love, was getting married or was pregnant. It wasn't that she was envious—she didn't think so, anyway—but such talk got a little bland when you had nothing to add yourself, so she was happy when Sage changed the subject.

"So, what about this year's honorary chair?" Sage all but drooled the question.

Now that was something, or rather someone, Selah could get excited about. "I know," she said smugly. "I've got an exclusive interview with him on Saturday."

Her friends glared good-naturedly at her.

"Seriously? You suck." Sage had always been a huge country music fan, and this year's rodeo chair, Jake Kohl, had been the star of many of her fantasies. Despite Dawson now having the starring role, she still held a candle for her celebrity crush.

"Do you need an assistant?" Jenny offered. "I'd be happy to volunteer."

Sage sighed. "And people think making chocolate for a living is glamorous, but it's got nothing on the perks of your job."

Selah laughed, but inwardly felt a little irritated. Her friends thought her job as features editor for *Charisma* fascinating and always liked listening to her tales of meeting celebrities at film premieres and fashion shows. *Charisma* was constantly inundated with samples of makeup, perfumes and the like, and occasionally Selah would send some of these to her friends.

She got the feeling they thought her job was one big party, but it wasn't always as exciting or as satisfying as they imagined. Serious journalists didn't receive handbags in exchange for the promise to write about them in a favorable light, and that's what she'd always wanted to be. A serious journalist.

"I thought you were here to write an article on the hotness of cowboys," Chelsea said, fanning her face a little.

"That, too," Selah said, trying to shake off her annoyance and simply enjoy being with her friends. "What can I say? It's a tough job, but someone has to do it."

"We'd be happy to help you with your research," Chelsea said with a naughty giggle.

"Yes," Jenny nodded, trying and failing dismally to keep a straight face. "Sage and I are particularly knowledgeable in that subject."

Selah couldn't help laughing alongside her friends. "Rodeo fever got you all good and proper last year, didn't it?"

"Sure did," said Jenny unashamedly. "In fact, if you wanted, I could get Colton to introduce you to some guys you could interview."

"And although Dawson isn't on the circuit anymore, he could assist you as well. You'd be hard-pressed to find cowboys hotter than ours," added Sage.

Selah rolled her eyes and shook her head. "You guys may be a little biased. Besides, I think *Charisma*'s readers would prefer single, *available* cowboys. Ones they can fantasize about seducing and luring into their webs."

"Fair enough." Jenny shrugged and gestured to Sage and Chelsea. "But if you want to write an article on how to tame a cowboy, we are your girls."

"Thanks." Selah took another sip of her drink and then said, "You know, not all the articles I write are so superficial. I've actually just finished a very interesting story about the regrets of the dying." She didn't add that it was languishing on her computer because her chief editor had told her it wasn't the kind of thing *Charisma* readers would be interested in.

Sage raised an eyebrow, Chelsea screwed up her nose and

Jenny said, "What? Who wants to read about that?"

Selah laughed. Maybe her editor had a point. "It isn't as depressing as it sounds. I interviewed some really inspirational people who've done some amazing things in their lives but are now terminally ill. I asked them what their one regret in life is. You know, what thing they would do or change if they could."

Selah spent the next little while telling her friends about the subjects of her story. They ordered another round of drinks and some onion rings to share, and as the liquid went down, conversation turned to the things the four of them regretted in their lives.

"That's easy," Chelsea said, scooping up an onion ring. "I regret ever dating that cheating scumbag Tod Styles."

As she popped the snack into her mouth, her three friends made sympathetic noises, all of them glad Chelsea had found someone who deserved her so much more than the local real estate sleaze agent.

Sage sighed. "I guess I regret sleeping with Dawson while he was married to someone else."

"You didn't know he was married," Chelsea said, her tone protective. "And anyway, it all turned out well in the end."

A smile burst on Sage's face. "Yes, it certainly did, and I definitely don't regret anything else when it comes to him."

Sage's happiness made Selah all warm and tingly inside. Her girls had done good when it came to their men.

Then it was Jenny's turn. She rubbed her lips together, taking a little longer over her answer than the others. "I'm not sure I regret working for Charles, because I learned a lot in that role, but I do regret squashing myself and trying to be less so that he looked good."

All four of them took sips of their Cosmos and a few moments for contemplation, but before too long Sage broke the silence.

"What about you, Selah?" she asked. "What do you regret?"

With three pairs of eyes trained on her, Selah racked her brain for something more significant than scarfing a whole bar of chocolate last night. Fact was, she mostly liked her life. Despite wishing she could sometimes write something with a little more substance, she enjoyed her job and liked the people she worked with. She had an apartment she loved, great clothes, great hair and fab friends. Sage, Chelsea and Jenny had all found Mr. Right, and she was stoked for them, but she didn't feel a desperate urge to settle down herself. She didn't see how she'd fit a permanent man in her busy work schedule. She'd had a couple of relationships—if you could call them that—with nice enough men, but the spark hadn't been there and, in the end, they'd both been more career-oriented than love-oriented.

However, if she had the chance for a do-over, there was one thing she would change. Her cheeks flushed at the thought, which although she'd contemplated many times in the last decade, she'd never voiced to anyone.

"What is it?" Sage demanded, not missing a beat.

"It's nothing. You'll all think it's totally silly."

"No, we won't." Chelsea sounded indignant.

"Promise," said Sage.

"Come on, spill," pleaded Jenny.

Selah sighed, trying to hide the grin that stretched upon her face at the thought of Levi Monroe, her first-ever serious boyfriend and, as far as she was concerned, the hottest guy to have ever graced the halls of Marietta High School. She leaned forward, about to whisper her confession, when the doors to Grey's opened, and she saw the man who had starred in many a torrid fantasy of hers stride into the saloon like he owned the joint. Startled, Selah jolted upright, knocking over her cocktail tumbler in the process.

Thankfully she'd already drunk most of it.

Jenny uprighted the glass, and Chelsea grabbed a stash of tissues from her bag and started mopping up the mess, but Sage followed Selah's gaze.

"Surprise! Didn't you know Levi was in town for the rodeo?"

"No." Selah gulped, heat flooding her body as she snapped her mouth shut and turned her head away before Levi noticed her. It wasn't like they'd have anything to say to each other after all these years.

"Oh, yeah," Chelsea said, catching on. "And rumor has it he might stay longer and help out a bit on the McCullough spread."

Barely taking in her friend's words, Selah fought the urge to turn and take another good look at her only regret. Her throat felt tight, her knees quivering and her heart racing so damn fast she'd be surprised if her friends couldn't hear it.

"Do you want me to call him over?" Jenny asked.

"No!" Selah covered her mouth the moment the word was out, thankful the noise around them drowned her shout. "No," she repeated quietly. It was simply the shock of seeing him just as she was about to say his name that had thrown her off-balance. She just needed a moment to pull herself together.

"Okay, relax." Jenny put her hand over the top of Selah's in a gesture of comfort. "Forget about Levi. This is a girls' night, and you were about to tell us your one regret."

"It's him." Her confession slipped out before she could think.

Her friends frowned.

"What do you mean?" asked Sage.

Selah took a deep breath and glanced at each woman staring intently at her. She tried to pretend Levi wasn't across the room, doing who knows what and talking to whoever. She forced a laugh, feigning nonchalance, and shrugged. "I wish I'd given him my virginity. That's all."

And then she grabbed Sage's half-full glass and downed the lot in a few seconds.

LEVI HAD JUST sat down at the bar with a bunch of cowboys he knew from the circuit and raised his glass to take the first mouthful of his beer when he heard hysterical giggles coming from a small group of women sitting at a table in the corner. Like almost everyone else, he turned his head to see what the commotion was about, and his heart jammed up into his throat as he recognized the perpetrators of the noise.

His drink spilled over his fingers, and he couldn't help but stare at the beautiful group of women. He'd gone to school with all of them, but one in particular had left an imprint on his life. During what had been one of the worst years of his life, Selah Davis had made him feel at home in Marietta. Almost from the moment he'd walked into Marietta High—pretending to be all cool and unaffected but secretly shitting his pants—she'd been his girl. Hanging out with Selah—talking to her, doing homework together, kissing like crazy teenagers do—had helped ease his worries about his sick mom. Selah had made being away from everything he'd known bearable, and he'd fallen head over heels in love.

Without Selah giving him a reason to get up in the morning and Em McCullough fussing over him, who knows what would have become of him that year?

Unashamed, his pulse finally slowing, he took a drag of his beer and stared over to where she sat with Sage, Chelsea and Jenny. The men around him went back to their conversations, but no way could he concentrate on their mindless chatter. Sage caught his gaze, leaned forward and said something to the others. Chelsea's and Jenny's heads snapped around to look at him, and he offered them a casual wave, all the while willing

Selah to turn a little. Her three friends giggled and waved back at him, but Selah appeared frozen.

Even from the side, her dark-chocolate hair falling like a veil across her face, she was still the best-looking woman he'd ever laid eyes on. And that was saying something. Since leaving Marietta and being on the road with the rodeo, he'd seen a lot of women. Not one had ever made the organs in his chest reverberate and his cock harden simply by thinking of them. Not the way Selah did.

This time, when he lifted the bottle to his mouth, he downed half its contents. He returned to Marietta every couple of years to visit Em or Cole, and he'd done the Copper Mountain Rodeo a few times as well. He'd run into Sage, Chelsea and Jenny at least once during these visits, but he'd never crossed paths with Selah. As far as he knew, this was the first time she'd ever bothered to leave her comfortable city existence for the rodeo.

He guessed dirt, horses and sweaty men just weren't her thing.

But people in small towns talked. And he may have cocked an ear to listen on the occasions he'd heard the name "Selah Davis" in conversation. According to local gossip, she was some hotshot journalist in Seattle, and didn't she just look the part? Her friends all wore dark, denim jeans, casual sweaters and cowboy boots, but Selah looked as if she'd stepped right off a Paris catwalk. Her smart jacket and tailored trousers were far too fancy for his liking, so why were his palms sweating and his heart racing at the thought of going over and saying hi? At the thought of sliding his hands into her salon-perfect hair and ruffling it up a little.

Unfinished business maybe? He downed the dregs of his beer and raised a finger to the barman. "Can I grab another?"

Within a few seconds, Reese had dropped a bottle down in

front of him, and Levi had handed over some cash. He glanced back at Selah's table. The women looked to be in deep conversation now, and he wondered about the topic of conversation. Could they be talking about him? He swallowed, his mind once again rewinding to the best and worst year of his life.

He and Selah had gone to the prom together. She'd worn this hotter-than-sin pink dress—Lord knew how she'd managed to get her dad's approval for that little number—and he'd bought her a corsage to match. Em had taken him to Married in Marietta and rented him a tux, insisting that Selah deserved a little effort on his part. He'd felt like some kind of fraud tugging that swanky jacket over his shoulders, but the moment he'd laid eyes on Selah, he'd decided he'd wear black tie every day for the rest of his life if it meant having her.

They'd been crowned prom king and prom queen, and twirling her in his arms around the dance floor had felt so good. He'd been filled with pride, lust and love, or at least, he'd thought that's what it was. Looking back now, he guessed it was more likely a case of rampant hormones.

But hormones, love, whatever it had been, he'd felt certain he'd get lucky at the after party. He'd bought the condoms and rented a cute little log cabin from a rancher who kept to himself and didn't ask questions. Although he'd never had an example of romance in his life, he'd done his damn best. There had been candles, flowers and chocolates, even some cheap champagne. Yet, still she'd resisted.

Back then, he'd thought Selah Davis was a cockteaser. She'd professed to love him, kissed him like a harlot, let him feel her up and suck her nipples (through her bra, mind you). She'd even given him a hand job, but she'd never let him go below her belt. Her excuse? She was saving herself for marriage.

Since marriage hadn't been on his agenda in the near future, and he had been a horny-as-hell seventeen-year-old boy, they'd broken up. He'd left school and headed back home to his sick mom.

Levi's grip tightened around his bottle, the frustration he'd felt so strongly back then rearing its ugly head. He'd regretted dumping her almost the moment he'd done so, but really, could she have expected him to wait indefinitely? He'd had nothing to offer a wife, and no way would he have let her end up like his mom, living in a broken trailer and having to clean and cook for other people because his no-hoper of a dad couldn't provide.

He sighed. The depressing thoughts had put him in a melancholic mood, and he found he didn't care for the company of cowboys right now. What he really wanted was to go over and talk to Selah, but she seemed intent on not looking his way. Taking one final mouthful of beer, he set his still nearly full bottle on the bar and slipped quietly away from the mates he'd arrived with.

A quiet night in his trailer wasn't a bad idea anyway, far more sensible a plan than staying in Grey's and getting sloshed before the weekend had even started. This was going to be his last rodeo, and he wanted to go out on a high. The last thing he needed was a distraction, especially not in the form of Selah Davis. Still, something niggled at him, and he found he couldn't leave the saloon without at least walking past her.

He took a detour to the exit, winding through tables and trying not to catch the eye of anyone he might know, until he came up alongside Selah's table. As his shadow fell over their drinks, all eyes glanced up. Even Selah couldn't pretend he didn't exist when he was standing right beside her. And as her eyes met with his, something shifted inside him. It'd been a long while since he'd felt a jolt of awareness upon seeing someone, but seeing Selah up close again felt as if he'd just crashed into an electric fence.

He did his damn best to hide his reaction and went for nonchalance as he smiled down at the group. "Hey, ladies. Selah."

Sage, Chelsea and Jenny all tossed him friendly smiles and chirpy "hi's," but Selah simply stared at him as if he were a ghost risen from the dead. Finally, when things started getting awkward, he dipped his head and continued on toward the door, feeling all kinds of stupid for thinking that, after all these years, she might actually have anything to say to him.

SELAH. THE WAY Levi had singled her out, the way he'd drawled her name in his still-delicious voice, had her insides twisting, right along with her tongue. Something in her brain registered that it was the done thing to reply, but her dry mouth just couldn't. She seemed incapable of doing anything but stare. So…it was still there…that incomparable crackle between them. That knock-your-socks-off, toe-curling lust. An attraction stronger than she'd ever felt for anyone else.

She suspected that her friends had returned his greeting with suitable ones of their own, but before she could pull her bamboozled self together, he'd dipped his head as if he wore his cowboy hat and was walking out the door.

Too late, her breath returned to her lungs, and she slumped against the back of the booth as the door to Grey's swung closed behind Levi. Sage, Chelsea and Jenny erupted into hysterics for the second time that evening.

"It's not funny," Selah hissed, suddenly struggling to remember why she'd been so excited about seeing them.

They made half-hearted attempts to smother their giggles, and then Chelsea said, "Oh, Selah, we're sorry, but it is."

"How apt that the moment you were about to admit your sordid regrets regarding him, he should walk in the door," Jenny added, helping Chelsea's her argument.

"A sign, I'd say." Sage nodded, pretending to be all serious.

Selah glared harder, trying hopelessly to forget how incredible Levi still looked and focus all her energies on being irritated with her friends instead. She made a tsking noise. "I don't believe in signs, and if I'd known how childish your reactions would be, I'd never have said a word."

Immediately, all three of her friends looked remorseful.

"We're sorry," said Chelsea, reaching out to take Selah's shaky hand.

"It just shocked us, is all." Jenny frowned. "We're your closest friends, and I don't know about Sage and Chels, but I thought you *did* sleep with Levi. The two of you were practically Siamese twins during senior year."

Sage nodded. "I would have sworn you admitted to much horizontal mambo with the Leve-star. We were all bursting with envy, if I recall. None of us had much luck with boys in high school, so we lived vicariously through you."

Selah looked down at the table, picked up the soggy cardboard drink coaster and started picking at the edges. Truth was, she'd never actually told anyone she'd slept with Levi, but she'd let her friends, and his, draw this natural conclusion. And, damn it, she'd wanted to make love with Levi more than she'd wanted to graduate high school with good grades so she could pursue a career in journalism, but she'd been scared.

"Oh, yeah." Chelsea sighed. "I don't think there was a girl in our class who didn't fantasize about Levi Monroe."

A sad truth that only amplified Selah's regret. She'd had that opportunity and she'd let it pass her by.

How many times had she almost given in to the lust that had raged between them? It hadn't been easy saying no to that face, not with his hands roving over her body as he told her how much he loved her, begging her to go the whole way, but every time she'd almost relented, she'd had a visit from her parents. Metaphorically, of course. Back then, she wouldn't have even held Levi's hand if her mom or dad had been within a mile. They'd heard rumors of course, but she'd always placated them with the sweet words of a good daughter. The good daughter. As far as her parents had known, she and Levi had just been friends, Selah doing her best to help him settle into Marietta and not miss his mom too much. As the minister of St. James Methodist Church, Jonathan Davis could hardly have asked his daughter to give up that charitable duty, but Selah had known she and Levi had to be careful.

The consequences of what could have happened if they weren't had been paraded in front of her face by her sister. The fallen daughter.

"It was all Magdalena's fault," she admitted, sounding far more vicious than she'd intended.

Her friends caught on immediately, aahing and nodding their understanding.

"How is Magdalena these days?" Jenny asked, and Selah grabbed on to the slight change in conversation.

She smiled. "She's good. She's started her own social media business and is doing really well for herself."

"That's great," Sage said, and the other two nodded their agreement. "Is she dating anyone?"

Since their own hookups at last year's rodeo, her best friends were almost fixated on the dating habits of those around them. It was like once they were happily paired, they saw it as some kind of duty to help Cupid with his aim. Oh, well, talking about her sister's love life was better than the alternative.

"Nothing serious. Her focus has always been Bella, but with Bella in high school now, I think Mags is considering getting more proactive in that department. Last time we talked, she mentioned signing up for Match.com."

That may have been a slight exaggeration, but Selah thought if she distracted her friends, they might forget about what had started this conversation.

No. Such. Luck.

"Cool, but back to Levi." Chelsea's eyes glistened in the way of someone who had recently been laid good and proper, someone who felt happy and smug with her place in the world. "If he is truly your one regret…you need to do something about it!"

Chapter Two

IN THEORY, A girl should get a fabulous night's sleep in the newly renovated, historic Graff Hotel. Its luxury was one of the many reasons Selah had decided to stay there rather than in her cramped old bedroom at her parents' place. She'd given them the excuse that as the magazine was paying, she might as well live it up, but now she regretted her decision. If she had been sleeping under her parents' roof, she could pretty much guarantee she wouldn't be having the torrid fantasies that plagued her now. Whichever way she turned, her head—too full of thoughts of Levi—refused to switch off and sleep.

She groaned and rolled over for the zillionth time since crawling into bed, hugging a fat pillow against her as she once again relived the conversation she'd had with her friends after her confession. Could she really do what Chelsea had suggested? Should she even contemplate it? Sage and Jenny had been equally as enthusiastic about Chelsea's idea, and now Selah was lying here in the dark, in a plush bed far too big for one person, and she couldn't stop her mind heading down that path.

Actually, sprinting would be the more accurate term.

"Levi Monroe!" As she said that scrumptious name out loud, heat kicked through her, making her body feel boneless.

She hadn't been entirely honest with her friends. Oh, the bit about him being her only regret was one hundred percent correct, but she hadn't told them the whole, depressing story. That although she'd slept with a few men, the only time she'd ever managed to achieve an actual orgasm was when she closed her eyes and thought of Levi.

She did so now, a smile spreading across her face and her lady bits standing to attention at the recollection of Levi pausing briefly at the entrance of Grey's as he surveyed the crowd. It was like her thoughts had conjured him up, and the reality of him trumped her memories and fantasies tenfold. He'd always been hot, but his years on the rodeo circuit and working the land had created the type of male spectacular that defied odds. Anyone who cared to look at him in his Wranglers and a Western shirt— and she bet lots of women did—could see that Muscles should be his middle name. His face had lost its boyish charm, and in its place was a strong jawline, serious eyes and a delicious spattering of stubble that made him look intense and a little dangerous.

Selah liked it, and she was pretty sure there was a law against looking that fine, especially if you were a redhead, as Levi was. She bit her lip, groaned again and glanced at the time on the digital alarm clock beside her bed.

Was two a.m. too late, or early, to go knocking on his trailer door?

Once she'd promised to give Chelsea's idea serious thought, Selah's friends had gone out of their way to help her find out everything she needed to know about her high school sweetheart. They'd made phone calls, checked Facebook and asked a couple of cowboys drinking at the bar a few pertinent questions. If they hadn't been so competent at their respective careers, they could possibly have made good journalists. Or private investigators.

By the time the closing bell had been rung at Grey's and the four of them had stumbled out onto the pavement, Selah knew this much: Levi hadn't properly dated anyone in years—thus, he was available; he worked for a rancher in Tulsa when he wasn't competing; apparently, he also knew his way around the stock market but had chosen to stay in his trailer on the rodeo grounds rather than with Em McCullough or any of his other friends in town.

If Selah had been truly dedicated to her work, these facts would have stimulated more questions, but the only thing she could think about where Levi was concerned was getting him naked and rewriting the past. The more she thought about this crazy, ridiculous notion, the more it grew on her. Her pelvic floor clenched, and her whole body trembled with anticipation.

But did she really have such courage? And how the hell would she go about it? Maybe she should lay it on him straight? Walk right up to him and say, "Hey, Levi, you know how we used to have a thing together? You know how you begged and pleaded, but I would never let you go past second base? Well, do you want to go all the way now?"

Or she could get him drunk and seduce him. There were always plenty of opportunities at a rodeo for such debauchery, or so she'd heard. Then again, Levi being inebriated might affect his performance—both in the rodeo and in the sack—and she didn't want either of those calamities.

Sometime between two and three, Selah fell into a restless sleep. Unsurprisingly, her dreams didn't bring a reprieve from thoughts of Levi. And by the time her alarm woke her a few hours later, she was hot, sweaty and possibly more turned on than she'd ever been in her life.

What she needed was a cold shower and a big bag of Sage's chocolates. Although, didn't chocolate contain the same chemical that was released in the brain when you fell in love? She didn't need that. Too busy with work, she wasn't in the market for love, but she had to admit she was in the market for

Levi. The article she needed to write would be the perfect ruse to approach him, and that opportunity was too good to refuse.

What happened after that? Well, she'd just have to see how receptive he was to her proposition.

THE LAST PERSON Levi expected to see while tending his horse, Ry, on Friday morning was the delectable Selah Davis. She'd been with him in his head all damn night as he'd tossed and turned in his bunk. He'd hoped to get another glimpse before the weekend was over, but he hadn't expected her to seek him out. Especially not here at the rodeo grounds on the outskirts of Marietta, where only those readying themselves for the weekend hung out.

The way she walked toward him now, her feminine hips swishing from side to side and her head held high, made her look purposeful, as well as her usual sexy. It made him curious.

He checked to make sure Ry's halter was hooked to the rope, crossed his arms and leaned back against the wall of the gooseneck trailer as she came to a stop a couple of yards in front of him.

"Hey." He gave her an unashamed once-over, happy to find her looking less citified than the night before. She should wear jeans more often, because they did so much more for her curves than the tailored stuff. Her fitted gray T-shirt left little to the imagination when it came to her breasts. And she smelled as if she'd just bathed in sugar.

"Hi, Levi."

At her husky greeting, he snapped this head back to her face and almost stumbled sideways when her smile hit him. It was warm, sweet and seductive and could still stop his heart. No matter how many miles or years had passed between them, standing so close to Selah now proved one thing: There was still something between them. The sudden tightness of his jeans only enhanced this theory.

"We didn't get the chance to talk at Grey's," she said, flicking her long, brown hair over one shoulder.

He bit down on asking whose fault that was.

"I admit to being a little bewildered at seeing you again," she said, "but I couldn't stop thinking about you last night.'

Levi raised an eyebrow, a little surprised—and, if he were honest, pleased—by her confession. It was nice to know he hadn't been the only one losing sleep.

Although he generally knew exactly what to say to women, his tongue failed him now. As he racked his brain for a reply to Selah's words, his gaze fell on her ring finger, and he couldn't help the jolt of joy inside him at the lack of any marital bling. He guessed he'd have heard on the Copper Mountain grapevine if she'd tied the knot. Em or Cole would have been sure to slip it into conversation. But just because she didn't wear a ring didn't mean she didn't have a significant other.

He wondered if she was still a virgin. Almost as soon as this thought landed, he dismissed it. No way she could have made it to thirty with her hymen still intact. Some lucky bastard would have worn her down. Levi's chest burned at the unfairness of that.

"Anyway"—she smiled, her cheeks flushed ever-so-slightly—"I'm writing an article on cowboys and the rodeo for the magazine I work for, and I was wondering if you'd give me an interview."

His heart sank. What had he expected? She'd come to seduce him? He chuckled at his stupidity.

"What? What's so funny?" Selah glanced behind them, as if looking for the source of his amusement. But all she would see was typical rodeo grounds—the yards, the chutes, the bleachers, bathroom blocks, canteens, sheds and the goosenecks of the competitors who'd already arrived—and Copper Mountain standing all tall and impressive behind everything. Even if he didn't have a history in Marietta, the Copper Mountain Rodeo would have been his favorite place to compete.

"Nothing." *Absolutely nothing.* And then, when he should have told her he'd be too busy competing and also pursuing the possibility of leasing land from Sam McCullough, he asked, "What exactly would this interview entail?"

He saw her swallow, adjust the bag on her shoulder and then slip her hand up to her hair, where she twisted chocolate-colored strands around her fingers in a way that always used to drive him insane. "A couple of questions. It wouldn't take long. Maybe an hour? Half an hour?"

"I've got plans today, and I'm competing tomorrow and hopefully Sunday, but if you want to take a drive with me out to the McCulloughs' place, I'll answer the best I can."

"Now?" Her eyes widened.

"It's the only window I've got." And call him childish, but it felt good to be the one calling the shots for a change.

"I'll take it."

SELAH SETTLED INTO the passenger seat of Levi's truck, her heart pounding and her hands sweaty as she fumbled to shove her seat belt into place. What game was she playing? He slammed the door shut for her, and she watched as he swaggered around the front of his truck, tipping his hat at a couple of cowboys and cowgirls who happened to be passing. The smile he tossed their way was easy and carefree, totally the opposite of the way he looked at her.

The driver's door opened, he climbed up into the seat beside her, and her heart stilled, yet her breathing sped up. Her eyes snapped to his strong thighs sitting only inches from hers, and she wondered how on earth she'd survive the fifteen-minute journey to the McCullough ranch in such close proximity to all that delicious masculinity.

"So," he said, not even glancing at her as he started the engine, "hit me with them."

"With what?" He had really nice hands, and her imagination fantasized about them being on her again, making it almost impossible to think about anything else. Her gaze traveled up his strong forearms to his impressive biceps and shoulders, and she bit her lip to stop from whimpering.

"The questions." Levi's sharp answer snapped her from her lusty-trance, and their eyes met as she looked up. Despite the frown that creased his brow, she swore there was heat in his gaze, too.

"Oh, right." Selah shifted in her seat as the truck crunched over the dirt tracks of the rodeo grounds, Levi navigating between the buildings, trailers and people setting up camp as they headed for the exit. Right, *questions*... As a journalist for more than ten years, questions generally came easily for her, but right now, her mind was blank.

"How long have you been on the rodeo circuit?" It was a lame question, one she could have answered herself with the help of her faithful friend Google, but Levi appeared satisfied.

"I started pretty much out of high school, so about twelve years, I guess. I won a place in a rodeo school back home and found I wasn't half-bad at it. The thrill of riding a bull, of battling such a massive beast and conquering, gave me a feeling like none other. I won the first contest I entered, and although the prize money wasn't huge, I decided it was something I could do to help Mom out. I—"

He'd been on a roll, but he broke off now as if he'd said more than he meant to. "How is your mother?" she asked.

"I thought this article was about cowboys."

"It is, I just…"

"Mom died a couple of years back," he provided with a sigh, the defensiveness gone from his voice.

"I'm so sorry to hear that." She resisted the urge to reach out and touch him. Aside from the McCulloughs, who were distantly related to Levi, his mom had been his whole family. His dad had died of a drug overdose long before Levi had been sent to Marietta, before he'd even met Selah, and he'd never spoken highly of him.

Levi shrugged. "It was probably for the best. The first stroke changed her, left her incapable of doing many of the things she loved, and if the second one hadn't killed her, she'd likely have ended up a vegetable in some awful institution. She would have hated that."

Although Levi said all this in a matter-of-fact tone, Selah detected the tiny wavering in his voice, and her heart went out to this big, strong and highly capable man. Her family might drive her crazy half the time, but at least they meant well. She blinked back tears, guessing Levi wouldn't appreciate her sympathy.

He turned right toward the center of town, and before Selah could come up with another question, he said, "I've just got to stop and grab something for Em."

"Okay." She smiled, nodded and then glanced out the window. It was far safer watching Marietta prepare for the busy rodeo weekend than looking at him.

The stores that lined Main Street were all circa nineteenth century with classic Western shop fronts, but they went that extra mile for the rodeo, each of them decorating their windows with rodeo-themed displays. In the streets, workers were setting up barriers for the three blocks considered the heart of town, readying for the events that complemented the rodeo. Although Selah hadn't been home for the rodeo since moving away from Marietta, nothing much had changed from what she remembered from her childhood. Tonight, there'd be a welcome dinner in the park. Tomorrow morning would see a pancake breakfast and then a parade, before the rodeo events kicked off in the early afternoon.

Even if you weren't into sweaty men, horses and/or bucking bulls, there was something for everyone in Marietta during the Copper Mountain annual rodeo weekend, and she'd be sure to get this across in her article.

In the last year or so, her friend Sage's chocolate shop had become famous in Marietta and beyond, and knowing how much Levi adored Em McCullough, Selah assumed they'd be stopping there for one of Sage's unique creations. Instead, the star of her fantasies found a parking space outside a new addition to town—The Copper Mountain Gingerbread and Dessert Factory—and looked to her as he killed the ignition. This time she saw the hint of a smile, and her insides melted. Maybe her plan wasn't so farfetched after all.

"You wanna come in with me? If you haven't had breakfast yet, Rachel's pastries will hit the spot. She was just starting out selling gingerbread when I was back at Christmastime, and I've been dreaming of the way it melted in my mouth since."

Selah wasn't sure she had an appetite for anything but him, yet the way he spoke about Rachel's creations tempted her. Thankfully, she'd heard this Rachel person was married to rancher Nate Vaughn, or no doubt, Levi's raving words would have sparked jealousy.

"That sounds good," she said, unclipping her seat belt.

Heads in the street turned as she emerged from Levi's truck. She smiled at the busybodies and made a mental note to expect a phone call from her parents within the next few hours. Word traveled fast in a town the size of Marietta, but she couldn't help the kick she got at being seen with this man. She no longer cared what people said. In fact, she hoped to give them plenty to gossip about.

They stepped in time as they walked along the sidewalk to the store, and Selah found herself relaxing a little. "You come back to Marietta quite often, then?" she asked.

"A bit. Em's not getting any younger—not that I'd ever say that to her face—so I like to visit as much as I can."

"You're a good man, Levi Monroe."

He snorted at that and then pushed open the door of the store they'd just arrived at, holding it for Selah while she stepped inside. Living in Seattle, she'd be forgiven for thinking manners and chivalry were a thing of the past, but it looked like Levi still had them. Warm with this thought, she inhaled the tempting aroma of freshly baked sweetness. She didn't need to taste any of Rachel's creations to understand why Levi raved and half the town appeared to be waiting at the counter. They stood in line together, Selah's senses overloaded with the smells of the bakery and the press of Levi's arm against hers as they stood close. It felt surreal to be with him again.

When they finally got to the front, they were served by Rachel herself.

"Hi, Levi." Rachel smiled. "Great to see you back in town. Is it true this is your last rodeo?"

Selah's eyes widened as she looked to Levi for his reply. From the way he walked to the way he dressed to the way he talked and tipped his hat, he oozed cowboy.

"Pretty sure." Clearly not that comfortable with talking about himself, Levi pointed at a sign advertising a dessert box. "Can I grab one of them, and can I get a ribbon on it, please?"

"Of course." Rachel retrieved a cardboard cake box from a shelf behind her and began filling it with treats from the display cabinet. As she worked, she looked to Selah. "I don't think we've met yet. Are you a friend of Levi's?"

"Um…" Selah looked to Levi for direction.

"Selah is Pastor Davis's daughter. We went to school together, and she's back in town for the weekend to write an article about the rodeo."

Selah's heart squeezed. While Levi's description of their relationship was technically accurate, she had a desperate urge to tell Rachel and anyone else in hearing distance about their romantic history. Of course, she swallowed it and smiled at the bright and cheerful bakery owner. "Nice to meet you."

"And you, too." Rachel closed the box and expertly wrapped curling ribbon around it and formed a bow, all the while engaging in conversation. "Your father is a darling. He married Nate and I only a few months ago. It was such a beautiful service."

"I can imagine," Selah replied, visualizing the woman before her dressed all in white, looking like one of the meringues she baked, and glowing from head to foot.

Rachel handed the box to Levi. "Anything else?"

"Do you want anything?" Levi asked Selah.

She surveyed the choices in the glass display—everything from elaborate tortes and cheesecakes to crumbly pastries and even some fudge. In the end, she settled for a couple of gingerbread biscuits in the shape of cowboy boots, which seemed fitting for her company and her reason for being in Marietta. They even had "Copper Mountain Rodeo" scrawled in tiny iced writing across the top.

After paying for their purchases, Selah and Levi stepped back outside onto the street, which was even busier than it had been when they arrived. The air buzzed with the excitement of the rodeo, but miraculously they made it back to Levi's truck without running into anyone either of them knew.

"Do you mind holding this?" Levi asked, offering the box to her as they settled back in the truck.

"Of course not." Selah reached out to take it from him, her

breath hitching as her fingers brushed against his in the exchange. She squeezed her legs together as hot, liquid desire swept through her.

"Thanks." Levi's voice was low, and she saw him close his eyes briefly as he turned back to the wheel. Had he felt it, too? That explosion of something hot when they'd accidentally touched?

"Next question?" he asked as he started the truck.

Selah swallowed, still trying to recover from that teensy-weensy brush with him. "Um…Rachel mentioned this might be your last rodeo. Why?"

"I guess it's time to settle down, secure my future," he said.

"By settle down, you mean what exactly?" Selah's heart pounded. Was there a girlfriend waiting on the sidelines for this next stage in his life? The thought didn't bear thinking about, but logically she knew it was a likely possibility. Levi—with his good looks, hot body and impressive rodeo history—must have women beating down his door.

"You know…consolidate a few things, work out a solid career that doesn't push my body to extremes. I'm not getting any younger. I've had success on the rodeo circuit, but I can't go on forever."

She tried to focus on the last part of his sentence, not the reference to his body, though with his denim-clad thigh only inches from hers, that was pretty damn tricky. "That sounds sensible. And have you got any ideas about what you might do next?"

"Well, I already play the stock market, and I'm not too bad at that, but I can't turn my back completely on the rodeo. I'm hoping to open a school for teens wanting to learn cowboy sports."

"Wow. Where? Back in Tulsa?"

"No. My friend and mentor, Lane Burke, already has that

ground covered. I've done some work for him during the rodeo off-season, and he's got a good concept going on. I'd like to do something similar in Marietta."

A funny feeling squeezed her chest. "You're going to move back here?"

"That's the plan." He tapped his fingers on the steering wheel, his gaze on the road ahead as he drove. "I've been talking to Sam McCullough about leasing some land on his ranch."

"Wow," she said again, aware that for a journalist she should vary her vocabulary, but he sounded so grown-up, so together.

Levi glanced briefly at her. "Shouldn't you be taking notes or something?"

"I've got a really good memory." It was the truth, at least where Levi was concerned. Besides, she could write an article about cowboys and the Copper Mountain Rodeo with her eyes closed.

"I'd love to hear more about your rodeo school plans," she said, "but I suppose I should get some more info on the life of a cowboy. Can you tell me about the highs and lows of being on the circuit? What's it like living the rodeo? The good, the bad, the ugly."

Levi chuckled, a sound that reverberated right through her body. "Geez, where do I start? How long do you have?"

She wanted to tell him that where he was concerned she had all weekend, but decided to play it cool for now. "How long till the McCulloughs'?"

Chapter Three

A S LEVI TURNED his truck onto McCullough land, he gave himself a mental shake. The journey out here with Selah by his side had been far more enjoyable than he'd imagined. After the initial awkwardness between them, they'd slipped into easy conversation, and although he knew she was writing an article, she also seemed genuinely interested in what he'd done with his life and his plans for the future.

He had to keep a grip on reality and remember what they had together was in the past and, even if things hadn't ended the way they had, they would have eventually fizzled out in the way of most teenage romances. Undoubtedly, she still made him hot and hard with one glance, and when their fingers had brushed against each other as they'd exchanged the box, he'd almost combusted on the spot, but he needed more in a woman now than simple off-the-radar chemistry. Once upon a time, he'd slept with anyone he found attractive—as long as they both knew the score—but lately he wanted more in a hookup. He wanted someone who could make him laugh, provide stimulating conversation, and perhaps most important, someone he could imagine going the long haul with.

Selah checked the first three boxes, but their lives were so far removed now that anything vaguely resembling commitment would be impossible. It was hard to make babies with someone who lived in another state, and from the way people talked, he couldn't see her exchanging her high-flying city career for life on a ranch in the middle of nowhere.

"Oh, look, there's Em." Hopefully oblivious to his thoughts, Selah pointed ahead as Levi slowed the truck. He'd driven past pastures, the bunkhouse, the old shed and the faded red-and-white barn on autopilot and now slowed in front of the 1970s wood-frame house that Em McCullough, her son Sam and his new wife Jane, called home.

Sure enough, his mother's second cousin, the woman who'd taken him in as a teenager the year his mom suffered a stroke, stood on the porch surveying the land before her like the matriarch she was. Dressed in her ranch clothes of jeans and a shirt, Em's familiar face lit up with a warm smile, one she used sparingly but sincerely.

Levi pushed aside thoughts of Selah and waved through the truck's open window.

"She looks so happy to see you," Selah commented as she unbuckled her seat belt. "I hope she won't mind me turning up uninvited."

"It'll be fine. Nothing fazes Em, and she always liked you." He grinned over at Selah before opening his door and rushing around to open hers, taking the bakery box from her before she could offer it up to him. This way, their hands didn't accidentally touch again and he had a hope in hell of being able to walk straight.

"I hope you're right."

He remembered Selah as sassy and outgoing, and her nervousness now made her seem slightly vulnerable. Levi felt a weird urge to protect her. Maybe bringing her out here to see Em hadn't been such a good move after all, but it was too late to back out now. Maybe where Selah was concerned, he'd never be able to think straight.

"I always am," he said, putting on a show of cocky.

She laughed and raised her beautiful brows as she closed the truck door. By the time they started up the path, Em was halfway down it, and Sam had appeared from the back of the house, wearing faded Wranglers, dirty boots and an ancient cowboy hat. Sam wasn't the type to get excited about much, definitely not visiting distant family, but he raised his hand in a wave and joined them anyhow.

Em, in comparison, threw her arms around Levi in a fierce hug. He only just managed to lift the box of treats out of the way, passing them back to Selah in the nick of time. But, damn, it felt good to be wrapped in one of Em's hugs. He swallowed the lump of emotion that rose in his throat as she laid her head on his chest and said, "It's good to see you."

Never one for long, over-effusive hugs, Em pulled back, gave Levi a once-over and a nod of approval before she turned her attention to Selah.

"And Selah, so lovely to see you, too. I bet your parents are pleased to have you home for a bit."

"I guess." Selah looked a little uncomfortable. "This is a business trip, though, so we won't have the chance to spend much time together."

"But you've managed to make time for Levi." Em's eyes twinkled in a way quite uncharacteristic to her, and she shot a questioning gaze between him and Selah.

Levi didn't have to be a mind reader to know her thoughts. Shuffling in his boots, he feigned ignorance, and Selah simply held on to her sweet smile.

Before Em could ask any of the questions she so obviously wanted to ask, Sam said gruffly, "I doubt Levi has all day. We should talk business."

Levi looked to Sam, his stomach clenching as he tried to

read the older man's expression. They'd spoken on the phone, and he'd sent a business plan for Sam to look at via email, but Sam hadn't officially said yes, and Levi didn't know what he'd do if he didn't.

"Yes. Over coffee." Em tsked, offering her son a look of reproach. It was clear she wanted to catch up for a bit first, and as usual, what Em wanted, she got. They all ended up traipsing inside, discarding their boots in the mudroom and then being ushered into the farm-style kitchen. Em and her husband had lived in the original log cabin that her father-in-aw had built on another part of the ranch when Levi had stayed with her all those years ago. But after her husband had died four years ago, she'd migrated to Sam's new house. Now Em's grandson Cole and his new wife, Nell, lived in the cabin. Although this house didn't have the character of the cabin, he could see Em had put her own touches on the place since she'd moved in. It had always been comfortable, but Em being here made it more of a home.

"Now what can I get you to drink?" Em looked from Selah to Levi as she gestured for them to sit down at the table, and Levi suddenly realized Selah was still holding the box from Rachel's.

"A coffee would be perfect," Selah said.

"I'll have the same, thanks. And I brought you something." Levi took the pretty-ribboned box from Selah and held it out to Em.

"Ohh, are these what I think they are?" she asked, that sparkle in her eyes once again. "With Sage's chocolates and now Rachel's bakery, I'll soon be the size of a house. But thank you." She kissed Levi on the cheek and laid the box on the table. "These will go perfectly with coffee."

Em turned to make the drinks, Sam scraped a chair back and sat at the table, and Levi pulled one out for Selah.

"Thanks." She gave him a quick smile as she lowered herself into the seat, and he caught a whiff of her scent again. He wasn't sure, but it smelled like an intoxicating cocktail of cotton candy and...was it watermelon Jolly Ranchers?

"Are you ready for your events?" Sam asked, a rare attempt at conversation.

Levi jumped on it, happy to have a distraction from Selah.

"Certainly am, sir. I've got steer wrestling first up and then the bull ride in the afternoon. Do you think you'll head into town for the rodeo?"

"I wouldn't miss it for the world," Em said over her shoulder, "and as I'm old and frail, I'll need someone to drive me in."

Everyone snorted at that. Em might be eighty, but she was about as frail as a champion heavyweight lifter.

"And I'm sure Jane will be there," Em said. "Won't she, Sam?"

"I 'spose so." Sam stared down at the table and, if Levi wasn't mistaken, a flush spread up his neck.

Levi caught Em's gaze, and she smiled smugly. Of course he'd heard that lone rancher Sam had hooked up with the head of the town's Chamber of Commerce, Jane Weiss. Aside from his initial shock at the news—Jane was a lot younger than Sam, and Sam was a man Levi'd thought would never marry again—Levi hadn't thought much about it. As he helped Em bring the drinks to the table, he stole another look at Sam and realized he did look different. He had less of a gray look around his mouth and had smiled at least once since they'd been inside. He'd had heart surgery recently, so maybe it was the new lease on life that caused the changes, or maybe it was love. Levi shook his head a little at the thought—wonders never ceased.

When Em finally sat down, Levi took a spot on the other side of the table from the women. Sam downed his mug almost immediately, and Levi couldn't help but notice his work-roughened fingers tapping on the table. He was sick of playing house, no doubt itching to be outside. Em and Selah had gotten to chatting quickly—Em asked after Selah's sister, Magdalena, and in turn, Selah inquired about Em's grandchildren, Jeff, Cole and Sadie. When the conversation turned to the possibility of Cole and Nell giving Em more great-grandbabies, Sam finally pushed back from the table and looked to Levi.

"Do you want to talk business or not?"

Levi nodded, comforted to see love hadn't changed Sam *too* much.

SELAH'S HEART QUICKENED as she listened to the low voices of Levi and Sam as they headed out through the mudroom. She felt Em's questioning gaze on her again and knew the older woman wondered what Selah was doing here with Levi and whether she should read anything into it.

She smiled at Em and then lifted her coffee cup to her mouth, only to realize it was already empty.

"I didn't know you and Levi were still friends," Em commented, the last word heavily weighted.

Selah swallowed and licked her lips. "Oh, we're not. Well, not exactly. I saw him at Grey's last night for the first time in years."

Creases appeared in Em's brow. "And you spent the night with him?"

"No!" Selah felt her cheeks flush, even though she was perfectly innocent of what Em insinuated. What was this? The Spanish Inquisition? She took a quick breath. "It's not like that at all."

Liar, screamed a naughty little voice inside her head. She wanted it to be *exactly* like that. Just the words "spent the night with him" had her insides tingling.

"No?" Em cocked her head. Conversation had flowed between two women when Sam and Levi were sitting alongside them, but Selah didn't feel so comfortable now.

She gave herself a mental talking-to. She had nothing to hide, nothing to be embarrassed or ashamed about—Levi himself didn't even know of her salacious plans. Whether she had the guts to actually proposition him was yet to be discovered, but she didn't plan to rehearse on his great-aunt, or whatever Em actually was to him.

"No." She smiled sweetly at the other woman. "Anything between Levi and me is ancient history. I'm writing an article on cowboys for the magazine I work for, and he kindly agreed to be interviewed."

Selah waited for Em to breathe a sigh of relief and her easy smile to return, but all she said was, "In that case, maybe we should go outside and join the men. You can see my cowboys in action."

"Great idea." Selah pushed back her chair and started clearing the table barely before Em had finished the suggestion. She didn't want to intrude on Levi's business with Sam, but then again, he had brought her out here.

"Leave all that." Em waved a hand at the empty coffee cups and the open, barely touched box of Rachel's treats. They'd been too busy talking to eat.

"If you're sure. Thanks." Selah smiled at Em as she, too, stood.

The other woman offered her a brusque smile—if there was such a thing—and then said, "Follow me."

Selah did as she was told, following Em back through the mudroom and out into the warm September air. Marietta couldn't have asked for a more perfect weekend for the annual rodeo.

"Has Levi told you about his plans?" Em asked as she

stooped to pull on work boots.

"He said he wants to open a rodeo school in Marietta."

"That's right," was all Em said before straightening and marching off toward an old truck. For an old woman, Em was sturdy and fit. Selah found herself walking fast to keep up.

When they arrived at the truck, Em yanked open the driver's side door and Selah did the same with the passenger's side, not wanting to be left behind. She found herself quite excited by the prospect of seeing the slice of land Levi wanted to lease from the McCulloughs. Or maybe she was simply excited at the prospect of seeing Levi himself. Her stomach tumble-turned at the thought as she remembered her real reason for being here with Levi.

Em started the truck and reversed quickly before taking a right turn and starting over a rough farm track. They passed a group of Angus cattle, and Selah looked out the window, admiring the impressive beasts. Although Selah hadn't said anything, Em filled her in.

"Those are Tom McKay's steers," she announced. "He's leasing some land off Sam. The land Sam and Levi have in mind for Levi's venture is at the southern side of the spread. Not too much of a ride."

"Thank you for taking me there," Selah said, transfixed by the scenery, so different from what she saw day in, day out in Seattle. Although a little dry following summer, the wide open spaces took her breath away. Only a certain type of folk could handle the isolation, though. It was easy to imagine Levi settling out here where conditions were sometimes harsh and the work grueling. He was a man's man who would never be suited to life behind a desk in some stuffy office.

"Not a problem." Em sounded friendly again now that they were on their way, and Selah thought maybe she'd been paranoid about her tone in the house. "It'll be good to have Levi back.

He's a good boy and a darn good bull rider, but a man can't do that forever."

Selah smiled, her heart warming at the love and pride in Em's voice. Other than yesterday, she hadn't seen Levi in well over ten years, so it was hard to know how to reply. Luckily, Em didn't seem to expect her to.

"I'm hoping once he's built his house and got his business up and running, he'll find a nice woman to settle down with." Em kept her eyes on the track ahead, and Selah didn't want to stare at her, so she couldn't tell if Em was warning Selah off or suggesting maybe she could be that woman.

Something low in her belly quivered at the thought, but she tried to ignore it. It wouldn't pay to start fantasizing about an impossible future with Levi. Besides, she didn't want anything to get in the way of a possible red-hot fling.

As Em had promised, it wasn't far to the land earmarked for Levi's venture, and pretty soon they crested a hill to see Sam and Levi in the distance. Sam stood leaning against a fence by an old, very run-down barn, and Levi looked to be pacing out measurements. As Em drove closer, Selah's breath caught in her throat as she watched Levi stride purposefully, his muscular thighs mouth-wateringly highlighted in his faded, fitted jeans. He looked up and waved when the truck approached, then stopped what he was doing and came over to help Em out once she'd parked behind his truck.

"Get away with you," Em said, waving away Levi's hand as she climbed out of the truck, but she looked secretly pleased by the gesture.

Levi chuckled and then looked to Selah as she made her way around the front of the vehicle. He grinned, and she almost stumbled by the strength of such a hit.

"You okay?" Levi frowned slightly as he reached out to steady her.

She swallowed and attempted a nod, trying not to be affected by the brush of his fingers against her arm. Even through the cotton of her top, her skin burned under his touch. The longer she spent around him, the more flustered she was getting. Maybe it was stupid to think she could be cool and sophisticated enough to proposition him for a one-night stand.

If he actually took her clothes off, she would likely combust.

"Made any decisions yet?" Em asked, looking past to Sam, who had also joined them.

He wiped his hands on his work jeans and nodded. "I think Levi and I will be able to come to some kind of arrangement. You think so, son?"

"If you'll have me," Levi replied with his cocky cowboy grin. "I reckon it'll be a great partnership. We're going to renovate the barn for inside work." He gestured to the derelict-looking building behind him and then turned to point toward the pasture. "I'll build an arena over there and some pens for the stock."

Selah smiled at Levi's obvious passion for his plans. And, hell, his ambition only made him all the more desirable.

"Where will you live?" Em asked. She could always be relied on to think of the practical. Sam and Levi both looked shocked. Em cackled. "Don't tell me you haven't thought of that yet."

Levi shrugged and offered her a sheepish smile.

Sam spoke up. "If you want, I'd be happy for you to build a small cabin on the land you lease. We can work something out."

Everyone was silent for a moment, no doubt thinking similar thoughts to Selah's, that that was a generous suggestion from someone who had a reputation for being a bit of a hard-nosed grump.

And then Levi replied with a simple "thanks," but his voice sounded a little choked. As if Sam's offer meant more to him than a simple piece of land.

"If that's it for now, I've work to do." Sam tipped his hat and looked to Levi. "I take it you'll take Selah back to town from here? Mom, can you give me a lift back to the house?"

"Of course." Em nodded. "We'll see you both tomorrow at the rodeo. I'm looking forward to it."

"Thanks, Em. See you then." Levi leaned forward and brushed a kiss against the old woman's cheek, and damn it, Selah felt a spark of envy flare within. She silently scolded her ridiculousness. For one, Em was almost triple Levi's age. For two, they were related. And three...the deal she had in mind for Levi didn't involve emotions such as jealousy. She needed to get a grip.

They waved Em and Sam off and then Levi turned to Selah. "I guess I'd better get you back into town. You've probably got a busy day ahead."

"I'm not in a huge hurry," she said, smiling as she gazed around them. "Your plans sound fabulous."

"Thanks." He adjusted his cowboy hat, giving her a glimpse of his rich red hair, which made her toes curl and her hands itchy. She wanted to run her fingers through it, so she jammed them in the pockets of her jeans instead. "There are still a lot of details to finalize, but getting Sam to agree was always gonna be the biggest hurdle."

"Looks like you jumped it."

"Yeah, I reckon I have."

Their eyes met, and they laughed. Levi looked so damn happy Selah contemplated hitting him with her proposal right there and then. Surely the lack of eavesdroppers in the vicinity made it the perfect spot, but she couldn't bring herself to do it. She was enjoying this time together, and she didn't want to ruin it.

Levi made a few more notes in a notebook and described in greater detail his vision for the area and the school, and Selah listened. His passion was contagious and his voice lyrically appealing, so that when he snapped his book shut and told her they should head back, she had to bite her tongue to stop from crying out in protest. She didn't want to go back into town, where he'd be consumed with the rodeo and she'd have to share him with all the other cowboy fans.

"Thanks for bringing me out here," Selah said as she clicked her seat belt into place and then looked at Levi shoving the key in the ignition.

"No worries." He reached over and took a little paper bag off the dash and handed it to her. "I had to rescue these from Sam."

She peered into the bag at her little gingerbread cowboy boots and laughed. "Thanks."

"What did you think?" Levi asked.

"Of what?"

"Rachel's cookies? You did have one at Em's, didn't you?"

She shook her head. "Too busy talking."

He nodded toward the bag in her hands. "Go on, try one now."

Willing to do almost anything Levi asked, Selah opened the bag and pulled out one of the beautifully decorated boots. She was all too aware of Levi's gaze on her mouth as she took a bite. The sugar melted on her tongue, but it wasn't its sweetness that made her warm all over.

"Well, what do you think?"

She finished her mouthful and licked her lips. "It's good, really good."

He didn't say anything in reply, just hit her with an intense, questioning gaze.

"What?" She touched her hand to her chin to check for crumbs. "Have I got something on my face?"

"No." He shook his head. "This is just weird, don't you

think? You and me chatting again after all these years."

Her belly tumble-turned, and she said something she'd been wanting to say for years. "I'm sorry at the way we ended things, Levi. I wasn't fair to you, I know."

He shrugged but didn't meet her gaze. "It's water under the bridge. From what I recall, I acted like a tool. It was unfair of me to pressure you."

She loved that about him, that he was willing to accept some responsibility for what she believed to be all her fault. He'd never asked of her anything more than any other teenage boy would have. But he'd treated her a hell of a lot better than most boys would have while they'd been together. When they'd broken up, she'd cried solidly for almost three months, certain she'd die of heartbreak. Everyone had assumed they'd split because he moved back home to his mother, but Selah knew the truth. Knew that if she hadn't been such a prude, if her parents hadn't branded her with the fear of God, it would have been a whole other story.

She wasn't naïve enough to think they'd have lasted the test of time, but...

"Do you think you've got enough for your article?" he asked, jolting her out of her thoughts.

She realized it was now or never. And she wanted him bad, so it had to be now. "I lied, Levi. I didn't simply want to interview you for my article."

And then the truth spilled ungracefully from her lips.

Chapter Four

LEVI COULDN'T HAVE been more shocked if Selah had yanked her T-shirt over her head, ripped off her bra and thrown herself at him in the truck. And he didn't manage to school that shock.

"What the fuck?" His grip tightened around the steering wheel. Had he heard her correctly? He couldn't believe his ears. In fact, it was quite possible he was dreaming, that he'd dreamed this whole damn episode of Selah turning up at the rodeo grounds to talk to him.

He felt her hand on his forearm and flinched. He'd been so startled, he hadn't even seen her reach out. "I'm sorry," she gushed. "I didn't mean that how it sounded."

"What? So you don't want to use my body for one sordid night of orgasms?"

"Well…" she began, but her voice drifted off before she could explain herself.

He'd never forget this announcement—learning that her one regret in life was not sleeping with him and that she wanted to rewrite history, to indulge in a red-hot one-night stand. While part of him was stoked she was so confident he could deliver the sexual highs she craved, he didn't like the idea of being used. And he'd put promiscuity behind him with the rodeo—well, that was his plan going forward from this weekend. The whole growing up, getting a real job and settling down thing meant finding a woman who wanted him for more than just his body.

"Are you still a virgin?" he asked, glaring at her as that one thought sent a strange pain shooting through his body.

She blinked her sensuous, big, brown eyes, her long, dark lashes fluttering in a way that tightened every muscle in his body. It was all he could do not to lean over and kiss her senseless. If all she wanted was meaningless sex, then his truck seemed as good a place as any.

"No." She shook her head.

"Who'd you give it to?" He was suddenly desperate to know this detail. Then he caught himself. It wasn't any of his business. "I'm sorry, I just…"

She rubbed her lips together, as if wondering whether to tell him, and the action only drove him more crazy. "No, you deserve to know. A man I met in college." A sigh. "It wasn't anything special. I had too much to drink at a party one night and decided it was time to get rid of it. I was the only virgin in my college class."

He cursed. Fresh pain washed through him at the thought she'd given what he'd so desperately wanted to some dude she felt nothing for.

"I'm sorry."

He didn't want her apology, damn it.

"I always wanted it to be you." Her choked words, indicating she was close to tears, eased his anger a little, and he took a moment to properly look at her. "You meant more to me than anything, anyone, and your touch never failed to set me on fire, but I was scared. We were young, my parents had just suffered through the scandal of Magdalena's teenage pregnancy, and I couldn't do that to them again."

"We would have been safe. I would have made sure of it."

Hell, he'd have walked through fire to look after her back then.

"I know," she whispered. "And I wish I hadn't been such a scaredy-cat."

"What's in it for me?" His question surprised even himself. Was he actually considering such a crass proposal?

She coughed and blinked again as color rushed to her cheeks. "Well, I would hope you'd find it enjoyable as well."

No doubt about that. Despite his fury, he was barely managing to contain his erection. He couldn't recall the last time he'd had such a blunt talk about sex with a woman, never mind one who drove him as wild as Selah did. He was torn between a resounding "Hell, yeah, let's do this" and a definite "No."

His cock was cheering for the sex, obviously, but a few niggly things held him back. His dignity, for one. And the fact she'd made him go without in high school. That was childish, maybe, but it was there. He couldn't deny it.

"Where are you staying?"

"The Graff Hotel," she answered, and he sent a silent prayer of thanks skyward that she wasn't staying with her parents. Even if he was willing to contemplate her proposition, he'd draw the line at taking her under the local minister's roof. And the single mattress in his trailer was no place to take a woman, not one like Selah, anyway.

"Let's do dinner there. I'll come to you." He finally turned the key in the ignition, and the truck's engine roared to life.

"Haven't you got the welcome dinner tonight?" She sounded a little uncertain, a little nervous, and he liked that. Maybe she was all talk. Maybe she wanted to shock him but never imagined he'd take her up on her proposition.

He raised his eyebrows. "Do you know how many of those things I've suffered through? Do you want to have dinner or not?"

In reply, she nodded her head furiously. "Yes, let's do it."

"Good." His lips curved into a grin. She obviously thought he'd made his decision in her favor. For the sex thing. Truth was, he still had a lot of thinking to do before he decided whether or not to hitch that ride.

AFTER LEVI DROPPED Selah off at the rodeo grounds, she climbed straight back into the car she'd rented at the Bozeman airport and headed into town to Sage's chocolate shop. As she drove, she called her gal pals on speakerphone and demanded an emergency meeting. They were the ones who'd gotten her into this fiasco, so they could help her prepare.

As she was in Marietta on *Charisma*'s time and money, she should have hung around the rodeo grounds a little longer and tracked down a few more cowboys to hit with questions. Once the festivities kicked off that evening and the events started tomorrow, it'd be harder to pin them down, but she couldn't worry about that right now.

Sage met her at the entrance to the shop. "I've got half an hour before I have to be back here, so I told the others to meet us at Java Café."

Selah nodded as Sage took her arm and they started down the sidewalk. Quite frankly, she didn't care where they went so long as they could get a table in a private corner so as not to be overheard. Hopefully, Sally Driscoll wasn't working today, for she had a reputation almost as bad as Carol Bingley's when it came to foraging for gossip.

"I'm so excited for you," Sage whispered. "And I heard a rumor this morning that Levi Monroe might be moving to Marietta, buying a ranch or something, so maybe he'll lure you back as well."

Selah rolled her eyes. "And the local grapevine strikes again. He is moving here, but he's leasing land from the McCulloughs to start a rodeo school. He's not buying a ranch. And even if we do sleep together"—she experienced a hot flush simply saying that out loud—"I'm not moving back. My career and life are in Seattle, and who's to say we have *anything* in common these days?"

"You have chemistry, don't you?" Sage wriggled her eyebrows up and down. "Trust me, that goes a long way. Besides, surely you don't have friends in Seattle as good as us."

"You got me there," Selah said, grinning. She got the feeling she was going to be doing a lot of that this weekend.

Jenny was waiting in front of Java Café when they got there. "Chelsea just messaged. Apparently, she can't make it, but wishes you the best of luck tonight."

"What's going on?" Sage asked, her tone a little annoyed.

Jenny shrugged. "She mentioned Jasper's brother or something."

"It doesn't matter," Selah said, pushing open the door of the café. Her friends followed her inside. Unfortunately, Sally was behind the counter whipping up coffees with her renowned barista skills, and they all put in their orders. Jenny ordered a large slice of carrot cake with her decaf latte, but Sage and Selah both ordered only coffee.

"Working with chocolate has turned me off all sweet food," Sage explained as they slumped into seats at the most isolated table they could find.

"Being pregnant has turned me into a monster where sugar is concerned." Jenny reached for the little packets of sugar that sat in a jar in the middle of the table, even though her drink hadn't arrived yet.

"Enough about food," Sage said matter-of-factly, positioning her chair so she could easily interrogate Selah. "Give us the lowdown about what happened this morning."

Selah sucked in a deep breath. "Well, I used the ruse of

asking him for an interview, and then we went for a drive out to the McCulloughs' spread. It was so damn hot hearing him talk about plans for his rodeo business, but we talked about other stuff, too. It was easy, good. He got a little nostalgic, said how bizarre it was to be together again like that."

"Aw." Jenny looked as if she were about to cry. Selah figured it was hormones.

She patted her friend's hand and continued, "I almost lost my nerve, then just as we were about to leave, I asked if he'd like to fuck me, to rewrite the past."

Sage snorted. "You what? In those exact words?"

Jenny laughed. Loudly.

Selah hung her head. "I know. I just blurted it out wrong."

Still stifling giggles, Jenny said, "Well, I can guess what his answer was to that."

"What male would ever say no?" Sage agreed.

"Say no to what?"

The three of them almost jumped out of their seats as Sally came over with a tray of steaming drinks.

"Nothing." Selah shot her a saccharine smile and gestured to their mugs. "Thanks so much for these. I dream about your coffee whenever I go back to Seattle."

It was an outright lie—the coffee wasn't that good—but it worked.

"Oh, shucks. Thanks." Sally beamed as she lowered each drink and then Jenny's cake onto the table. "You girls yell if you need anything else."

"Will do," they said in unison.

Selah cursed. "How much do you think she heard?"

"Only the last bit, I'm sure," Jenny said. "Now, where were you?"

"His reply," prompted Sage.

"He asked me out to dinner at The Graff."

"Oh, he wants to wine and dine you with fine food first."
Sage laid a hand upon her chest and sighed. "I like his style."

Another smile burst on Selah's face.

"Hang on," Jenny said, a forkful of cake halfway to her
mouth, "but doesn't that kind of ruin the just-sex deal? It adds
romance. It ups the stakes."

"Yay. Go, Selah." Sage punched the air.

Selah bit her lip. She hadn't thought of it in those terms.
And she was certain Levi hadn't, either. That would complicate
things, and she didn't want to complicate things. "I don't think
so. I guess the man just wants to get his strength up before
we…you know."

Her friends giggled. "Oh, yeah, we know," Jenny said.

Sage glanced at her watch. "Really sorry, but I'm going to
have to bail soon. Shall we discuss tactics?"

By tactics, she meant whether Selah should book an appointment today at the salon to get waxed or whether shaving
would do. Whether she'd packed appropriate undergarments or
needed to take a quick visit to Married in Marietta, which, in
addition to beautiful bridal gowns, also sold an array of hot
lingerie.

"I don't want to look too desperate," she said, secretly imagining the look on Levi's face if she stood before him in a slinky,
little, red or black lace number.

Sage nodded. "Besides, it's not worth spending dollars on
something that he'll rip off in a matter of seconds."

A shiver whispering through her, Selah agreed, but when she
said goodbye to her friends ten minutes later, she made a beeline
for Married in Marietta. Due to most people being busy with
rodeo fever, the shop was empty, and Lisa, the owner, was eager
to attend her.

"Got plans for tonight?" she asked suggestively as she directed Selah to the "extra sexy" section.

"No." Selah laughed as if the idea was preposterous. "I've got my eye on someone back in Seattle, and I know you stock quality garments."

Lisa's eyes twinkled. "Say no more."

Selah was getting good at this lying thing. Her father would have been appalled, but she couldn't summon any guilt. Just half an hour after stepping into the boutique, she exited with the most provocative black bra and panties she'd ever bought in her life. And of course, just as she'd been about to leave, she'd realized that she hadn't brought a *wow* dress with her from Seattle. Wanting everything to be just perfect that night, she turned back and added an amazing, black-and-white lace number to her purchases. It fitted like a second skin and finished just above the knee, but both Selah and Lisa agreed it still managed to look classy.

Obviously, such a dress required shoes to match, and she was pleasantly surprised to find the perfect pair at Main Street Shoes, which in her recollection had always sold mostly grandma shoes. Stoked with her purchases, she walked back to her rental car, bags swinging at her sides, feeling like a kid counting down to Christmas. This was turning out to be the best business trip ever.

How on earth she'd get through the next few hours, she had no clue!

Chapter Five

L EVI WAS MORE than a little pissed off when he walked up the steps to the recently refurbished—more accurately, saved from the brink of demolition—Graff Hotel. He'd heard anecdotes from Cole and Em about what Troy Sheenan had done with the place, but this was the first time he'd gotten close enough to take any real notice. It looked almost regal from the outside, and when he stepped into the lobby, it became clear Troy had spared no expense. But Levi couldn't give a damn about the palatial mahogany furnishings, lavish rugs and opulent marble floors. All he could think about was the woman waiting for him somewhere inside. *Selah.*

The woman who'd refused to leave his mind all day and had made it impossible for him to get anything else done. He'd planned a little training with his horse and to devote some time to the business plan he needed for the bank, but all that had flown out the window with Selah's surprising proposition.

Would he like to fuck her?

Hell, yeah.

Would it be a smart move?

Despite spending all day agonizing over this question, he hadn't yet decided.

He was glancing around, looking for the restaurant, when he

saw her walking toward him from the elevators on the other side of the lobby. Actually, sashaying would have been the correct term. A killer smile on her face, her shoulders held back and her chin high, she looked confident and drop-dead sexy in a black-and-white dress that left little to the imagination and made his mouth go dry. Heels so high and pointy they could have been used as weapons punctuated her steps, click-clacking across the marble floor. He certainly felt defenseless against them.

Her whole outfit—from those f-me shoes, the dress, right up to the chunky heart pendant that sat snugly in her cleavage— told him that, to Selah, dinner was merely a formality, that her investment was in what might came after.

He was going to have to keep his wits about him.

With that thought, he puffed up his chest and pasted an easy grin on his face. "Hi there," he said, dipping his head, despite not wearing his cowboy hat. He felt a little naked without it, and the fact he was wearing clothes that rarely saw the light of day didn't help either.

"Hi." She beamed at him as he leaned in to kiss her politely on the cheek, and he tried not be affected by the suggestive tone she put in that one, supposedly innocuous word, or the feel of her soft skin against his lips. "It's good to see you again."

"Yeah." Damn, she smelled good. Leaning close gave him another whiff of that sweet fragrance. Theoretically, the scent should have been nauseating, but on her it had the opposite effect. It made him hungry—not for cotton candy or Jolly Ranchers, not for the fancy dinner they were about to be served, but for Selah. The hunger had lain dormant for years, but the moment he'd laid eyes on her again, he'd realized it had never actually died.

They stood in the lobby, staring at each other for a few long moments. It would have been so easy to be lost in her warm, brown eyes. To grab her hand, forgo the pretense of dinner and ask her what number her room was. His body liked that idea a whole lot, but he refused to stumble at the first hurdle.

"Shall we head into the restaurant?"

She nodded, and Levi resisted the urge to take her hand or offer his elbow as they walked toward their destination. It was bad enough simply being near her. Touching her again would have been his downfall.

"Good evening, sir, madam." The maître d', dressed in a fine black suit and a deep crimson tie to match the tablecloths, bowed his head and smiled at them. "You have a reservation?"

Levi nodded. "Under Monroe." Not that it looked like they needed one tonight. Although already eight o'clock, hardly any of the tables were occupied. Levi hoped that was because most of the town was at the fund-raising steak dinner and not because the hotel was struggling. He liked Troy Sheenan and wanted his venture to be a success.

The maître d' settled them at their table, first pulling back their chairs and then flourishing their napkins in the air before settling one onto each lap. Levi vaguely registered a question about drinks, and judging by the wine delivered to their table not long after, one of them must have answered, but he didn't remember any of that.

He was too consumed by the beautiful woman across the table. A small table, so that he could easily reach out and take her hand or begin a game of footsie.

"Have you been here before?" he asked, glancing down at the menu in front of him but not really taking any of it in.

She flicked a few strands of that luscious chocolate hair over her shoulder and shook her head. "I don't come back to Marietta often, but when I do, I usually hang at Grey's or the diner with the girls, and of course, I have to eat at home some nights."

"How are your parents?"

She rolled her eyes. "Same as ever. Their lives still revolve around the church and their obsession with finding me a suitable guy to settle down and have babies with. Marriage first, of course."

He couldn't help laughing. "And you don't want that?"

She shrugged and rubbed her lips over each other again in that way that did something to his groin. He shifted in his seat as she replied. "It's not that I'm opposed to the idea of marriage or children, but I've kinda been too busy to find a suitable candidate. I've been focusing on my career instead."

He nodded, then teased, "You could always get Pastor and Mrs. Davis to find a husband for you. I'm sure they'd have people lining up for the vacancy."

She glared at him with her feisty eyes, and he thought she might actually reach across and whack him on the arm. His muscles tightened in anticipation of the connection, but a damn waitress arrived and Selah tucked her hands under the table instead.

"Good evening," she said, with a chirpy smile. "Are you ready for me to take your orders?"

"That'd be lovely." Selah glanced down at the menu, before picking it up and closing it. She looked up to the redheaded waitress and said something about chicken. Levi only realized when the waitress looked at him expectantly that he'd been too busy staring at Selah to a) listen to what she'd actually asked for or b) pay any attention to the menu himself.

"I'll have the same." He closed his own menu and handed it to the waitress, hoping she'd hurry the hell away. They hadn't been here long, but he was already enjoying himself immensely. The waitress gave them another smile, asked if she could get them anything else and then scurried off, much to Levi's joy. He turned back to focus on Selah. "Where were we? Your parents?"

She blew air between her lips, flicking up strands of her dark fringe. "The most boring topic on the planet. I didn't come here to talk about my folks, Levi," she said as she leaned a little toward him.

Again, suggestive undertones oozed from her words, reminding him exactly why she'd wanted him to come. He swallowed and looked right into her eyes to stop his gaze from drifting down to the pendant and the way it hung between her two awesome breasts. "If you're not dating, what do you do when you're not working, not writing?"

"I didn't say I didn't date, just that nobody has fulfilled my fantasies in the bedroom or made me want to race up the aisle."

He wanted to talk about those fantasies. Hell, he'd like to enact some of them right this second, because no matter what they were, if they involved Selah, they'd be smoking hot.

Instead, he impressed himself by saying, "Hobbies?"

She sighed, as if irritated he wouldn't easily succumb to her desire to take the conversation somewhere sordid. "I bake cakes. You haven't lived until you've tasted my caramel mud. I watch a fair bit of television."

"What? Scandal? The Good Wife?"

Again, she looked as if she wanted to hit him. "As it happens, *Levi*, I like watching documentaries."

Now he was intrigued. He didn't watch much TV himself, but when he did or when he picked up a book, he liked true stories, stuff that made you think. "What type?"

"Human interest stuff mainly—how advertisers trick us into buying things we don't want, travel shows about places I'd like to visit and true crime. That stuff terrifies me at the same time that it fascinates me."

"I love that shit, too," he admitted, surprised to find this much in common already. "I saw one recently about this outlaw gang who were conned by a bunch of old ladies."

She snapped her fingers at him. "I saw that one, too. It was hilarious."

He couldn't help but grin at her laughter, which washed through him like liqueur. "So, baking and TV?" Seriously, what more could a man want in a woman? Besides hot sex, which was all she was offering him.

She nodded. "And yoga. I love my yoga."

Damn it, his mind shot straight to the gutter at the mention of yoga. All sorts of images of Selah's clearly flexible body in kinky sexual positions tortured him. He picked up his wine glass and gulped half of it down. How the hell was he going to get through the main course, nevermind dessert, without leaning across the table and covering her mouth with his? All he could think about was slipping his hands up into her hair and caressing the nape of her neck while he kissed her.

"Do you do any other sport aside from the rodeo?" she asked, twisting her wine glass in his fingers.

He took a breath and focused on the question. "Nothing structured. The horses keep me busy, but I occasionally get out and run. Team sports were never really my thing."

"Not enough blood and gore?" she asked, referring to the dangerous nature of the rodeo.

He chuckled. "Something like that."

Their conversation flowed far easier than Levi had imagined it would. Their meals arrived—chicken fettuccine Alfredo, not what he'd have chosen if he'd been paying attention—and between mouthfuls, they continued learning about each other. Although he'd known Selah for years, in many ways this felt like the first getting-to-know-each-other date, but without the awkward silences that frequented so many of those. He genuinely liked hearing her anecdotes about life and work, and they had fun discussing their former classmates and what had become of them.

"Shall we get dessert?" he asked as the waitress cleared away their main dishes.

"Dessert?" Selah hoped Levi didn't hear the disappointment in her voice. Truth was, she'd been hoping she'd be his dessert. Then again, the way they'd been laughing and bantering across the table for the last hour or so had to be a good omen. Surely, he wouldn't want to spend so much time with her if he wasn't still a little interested. She could almost see the sexual tension sizzling between them across the table and felt confident her new sexy lingerie was not going to go to waste.

He picked up the dessert menu the waitress had left on the table and perused it a moment. She liked the way tiny creases formed in his forehead as he contemplated. Then he looked up. "I'm thinking the crème brûlée or the molten chocolate cake."

She smiled. "You can't go wrong with chocolate, but I'm not sure I could eat a whole one. Should we share?"

Levi raised one eyebrow, as if telling her he saw right through her plan, but then he grinned, closed the menu and said, "Good idea."

The waitress, who seemed to have some kind of instinct telling her exactly when they needed her, appeared as if from nowhere. "Do you need any recommendations?" She spoke only to Levi, her lips stretched into such a big aim-to-please smile, Selah worried they might snap.

He's mine, she thought, glaring at the woman.

"We've decided on the chocolate cake," Levi told her.

"Good choice." She picked up the menu and hugged it close.

"To share," he added, looking only at Selah as he did so and causing her heart to go a little crazy.

The waitress went away, but Levi continued gazing at Selah in a manner that was both thrilling and disconcerting. In many ways, she was glad he'd chosen do things a little more classy—she'd enjoyed dinner and his company immensely—but the longer it took to get to the bedroom, the more nervous she was getting. She had no doubt he could give her exactly what she'd been missing all these years, but what if *she* disappointed *him*? Her experience at this kind of thing was limited, to say the least. How could she be both insanely excited and terrified at the same time?

"What?" she asked, her chest heaving with a big breath as she wondered what kind of scrape she'd gotten herself into.

"You're beautiful," he replied simply, then reached out and brushed his thumb over her cheek, cupping her chin and holding his hand there a moment. "And I'm so damn glad you sought me out again."

While his seductive, very complimentary words and his touch sent shivers down her spine, and to much more feminine places, she told herself to take it all with a grain of salt. The last thing she needed was to start falling for Levi Monroe all over again. To start thinking of him as something more than the man she wanted to bed.

She swallowed, resisting the urge to shift her head slightly and kiss the palm of his hand. "Me, too. I've had a great night."

"It's not over yet." He put his hand back on the table, but suggestion dripped from those four words.

The butterflies that had been fluttering in her stomach flew away as her excitement kicked up. She squeezed her thighs together to stop from crying out in anticipation and silently reminded herself they were still in public. But, hell, the chocolate cake couldn't come fast enough. She wanted the man sitting opposite her more than she'd wanted any other man before.

"Tell me more about your work," he said, lifting his glass again and taking another sip.

Selah blinked, wondering if she'd just imagined their little near-public-display-of-affection. She took another sip, more like a gulp, of her own wine and then replied, "What do you want to

RACHAEL JOHNS

know?"

He shrugged. "The articles you've mentioned writing so far and the one you're doing on cowboys don't seem to suit you."

She frowned, confused and unsure what he meant.

"No offense. *Charisma* sounds like a fun sort of magazine, a great place to work, and I'm sure your articles are well-written, but your interests run deeper. Don't you ever want to write about something grittier than the latest handbag styles?"

The funny thing was, coming from anyone else she *would* have been offended by such a comment. But Levi's words didn't put her on the defensive. It was as if he'd reached right inside her and found a truth she'd not shared with anyone yet. "Yes," she answered forcefully. "To be quite honest, I'm bored out of my head. I always wanted to be a serious journalist, but I've been writing for fashion magazines for so long, I..."

She let her words fade off, not wanting to admit to a man who rode bulls for a living that fear was keeping her back. She was a small-town minister's daughter, and although she'd traveled widely and lived a somewhat glamorous life, she still felt like a country girl. Being back in Montana with her friends made her realize even more that her life in Seattle wasn't all it was cracked up to be. She missed the friendliness and community that a place like Marietta had to offer.

"Why not write something for you?" Levi suggested. "If you could write about anything in the world, what would it be?"

Considering she'd all but offered him sex on a platter, Levi seemed to be taking a great interest in finding out about who Selah was now. She couldn't help but like him more for it.

"I'd write human-interest stories about ordinary people who do extraordinary things."

"Have you got anyone in mind?" he asked as their waitress delivered the most amazing-looking chocolate dessert to their table. She placed it between them and set two tiny forks on the

62

edge of the plate.

"Enjoy," she said, but Selah swore there was an edge to her voice and that she gave Selah an evil glare as she stalked off. It made her feel happy and smug. If she had to witness another woman dining with this sexy cowboy, she'd be spitting with jealousy, too.

When Levi dug his fork into the chocolaty, gooey goodness, Selah forgot all about their conversation. She forgot she had ambitions and dreams and desires that didn't revolve around him. Her breath halted as she waited for him to taste the first mouthful, to watch his Adam's apple work as he swallowed. But, instead, he stretched out his arm and offered the forkful to her.

"Open your lips." His voice was low, and for a moment Selah swore he'd told her to open her legs. She would have obliged either way.

Her mouth opened, her heart strumming a quick beat as Levi slipped the fork into her mouth. Her taste buds exploded as the chocolate melted on her tongue, but it was the intimacy of Levi feeding her that set her on fire.

He withdrew the fork and looked expectantly at her. "Well?"

"It's good," she all but panted and then reached out to gulp from her water glass.

Levi shoved his fork back into the cake and devoured a chunk himself. Wanton need shot through Selah at the realization that that fork had been inside her mouth only moments earlier. It wasn't anything like sex, but it felt as intimate as they could get in a respectable restaurant.

"I see what you mean." Having finished his first mouthful, Levi dug his fork in again and offered her another. They finished the cake in this manner, each mouthful setting Selah more and more on edge, so that by the time the plate was empty, she felt like a desperate, panting mass of need.

"Shall we get the bill?" she asked, code for "Are you ready

to take me to bed?"

"Good idea." Levi glanced around and caught their waitress' eye. He gestured that they were ready to go.

Selah felt like an impatient child as they waited for the bill. It was all she could do to stop herself from squirming in her seat. Neither of them said anything, as if they were both thinking about what was about to follow, but Levi whipped out his wallet the moment the bill was delivered.

"We can just put it on my room," Selah suggested, anything to save time.

"No, this is my treat." Levi retrieved a few bills from his wallet, leaving a generous tip before standing. "Shall we go?"

"Yes." She hadn't meant to sound so husky or so excited, but his grin said he didn't mind.

"I'll walk you to your room." He took her hand in his as they weaved through the other tables to the exit, and as they crossed the lobby, she prayed the elevator would be fast tonight.

As if God were on her side, the doors peeled back the moment Levi pressed the up button. They stepped into a thankfully vacant elevator, and Selah turned to him the moment the doors slid shut behind them. She licked her lips as he took a step toward her and did exactly what she'd been dreaming of all night. Well, the beginning of said sordid fantasy.

He put his hands on her waist and tugged her against him, his hands sliding around and up her back as he bowed his head and kissed her like he would die if he didn't. She was thankful he had a good grip on her, for the feel of his tongue sliding along hers left her weak. It could have lasted only a matter of seconds, but it was the hottest kiss she'd ever participated in, and when the elevator opened again, she broke free and tugged him along behind her like some kind of sex-starved nympho.

"Praise the Lord," she uttered as she slipped her hand into her bag and found the room card immediately. She swiped the door unlocked, and Levi pushed it open, lust and hunger visible in his eyes as he gazed down at her.

Not waiting for them to get decently inside, he stepped close again, pinning Selah against the door as he slid his knee between hers. His mouth went to her neck. She groaned at his touch and anchored her fingers in his hair, drawing him even closer. Not wanting him to ever stop kissing her.

Then, as quickly as it had started, Levi broke free. He shoved his hands in his pockets and grinned as if he'd just won the lottery.

"See ya later, Selah."

Her mouth dropped open, her hand flying to her chest as he turned and swaggered off down the corridor back toward the elevator, dashing all her hopes, dreams and desires for that night.

Chapter Six

SELAH WOKE TO the alarm on her cell phone and flapped her arm out to turn it off without even opening her eyes. It was Saturday—the first official day of the Copper Mountain Rodeo. She had old friends to meet, greasy rodeo food to eat, cowboys to ogle and a pretty damn hot country music singer to interview, but after last night, none of those things was enough to make her want to drag herself out of bed.

"Oh, God." She rolled over, wrapping the covers around herself and pulling a pillow over her head. If only that embarrassing fiasco with damn Levi Monroe had been a dream, or rather, a nightmare.

She was still wearing her sexy underwear, having only just managed to rip off her own dress while sobbing uncontrollably. She could still taste him on her lips, and the skin on her neck felt a little raw from where his rough stubble had brushed against it. And her insanely sexy high heels were discarded on the floor like clues from a crime scene. All painful reminders of the way she'd thrown herself at Levi, and he'd teased her, led her on and then dropped her like a hot piece of coal.

Had he ever planned on following through? On taking her up on her proposition? Or was the facade of dinner, the undeniable flirting, all his idea of a sick joke? Something inside her snapped, and her humiliation led to anger. How dare he play her like that? Well, two could play at that game.

Spurred on by this thought, she threw back the covers, all but jumped out of bed and headed for the shower. Under the water, she contemplated her outfit—she didn't want to look like she was trying too hard, but if Levi saw her (and Copper Mountain wasn't that big, so he likely would), she wanted to be sure he knew what he'd turned down. She wanted to make him regret his decision to play her for a fool, and if her distraction put him off his game, well, that would be payback for kissing her stupid and then walking away.

After toweling herself dry, she put on her underwear and stood in front of the mirror to blow-dry her hair to perfection. Then came her outfit, which consisted of dark, skinny jeans that fit like a second skin but were surprisingly comfy, a fitted Western shirt that she wouldn't have been seen dead wearing in Seattle and knee-high boots that had cost her a whole week's salary a couple of years back. Man, she loved those boots. A deep-pink leather adorned with tiny embroidered flowers, they were sexy and feminine at the same time, and when she wore them, she felt as if she could conquer the world.

"Watch out, Levi Monroe," she told her reflection as she appraised the finished product in the mirror and perched her cowgirl hat on her head. Although a city chick now, she hadn't grown up in Marietta without acquiring such accessories, and she'd dug this one out for her return.

After grabbing a quick omelet for breakfast in the hotel restaurant, Selah returned to her room for her voice recorder and camera and then headed out to her car.

Due to prior commitments, country music star Jake Kohl hadn't been able to get into town until late last night, which was why the rodeo committee had switched the annual dance on Main Street to tonight, instead of holding it after the welcome dinner like they usually did on Friday. As honorary chair, he'd be needed during the parade, but Selah had scheduled an interview with him at midday, hoping they'd have plenty of time to talk before the opening ceremony kicked off the events in the afternoon.

Theoretically, she didn't need to be at the rodeo grounds until that time, but she figured she'd get to catch up with old friends and maybe grab a couple of cowboys to chat with for her other article. Of course, there was also the chance she might run into Levi. Her stomach tightened at the thought. After the way he'd led her on last night, she shouldn't still want him like she did, but she couldn't help it.

From the moment she parked her car in the designated area at the rodeo grounds, every cell in her body was on high alert, looking out for him. The grounds were busier than when she'd visited Levi yesterday. People who'd likely been to the pancake breakfast in town were starting to arrive for the official opening parade, which would kick off soon. As she walked through the gathering crowds, she tried to focus on the smells and sounds of the rodeo instead—things she hoped to use in her article to convey the atmosphere—but each time she saw someone in the distance wearing the classic cowboy uniform of Wrangler jeans, dusty boots, Western shirt and work-weathered hat, her insides quivered. Sooner or later, it would be him.

"Selah?" She turned at the sound of a woman calling her name, relieved to have a distraction.

It was Jenny, wearing a smile like a rainbow and her hand linked with her new hubby, Colton Thorpe, who was eating a corn dog. Selah waved and walked toward them, happy for the chance to see Colton again.

"Hi, guys." She came to a stop alongside them and smiled.

"Morning, Selah. Great to see you." Colton tipped his cowboy hat and grinned at her. "Jenny said you're here for work, writing articles or something?"

For a second, Selah didn't know what Colton was talking about, but then she remembered her real reason for coming to Marietta and nodded.

"Let me know if you need any information," he offered. "I'm not competing this year, but I'm happy to help if I can."

"Thanks."

"So," Jenny hissed as she dug Selah in the side, "last night?"

Fresh humiliation washed over her at the thought of having to tell Jenny and the others exactly what had happened. Or rather *not* happened. Colton and Jenny took her flushed face the wrong way, and he held up his hands and said with a laugh, "Whoa, spare me the details. I'll leave you ladies to chat and go catch up with some of the dudes."

Jenny laughed as Colton all but ran off toward the camp where the competitors kept their horses, trailers and goosenecks. Then she grabbed hold of Selah's arm. "I know I should wait for Sage and Chels before I hound you for details, but Sage is working this morning, and Lord knows what's going on with Chelsea at the moment. Shall we go grab something to eat and find a quiet spot to chat?"

Even if Selah hadn't enjoyed a good breakfast at The Graff, she wouldn't have wanted to eat now. Greasy rodeo food had never enticed her, and besides, the knowledge that Levi was around here somewhere killed any appetite she might have had. As for a quiet spot? With cowboys and cowgirls gearing up for their events, parents chasing overexcited kids who were running around like crazy and the calls of the carnival folk who'd set up a few rides for the weekend, such a place seemed unlikely.

"There's really nothing to tell," Selah said, glancing around for an excuse to escape Jenny's clutches.

Someone who didn't know her that well might have mistaken these words for not wanting to kiss-and-tell, but Jenny saw the truth immediately. She looked into Selah's eyes, and Selah felt tears welling up at the look of concern on her friend's face. If she were honest, it wasn't simply embarrassment over what had happened. There was a little heartache, too. Stupid when she'd only just reconnected with Levi, but she'd thought they'd been enjoying each other's company last night. Talk about foolish!

She blinked and swallowed. "Please, Jenny, I really don't want to talk about it here. I have work to do."

Jenny hesitated a moment before pasting a smile over her concern. "That's right"—she wriggled her eyebrows—"you've got your interview with Jake Kohl soon, haven't you?"

"Yep. After the parade. And I need to chat with some of the competitors as well." She pulled her camera out of her shoulder bag. "And I should get some snaps. Reckon I'll be able to sweet-talk a few cowboys into having their photo taken?"

"Are you kidding?" Jenny made a theatrical show of looking Selah up and down. "They'll be falling all over themselves to please you."

Selah tried to laugh but failed dismally. If only the cowboy she actually wanted had been so eager to please. She walked through the crowds with Jenny, trying to resurrect some of her kick-ass attitude, as they passed the stalls selling hot dogs and barbecue and headed for the arena where the parade would soon start.

"Ladies," Colton, hanging out with a couple of men on the bleachers, called to them. "Can I introduce you to Brendan Reid and Ryder Black?"

"Hi," said Selah and Jenny at the same time.

"Jenny is my better half," Colton said, proudly wrapping an arm around her and pulling her into his side. "And Selah's an old friend of Jenny's. She's writing an article about cowboys. I know these two from the circuit, and they're as good as you'll get,

Selah."

"Nice to meet you." Brendan, a tall, dark-haired man who looked a little too thin for a cowboy, held out his hand, and Selah took it. He had a firm shake and held on a fraction longer than was decent. "Selah? That's a pretty name. You from around here?"

She shook her head. "Not anymore, although I did grow up in Marietta."

"And where do you call home now?" Brendan asked, leaning a little too close and tossing her a practiced cowboy grin. He was kinda cute when he smiled, and she imagined it worked well for him with many a girl, but he had nothing on Levi. It didn't make her toes curl or her insides twist.

As that thought darted through her head, Selah happened to glance sideways, and her heart flipped at the sight of Levi only a few yards away. He was leaning back against a bleacher, his arms crossed over his chest, watching them. Their eyes met, and then he waved a hand, as if acknowledging a casual acquaintance.

Grr. He made her blood boil. How dare he wave at her like that after last night?

Flicking her long hair over her shoulder, she turned her attentions back to the conversation and pasted a flirty smile on her face.

"Selah lives in Seattle now," Jenny was saying, pride shining through in her voice. "She's a journalist, so if you don't mind, she'd like to ask you a couple of questions. Maybe take a few photos? Make you famous."

"Sure." Brendan laughed and turned to Ryder, his blond friend. "Which do you think is my best side?"

"Neither." Ryder snorted and then held out his hand to Selah. She fluttered her eyelashes at him as she took it, purely for Levi's sake, of course. "Don't waste your time with this loser, he barely knows one end of a horse from the other, and his mug's far too ugly. It'll break your camera."

"Funny guy." Brendan glared good-naturedly at Ryder. "Careful or I won't partner you in the steer wrestling."

"I'd like to interview you both," Selah told them, flicking her hair again and secretly hoping Levi was still watching the interactions, "and I'm sure my camera will love you."

They made arrangements to meet after Selah had interviewed Jake Kohl, and then Ryder and Brendan swaggered off in search of food. Selah couldn't resist any longer. She turned back to look at Levi, her heart feeling as if it were physically deflating when she realized he was gone. She sighed. So much for trying to make him jealous or regret missing out. Her little show with Ryder and Brendan had been for nothing. Why she'd thought Levi would care, she had no clue.

If he felt anything for her, he wouldn't have led her on last night. Vowing to try to forget about him and her ridiculous proposition, to enjoy the rodeo and catching up with old pals, she summoned a smile from deep within and sat down with Jenny and Colton to watch the parade.

HAD ANY WOMAN ever looked hotter in jeans, boots and a cowgirl hat? Levi wondered, glowering as he strode away from the bleachers. Of course, the answer was no, and he wasn't the only one who'd noticed. The memory of Brendan and Ryder laughing and leaning in close to ogle Selah's magnificent cleavage made his fists clench, and he hadn't been able to bear standing around and watching. He knew both men from the circuit and although they were reasonably good guys, they were all about the thrill of the ride—where the rodeo *and* women were concerned. No doubt, they were already placing bets on which one of them could lure Selah into his bed, and the thought had Levi seeing red.

He'd felt so good, so empowered last night after kissing Selah and then walking away, but it had lasted all of five minutes. He hadn't even been back at the rodeo camping grounds before he'd started feeling like a total shit. Not only had he treated Selah badly, but he'd spent all night tossing and turning on his bunk, wondering if maybe he'd cut off his nose to spite his face.

Needing a few moments to pull himself together, he was heading for his trailer when he almost crashed into a laughing couple as they came around a corner.

"Hey, watch where you're going, loser."

Levi looked up to see Cole McCullough, Em's grandson, still laughing, despite his harsh words.

He tried to shake off his frustration and grinned at Cole. "Maybe you should watch where you're going," he shot back.

Then they both leaned in for a quick man hug. Neither of them were the hugging type, but Levi hadn't seen Cole for about a year, back when he was still a single man about town. "Congratulations," Levi said, pulling back. "And to you too, Nell." He leaned over and kissed Cole's wife on the cheek. He'd met her at the Wilsall Rodeo at the same time as Cole, but had been as in the dark as everyone else about their relationship status. "I couldn't believe it when Em told me you two had tied the knot in secret. But I'm really happy for you both."

It was the truth, but it left a weird ache in his gut. He desperately wanted what Cole had found. He longed for a woman who wanted to be his partner in everything. Nell had a successful career in reality television, but she and Cole loved each other enough to make it work. The way Em told it, Nell had fought for him.

"Aw, thanks, Levi." Nell smiled and linked her arm with his. "That means a lot. Wanna come watch the parade with us?"

"And then we can grab some lunch," Cole added. "I want to hear all about this rodeo school you're planning."

Levi looked off into the distance toward his trailer and his horse. He could go off and sulk, or he could hang out with Nell and Cole and try to enjoy his last rodeo as a competitor. That had been his goal until Selah had come along and thrown a mammoth spanner in the works.

"Sure, that sounds good. Do you know if Em's here yet?"

"Dad and Jane were bringing her. Not sure they'll be here for the parade, but Em said nothing would keep her from watching your events. We'll all be rooting for you."

"Thanks, man." Feeling a little more relaxed after the conversation with Cole and Nell, Levi headed with them back toward the arena where the parade was about to kick off, a decision made as he walked.

The evening with Selah had been the best night he'd had in a long while, and he was no longer proud of himself over how it ended. He needed to apologize to her for the jerky way he'd acted and maybe explain why he hadn't accepted her very tempting offer. Just because he didn't think it was a smart idea for them to sleep together didn't mean he wanted things to end badly between them a second time.

All through the parade, Levi was semidistracted as he went over in his head what he could say to clear the air. He noticed Brendan and Ryder in the bleachers and couldn't help a sigh of relief when he didn't see Selah with them.

Although on the lookout for her so he could try to catch her before the afternoon's events arrived, he didn't see her again until he was sitting down eating lunch with the McCullough clan. Trying to pay attention to the conversation, led mostly by Nell, Em and Jane, Levi watched out of the corner of his eye as she laughed with a couple of local girls—Mandy Wright and Trinity Cash, if he recalled correctly. Both girls had been a few years behind them at school, but Mandy was Selah's friend Jenny's little sister.

The moment she began to walk away, he made his excuses, leaped up and hurried after her. She was walking briskly toward the temporary offices set up for the rodeo, and although he would usually be able to keep up with her easily, Levi lost ground navigating the growing crowd.

He was about to call out to her when she raised her hand and knocked on the office door. He cursed and kicked up some dirt on the ground as a man dressed like a cowboy but far too polished-looking to be a real one stepped out. The man and Selah exchanged a few pleasantries, judging by the looks on their faces, then shook hands before he ushered her inside and closed the door.

"Can I help you?" asked a woman, coming up behind him. She was wearing a rodeo committee badge.

"It's fine." He shook his head and gestured toward the office. "I was trying to catch up with my friend, but it looks like she's busy."

"You mean Selah?" The woman beamed. "She's interviewing Jake Kohl for that magazine she writes for. We're all so excited to have him here."

Levi racked his brain for why the name sounded familiar. And then it hit him. Jake was a country music heartthrob. One of the female wranglers who worked for his friend Lane had all his albums. By all accounts, he was an all-around nice guy and great singer and owned a face and body that made women crazy.

Something tightened inside Levi at the thought of Selah all alone with this man, but he could hardly voice his discomfort.

"Ah, that's right," he said to the woman, feigning nonchalance. "I'll catch up with her later."

Vowing to put all this pent-up tension to good use, Levi went off to prepare his faithful steed for his first event, steer wrestling. He was in no mood for the dramatics of the opening ceremony, but ventured back toward the action just before the calf-roping was due to start to see if any of the competitors in this event would be competition for the title of All-Around Cowboy. Earlier, he'd seen a cowboy unload a big black horse from a trailer. While the horse had appeared half-asleep, his gut told him the horse was whip smart and the cowboy a seasoned competitor. Considering this would be his last rodeo, he'd decided winning the All-Around Cowboy title would be a good finale to his career. The prize money would also come in handy for his new venture, so he planned on giving it his best shot.

Heading toward the arena, he saw Selah, a camera slung around her neck, walking a few steps ahead of him as if she, too, had had business in the camp.

"Hey, Selah," he called, and began jogging toward her before he could think better of it.

She turned, and the breath caught in his throat as her gaze connected with his. Her long, chocolate-brown hair blew across her face in the wind, and he seriously couldn't recall having ever seen anything or anyone as beautiful as she was.

"Levi." Her tone was guarded and her look wary as she tucked her errant hair behind her ears and readjusted her hat. It wasn't exactly a friendly greeting, but what had he been expecting?

"Can we talk a moment?" he asked, stopping just in front of her.

She folded her arms across her chest and glanced behind them toward the arena. "I don't have long. I need to get some photos of the calf-roping."

"This won't take long," he promised, shoving his hands in his pockets, because right now all he wanted to do was pull her against him and apologize in the most basal way possible. Not with words, but with kisses. Yet, standing before her now only emphasized the fact he'd made the right decision yesterday. He may have gone about it the wrong way—he should never have teased her and led her on—but Selah wasn't the type of woman he could sleep with and then walk away. Even after all this years, she still did something crazy to him. "I wanted to apologize for last night."

She held up her hand, a decided flush rushing up her neck and spreading into her cheeks. "It's fine, Levi, you don't owe me an…"

Her next words were drowned out by the thundering of a horse's hooves heading toward them. He turned in the direction of the noise to see a riderless bay cantering toward them, its stirrups thrashing against its belly and the reins dangling free. Instinctively, he grabbed Selah, yanking her against him and pulling them both out of the path in the nick of time.

His heart thumping, he held Selah close. Her hat had fallen onto the dirt in the commotion, and he rested his chin against her silky hair, relishing its softness as he praised the Lord the horse hadn't hurt her. The thought left him cold, and the intensity of his feelings scared him. The shock flooded his senses, resurrecting memories of their time together. She still fit perfectly against him.

But however good they were in the past, and despite the fun they'd had together last night, he had to remember things were different now.

They were older, more worldly. And the biggest difference of all—Selah had made her career and a life for herself in Seattle, whereas he wanted to make a home right here. Her proposition hadn't included a relationship, just sex.

Coming to his senses, Levi pulled away. "Are you okay?" he asked her.

Although Selah looked a little shaky, she nodded, and then shock crossed her face as she brought her hand up to cover her mouth. "Did the horse knock over that baby carriage?"

He followed her gaze, his heart clenching again at the sight of a baby carriage lying on its side. "Shit," he cursed before they both noticed a young mother stepping out from behind a trailer, clutching a chubby baby on her hip, horror sprawled across her face as she gazed at the baby carriage, likely contemplating what could have happened if her baby had been in it.

"Thank God," Selah breathed out beside him.

Not trusting himself to stick with Selah any longer after the thoughts that had just been running through his mind, he scooped her hat off the ground and handed it to her. "I'd better go see if anyone needs help with the runaway horse," he said, snatching the excuse to get away.

"Thanks," she called after him.

And he didn't know whether it was for the hat, for saving her from getting trampled or for his half-finished attempt at an apology. Either way, he hoped she'd forgiven him for acting like a jerk.

Chapter Seven

SELAH'S MOUTH WENT dry as she watched Levi jog away from her. Despite still shaking after their encounter and the incident with the errant horse, she couldn't deny that the sight of his delicious ass encased in faded denim was a sight too good to be ignored. She rubbed her lips together to stop from drooling.

Damn, he was hot, and even after the humiliation of last night, she still wanted to nail him. She clutched her hat to her chest, stupidly inhaling in the hope of catching a whiff of Levi's raw, masculine scent and torturing herself by wondering what exactly he'd started to say to her. Maybe it was a good thing the horse had charged by when it had, for it saved her the further mortification of listening to him explain why he'd rejected her. What if he'd been planning to follow through until they'd kissed, and the spark hadn't been there for him? Or maybe he simply didn't find her attractive?

The awfulness of these thoughts sparked uncharacteristic tears at the corners of her eyes, and she prayed she'd get through the weekend without another brush with Levi.

"Are you okay?"

At a female voice behind her, Selah blinked away her tears and snapped her hat back on her head. "I'm fine," she lied, turning to find Marly Akers, who'd recently taken over from her mother, Angelina, as editor at the *Copper Mountain Courier*, a paper that had been in their family for generations. "Great to see you, Marly," she said, trying to keep her voice even.

Marly nodded in the direction the horse had flown. "That is *so* going in the *Courier*, but thank God no one was hurt."

That was debatable. Selah's heart felt as if it had split down the middle, but of course she didn't say that. "Bit of excitement to kick off the rodeo. Oh, and congratulations on your baby"— she glanced down at the other woman's burgeoning bump— "and your upcoming nuptials. Drake's a lucky man."

Marly beamed in the way pregnant women and blushing brides were renowned to do. Selah had already congratulated her on the phone when she'd offered the article she was going to write with Jake to the *Courier* as well, but it felt right to say it again in person.

"I think I'm the lucky one," Marly said. "Amazing how your luck can change in an instant."

"Yes." Selah tried to smile, though she felt anything but lucky this particular instant.

"How'd your interview with Jake go?" Marly asked, absent-mindedly caressing her bump.

"Good." Selah smiled, happy to have something to talk about that would take her mind off of Levi. Jake had been very obliging, flirtatious even. "He's as lovely as everyone says he is, and I think it'll be a great article. I'm going to take some photos tonight when he's singing at the dance. I'll send the article and the images to you early next week. Is that okay?"

"Perfect. I'm just so pleased you offered them to us. The pregnancy is affecting my brain lately, and I didn't even think about requesting an interview myself."

"It's fine. It'll be nice to finally have my byline in the local paper after all these years."

"Speaking of your byline in the local paper," Marly began,

her lips curving into an even bigger smile, "any chance we could lure you away from that big-city magazine?"

Selah blinked, the offer completing blindsiding her. "What do you mean?"

"It's probably a long shot, but I'm going to have to go on maternity leave soon, and I want someone I can trust to take over as editor while I'm away. You've got the experience, and you know the area and the people from having grown up here. You'd be perfect, but I understand if it's not something you're interested in at the moment, as I can only offer you a temporary position."

"Move back to Marietta…"

Selah didn't realize she'd said the words aloud until Marly nodded. "Yes, I'm sorry, but I think you'd have to, it's not really a job that can be done long distance."

Since leaving ten years ago, she'd never contemplated the idea of moving home, but she had to admit that lately, she'd been feeling a little disgruntled. And she was missing out on so much here. Although she'd return for Sage's wedding in a few weeks, she wouldn't be able to get away for the bachelorette party as well. And then there was Jenny's baby. She'd miss watching her bump blossom like Marly's, and she'd miss watching the baby grow up. Likely, Chelsea and Jasper would marry soon and start a family, too, and her parents weren't getting any younger. Since they were barely on speaking terms with Magdalena, the job of looking after them if they needed help would likely fall to her.

Then she thought of Levi, and her whole body tingled. He was moving back himself. Would there be any possibility of rekindling that old spark if she returned as well? A hot flush swept through her at the thought, but she quickly dismissed that ridiculous notion.

Hadn't they just established Levi wasn't interested?

"Wow." She sighed, her head suddenly throbbing. "That's a temping offer, and I'm honored that you'd think of me…"

"But?" Marly asked, anticipating her refusal.

Selah found she couldn't actual do it. "Can I have some time to think about it?"

"Sure." Marly's eyes lit up with hope. "I know it'd be a big change for you, and I've still got a few weeks of work left in me. Let me know as soon as you can, okay?"

Selah promised to do exactly that and then continued on toward the arena, hoping to find one of her friends to sit with while she watched some of the events. In the end, it was Chelsea who found her.

"Selah." She threw her arms around her friend and whispered, "Come sit with me. I need a break from Jasper's evil twin and his supposed girlfriend, who acts more like his minion."

"What?" Selah looked questioningly at Chelsea as her friend started dragging her toward the bleachers.

"It's a long story. One I don't want to talk about right now. Let's enjoy the rodeo instead, okay?" Chelsea delivered these lines in her school teacher's voice, and Selah knew there was no point arguing. Besides, she didn't know if she could handle Chelsea's issues while grappling with her own. Maybe later she'd tell her friends about Marly's offer, but right now, she just wanted to lose herself in the rush of the rodeo.

They stopped at a stall next to the bleachers to grab drinks and a hot dog each, and then Chelsea led her to a row right at the top, where they'd be hard to find. The calf-roping was fun to watch. Selah didn't know many of the competitors, aside from Rhett Dixon, who'd been a few years behind her at school and, according to her father, had recently been hanging out with the Taylors and getting into a bit of trouble. One poor cowboy got off to an unfortunate start when his horse broke before the calf. That earned him a ten-second penalty, but a dark-haired guy named Cordell Morgan followed and got an awesome time.

"He's staying with Payton Hollis out at Beargrass Hills Ranch at the moment," Chelsea whispered. "I wonder if anything will happen between them. Payton swears she's too busy with her cows to have time for a man."

Selah only vaguely knew Payton—she'd been a few years behind them at school and was friends with Jenny's sister, Mandy—but she'd seen the cowgirl talking to the good-looking cowboy earlier. And by the way Trinity and Mandy had rushed over to speak to her, leaving Payton alone with Cordell, she suspected Payton's friends had hatched a Marietta matchmaking plan.

She shrugged and made no comment.

It was fun watching, but she didn't really feel invested in any of the events until it was Levi's turn in the ring. Then, no matter how hard she tried, she couldn't take her eyes off him. The way he rode his horse and the control he had over the steer were things of beauty indeed. None of the other competitors stood a chance, and when Levi came out with the best time in his first event, Selah couldn't help feeling a burst of pride.

He wasn't hers, she reminded herself. Unfortunately, Chelsea chose that moment to remember her Levi plan. She dug Selah in the ribs. "Hey, you haven't told me about last night. Was he as good a ride as he looks?"

"I can't talk about it here," Selah hissed, semishocked at Chelsea's dirty question. Jasper had certainly loosened her up some.

Chelsea gave her a knowing smile and then wiggled her eyebrows. "Fair enough, but I want all the details later."

"Deal." Selah sighed, hoping that something drastic would happen to make Chelsea forget to ask again. She really didn't want to hash over her disastrous Friday night again.

During the ladies' barrel racing, Chelsea went off to look for

Jasper, and Selah went for a stroll. She contemplated going into town—maybe even visiting her parents, who had never embraced the whole rodeo thing—but she found herself hanging around, chatting with old friends and generally soaking up the buzz of the rodeo. A sucker for self-punishment, she ended up back at the arena with Sage, Dawson, Jenny and Colton for the final event of the day—the bull riding. This time, they sat closer to the action, and her heart felt as if it were pounding in her throat as she waited for Levi's turn with the mammoth beast.

Then he and the meanest-looking bull she'd ever seen came bursting through the chute.

Despite not wanting to care, Selah was on the edge of her seat the whole time she watched him compete, her insides churning and her teeth cutting into her lower lip for what seemed like the longest eight seconds of her life. As Levi dismounted after a very successful ride—in which he'd managed to stay on the bull until the buzzer sounded—she let out a sigh of relief and smiled. She didn't know how women in love with pro cowboys didn't lose their hair or at least turn prematurely gray.

As the crowd erupted around her and other spectators started talking about Levi's skill, he turned and met her gaze. They locked eyes for a few moments, and she mouthed, "Well done," a warmth spreading through her when he rewarded her with a smile. If only she hadn't listened to her friends, if only she hadn't attempted seduction, then maybe she and Levi could have salvaged some kind of friendship this weekend. Feeling as if she might recover from her mortification, she vowed to congratulate Levi if she saw him later at the steak dinner or dance.

COLE AND NELL had persuaded Levi to attend the dinner and dance on Main Street. Although it was his last rodeo, he hadn't been that enthused about anything but the events. Over his last ten years on the circuit, he'd partaken in his fair share of celebrating (aka drinking himself stupid and then finding a pretty girl to share his trailer for the night), but he was bored of that lifestyle now. He'd planned on going out to the ranch to have dinner with Em, but after congratulating him on his events, she'd mentioned she was tired and planning an early night.

"Come to the dance with us," Nell had said, sounding like an excited child as she tugged on Levi's arm. "I'm sure there'll be lots of pretty cowgirls there eager to dance with today's star."

"I'm not much of a dancer, Nell," he replied, thinking that he'd likely blown his chance with the prettiest girl in town. He didn't even know if Selah would be there tonight, but as she'd come to town specifically to write about the rodeo, he guessed she probably would be.

"The food's good," Cole added.

"All right, you twisted my arm," Levi said, allowing Nell and Cole to think it was the food that had won him over. Truth was, despite the adrenaline rush of riding the rodeo that afternoon, he hadn't been able to get the memory of Selah pressed against him when he'd pulled her out of the runaway bay's path out of his mind. And somehow, whether wise or not, that memory had him throwing himself in the shower and then yanking on his best jeans and a clean shirt.

He sat with Cole, Nell and a couple of guys he'd gone to high school with during dinner, munching on overcooked steak and potato salad, half-listening to talk about cattle prices and drought, all the while keeping an eye out for Selah. He didn't know what he would do if he saw her, but he couldn't help wanting to. Knowing she'd been watching his bull ride this afternoon had spurred him on to the best ride of his life. Yet the thrill of victory had been nothing compared with her smile as he'd exited the arena. It gave him hope that she'd forgiven him, and call him insane, but he wanted another hit.

"Are you looking for someone?" Nell asked as the first croons of Jake Kohl wafted across the crowd, signaling the beginning of the dance.

Why did women have to be so damn perceptive? None of the men had noticed his distraction. Unfortunately, Selah had so far proved elusive, and he was just about to deny he was looking for anyone when he saw her standing at the edge of the temporary stage, snapping photos of the country music star. She lowered the camera, and he saw her face light up with a massive smile as she bopped along to what he had to admit was a very catchy tune.

"Oh, I see…" Nell's tone was all knowing beside him. "Who is she?"

"I don't know what you mean," he said, tearing his gaze off the stage, off Selah and back to Nell.

But Cole had chosen that moment to abandon the ranch chat. "Who is who?"

Grinning like the Cheshire cat, Nell leaned into Cole as she pointed toward the stage. "That gorgeous woman taking photos of Jake."

Cole registered who Nell was looking at, then looked at Levi and back at his wife with a cocky grin. "*That* is Levi's first love. Selah Davis."

"Really?" Nell was far too excited for Levi's liking. "Is she from around here? I don't think I've met her yet."

"No," Cole supplied, "not anymore. But she used to be, and she and Levi were the hottest couple in senior year."

"You should ask her to dance," Nell suggested, nudging Levi as if she wanted him to march up to the stage and do so right that moment.

"She's busy." Levi shrugged, glancing back at Selah, his chest squeezing at the look on her face, directed right at Jake, who appeared to be looking back as if the love tunes he sang he'd written specifically for her. Levi clenched his hands into fists.

"I'm going to get a drink." Levi marched off to find the bar, ordered himself a beer and all but poured it down his throat in one shot. This rodeo weekend was not at all turning out as he'd expected. He was contemplating the unfamiliar and unwelcome feeling of jealousy when three young cowgirls came up to chat.

"Hi, I'm Cindy." One of them offered her hand, giggling in an irritating manner as she did so. "We saw your bull ride earlier and just...wow."

"Yeah, wow," echoed her two friends, also giggling.

"Thanks." Levi tried to swallow his bad mood and remember his manners as he offered his hand to each of them. "Pleased to meet you. Are you ladies here to watch or compete?"

Cindy announced that she'd competed in the barrel racing but hadn't done as well as she'd hoped, and her two friends— Layla and Louise—declared themselves her cheer squad.

"Will you come dance with us?" Layla asked.

In his youth, three gorgeous women would have been a fantasy come true, but right now another beer sounded much more appealing. Still, figuring it wouldn't kill him to give them one dance, he let them lead him out onto the dusty dance floor.

Jake appeared to have finished his couple of songs, and a DJ had taken over. Loud country tunes blasted from speakers at each corner of the dance floor, which was already jam-packed with sweaty bodies writhing to the music. As his three young cowgirls gyrated around him, Levi glanced toward the stage where Selah had been ten minutes earlier, the tension in his body ramping up a notch when he could see neither her nor Jake.

He smiled at the girls and tried to relax, but that possibility flew out the window when a few moments later he caught sight of Selah and Jake dancing a few yards away. Torturing himself, he watched as they chatted and laughed while they danced, seemingly having a splendid time together.

If he hadn't been such a fool last night, he and Selah could have been in bed now. Instead, she was dancing with Jake Kohl. As Jake's hands moved lower on Selah's waist, something inside Levi snapped. Just because they might not have forever, didn't mean they couldn't have one night. No way did he want Jake getting what she'd offered him first.

Peeling the arm of one of the girls from around his neck, he strode through the dancers, over to Jake and Selah.

"Can I cut in?" he asked, tapping Jake on the shoulder, prepared for a fight if he refused.

The singer looked shocked and stepped back, and by the time he seemed to register what had happened, Levi already had his arms around Selah, and no way was he letting go.

"Levi?" Selah looked questioningly into his eyes as he danced her away from the crowd. "What's going on?"

"I thought you wanted to fuck me," he hissed. Raw lust combined with frustration and jealousy had caused him to repeat the exact words she'd used to proposition him on Friday morning.

Her eyes widened, and he saw the muscles in her slender neck move as if she'd swallowed. Yet when she spoke, she held her chin high. "Yes, that is what I want."

"Then what are you doing in Jake Kohl's arms?" he asked gruffly.

She tipped her head to one side. "Your actions last night told me you weren't interested."

"Damn it, Selah, I was trying to teach you a lesson. You made my balls blue in high school by refusing to sleep with me. I thought maybe I'd give you a little of your own medicine," he told her, shocked by his own raw admission.

She was silent for a few moments, and then she laughed. "So

you do still find me attractive?"

He groaned and rested his forehead on hers, and his hands slid down to cup her butt. "There's no woman on this planet that makes me as hard as you do."

"Really?"

In reply, he kissed her forcefully on the lips, his cock tightening with the feel of her body once again pressed up against his. "Is your offer still open?"

"Oh, yeah, it most definitely is." She sounded breathless, and the thought of what else he could do to make her sound that way set him on fire.

"Then let's get out of here." Levi grabbed her hand, and not stopping to say goodbye or talk to anyone, they hightailed it out of the party area. They established they'd both walked to Main Street for the dinner and dance and that her room at The Graff was closer than his trailer at the rodeo grounds. Although, the way he felt right now, he'd have taken her up against the wall in an alley if there hadn't been another option.

Judging by the way she ran alongside him, the way she all but slammed her fist against the up button when they reached the elevator and the way she threw herself against him once inside it, he felt fairly confident Selah felt the same way.

"This isn't going to be a repeat of last night?" she asked, pulling back from his kisses as the door to the elevator pinged open on her floor. "Because that was just cruel, and if you try it again, I might actually kill you."

Chuckling, he tugged her out of the elevator and yanked her against him once again, taking delicious liberties as he ran his hands up her body to cup her face. "Sugar, I'd kill myself. Now where's your room key?"

Chapter Eight

*S*EX WITH LEVI. *Sex with Levi. Holy hell, she was* finally *going to have sex with Levi.* What was it that Marly had said about luck sometimes changing in an instant? Selah grinned, feeling like the cat who was about to meet the cream. Jake Kohl was a sweet guy, undeniably cute if you liked the shaggy-musician look, but all the while she'd been dancing with him, all she'd been thinking about was Levi.

Her heart raced as she fumbled in her oversize bag—she'd had to carry her camera as well—to find her room card. Images from that afternoon when Levi had been riding the mammoth bull flashed through her head, causing another wave of desire to sweep over her as she anticipated him riding her instead.

"Here, let me help." Levi all but snatched the bag from her grip and then peered inside. "Bingo." He held the card up as if he'd just conjured it from nowhere, unlocked the door and pushed it open.

This time Selah grabbed his hand and pulled him inside, kicking the door shut behind him before he could have second thoughts. "No escaping now," she said, giving him a reproving glare as they stood staring at each other.

"I wouldn't dare." Levi took a step toward her, closing the gap that hadn't been that big in the first place.

Her mouth went dry at the ravenous expression on his face as his gaze swept over her. Aiming to keep things light, she said, "If I had a scarf, I'd tie you to the bed to make sure."

He cocked an eyebrow. "I never knew you were such a bad girl, but if we're going to play that game, rest assured I'll be the one tying you up. Is that what you want, baby?"

Light went by the wayside as the idea of Levi dominating her made her pelvic floor quiver. It was on the tip of her tongue to say yes, this was a fantasy after all. She wanted Levi to give her what no other man had, but then she remembered the lingerie she'd bought especially for this moment.

"Maybe." She held up her hands, flattening her palms against his chest. "But hold that thought a moment, I need to…" What? If she told him about her underwear, it would ruin the effect. "Freshen up," she said instead.

"Selah." His hands landed on her hips, and she felt his hot breath on her forehead as he looked down at her. "You're perfect as you are. We don't need scarves, we don't need games and if you insist on freshening up, then let's do it together."

"You mean…" She licked her lips, imagining.

He nodded as his fingers started on the top button of her shirt. "I've heard the showers here are something else, or we could test out the spa?"

Although not at all rough, he worked fast, and before she could reply, he'd slipped her shirt down over her shoulders. She shivered, more with anticipation than nerves, as he looked his fill at her breasts. Her nipples tightened, and she knew they were poking through her bra, announcing her desire, but she couldn't give a damn. She just wanted him to touch them. Preferably with his tongue.

As if a mind reader, Levi reached around to unclip her bra. She shrugged her shoulders, and as it fell to the floor, he swept his palms over her bare décolletage and then down over her breasts. Her breath caught in her throat as his thumbs teased her hard nubs. She groaned, already so hot for him she felt unsteady on her feet.

"I missed this," he uttered, before lowering his head and taking one of her burning nipples in his mouth.

"*Oh, God.*" So had she. As he swirled his tongue around the nub, his hands moving up and down her back, Selah wondered how she'd ever resisted him. They'd gone this far all those years ago. She'd even given him a hand job a couple of times, but she'd always made an excuse before they'd gone the whole way. Fear had ruled back then, but this time she was a grown woman who no longer wanted to ignore her needs.

And she needed Levi. She needed his mouth and hands on her bare skin. She needed to feel him moving inside her in the way she'd dreamed of all these years.

Giving her exactly what she needed, he slid his hand down into the front of her jeans, causing her to cry out as he breached her cotton panties as well. He held her there a moment, his palm pressed tightly against her sex. If he'd ever had any doubt about what she felt for him, there would be none now.

"You're so hot, so wet." Cockiness soaked his words as he slipped one finger inside her. Embarrassingly, it wasn't long before she was panting and writhing beneath his magic touch.

She was so damn close to the edge, but she put her hand on Levi's, halting him. He looked at her, his cocky grin slipping for a second. "You okay?"

She nodded, barely able to form the words to answer. "More than. But I want us to do this together."

Reaching out, she yanked his shirt out from his jeans and tugged it up over his head. Kissing, their fingers tangling in each other's hair, Levi walked her back toward the bed until she tumbled down on it. She watched, overcome with lust and admiration as he quickly rid himself of his boots, jeans and underwear. Last time she'd seen him without his shirt, he'd been gorgeous, but the years had been kind to him, and now gorgeous didn't come close to doing him justice. He'd filled out, his chest wider, his shoulders broader, and he had a delicious smattering of ginger hair in all the right places. She followed the trail of hair downward and swallowed at the sight. Oh, yeah, Levi Monroe had grown up.

When he knelt in front of her on the bed, she realized it would have saved time if she'd undressed herself while he'd been busy, but Levi seemed quite happy to do the honors, and Selah relished the feeling of being unwrapped by him. He tugged off her cowgirl boots, hurling one and then the other over his shoulder, before unbuckling her belt and peeling her jeans and panties down her legs.

He looked his fill down her naked body and then joined her on the bed. His work-muscular, gorgeous body hovering over hers, he grinned down at her and then kissed her hard. Although she was more than ready to do this, Levi seemed intent on making it last. He kissed and caressed her all over, driving her more and more insane, making her more and more desperate, before he finally left her just long enough to grab a condom from his wallet.

Then he was looming over her, as wild, rugged and big as the beast he'd conquered in the arena that afternoon. Yet, his gaze was incredibly tender as he looked down at her, stroked his fingers through her hair and then cupped her cheek.

"Have I told you how gorgeous you are?" he asked.

She smiled up at him. "Not in those exact words. But let's not waste time talking now. Why don't you *show* me instead, Levi?"

And so he did.

He brought his lips down on hers at the same moment as he thrust into her. Selah clung to him, her hands pressed against his buttocks as she urged him on to go faster, harder. It wasn't long before she felt her orgasm rising again, and Levi's breathing changed, indicating he was just as close. They came together, their hearts pounding in time and smiles spread right across their faces.

Levi was right, Selah thought. They didn't need anything but the two of them.

"WAKE UP, SLEEPYHEAD."

At the sound of Selah's soft voice, Levi opened his eyes to find light blaring in through the cracks in the curtains and Selah gazing down at him, her sweet smile the best wake-up call ever.

"Hey." He pulled her down into his arms. Snuggling close, she rested her head against his chest, and he kissed the top of her head, that tantalizing scent penetrating his senses. "What *is* that?"

"What?"

He inhaled deeply, smiled and ran his fingers through her long, silky hair. "You smell incredible. I noticed it the other day when you were in my truck as well."

She laughed. "Must be my shampoo. It's called Cotton Candy and is designed by a friend of mine in Seattle who has a small business making skin care and hair care."

"It makes me want to eat you up."

Again, her laughter wrapped around him like sunshine, and he couldn't help himself. He reached out and put his thumb under her chin, gently turning her head so he could cover her mouth with his. She was like a drug, an addiction, the more he had, the more he wanted. Her fingers slipped into his hair as she rolled toward him and gave herself wholeheartedly to their kiss.

It didn't take long for things to get heated. Again. They were already naked, and his morning hard-on pressed against her soft belly, desperate for release. Selah wrapped her hand around its length as she climbed on top of him. He had the best view ever—her perfect breasts bobbing up and down slightly—as she worked her hand, teasing him. He couldn't help but touch them. They fit perfectly in his hands, and he loved her moans when he flicked his thumbs across her nipples.

He was close to the edge, and she knew it. "Are there any condoms left?" she asked, her tone desperate.

He'd lost count of the number of times they'd taken each other throughout the night. The two condoms he kept in his wallet were long gone, but thank God Troy Sheenan was a man of the world and stocked condoms in the minibar.

Taking his hands off of her for merely a second, Levi grabbed their last foil packet off the bedside table. He handed it to Selah, grinned as she ripped it open with her teeth and groaned when she slid it down over his cock.

Then, she repositioned herself above him and rode him.

As he came down from what was undeniably the best sex of his life, Levi held Selah against him and realized this was it. The end of their amazing night together. The thought left a bitter taste in his mouth and a pain in his chest.

He didn't want to climb out of bed and leave her. Suddenly, winning All-Around Cowboy didn't seem half as important as making love with her again, but they'd run out of condoms, and going without would lead them into territory neither of them had agreed to go.

"I guess we'd better get ready," Selah whispered, not lifting her head from where it rested on his shoulder. Was she as reluctant as he was to end this thing? "You wouldn't want to miss your events after the success you had yesterday."

Right now he didn't give a damn about his events, but they couldn't stay holed up in this fantasy land forever. No matter how much he wanted to, Selah was only in Marietta temporarily, and she'd only ever offered one night.

He groaned. "Suppose so. Are you gonna watch me today?"

Starting to climb off of him, she looked down and smiled. "I wouldn't miss it for the world. I'll be the one cheering the loudest. Do you need a shower before you head back to the grounds?"

"Will you be having one, too?"

"I wouldn't function without my morning shower. And considering the amount of sleep we got last night—or, rather, didn't get—I think today I need it more than ever."

Levi climbed out of bed. "In that case, we should be water wise and share."

"I couldn't agree more." Selah's lips curved up into an irresistible grin as she turned and padded toward the en suite.

Although they didn't have another condom, they were inventive beneath the hot shards of water, and Levi knew he'd never have another shower as rewarding as this one. So much for water wise...they stayed in there, washing each other until the water ran cold, and then they toweled each other dry, stealing kisses as they dressed. Although there were plenty of places to eat in town, they ordered room service, talking, laughing and kissing some more as they ate.

And when it was time to go, Levi felt a strange kind of anxiety he'd never felt before when saying goodbye to a woman. It was on the tip of his tongue to ask her if she'd still be around that night, if she wanted to have dinner with him after the rodeo was over, but common sense saved him in the nick of time. After dinner on Friday night and the conversations they'd shared in the early hours of the morning between episodes of hot sex, assumptions he'd made about her had been busted. Although she lived and worked in the city, she wasn't stuck-up, as he'd imagined, and he already liked her way more than he should. Spending more time with her would have been dangerous.

"I'll drive you to the rodeo grounds if you like," Selah said, as she packed her handbag with the things she'd need for the day. She sounded so carefree, so totally unaffected by the knowledge that this was the end of what they'd shared.

"What if someone sees us?" he asked, tugging on his boots.

She shrugged and tossed him one of her flirty smiles. "Good for them. I no longer care what people think about me, Levi. If they wanna talk about us, let them."

He wasn't gonna argue with that. If she was happy to be his girl for the day, he'd take it. To hell with the pain, he'd deal with losing her again tomorrow.

"Let's do this." Levi wrapped his arm around Selah and pulled her to his side as they left her hotel room and walked to her rental in The Graff parking lot. He kept his hand on her knee as she drove, and when they arrived at the grounds, he kissed her on the lips—hoping it wouldn't be the last time—before heading off to his trailer and his horse.

WHAT HAD SHE done?

Selah managed to keep herself together until Levi was out of sight, and then she made a mad dash to the public restroom. She closed the door behind her, slammed the lid of the toilet down and then plonked herself on top of it. Right away, tears sprang from her eyes.

She wanted to feel happy today, to be able to bask in the memories of the hottest night of her life, but who had she been trying to fool? In hindsight, the reason she'd regretted not sleeping with Levi the first time was that she'd wished for that one memory to cling to. But now that she had it, it would torture her forever. She wasn't a one-night stand kind of girl, but to have one with Levi—the only man she'd never been able to forget—had to have been the dumbest thing she'd done in her life. That thought was interrupted by the buzzing of her cell phone somewhere in the depths of her bag.

With a sigh, Selah dug it out and glanced at the caller ID. *Chelsea.* No doubt, her friend had seen her rush off with Levi last night and wanted details. She let the call go to voice mail and tossed her cell back in her bag. The last thing she felt like doing now was spilling the beans on her amazing night with Levi. Reliving it, saying it aloud to her friends—even if only the bare minimum—would make her too sad, and she didn't want to be sad today. She wanted to pick herself up, powder her nose and hope like hell that when she left the restroom, nobody would be able to tell she'd been crying.

She wanted to watch Levi in his events, to cheer him on at the top of her lungs, to maybe pretend for a moment that being with him was real. With that thought, Selah pulled herself together and went back to join the crowds gathering for the Sunday afternoon events.

"Hey, sexy." She was approaching the arena when a deep voice called to her from off to one side. Although she didn't see the owner of the voice at first, her insides twisted at the sound, her whole body reacting in recognition.

She spun around to see Levi looking all rugged and beddable, the biggest, blackest horse she'd ever seen at his side. Of course it'd been the horse he'd used in the steer wrestling yesterday, but she'd been more focused on Levi then. Now, only a few yards away from her, it was hard not to notice the beast's size.

"I like your horse," she said with a smile.

Levi looked proudly at the stallion. "Yeah, Ry's a good'un. Now, are you gonna give me a good-luck kiss before my first event?"

A delicious thrill swept through Selah at that thought as she glanced around them.

"I thought you didn't care what anyone thought," Levi said.

She didn't. But she was a little worried about her heart. She was pretty certain she was over halfway in love with Levi again—maybe her feelings had never completely died—and she didn't know how many of his hot kisses she could take before she went flying over the edge. Then again, if today was all they'd have together, shouldn't she make the most of it? Decision made, she took a few paces to close the distance between them, pushed up on her tippy-toes and kissed Levi on the lips.

He wrapped one arm around her and drew her tight up against him. Her spine tingled and goose bumps covered her skin as his hand moved lower to cup her butt, and his tongue danced with hers. She never wanted the kiss to end.

"Now *that*," Levi announced, finally coming up for air, "was one hell of a good-luck smooch. Wanna walk with me to the arena?"

Too tongue-tied by arousal to talk, Selah nodded and took Levi's offered hand. She walked with him and Ry—waving at a few curious locals as they passed—to where the competitors were congregating for the steer wrestling and then rushed off to find a good vantage spot in the bleachers.

"Hey, Selah! Over here!"

At the sound of Jenny's voice, Selah looked around and saw Jenny and Colton sitting a few rows back from the front. Jenny gestured to the space beside her, and Selah made her way over to sit with her friends.

"Where were you last night?" Jenny asked the second Selah's butt hit the bleachers.

Selah blinked. If Colton hadn't been sitting with them, she might have confessed, but she couldn't bring herself to talk about her hot one-night stand next to her friend's husband, even knowing Jenny would probably tell him later anyway. "I was tired." She added a yawn for good measure. "It's been a busy weekend."

Jenny raised an eyebrow and then exchanged a look with Colton. "So the fact we just saw you lip-locked with Levi had nothing to do with it?"

Selah swallowed, unable to control the heat that rushed to her cheeks. Thankfully, at that moment Jake Kohl's voice blasted over the loudspeakers, announcing the start of the steer wrestling and introducing the first competitor.

"Don't think I'm letting you off the hook that easily," Jenny whispered into Selah's ear. "And have you spoken to Chels yet this morning?"

"No, why?" Selah shook her head, thinking of her earlier phone call.

Jenny grinned. "I'll let her fill you in later."

After refusing to share her Levi business with Jenny, Selah could hardly grill Jenny about what was going on with Chelsea, but she vowed to return her friend's phone call after the steer wrestling ended.

"Man, that was close." Colton whistled, and Selah pushed thoughts of Chelsea aside to concentrate on what was going on right before her eyes. One of the competitors had just stumbled and only escaped being trampled by the steer in the nick of time. Although Selah didn't want anyone to get seriously injured, she couldn't help a slight smile that this guy wouldn't be serious competition for Levi.

As she watched a number of fairly competent cowboys wrestle steers to the ground, Selah found her mind drifting to Marly's offer from yesterday. It seemed like so much longer since she'd chatted with the *Courier*'s editor. So much had happened, and although she was scheduled to return to Seattle tomorrow morning, her life there seemed a distant memory. The *Copper Mountain Courier* didn't have a huge readership and would likely be considered a big step down from her current position as features editor at a national magazine, but she would be in charge.

That notion sent a rush to her head.

But was she seriously considering this only because of Levi? Maybe her hormones and her heart were angling for a vote in what should be a decision made by her head. And she needed a clear head to make such a decision. Would she have been leaning toward what some might see as a backward step in her career if Levi hadn't been moving back to Marietta as well? Trying to leave him out of her decision-making process, she thought of the other things in favor of Marietta. Her family, her friends and the chance to spread her journalistic wings a little. She guessed the *Courier* job wouldn't be all that demanding, and maybe she'd have time to explore some freelancing opportunities as well. She could build up a portfolio of more serious articles that would stand her in good stead for finding another job once Marly went back to work.

Argh! Thinking about this on the amount of sleep she'd had last night, the memory of Levi's fingers on her skin still raw in her head, probably wasn't the smartest move, either.

"Levi's next." Jenny dug her in the ribs, her tone smug, as if she expected a reaction from Selah.

Trying hard to keep a straight face—devoid of all the emotion churning through her head—Selah nodded. But her heart picked up speed as she waited for the chute to open and Levi and Ry to burst through.

"And they're off," Jake announced over the loudspeaker.

Perched right on the edge of the bleacher, Selah bit her lip, every cell in her body wishing and hoping for Levi's success. Pride soared through her as he came up alongside the caramel-colored steer. When he glanced up and smiled at her, she thought she might burst with happiness.

She knew he could do this, knew he could win this event

and likely All-Around Cowboy as well, so she couldn't have been more shocked when Levi misjudged his leap onto the steer and came crashing down onto the dirt.

Around her, the crowd gasped. The animal turned, its horns aimed at Levi, and Selah screamed as she shot to her feet. Her heart felt as if it had exploded out of her body and was lying alongside him on the ground. She prayed he'd get back up or someone would take hold of the steer before it trampled him.

"Please, somebody do something," she shouted, frantically looking around her for an escape route so she could get to him. If she had been closer, she'd have taken the animal on herself.

"It's okay." Jenny's arm wrapped around Selah as the chaos in the arena was brought under control. Relief flooded through Selah as the steer was captured and led away from Levi.

"I need to go to him," she breathed, clutching Jenny's hand tightly. Because, although the steer had been removed, Levi still lay curled up on the ground, and Selah suddenly knew with absolute certainty that there was no place in this world for her if it wasn't by Levi's side.

Chapter Nine

LEVI WINCED AS he tried to push himself up off the ground, but pain throbbed in his shoulder and his arm wouldn't do as he required. He couldn't believe he'd made such a simple error of judgment, and he wasn't just talking about this event.

Footsteps pounded toward him across the dirt, and he looked up to see two paramedics—man-about-Marietta Daniel Garrett and a woman he didn't recognize.

"Are you all right, Levi?" Daniel asked, peering down at him.

"I've hurt my shoulder," he replied, realizing that the pain in his shoulder was nothing compared to the thought of Selah not being in his life. Forever. It was thinking of her that had caused him to fall. He'd done something he'd never done before during an event—he'd glanced up into the crowd and searched the faces for hers. She'd smiled back the moment he'd needed to jump from Ry to the steer, and although he'd done so, he'd been distracted and misjudged the distance or some crap.

"Is that it?" Daniel knelt beside him.

"Yeah, and I've got a bit of a headache." He pressed his good arm to his forehead.

"Not surprising." Daniel chuckled. "You went down pretty hard. Lucky you've got a tough skull. Let's get him onto the stretcher," he added, turning to the female paramedic.

"I'm sure I can walk." Levi didn't fancy being wheeled out through the crowds. No chance of All-Around Cowboy now, but he didn't want to draw any more attention to his accident than he already had, as such a stupid error wouldn't look good when he started advertising his rodeo school.

"I don't think so." The female paramedic laughed and rolled her eyes. "You rodeo guys think you're so tough, but until we've had the doctor check you over, we're not taking any chances."

Levi looked at Daniel pleadingly. "I'm fine. Really. I just need a hand up and then I can walk out of here."

"Sorry." Daniel held his hands out in apology. "But I can offer you some good pain relief."

"Okay," he relented, figuring that if he took the drugs, he might be in a better position to convince the paramedics he was fine. And then he could track down Selah.

Levi looked the other way as Daniel's partner held a big needle up to his arm, checking that Ry had been taken care of. He breathed a sigh of relief when he saw that Cole had entered the arena and was standing beside Ry, holding his halter and talking softly.

"You all right?" Cole called across to Levi.

"I'll live," he tried to yell back, but the needle jabbed into his arm at that moment, and he feared he groaned instead.

"I'll take care of him," Cole promised, referring to the horse, "and then Nell and I will follow to the hospital."

"Hospital?"

"Yes, Levi, the hospital," said the female paramedic, amusement evident in her voice. "Where did you think we'd take you? A resort in Hawaii?"

"I'm fine," he argued, but no one listened to his protests, and he found himself being gently lifted off the ground and onto a stretcher.

Panic filled his chest as he glanced at the faces surrounding him. What if they wheeled him away, shoved him in a hospital and by the time he was discharged, Selah had gone back to Seattle? The pain traveled from his shoulder into his chest, and he thought he might be having a heart attack.

A group of concerned competitors and rodeo committee people had gathered, making it hard to see past into the crowd. Not caring about his injury, he tried to sit up again, but Daniel forced him back down. He was about to tell Daniel to back the hell off and step aside when he heard Selah's voice.

"I need to see him. Let me in." She sounded as panicked as he felt.

"Selah!" he cried out, and the officials trying to keep her out must have heard his plea, for seconds later she was beside him.

"Oh my God. Are you okay?" She grabbed hold of his good hand and brought it up to her face, kissing his knuckles as tears spilled down her cheeks. He wanted to lift his other hand to wipe them away, but it hurt too damn much.

"I am now," he replied. Her beautiful face was better than any pain relief the paramedics could offer him.

"We're going to have to clear the arena," came an official-sounding voice.

"We'll drop him off at the hospital and then bring the ambulance straight back," Daniel told the man.

Their voices sounded like a distant echo. Levi couldn't take his eyes off of Selah. She was beautiful, now and ten years ago, and if he was honest, he'd never managed to find anyone else who could make him feel the way she did. She turned him on, she made him laugh and he could talk to her for hours and never get bored.

"I'll come to the hospital," she said, walking alongside the stretcher as Daniel and his partner started to wheel him away.

"Marry me," he blurted out, loud enough that Selah and all

the people milling around to watch the show heard.

She blinked and snatched her hand away. "What?"

He wasn't sure whether the look on her face was one of shock or surprise—there was a vast difference—but either way, he wasn't backtracking now. He'd already made a fool of himself on his horse. If he made a fool of himself for love on top of that, so be it.

"Marry me," he said again, realizing the paramedics had stopped pushing the stretcher and were listening eagerly, along with everyone else. "If you don't want to live in Marietta, we'll make the long-distance thing work somehow, or I'll find land for my business closer to you. But I love you, Selah Davis. If this weekend has showed me anything, it's that there's never been anyone but you."

He'd almost forgotten to breathe as he rushed out the proposal, and his hands felt clammy now as he waited for her response. Around them, people whooped and hollered. Someone called, "Come on, Selah, don't kick a man when he's already down."

Looking at him as if they were completely alone, she whispered, "Are you serious?"

He nodded. "I've never been more serious about anything in my life."

In reply, Selah leaned over the stretcher and gently touched her lips to his. "Let's get you checked over and then we'll talk."

AFTER ALL THAT had just happened, Selah was too shaky to drive, so Jenny got behind the wheel so they could follow the ambulance the very short distance to Marietta Regional Hospital.

"You've got some serious explaining to do, missy," Jenny said, glaring at Selah as if she were years older instead of six months younger.

"Keep your eyes on the road," Selah chastised as her friend reversed the rental car out of its parking space.

Ignoring her, Jenny continued her ambush. "What the hell happened between you and Levi last night? Last I knew, your date had been disappointing and nothing was going to happen between you. And now he's asking you to be his wife?"

Taking a deep breath to try to regulate her breathing, Selah gave Jenny the condensed version of what had happened over the past twenty-four hours. Everything from Levi supposedly turning down her salacious proposition on Friday evening to practically dragging her from Jake's arms last night. Everything right up to Levi asking her to marry him in front of half the town plus many more people who'd come for the rodeo.

"That is *so* hot," Jenny said as they turned into the hospital parking lot. "So what are you going to do?"

"He probably didn't mean to say it." Selah's heart broke as she said this, but she had to acknowledge this very real possibility. She'd seen the female paramedic inject him with something. Maybe it had been drugs speaking. "He might have a head injury. It's likely just a concussion talking."

"That's not what I asked," Jenny said firmly. "Do you *want* to marry him?"

For as long as Selah could remember, she'd been more focused on her career than looking for a man she might want to settle down with. Despite her religious upbringing, or maybe *in spite of it*, she hadn't been sure she'd ever get married. It was just a piece of paper, after all. But when she'd been staring down at Levi on that stretcher—when he'd asked her something she'd never even dared to hope—she'd realized something.

Oh, yeah…she wanted to marry him.

She wanted it more than she'd ever wanted anything in her whole entire life. She wanted Levi, she wanted Marietta and she wanted the life they could build together here, out on their own slice of the McCullough spread.

"I think maybe I do," she told Jenny simply. But she was terrified he hadn't really meant any of it. Her hands still shaky, Selah unclicked her seat belt and pushed her door open. The ambulance entrance was around the side and not accessible by the general public, so she marched toward the main ER entrance. Jenny had to run to keep up with her.

"I'm here to see Levi Monroe," she told the matronly woman behind the desk. Although she looked old enough to have been there forever, Selah didn't recognize her. "The ambulance just brought him in from the rodeo."

"You can go sit in the ER waiting area." The receptionist pointed down a corridor toward an area with a few rows of plastic chairs and a television set on the wall playing some old black-and-white movie. Jenny sat, but Selah couldn't do anything but pace. She wasn't patient at the best of times, but this felt like agony.

Levi hadn't seemed too injured, but she'd seen his head connect with the ground, and it hadn't been pretty. She wanted him checked over by a doctor, and then she wanted to run her hands over every bone in his body to make sure he was okay. And then she wanted to know if he'd meant even a fraction of what he'd said on the stretcher.

She'd barely been pacing two minutes when the entrance doors opened again, and in came Cole and Nell with Em McCullough, her son Sam and his new bride, Jane.

"Has he seen the doctor?" Em demanded.

Selah shrugged. "I guess that's what's happening now."

Em nodded curtly, sat down on a seat and then looked up at Selah. "I was at the top of the bleachers, but word has it Levi just asked you to marry him. Are congratulations in order?"

Selah felt as if six pairs of eyes were boring into her waiting for an answer. She desperately wanted to say yes, but she didn't want to put Levi in the position of feeling as if he had to follow through on a proposal he may not have meant. "Let's hold off on the champagne until we know Levi is okay."

"He'll be all right." Cole waved a dismissive hand. "He's had worse injuries than this one. Can I get anyone a coffee while we wait?"

Selah didn't think she'd be able to hold her hand still long enough to bring the cup to her mouth, but she was thankful for the distraction Cole appeared to have given everyone. He and Nell went off to find a coffee machine, and Sam and Jane sat down beside Em on the plastic chairs.

Selah waited for someone to grill her again, but Levi's relatives went quiet. Just when she thought maybe she'd have five seconds to try to get her head straight, the entrance doors opened again and in walked her parents.

Just fabulous.

At the horrified look on Selah's face, Jenny giggled. "Good news sure travels fast in this town."

"Selah, have we just heard correctly?" demanded her father.

Her mother's forehead looked pinched. "Carol Bingley just called and said you were getting married."

Not sure how to answer, Selah couldn't have been happier when the ER doors swung open and out walked a man wearing scrubs and a stethoscope around his neck. She didn't recognize him, but she hadn't been to see a doctor in Marietta in over ten years.

"Are you all here for Levi Monroe?" he asked, surveying the small crowd.

Everyone nodded, including her parents, for some bizarre reason.

The doctor smiled warmly. "Levi has dislocated his shoulder. We're going to do some X-rays to make sure nothing is broken, and he won't be riding a bull or wrestling a steer for the next few months, but I'm confident he'll make a full recovery."

Selah let out a sigh of relief that his injuries weren't more serious. "And what about the concussion?"

The doctor frowned. "What concussion?"

"His head. Didn't he knock his head?"

"I can't see any evidence of a head injury, even a mild one. Levi's a lucky guy, but I'll keep him for a few hours just for observation."

"And the pain relief?" she asked desperately. "Would it cause him to say weird things?"

The doctor looked at her like she was the one in need of medication. "Not generally."

"So he's not delusional?"

This time, the doctor laughed. "Not that I know of."

Her knees giving way beneath her, Selah finally flopped down onto one of the hard plastic chairs as hope sparked in her heart. Could she dare to hope that Levi had meant every word of his marriage proposal?

"Can we see him?" asked Em McCullough.

The doctor glanced between them. "Which one of you is Selah? I'd prefer we give Levi a chance to rest and limit visitors until after his X-rays, but he's refusing to have them until he sees Selah."

She couldn't speak. Her eyes had filled with tears again. She couldn't remember the last time she'd cried in Seattle, but over the last forty-eight hours she'd run the whole gauntlet of emotions and shed every kind of tear possible. All of them because of Levi.

Jenny nudged her in the side, and Em said, "You're not going to keep the poor guy waiting, are you? Go and put him out of his misery."

Not needing any further encouragement, Selah stood and followed the doctor into the ER. A nurse was filling out paperwork in the corner of the room, but Selah had eyes only for Levi.

"Hey there." She risked a smile as she crossed the room to stand beside his bed.

"Hi." With his good arm, he reached out, took her hand and looked right into her eyes. "Have you been crying?"

She sniffed and shrugged one shoulder. "You gave me a fright."

"Yeah, I guess I'm not gonna win All-Around Cowboy this year."

She laughed. "Possibly not the best way to go about it."

"I don't care, you know." His voice was low, and the way he looked at her made her bones quiver.

"You don't?"

He shook his head. "I came back to Marietta for the Copper Mountain Rodeo, hoping to win a few events and end my career on a high. I came back to set up a business and make some kind of life for myself. Two days ago, that dream didn't include you, but now I can't imagine doing any of it without you."

A lump formed in Selah's throat. No poetry could ever have been as beautiful as Levi's raw declaration. She couldn't speak, but he continued.

"Last night was beyond anything I could ever have fantasized. You blow my mind in every way, and there's no one else in this world I'd rather spend my life with. I meant what I said back there at the rodeo. So what's your answer?"

"You really want to marry me?"

He nodded. "It might seem hasty to some, but when something's as right as we are together, you don't question it. No way am I losing you a second time. Besides, I reckon you'd look pretty damn fine in a white, virginal wedding gown, and I'd enjoy myself immensely taking it off."

At the thought of Levi undressing her, Selah shivered. "You

know, for a rough-and-ready cowboy, you certainly have a way with words."

"Are you falling for them?" He gave her his cocky cowboy grin, and her heart swelled even more.

"I reckon I might be."

He drew her hand up to his chest. "Is that a yes, Selah Mary Davis?"

"You remember my middle name!"

"Selah," he said, his tone and eyes serious, "I never forgot one thing about you. I don't know if I'd ever have gotten through that year my mom had her stroke without you, and to be quite frank, I don't want to go through anything ever again without you."

To try to stop the tears barreling loose again, Selah leaned over the bed and kissed him. On the lips. With perhaps a little more passion than strictly appropriate for a pubic place like a hospital. She didn't care. This was the best day of her life, and if she wanted to kiss her future husband, then just let anybody try to stop her.

"Is that a yes?" Levi asked with a chuckle when she finally pulled back.

She shook her head. "No, Levi Jonah Monroe. It's a 'hell, yes.'"

Epilogue

Six Weeks Later

S ELAH WAS JUST putting the final touches on her very first edition of the *Copper Mountain Courier* when the door to her office opened. Glancing away from the birth announcement on her screen, she looked up to see Levi standing in her doorway. As usual, her heart danced a jig in her chest as she looked her fill of the sexiest cowboy to ever have graced God's earth.

"Good afternoon, good-looking." Grinning, he held up a very fine-looking bottle of sparkling wine and two crystal flutes as he stalked around her desk to get to her. He put the bottle and glasses down next to her computer, placed his hands on the arms of her swivel chair and spun her round to face him, before dragging her up and into his arms.

As was becoming a little bit of a habit—but not one she planned on trying to kick—she melted into his kiss. When things threatened to get more heated than they should in her place of employment, Selah pulled back and gestured to the bottle on her desk. "What are we celebrating?"

"Your first edition, of course."

She laughed. "We still have to print it. It's not out until tomorrow. Anything could go wrong."

"As if." He rolled his eyes, then reached for the bottle. "It'll be the best paper this town has ever seen, and once it hits the stands, you'll have every man and his dog wanting to offer you congratulations."

She opened her mouth to object, but he raised an eyebrow at her as he popped the cork. "Don't tell me Chelsea, Sage and Jenny haven't already planned dinner and cocktails."

And of course he was right. Her friends, who complained they hadn't seen nearly enough of her since she'd moved back to town two weeks ago, had called that morning and told her they'd booked a table at The Graff for tomorrow night. Levi was invited as well, of course. Jasper, Dawson and Colton would also be in attendance, as would the McCulloughs and Selah's parents, who'd quickly come round to the idea of Selah marrying a cowboy when they'd realized it meant she'd be moving back to Marietta. Apparently even Marly, Drake and their tiny, week-old baby girl, Violet, were planning on coming, and Selah wouldn't be surprised if there were a few more additions between now and tomorrow night.

The locals had embraced her homecoming, her new job and her and Levi's engagement in the same way they embraced the rodeo that had brought them together. And whatever happened down the track, whether there was a job for her on the paper once Marly returned from maternity leave or not, Selah knew two things.

She was glad she'd found Levi again and proud Marietta was the place they called home.

THE END

Cherish Me, Cowboy

A Montana Born Rodeo Novella

Alissa Callen

DEDICATION

To fabulous Jane Porter and the marvelous Tule Publishing team.
Pure magic happens in Marietta, Montana.

Chapter One

THE NEXT TIME Payton Hollis went to a wedding she'd wear boots.

Her work-roughened fingers fumbled with the delicate clasp of her sky-high sandal. "Dammit."

It would be Christmas before her foot slipped free from its candy-pink prison. She chewed the last of the gloss from her bottom lip and glanced at the prone body of the newborn calf on the other side of the wire fence.

"Hang in there, buddy. I'm coming."

She pulled hard at the diamante buckle winking in the late afternoon sunlight and the clasp finally surrendered. Her sigh of relief blew the strands of brown hair out of her eyes. The next wedding she went to she'd also wear her hat.

Payton tossed the sandal to join its partner on the battered passenger seat of her pickup and rummaged around for her old boots. Her favorite pair had split above their worn heels and she'd stored them in her truck for when she found the money to fix them. They'd been there a while.

She pulled on the soft leather and her feet sighed. Mandy Wright could remind her a thousand times what a bargain the strappy pink sandals were but next trip to Marietta she'd donate them to the thrift store they'd found them in.

The dry autumn wind tugged at her loose hair as she slid into the driver's seat. Through the dusty windshield, the rugged Absaroka mountain range pushed out of the rolling green foothills of Paradise Valley. She only had to look a little to her left to see where the green faded into a parched brown. Her great-grandfather may have named their ranch after the local white conical wildflower but no flowers, let alone grass, swayed in the breeze. Beargrass Hills Ranch had missed all the spring storms as well as the summer squalls. The prairie was bare, the cattle hungry and her water supply critical.

She turned the ignition key. She'd swing out across the road, back up to the fence and lower the tailgate so she could jump from the platform over the fence. The truck engine idled as she waited for a silver car to pass.

Out her side window, Payton checked on the black Angus cow suckling a tiny calf. When she'd left for Eliza's wedding she'd known the cow would calve that afternoon but if she'd known she'd deliver twins, she'd never have left her alone. At least the twins had arrived safely and one of the newborn calves was doing okay. It wasn't uncommon for the second calf to be rejected and Payton had a few tricks up her cowgirl sleeve to ensure the calf would survive. But before she could do anything she had to get the calf to the barn and make sure the little critter had a feed of antibody-rich milk.

Her thumbs tapped on the steering wheel as the silver car drew closer. "Move along," she muttered as the glossy sedan slowed, "there's nothing to see here."

Her stomach grumbled as she breathed in the rich aroma of the plate of foil-covered prime ribs safe on the floor of the truck. Her early lunch was little more than a vague memory. When she'd told Eliza she was worried about the cow and couldn't stay for the reception held at The Graff Hotel, her kind-hearted friend had organized a plate of food for her to take home. She smiled. Seth was one lucky cowboy and Eliza was one happy cowgirl.

Payton's smile died as she stifled an unexpected pang of loneliness. Where had that come from? The joy shining in Eliza's eyes as she'd said her wedding vows must have affected her more than she thought. She had no time, or room, in her life for a man let alone to feel lonely. She had her friends, ranch and cows. That was all she needed, wasn't it?

The male driver pulled off the road and parked the silver sedan on the verge. She released a tight breath of frustration. Now was not the time for some bored wedding guest to make a stop on their scenic Montana tour while the bride and groom had their photographs taken. She had a calf to feed and then re-mother.

Payton switched off the engine. She'd fielded her share of curious questions when her father had turned Beargrass Hills into a dude ranch during her teens. She rolled down her window. She'd dig deep into her well of zen calm and send the out-of-towner on their way.

A broad-shouldered and lean-hipped figure uncurled himself from the driver's side seat. She briefly closed her eyes. City-slicker. Then she took another look. This man might wear fancy shoes and a tailored suit but there was nothing soft about the hard line of his jaw or the swagger in his stride.

"Everything okay?" he asked, his deep voice low and slow as he reached the truck's open window. He pushed his designer sunglasses onto the top of his short, dark hair.

Payton stared into blue eyes as clear as a spring-fed summer lake. For an endless second the world fell away before the breeze carried the scent of high-end aftershave and reminded her she already had more than enough blue-eyed masculine trouble.

"Fine, thanks."

From long practice, she held his gaze. First impressions were created in ten seconds. This wedding guest needed to see past her fine bones and small size to her strength and capability. She'd fought hard against the genetic card she'd been dealt. Mandy might envy her petite figure but she refused to be treated as though she were spun from fragile glass. She was as tough and as able as any man.

The stranger's eyes narrowed. She didn't look away.

"So you don't want any help with that lone calf over there."

She blinked. Since when did a businessman notice abandoned calves.

"Nope."

"Are you sure?" She didn't know if it was the slight drawl to his tone or the quirk of the corner of his mouth that caused her breath to catch. "Because I'm sure pink cocktail dresses aren't in a cowgirl's manual of what to wear when jumping over a barbed wire fence."

Despite herself, she smiled. Funny as well as gorgeous. Mandy had sure missed this guest at the church when she'd bemoaned the lack of fresh eye-candy.

She clipped on her seat belt and glanced at the strapless and flimsy dress that was as impractical as a show pony in a barrel-race.

"So would that be the sassy and modern cowgirls' manual? Because on page three it clearly says anything pink goes. Now if you don't mind, I have a calf to rescue."

The man dipped his head and grinned. "Be my guest."

Her gaze lingered. She had the strange impression he'd look right at home doffing a cowboy hat.

"Enjoy your visit to Montana and … thanks for checking everything was okay."

His blue eyes crinkled at the corners. "Don't mention it. And you're not getting rid of me just yet. You'll need a hand to back your truck."

Before she could say she'd backed trucks for almost as long as she'd ridden horses, he strode over to the fence and waited for her to swing the truck into position. She refused to look at him as she reversed. No matter what life threw at her she wasn't a helpless damsel in distress. She didn't need help. Period.

Despite her best intentions, she snuck a quick look as he waved at her to continue reversing. She'd seen plenty of attractive masculine profiles from her two years at Montana State University, there was no reason for blood to rush through her veins and render her light-headed. She really needed to eat.

"Whoa," he called out even as she applied the brakes.

Chin tilted, she quit the truck. Show time was over whether this man liked it or not. He needed to head to Marietta and then over the mountain pass to Bozeman to catch whatever chartered jet he'd arrived on.

From the corner of her eye, she caught a glimpse of charcoal-grey and white as he leaped over the wire fence. She swung around only to see that he'd thrown the canvas horse rug from the back of the truck over the barbed wire and that his jacket and tie now hung from the side of the truck.

She ground her teeth.

Just. Awesome.

The city-stranger had let the fresh air of the Big Sky Country get to him and now relived his Boy Scout days. He'd no idea what a dead weight a calf could be. It didn't matter if the fine weave of his white shirt stretched over the taut width of his back, his gym-honed muscles weren't built for country life. It would be her luck he'd pull a muscle and then how was she going to get him over the fence? Her other good friend, Trinity Redfern, might relish any opportunity to get up close and personal, but Payton had a ranch to run and no time to indulge her hormones.

"Thanks," she shouted, "I've got this." But the north wind

stole her words.

Muttering beneath her breath, Payton let down the truck's tailgate. The capricious breeze whipped hair across her cheeks and lifted her lightweight dress. She muttered again, caught the hem before it made it past her thighs and tied a firm knot to ensure the full skirt wouldn't balloon upward again. She couldn't give Trinity back her impractical dress quick enough.

She turned to see the man heading her way. He'd rolled up the sleeves of his shirt and his strong arms easily carried the calf. His lips curved as he spoke soundless words of reassurance. The wind mussed his neat hair and his shirt gaped to reveal the tanned, strong column of his throat.

A fleeting memory teased her subconscious. The white flash of his smile reminded her of someone. But as he neared the fence and lifted the calf over the rug-covered wire and onto the tailgate, the memory fled. She took hold of the calf and eased him into the truck.

"Easy," she crooned as the calf struggled. She'd wrap the horse rug around his vulnerable body. She reached for the horse blanket on the fence at the same time as the stranger. Their hands tangled. Her eyes flew to his.

It didn't matter that he wore an expensive suit or drove a town rental car, she'd felt the calluses on his palms. She'd wager a new pair of boots. This man was no city-slicker.

He was a cowboy.

CORDELL MORGAN GAZED into thick-lashed eyes that he still couldn't decide were brown or gold. One minute they were the hue of an aspen leaf in the fall and the next they were chocolate-dark, like now.

Self-preservation told him to look the hell away. Nowhere in his five-year-plan did it include being intrigued by a woman who was as untamed and free-spirited as a wild mountain mustang.

She was slim-limbed to the point of fragility and her heavy, long brown hair framed delicate features. But she was more than a pretty face. Her direct gaze and the angle of her chin left him in no doubt her will was as strong and resolute as the granite embedded in the ground beneath his feet. The make-up and the girly cocktail dress didn't fool him. From the top of her windblown head to the toes of her scuffed boots she was a working cowgirl.

The calf struggled to its knees and as one they turned to make sure he didn't fall from the truck. With gentle words and efficient hands the woman tucked the horse rug around the calf and closed the tailgate.

She faced him and as the breeze toyed with her hair he caught the scent of fresh flowers. His jaw locked as he fought to keep his eyes on her face. The bodice of her strapless dress had slipped and now skimmed the tops of curves that would neatly fill his hands.

He reached for his jacket and tie and draped them over his arm. His testosterone could tantrum all it wanted, he had to leave. He'd already stayed too long if he noticed more about this cowgirl than the fact she had a calf needing mothering.

"Thanks again," she said with a sweet smile that reminded him of the sun's rays after a city winter's night. "I'll get going and take him to the ranch."

"A good feed of colostrum and he'll spark right up."

Her eyes searched his. "You haven't always been a city-boy, have you?"

He flexed his shoulders beneath the tailored shirt that, no matter how much it cost him, never felt comfortable.

"No."

There was no need to elaborate. But this unaffected woman would soon be nothing but a Montana memory and the knowledge loosened his tongue.

"No," he repeated, "I haven't. My twin brother and I grew up on a ranch outside Colorado Springs."

"It's a pretty part of the Rockies. Has your brother moved to the city too?"

Cordell shook his head. "The ranch wasn't big enough to support the two of us. He stayed and I moved away."

The cowgirl stood on tiptoes to reach into the truck and adjust the horse rug to better protect the calf from the wind. She spoke over her shoulder. "No wonder you're driving around sight-seeing while Eliza and Seth have their photographs, the mountain scenery would remind you of home."

He blanked out the way her dress inched a little higher up the cowgirl's smooth thighs. What was she talking about?

"I'm not driving around sight-seeing or even here to go to any wedding. I'm here on business."

She swung around, eyes dark and sharp. "You're here for business, not for today's wedding?"

"Yes." He looked toward the ranch buildings clustered on a distant hill.

She followed the direction of his gaze and folded her arms.

"If by business you mean you're going to see old Henry Watson, good luck. A century ago he'd have had run you out of town. He doesn't take kindly to strangers enquiring about his land."

Cordell didn't look away from the ranch dwarfed by the high-country backdrop. "So the stories are true?"

"It depends who's telling them. I only know him as a good and decent man." She inclined her head toward the pasture behind the truck. "This section isn't part of my ranch but Henry lets me use it because I'm all out of feed." She paused and when she spoke again her tone had hardened. "He doesn't suffer fools easily. He also rightly doesn't see the fall he had last winter, or his lack of family, as grounds for an early retirement or a land grab. So, I'll give you some friendly advice. Cut your losses and return to town. The only way Henry will leave Larkspur Ridge Ranch is in a pine box."

Cordell slung his tie around his neck and shrugged on his suit coat. "Good advice but I'm not here to buy his land, I'm here to lease it."

"Lease?"

"Yes, Henry won't need to go anywhere and will have use of whatever land he wants. I'll then pay to use the rest. I've already spoken to him on the phone and he seemed agreeable in a terse, non-committal way. So I've come to meet with him face-to-face."

Her frown didn't ease. "There's other ranches for sale, why lease Larkspur Ridge when you could own another outright?"

He kept his expression neutral. This working cowgirl was as smart as a whip. He couldn't have her perceptive gaze pry free his secrets. "Larkspur Ridge is the right location and the right acreage. I also don't want to be locked into anything long-term. Unlike my brother, I … like to move around."

"Fair enough." She glanced at the calf and unfolded her arms. "You know, you and Henry might get along. I've known him to wade into mud waist deep to rescue a calf. And I'm also sure it will do him good to have some company." Her eyes sparkled pure gold. "Even if something tells me there will be times the two of you will butt heads."

She turned and leaned into the cabin of her truck. The skirt of her bunched dress hitched higher.

Mouth dry, Cordell glanced away. Never again would he look at a short pink hemline and not see long, shapely legs encased in cowboy boots.

"Here." She passed him a foil-covered dish. "Give him this to sweeten the deal. He loves his prime ribs and it might buy you five minutes before he shows you the door."

He accepted the plate. "Thanks. Who shall I say it's from?"

She held out her hand. "Payton ... Payton Hollis."

He covered her small hand in his. Her hand remained still and then her fingers curled around his. The warmth of her palm seeped into his bones.

"Cordell Morgan," he said, hoping his voice didn't emerge a husky rasp. Touching Payton left him as disorientated as a fall from a badass rodeo bull.

She nodded and slipped her hand free.

She turned before he could identify the emotion washing across her face and settled herself into the driver's seat. Her serious eyes met his through the open window. "Henry's a generous and honorable man; be straight with him and who knows, we might end up being neighbors."

Cordell watched until her rust-red pickup disappeared over the gentle rise, a faint trail of bleached dust in its wake.

He strode toward his rental car. Neighbors or not, he wouldn't be seeing Payton Hollis again. Their paths couldn't cross. No matter how much he wished they could. The unspoilt cowgirl had caused something to unravel deep inside him and he needed his emotions to remain hog-tied. There was a reason why he never settled in one spot and kept his life entanglement free.

Just like there was a reason why leasing land wasn't the sole motive behind his coming to Marietta.

Chapter Two

~

THE PERSISTENT BARK of a black-and-white Australian Shepherd welcomed Cordell to Larkspur Ridge Ranch. He slowed on the graveled driveway as the Shepherd raced close to his wheels. The dog's instinct to herd might be invaluable out on the range but when it came to chasing cars it could become a liability. When he was sure the dog was again a safe distance away, he stopped and pulled on the emergency brake.

A double-story wooden building filled his windshield-framed view. While the ranch house had looked small and insignificant from the valley below, it now appeared as rugged and as stalwart as the mountains themselves. Movement drew his eye beyond the sprawling house and outbuildings to a corral where a buckskin mare paced. The dog's high-pitched barking intensified and the buckskin tossed her head, her black mane lifting in the wind.

Longing cut through Cordell like the lash of a bullwhip. What he wouldn't give to swap his suit for jeans and chaps and to throw a saddle on the restless horse. He understood how the corralled mare felt. Freedom was beyond both their grasps. He slid the silk knot of his tie into position. But he'd made his choices and now he had to live with them.

He tore his gaze away from the buckskin who held her head

high, scenting the breeze coming off the snow-capped peaks. He might be the eldest by only a minute but it was his duty as the first-born son to look out for his twin brother. Serious and steady Ethan wasn't a risk-taker. He could spot a sick heifer a hundred yards away but he could no more head to the city to secure their financial future than the now tail-wagging dog could abandon its natural instincts.

Cordell opened the driver's side door and stood. The dog grinned and wriggled forward as though angling for a pat, except the Shepherd's bright eyes were centered on the foil-covered plate on the passage seat.

"You can't fool me," Cordell said with a chuckle as he bent to tickle behind the dog's silken ears. "It's not me you're overjoyed to see."

The dog dropped to the ground and rolled onto his back to expose the fluffy white underside of his belly. He rubbed the dog's stomach with the toe of his city-shoes. "And looking cute won't get me to slip you a rib. Payton would have my hide if I didn't deliver the whole plate to Henry."

Sensing, rather than hearing, someone approach, Cordell looked up. A tall, unsmiling, white-haired man stood a short distance away. Faded grey eyes locked with his. He went to remove his Stetson then remembered his felt hat lay packed in a box in his Denver condo. With a last rub to the dog's belly, he walked forward, his hand outstretched.

"Hello, Henry. I'm Cordell Morgan. We spoke over the phone."

The old man grunted, his fixed stare never wavering. Just when he thought Henry wouldn't shake his hand, the gnarled strength of the rancher's fingers grasped his. He concentrated on matching the power of Henry's handshake and on reading his face. The old rancher's craggy features may appear as if carved from stone but the laugh lines around his eyes and mouth spoke of a life well-lived. Payton had spoken the truth. Henry was a hard but decent man, a man to ride the river with.

A hint of acknowledgment softened Henry's gaze. Cordell hadn't been the only person making a snap character assessment.

The handshake ended and he lowered his arm. "Sorry I'm late. I stopped to help your neighbor Payton with a calf."

"You helped Payton?"

'Yes.'

Skepticism creased the old man's brow. "And she let you, just like that?"

"Actually, to be honest I didn't give her a choice. It didn't seem right her jumping over the fence in her dress, even if she had her boots on."

"So you jumped over in your suit instead?"

He shrugged. "As you do. I did take off my jacket and tie."

A faint smile touched Henry's mouth. "As you do. And how did Payton take to you butting in?"

Cordell remembered the cuss words he couldn't hear but could see her lips form when he'd turned to make sure she didn't follow him. "Fine, considering she's used to doing things on her own."

"That she is. Anna and I weren't lucky to have children so Payton's the closest thing I have to a daughter. But even then, she's reluctant to accept help from me."

"Maybe I caught her in a soft moment but ..." Cordell swung away to retrieve the plate of prime ribs from the car. "She did wish me good luck and gave me these to buy five minutes of your time."

The dog's tail thumped on the gravel as he handed the plate to Henry.

The old man's eyes twinkled and Cordell had the impression he'd passed some sort of test before Henry's face resumed its impassive lines.

"Well then, you'd better come in."

Henry turned and for the first time Cordell realized his ramrod straight back belied a body twisted with age and pain.

He matched his stride to Henry's slower one as they walked toward the front doorsteps. From the corral a piercing whinny sounded.

Cordell stopped to gaze at the buckskin. He then glanced back at Henry and noticed the old man had stopped too, but it was Cordell whom he examined and not the restless horse.

Henry inclined his head toward the buckskin. "Payton and I adopted this mare from the Pryor Mountain horse range. She's a mustang through and through and hasn't yet taken to her new home. I'm waiting for a truckload of hay to be delivered to Payton and then she'll go to Beargrass Hills. She'll be happier out of the corral."

Cordell nodded and erased all empathy for the mustang from his face. The man waiting for him held the reins of his future in his time-worn hands. He had a promise to keep and to do so he had to gain access to the lush pastures carpeting the rolling foothills below. But first he needed to get his act together. Payton had distracted him and now the mustang's yearnings continued to stir emotions he'd long ago buried.

Shoulders squared, he followed Henry up the steps, through the front door and down the hallway into the large kitchen filled with the pure mountain light. The huge windows, exposed beams and stone feature wall, all bespoke of an attention to detail and a desire to bring the natural beauty of Montana indoors. A light-fixture made from a circle of old lanterns hung over the table, but no homely knick-knacks or family photographs sat clustered on shelves. If a woman had lived here, her presence had long since faded.

"So," Henry said as he carefully settled himself into a chair, "you'd better start talking, your five minutes starts now." He tousled the Australian Shepherd's head as the dog rested his head on his knee.

Cordell sat opposite Henry and leaned back in his chair. "I don't need to talk. You do. What do you want from a lease agreement?"

Respect glinted in Henry's slate-hard gaze. "You're a cool customer, aren't you?"

Cordell didn't answer. He wasn't going to waste time talking or feeling. He'd learned life's lessons all too well. Emotions were synonymous with weakness. To survive he couldn't allow himself to feel. No matter how high the stakes were.

"Let me see ..." Henry stared out the windows to where the waning sunlight caught in the blue of the lake Cordell had passed on the drive in.

"I'm not leaving here until they carry me out. I don't want people poking their noses into my business. I like my peace and quiet too much to hire a ranch foreman and to fill the bunkhouse with strangers. I have more than enough money. I want to read and to fish. I want to see cattle grazing but don't want the responsibility." He paused, mouth tense. "I want to end my days with no regrets."

Cordell again remained silent, not wanting to intrude on the old rancher's memories as he continued to stare out the window as though lost in another time and place. As the silence swelled between them, he wasn't even sure if Henry remembered he was there. But when Henry's sharp gaze zeroed in on his, Cordell realized Henry knew exactly where he was and whom he was with.

"So if you can deliver on these things," he continued, his tone gruff, "you might have yourself a deal."

"I can. You'll have no regrets about leasing me your land."

"Maybe."

Henry rubbed at his thigh. Pain pinched his features.

"The pastures closest to Payton's ranch are off-limits. She has full use of them for as long as she needs."

Cordell nodded.

"*If* I let you have my land what will you use it for?"

"I've two truckloads of hungry cattle leaving Texas next week."

"Herefords?"

"No, black Angus."

"I'm not surprised they're hungry. Payton's part of the range might be dry but Texas is doing it real tough. The drought there just won't break."

"I know." The despair Cordell had witnessed when he'd visited Texas three weeks ago still kept him awake at night. "And it's not only the cattle suffering. If I could, I'd make it rain."

Desperation must have seeped into his words because Henry's eyes narrowed.

Cordell cleared his throat. If he had any chance of leasing Larkspur Ridge Ranch he had to get himself under control. "So, I'll have my lawyer draw up a draft lease agreement and then –"

Henry came to his feet.

"Not so fast. This is far from a done deal." He looked at the foil-covered plate. "Rocky and I have some ribs to eat. See me tomorrow morning and I'll make my decision then."

Cordell pushed back his chair, using the simple movement to mask his tension. He'd lasted more than five seconds but he still had to pick his battles. He'd award round one to Henry but tomorrow there would be round two.

"No problem," he said as he too stood. "I'll come at nine."

"With some of Payton's chocolate-chip cookies."

"Sorry? Payton's cookies? I won't be seeing her again."

A ghost of a smile curved Henry's lips. "Where do you think you'll stay tonight?"

Cordell's tie suddenly choked like a silken noose. "Marietta?

The woman at the rental car place at Bozeman said I didn't need to book ahead."

"Well, this weekend you do. Rosa, my housekeeper, says all the accommodation in town is booked out thanks to the wedding." Henry shuffled toward the kitchen door leading to the hallway signifying Cordell's time had more than expired. "Payton won't mind if you bunk in her bunkhouse. Beargrass Hills has plenty of beds since her dad ran it as a dude ranch."

Cordell followed Henry along the hallway. As Henry held open the front door, he briefly turned, mouth hard. "And if you don't want a black eye like that cowboy Rhett Dixon, remember Payton is only interested in one thing – her ranch."

"EASY THERE, BUDDY," Payton said as she lowered the bottle to reduce the milk flow to the hungry calf. She tightened her grip to make sure the calf didn't pull the plastic bottle from her grasp. It might have taken patience and persistence to encourage him to drink but once he got started there was no stopping him. She smiled at the expanding contours of his round belly. She'd like to see Cordell lift him now. The calf had almost drunk his own body weight in colostrum.

She glanced across the barn to where a black cow stared at them, her tail twitching. She hadn't liked being milked even though the action had reduced the pressure on her swollen udder. The cow had given birth to a stillborn heifer yesterday and Payton had brought her into the barn to make sure she caught any early signs of mastitis. As kind and as generous as Dr. Noah Sullivan was, she didn't need the expense of a vet bill should the cow's udder become inflamed. With any luck the cow would now accept the abandoned calf.

The little bull calf's sucking noises changed as the bottle emptied. She slipped the teat from his milk-frothed mouth. He took a step toward her and then sank to the straw-covered floor before closing his eyes. She chuckled. Now he'd been fed the calf wouldn't be able to do anything but sleep. She'd wait until he grew hungry again and then she'd see if his new mother would let him suckle.

Bottle in hand, Payton left the barn. The evening breeze buffeted her and she dragged her denim jacket closed. It had felt so good to ditch the pink cocktail dress and pull on her faded jeans and warm blue plaid farm shirt. Fashionista Trinity would be horrified at her wardrobe choice but Payton dressed purely for practicality.

Payton's gaze strayed toward the high peaks that framed Henry's ranch house. Cordell had to be on his way to Marietta. She'd give him ten minutes tops before Henry would have sent him on his way. Her eyes lingered on the snow-crested slopes. The prospect of Cordell being gone shouldn't make her feel so … empty. By his own admission he said he didn't stay in one place for too long. But there was just something about him that made a small, hidden part of her want a chance to get to know him better.

Was that dust on the road? She strained to see into the gloom and caught an unmistakable flash of silver. She swallowed. It was as though her thoughts had conjured Cordell out of the indigo shadows. From over near the kennel beneath the pine tree, Baxter barked and pulled at his chain confirming they'd soon have company. The liver-colored kelpie had been fed early and tied up to make sure he didn't spook either the cow or the calf.

Payton lifted a hand to her tangled hair, only to quickly lower it. What was she thinking? It didn't matter if her unspoken wish to see Cordell again had been granted or that she looked a mess. She had no room in her life for a man. But still her right hand sneaked to the backside of her worn jeans to check that the rip she'd torn when milking the un-cooperative cow hadn't ripped further.

Cordell slowed and parked beside the barn. He dipped his head in greeting as he left the rental car. Despite the gathering chill, he'd discarded his jacket and tie. In the waning light, his white shirt accentuated the width of his shoulders and the honed contours of his chest. "Hey, Payton."

"Hey," she said, hoping her voice didn't betray how much her breathing had accelerated in the past three seconds. "The prime ribs seemed to have worked. You must have lasted at least five minutes."

Cordell stopped in front of her. The subtle scent of his aftershave teased her senses. He chuckled. "Yes, they did. Not that I was counting, but I would have been inside the ranch house for at least seven minutes."

The tightness constricting her chest intensified. His easy laugh was rich and genuine, with the power to stir yearnings she thought long dead.

"Wow. Henry was sociable." She searched Cordell's face for a sign of how their talk went but all she glimpsed was a deep weariness touched with a strange wariness. She arched a brow. "So ..."

"So ... I'm to come back tomorrow morning ... with some of your chocolate-chip cookies."

She shook her head. "He's such a rogue. Wait until I see him. You haven't just come for chocolate-chip cookies, have you? Let me guess, you need a place to stay?"

Seriousness dimmed the smile in his eyes. "Yes. If it was no trouble. Henry said Marietta would be booked out with wedding guests." He glanced toward the large tin-roofed building to his left. "And he assured me you have plenty of beds."

She hesitated. "I do ... it's just the bunkhouse has no running water. My foreman and his wife left yesterday to visit their daughter and I swear as soon as they drove through the main gate the windmill stopped. The bunkhouse water tank is bone dry so there's no chance of you taking a shower." She fought the heat sweeping into her cheeks at the sudden image of water sluicing over the hard-packed torso only an arm's length away. "There are plenty of beds inside if you don't mind a room with floral wallpaper, carpet and drapes. My mom had a thing for flowers."

"Thanks. I wasn't looking forward to sleeping in my car." The corner of his mouth curled in a smile. "I'm secure with my masculinity, I think I can handle a flower or too."

Her own lips twitched. "Well, that's good to hear. Luckily for you, Maria also left a freezer full of food, otherwise grilled cheese sandwiches would be the only item on the dinner menu."

"It's sleep not food I need, so a grilled cheese sandwich actually sounds pretty good. I don't want you to run short of meals."

"It's fine. Trust me. You'd much rather eat Maria's food. Even Baxter thinks twice before scoffing my meat loaf. Maria and Joe might be away for a fortnight but she's left me enough meals for a month."

Cordell nodded before his gaze dropped to the forgotten bottle in her hand. "How's the calf?"

"Good. When he's ready for his next feed I'll see if the cow that lost her calf yesterday will let him suckle. And if she doesn't I'll try the Vicks trick."

"I know the Vicks trick well. The strong smell will mask the scent of an unfamiliar calf. Your mother might have liked flowers but mine liked Vicks." Cordell pulled face. "Both for abandoned calves and sick boys."

Payton's laughter filled the small space between them. For a brief moment the weight of responsibility and the desperate need for rain didn't press so hard on her shoulders.

"I take it you didn't get a cold or the flu often?"

"No. And our cat soon stopped scratching the lounge. It seems Vicks has uses only my mother knew about." Cordell glanced toward the closed barn door. "Ethan actually uses another trick to re-mother his calves. He wets the calf and covers it in grain. After a night spent licking the feed off the calf, by morning the cow has then bonded with her new baby."

"What a great idea. Perhaps my Vicks days will be over too. I'll try it tonight if Miss-Cranky-Pants won't play nice with the small bundle of cuteness I just fed."

He smiled. "If you need a hand, let me know."

"Thanks, I'll be fine. You'll need your beauty sleep if you're to face Henry tomorrow."

"Well, if you change your mind, you'll know where I'll be. I'll grab my bag and follow you inside."

She nodded and made her way over to where Baxter lay, his head on his paws and bright eyes never leaving Cordell. She unfastened the chain from his red leather collar. He bolted over toward their guest. She didn't whistle him to her side. Cordell would cope with Baxter licking him to death.

She tucked the milk bottle under her arm and headed toward the front porch of the single-story ranch house. The desert areas of Montana would ice over before she'd change her mind about Cordell helping her with the calf. And she didn't need any reminder about where he'd be. Her stomach did a strange little flip.

He'd be three doors down the hall.

Chapter Three

PAYTON SMOTHERED A yawn and worked quickly to fill the plastic calf bottle with the last of the colostrum. After dinner Cordell had spent an hour on the phone before he'd gone to take a shower. She needed to get to the barn before he decided to help her with the calf and before she heard the sound of running water in the guest bathroom. Her hormones already fixated on the fact Cordell would soon be naked.

She pulled the rubber calf teat onto the bottle. Her cheeks radiated as much warmth as the cooker on which she'd heated the milk. For some reason sitting across the table at dinner in the small, cozy kitchen from a smiling Cordell had raised her body's core temperature. And it hadn't yet subsided. She dragged her unruly hair off her face. She needed to get back to reality. She had a ranch to run and a drought to survive. Remaining hyper-aware of Cordell, no matter how gorgeous he was, wasn't going to get her chores done. Her teenage-crush days had ended a lifetime ago back in high school.

She collected the bottle, strode along the hall to the mud-room where she collected her worn denim jacket from off the coat rack. What had Henry been thinking suggesting Cordell bunk with her? He probably thought Cordell would at least be safe around her. It was common knowledge Payton coped just fine on her own. Even if blue-eyed cowboys like Rhett Dixon were determined to challenge her independence and single-status.

She set the bottle on the floor. The upside of Cordell's visit was that he'd only stay a night. A night that was at least a third of the way through. Come morning her life would resume its safe, solitary and predictable routine. She shrugged on her coat and pulled her too-long hair out from beneath the collar. One of these days she was going to have to sit still for Mandy to give her a quick trim. A floorboard behind Payton creaked. She swung around. She'd left making her escape too late.

"Sorry," Cordell said with a weary grin. "I didn't mean to surprise you."

"It's fine." She frowned. "I thought you were taking a shower."

He nodded. "I didn't want to waste your water, so I kept it short."

As he stepped closer she could see his damp hair. He was dressed in a simple grey T-shirt and dark denim jeans and his feet were bare. Her frown deepened as the clean scent of soap filled her lungs. She needed to get out more. She never knew a man could smell so good. Or that the tight stretch of a cotton T-shirt could empty her head of all rational thought.

"Thanks. I appreciate it." She bent to pick up the milk bottle. "Water is like liquid gold around here at the moment." She inclined her head toward the kitchen. "There's coffee in the pot. Make yourself at home. I'll be in the barn a while if the cow's temper hasn't improved."

"Wait. I'll grab my shoes and come too," he said as he turned to retrace his steps.

"No, you don't have to —"

But like at the roadside, Cordell appeared to have selective hearing and disappeared down the hallway. She stomped her feet into her boots.

Cordell soon joined her, his mirror-polished shoes looking out of place with his jeans.

She planted her hands on her hips. 'Thanks, but I really don't need any help.'

"I know." His lips curved. "I'm not coming to help, I'm coming to watch."

"Watch?"

"Yes. My money's on the cow if you try to milk her again."

"And why would you think I can't handle one grouchy cow?"

Laughter gleamed in the blue of his eyes. "Because the back of your jeans tells me you've landed on your butt more than once this afternoon."

She failed to catch her own smile. She'd checked the state of the rip but hadn't dusted off the seat of her jeans. Several well-timed kicks from the unimpressed cow had sent her butt-first onto the dusty barn floor.

"Okay. Yes. There were a few pecking-order issues but it will all be fine now. Besides, the cow might accept the calf and I won't have to milk her."

Cordell headed for the door. "Let's go and find out."

"You know your fancy city shoes will get trashed in the barn," she called after him. But as her gaze slid from his broad shoulders, down to his Wrangler-clad butt, all reasons why he should stay inside fled. Muttering beneath her breath, she grabbed her father's old sheepskin coat and followed Cordell out into the darkness.

"Here, put this on," she said as they reached the red barn door. The coat wasn't so much to warm Cordell against the night air but for her piece of mind. Something had to be wrong with her? Lean, long-legged cowboys were nothing new in her world, so why did this cowboy's smile have the power to make her breath hitch?

She handed him the coat. She didn't need to be distracted by the flex of a smooth biceps. She wasn't landing back on her butt on the barn floor around Cordell anytime soon.

"Thanks."

His white grin flashed in the moonlight as he slid on the jacket.

She opened the barn door and switched on the barn light that would illuminate the entrance and leave the pens shadowed. The rustle of straw sounded as the cow stood and turned to look at them.

Payton entered the calf's pen and ran a hand along his soft black back. He blinked his wide eyes open to stare at her. She'd take the edge off his hunger before she let him loose on the cow's full and tender udder.

"Hey buddy, it's dinner time."

The calf scrambled to his feet and head-butted her knees looking for milk. She guided the teat into the calf's mouth. When he sucked strongly, she glanced toward the still quiet cow and then to where Cordell leaned his hip against the wooden pen rail.

"Sorry to disappoint you but there could be no show," she said with a grin. "Miss-Cranky-Pants over there is half asleep and appears quite amiable. She might adopt the calf without a fuss and then I won't have to milk her."

The corner of Cordell's mouth kicked into a half-mile. "Or she's lulling you into a false sense of security."

"Thanks. You're a regular ray of sunshine."

His rich laughter rippled through the fine hairs on her nape. He moved away from the wooden rail. "How about I go and find some grain for our Plan A. There looks to be feed bins over there to the right?"

She nodded, her attention diverted as the impatient calf butted the bottle wanting a quicker milk flow.

Cordell returned with a grain-filled bucket.

"He's a lucky little critter. I was in Texas a few weeks ago and a calf like him wouldn't have stood a chance. Cow's didn't have the strength to stand let alone milk for a newborn."

"That's dreadful." Her eyes lingered on Cordell's drawn features. The rawness of his words hinted at a fatigue that bit deeper than physical exhaustion.

Cordell stared at the calf. "That's why I need Henry's land. He hasn't run cattle for years and pasture-rich Larkspur Ridge is a hungry Texan cow's idea of paradise."

"So you've bought some cattle to fatten?"

She again concentrated on feeding the calf. Cattle-trading was a common ranch practice but it didn't feel quite right Cordell making money off someone else's misfortune. He would have purchased the starving cattle for a pittance and would make a healthy profit once they grew sleek and fat.

"I haven't bought them. I'm helping out an old friend." Cordell paused. "Luke gave me a place to stay when I needed one and it's the least I can do to save the last of his breeding stock. His family has bred cattle for four generations and the financial pressure of no rain has cost him his marriage. I now can't let him lose everything. I said I'd take care of the cattle until he got back on his feet."

From the gravity of Cordell's words she knew such a thing could take a while even if rain were to fall across the Lone Star State.

"This little critter might be lucky, but your friend is lucky too; he has you."

"Maybe." Cordell rubbed a hand along his jaw. "He swears his grey hair is a result of all the things I dragged him into when we were youngsters on the rodeo circuit."

"Boys will be boys."

Cordell smiled but even in the poor light she could see his

smile didn't reach his eyes. "Some boys took more risks than others. My Denver agricultural consultancy business can run itself for a while. I owe it to Luke to get my hands dirty and to safeguard his, and his infant son's, future."

The calf sucked the last of the milk from the bottle, his appetite in no way satisfied.

"Okay," she said as she opened the wooden pen gate and slipped through before the calf could follow her. "Let's see if your brother's trick works. Do your water and grain thing and we'll introduce the cow to her new, beautiful baby."

"PLEASE TELL ME I'm not seeing things," Payton said the next morning from the barn doorway. Cordell turned away from the sight of the calf feeding from the contented cow. He narrowed his eyes as the bright early morning light poured through the door Payton had left open behind her.

"No, you're not. Your cranky cow has turned into a doting mother."

"My Vicks days are behind me. The grain trick really works," Payton said as she rested her arms beside his on the top timber rail of the cow's pen. He breathed in her sweet floral scent and felt the companionable pressure of her arm against his. "Look at his little tail wiggle, he's so happy, and look at the size of his belly. He can't possibly be hungry any more."

Cordell only nodded. He needed another second or two before he could speak. The beauty of Payton's smile delivered such a jolt to his senses he knew the water and grain plan was the only thing to have worked. He'd thought a sleepless night would blur the effect this Montana cowgirl had on him. His jaw clenched. He'd been wrong. Her happiness danced through him like the dust swirling through the streams of barn light.

"Your brother is one clever cowboy."

"Yes, he is."

She was so close he could see the thick length of her dark lashes, the satin hue of her skin and the natural pink of her full lips. Her hair was pulled back into a ponytail and her fine-boned face was all high cheekbones and large eyes. But as fragile as she appeared, the strength of her spirit shone from her intelligent brown gaze.

He straightened so their arms no longer touched. He had to get out of the barn and away from all temptation to tug her close and explore the soft skin below her jawline with his mouth. He'd come to Montana to lease Henry's land and to make peace with the past. Not to have his self-control desert him.

He forced himself to remain still while she reached out to touch his jacket collar. When she lowered her arm he saw straw caught between her fingers.

"Did you sleep here?"

He stiffened. He'd hoped she wouldn't discover where he'd spent the night. The knowledge would only lead to questions he didn't want to answer.

"Yes." He forced a casual smile. "I lied when I said I could handle sleeping in a room full of flowers."

"But I came in at one and again at four and you weren't here?"

"I was. You brought a flashlight. I didn't want to scare you or talk in case I spooked the cow."

"You slept here *all* night?" she said frowning at a pen filled with clean straw.

"And it was quite comfortable compared to some of the places I've slept on the rodeo circuit."

"But why stay? You were dog-tired and I had everything under control."

"I know you did." He scraped a hand through his city-short hair. "I couldn't sleep so thought I may as well be on hand if the cow didn't share your view of the calf being cute enough to be her own."

Her frown cleared but the intensity of her stare didn't waver. "Thank you."

"You're welcome."

"Do you often not sleep?"

"It depends on where I am." He swung away toward the open barn door. His secrets, along with his emotions, had to remain hidden. "I don't know about you, but I hear the coffee pot calling."

He stepped into the new day and strode toward the ranch house. But as fast as he moved he couldn't outrun the darkness of the memories that stalked his dreams no matter where he slept.

TWO COFFEES LATER, Cordell drove through the wooden archway of the Larkspur Ridge main gate. Heavy dew clung to the gossamer cobwebs strung between the wire of the fence either side of the road. Behind him pockets of mist lazed in the valley hollows. Winter would soon throw its blanket of white over the mountains but Henry's land would provide perfect wintertime grazing. The draws and gullies would offer protection from the snow and the pine trees respite from the wind. The Texan cattle would soon grow thick coats and adapt to their new environment.

He swallowed. If only he could be so resilient. The knot in his gut told him he could stay at Payton's ranch countless winters and still his self-control would hemorrhage. Never before had he found it so difficult to remain on task or to keep his feelings in check when around a woman. It wasn't just how she looked. Sure her smile kicked him harder than a stallion's hoof, but she was so much more than a beautiful face. Her strength, her kindness and her generosity humbled him.

She'd insisted he wear her father's sheepskin jacket to see Henry. She argued that Henry would relate to him more than if he wore his suit. Cordell's grip firmed on the steering wheel. But when he then returned the jacket, his visit to Beargrass Hills would have to be his last. Even if Henry agreed to the lease proposition and he and Payton became neighbors, he had to put distance between them before he forgot who he was and why he'd come to Montana. Once Luke's cattle were settled, Cordell could split his time between Marietta and Denver until the pieces of his friend's life slotted back together.

He approached the ranch house and just like before, Rocky dashed toward the rental car. But this time, a shrill whistle sounded and the Australian Shepherd retraced his steps to where Henry hobbled away from the corral. Behind him the buckskin had her nose deep in the bucket of food Henry had delivered.

Cordell parked the sedan, collected Payton's container of chocolate-chip cookies and made his way over to the old rancher. The buckskin lifted her head, her nostrils flaring, before returning to her feed.

Henry eyed off Cordell's mismatched city-shoes, jeans and sheepskin jacket. "Coat Payton's idea?" A suspicion of a smile warmed his grey gaze.

"Yup. The things I do to get you your cookies. It was no coat, no cookies."

Cordell bent to rub the Shepherd's ears. "Sorry, no ribs today, Rocky."

"For someone who slept in a bed you look like hell," Henry said as Cordell carefully straightened, "and you move like you're as old as me."

He rolled his bad shoulder. He'd once come off second-best riding a black bronc that was more devil than horse.

"We re-mothered the calf last night, so I slept in the barn."

Henry grunted, the brief dip of his head telling Cordell that the sound was more one of approval than disinterest. "Did you use Vicks?"

"No, grain and water. My brother swears by it."

Henry's eyes narrowed.

"Smart man. Younger brother?"

"Yes, by minutes."

"That figures. Identical twins?"

"No. But we do look similar even if we are then very different."

"Let me guess." Henry's stare zeroed in on Cordell's stiff shoulder. "He's not so knocked about?"

Cordell grinned. "True. But while I might have a few more aches and pains than Ethan, there's plenty of life left in me yet. I could still go a bareback bronc round or two."

Henry chuckled. "You and me both."

The old rancher's laughter shaved decades off his face. The rigid line of his jaw relaxed as memories returned him to an earlier life. Cordell's own rodeo memories stirred. The smell of leather, dust and sweat. The intense quiet as the chute opened. The rush of adrenaline as the horse beneath him exploded into life.

A gust of cold wind funneled down the back of his neck and returned him to the present. There were no more rodeos. Just promises to keep. He adjusted the sheepskin coat collar. "Henry," he said, voice now quiet, "I know what you're up to. It won't work."

An indefinable expression flashed across his weathered face, before his mouth tensed. "And what's that?"

"Payton is like a daughter to you and so it's only natural you want to help her."

"That might be so but we both know that Payton accepting help is as likely as a blizzard in summer."

"But it doesn't stop you ... and me ... from trying. You delayed making your decision last night so I'd stay with her, didn't you?"

Henry's only answer was a scowl that would have sent a lesser man hightailing it to his car.

Cordell held his sub-zero gaze. He'd dealt with men far frostier than Henry. "I agree, in a perfect world Payton wouldn't be on her own and responsible for running Beargrass Hills. But I'm not the answer. The truth is I'm no good for her." He swallowed past an unexpected sense of loss. "I have trouble staying in one place and she needs someone steady and reliable like my brother."

"She doesn't need someone like your brother. She needs someone who understands her. Someone who will risk everything for her." Henry rubbed at his thigh and inclined his head toward the valley to their right now bathed in the bright morning light. "Walk with me."

Cordell nodded and walked beside him, matching his slow pace. What had he been thinking bringing Payton into the conversation? Sleep deprivation was no excuse for acting on the impulse to make sure Henry didn't send any more would-be suitors in Payton's direction. Losing focus and allowing his emotions to sidetrack him wasn't going secure him the land that now rolled before him in a sea of windblown green.

Henry stopped at the edge of the driveway and together they stared out at the empty pastures dotted with pine trees instead of glossy-coated cattle.

"The land's yours," Henry said in a husky voice, without looking at him.

Cordell remained silent for a moment. "Just like that?"

"Yup." Still Henry didn't make eye contact. "Take it or leave it."

"I'll take it."

A smile touched Henry's mouth as he turned toward him. "I thought so. There's two conditions."

"Name them."

"Payton's chocolate-chip cookies."

He handed the container of cookies to Henry. "And?" He clenched his teeth. He already knew what was coming.

"There's an old cabin but it's inhabitable. The quickest way in, apart from through here, is the gate you passed on your way from Payton's."

"So when I return in a week, you want me to stay at Beargrass Hills Ranch?"

"Yes and I want you to pay board. Payton needs the money. She has a heart as generous as her mother's so she'll refuse to accept payment but I'm counting on you to make sure she takes it."

"Done." He matched Henry's brusque tone. "But I'm putting it on record that it doesn't matter how much time we spend together, I won't ever be right for Payton."

"Maybe and maybe not. One person who isn't right for her is Rhett Dixon." Henry shook his head. "Now there's a set of twins that couldn't be more different. Rhett could do with some of his twin sister's sense. Kendall's just as worried about their sick mother but she knows better than to hang around those troublesome Taylor boys." Henry paused and held out his hand. "So shall I expect to hear from your city-lawyer this afternoon?"

Cordell shook Henry's hand. "Yes, I'll call him on my way out."

But as his arm lowered to his side and he gazed out at the foothills that were now his, unease shouldered aside his relief. He'd secured the land he needed but at a price.

He'd be living with the one woman he had to stay away from.

Chapter Four

"**N**OW *THAT'S what* I'm talking about," Trinity said, her words ending in a drawn-out sigh.

Payton didn't have to look up from scanning the rodeo program to know her friend salivated over a man. Trinity had only come to the 76th Copper Mountain Rodeo for one thing – cowboys. Luckily Payton had come for the events. She read the list once again. She'd run late helping a cow calve and if Trinity and Mandy didn't stop dawdling to look at the masculine scenery they'd never make it to the main arena to catch the tie-down roping.

"I hear you," Mandy replied from Payton's left, a dreamy note in her voice. "Come on Pay, take a look. You can't be all work and no play. The view will make your day."

Payton sighed. She'd have no peace until she threw a token glance toward the cowboy. She looked up from the program. "You guys, the only thing that will make –" Her jaw dropped.

The cowboy, dressed in jeans, chaps and a blue western shirt, who tied a black horse to the side of a trailer was the last person she'd expected to see.

Cordell.

Mandy giggled. "Trinity, mark this day. Payton's mouth is hanging open and she isn't checking out a nice piece of horseflesh. Eliza might be on the other side of the world honeymooning in Australia, but I'm going to have to call her."

Cheeks burning, Payton snapped her mouth shut. "No, you don't. Leave Eliza and Seth in peace. It's not what you think."

"So tell us what it is like, then," Mandy said with a raised fine brow.

"That's Cordell."

"You *know* him?" Trinity asked, green eyes round. "Because I can guarantee he's not from around here."

"He's not. That's the cowboy leasing Henry's land."

Mandy grabbed her arm. "The one *staying* with you."

"Yes. Three doors down the hall."

"We are so having a girls' night in at your place," Mandy said. "How does next Friday sound?"

Payton laughed. "No way. I'm not sitting through one of those chick flicks with you again. But I might consider cooking dinner one night if you let go of my arm before I lose all feeling in my fingers."

"Sorry," Mandy said with an unrepentant grin, releasing her. "I can't believe you were holding out on us."

"I wasn't. I told you about him."

"You did, but you left out a few important details." The laughter in Trinity's eyes dimmed. "He might look good in his Wrangler jeans but is he a good guy? You shouldn't be out there alone with him, if he isn't. When are Joe and Maria back?"

"Joe and Maria won't be back for another week but it's fine, Trin. I can take care of myself. And, yes, he's a good guy. I wasn't expecting him for a couple more days. I guess that's why I looked ... surprised."

A dimple flickered in Trinity's cheek as she smiled. "Yes, the expression on your face was pure ... surprise."

"Don't look now," Mandy said, "but your gorgeous, good guy is staring at us."

"He's not my guy. You both know I've only time for my ranch." Despite her words, fresh heat surged in her face as Cordell lifted a hand in a brief wave. "Now you two, behave," she warned as he strode toward them.

Cordell's smiling blue eyes touched each of them in greeting before he doffed his felt hat at her. "Payton."

"Hi." She quickly spoke, even knowing her voice would emerge far too high. She was pretty sure Trinity and Mandy, for once, would be speechless. A man shouldn't look so damn fine.

"Cordell, these are my good friends, Trinity," Payton inclined her head toward the smiling brunette on her right, and then toward the beaming blonde to her left, "and Mandy."

"It's nice to meet you both." He smiled a crooked grin. "Great job getting Payton off the ranch and away from her cows."

"Hey, I like my cows."

But her words were lost beneath Trinity's and Mandy's breathless giggles.

Just. Perfect. Her two besties were already besotted. And they hadn't even seen what Cordell looked like on a horse yet.

Trinity cast an eye over Payton's conservative small belt buckle and her plainly stitched boots. "We're still working on her wardrobe but we are making progress. She wore a dress last weekend."

Cordell's mouth curved. "I know."

The dark flash of appreciation in his eyes caused Payton's toes to curl.

She silenced a groan as Trinity's and Mandy's bright and curious gazes centered on her. As soon as they were alone, Payton would be in for a grilling. There were a few details about Cordell she hadn't yet mentioned, least of all how they'd met and what she'd worn.

"So," she said, tone firm trying to regain control of the

conversation, "what brings you to the 76th Copper Mountain Rodeo? I didn't think you were due in town for another day or so."

'I wasn't but seeing as I'll be working cattle soon I thought I'd freshen up my roping skills." He paused. "I did leave a message on your ranch phone. I don't have your cell number."

"Sorry, with Maria away I keep forgetting to check for messages."

"No problem, I only expected a call if it didn't suit for me to arrive today."

She nodded and forced herself to hold his gaze. She'd forgotten how crystal clear his blue eyes were and how strong the line of his jaw. Her fingers had the sudden urge to trace the stubble-blurred curve from his chin to his mouth. She jammed her hands into her jeans pockets and forced her breathing to slow. She'd soon have some explaining to do. Her friends would know when she was flustered. And when it came to the cowboy in front of her, all he seemed to do was upset her rock-steady equilibrium.

Trinity looped her arm through Mandy's and pulled her away from Payton's side.

"Nice to meet you, Cordell," she said, "good luck in the tie-down roping. We'll make sure we cheer for you." Trinity glanced at Payton, her eyes innocent. "Mandy and I need to catch up with Selah over there and we'll meet you in the stands."

Then before she could even assemble the words, "I'm coming with you," Trinity and Mandy had walked away.

Payton looked back at Cordell and found his intent gaze on her.

She wet her dry lips. At least her precious cows never left her alone with a cowboy whose smile scrambled her thoughts. Wait until she saw Trinity and Mandy. They'd already caught up with dark-haired Selah Davis as they'd been talking to the gorgeous Seattle journalist when Payton had arrived. Selah had returned to cover the rodeo for her women's magazine, Charisma.

"How's the calf doing?" Cordell asked, voice low and casual.

"Good, thanks." Then realizing her reply sounded far too formal, she smiled. "You won't believe how much he's grown."

"I bet he has. He was a greedy little critter."

Cordell's words were warm but still a strange seriousness tempered his gaze. It was as though he was as uncertain as she was about being alone with her. Get real. Cordell might not stay around for long but when it came to women his cowboy swagger and grin would leave a trail of languishing hearts behind.

She searched for something to say. "When are you expecting Luke's cattle?"

"In two days. That will give me a chance to check Henry's fences and water." His eyes examined hers. "Are you sure it's okay me arriving early?"

She ensured her expression remained neutral. She'd counted on the extra days to make sure her self-control would be watertight. But if her earlier open-mouthed reaction at seeing him was any indication she'd have needed extra weeks.

When Cordell had returned her father's sheepskin jacket and asked if he could bunk with her while he leased Henry's land, she'd agreed. Her self-preservation had hyper-ventilated at the thought of him staying longer than one night but Beargrass Hills Ranch was the logical location to base himself. The starving cattle would need attention and time and Cordell would be close enough to provide both.

"It's fine. You'll just have to suffer my cooking and sleeping in the main house until Maria and Joe are back next week. Joe can then tinker with the windmill so there'll be running water at the bunkhouse again."

"Sounds like a good plan. I'll be coming and going at all

hours and so won't disturb you over there. But you don't need to cook for me while I'm in the main house. I'll take care of myself."

She frowned. "That doesn't seem fair. I feel bad enough as it is about accepting money for having you stay. How about if you cook, you don't pay board?"

Cordell's jaw hardened. "We went over this before I left. I'm staying and so I'll pay."

She slipped her hands from out of her jeans pockets. Now she was on familiar ground and in her comfort zone. Arguing with a strong-willed cowboy she could handle. It was the uncertainty and confusion she felt around him that ruined her composure.

"Actually, I don't think we resolved our earlier discussion."

"Yes. We did. I'm paying."

A horse's impatient whinny punctuated his words.

Cordell turned to look at his trailer.

"That would be His Lordship telling me to get a move on. I'd best get him saddled and warmed up."

"Outside the main arena there's a smaller space where you can put him through his paces."

"Thanks." Cordell pushed his hat brim a little higher so their eyes could fully meet. "Listen Payton, you know I have to pay, as well as stay. That was part of Henry's conditions to lease his land."

"I know, as I said before he's such a rogue. Thank you again for being honest with me." She sighed. "I still don't feel comfortable about you paying but I concede defeat ... this time."

"MOSSY, STOP LOOKING at me like that," Cordell said as he approached his restless horse. "Yes, I talked to Payton for too long. And yes, I need to stay away from her."

Mossy's ears flattened and he aimed a kick at Cordell that would have hit a fly on a wall. He automatically side-stepped Mossy's hoof. The horse's show of bad temper was nothing but a game, a game that could still leave him bruised if he didn't keep his wits about him.

He collected Mossy's saddle blanket and saddle from inside the trailer. And it wouldn't only be Mossy's teeth or hooves that would pack a wallop if he didn't concentrate. His own conscience would give him a hiding if he lost sight of why he'd come to Marietta. The five days away from Montana had in no way diluted his response to Payton.

When her friends had left the two of them alone, he'd been strangely tongued-tied. For a man never lost for words, all it took was tousled brown hair and the tight hug of faded denim and he was as incoherent as a schoolboy. And it had to stop. Once at Beargrass Hills he'd keep himself so busy their paths wouldn't cross. Thanks to old Henry, they might be living in close proximity but he'd meant what he'd said that Payton deserved better than him.

He exited the trailer, saddle blanket and saddle slung over his arm. Hooves drummed to his left and he swung around. Rodeos would test an anxious horse. The crackle of the loudspeaker or the squeal of an excited child could all trigger a horse's instinct to run.

He tensed as he caught sight of a riderless bay galloping toward him. Stirrups flapping and reins dragging, the horse ducked and weaved through the thin crowd as he headed for the open space of where the trailers congregated. Cordell dumped the saddle, reached into the trailer to grab Mossy's half-full feed bucket and glanced in the direction Payton had walked. His mouth dried. She stood talking to Henry near a goose-neck trailer, both of their backs toward the runaway horse.

A scream sounded. He high-tailed it over to the dirt road along which the horse travelled. A young mother, a chubby baby on her hip, abandoned the pram she was pushing to run behind a trailer as the horse bore down on them. The horse clipped the navy pram as he sped by and it toppled over.

Cordell stepped onto the road, making sure he didn't fully block the frightened horse's escape route. Talking softly he called to the bay, held out the bucket and then shook it so the rattle of grain sounded. The horse didn't slow or appear to notice him standing there. Cordell remained where he was. Shoulders relaxed and voice calm, he continued to call to the horse and shake the bucket. Just when he thought the bay would race past, the gelding swung around to face him and pulled to a jarring stop. Head high, he snorted, his sweat-darkened flanks quivering.

"Steady boy," Cordell crooned.

The horse took one and then two steps toward him and sank his nose into the bucket. He snatched a mouthful of grain and then flung up his head. Knowing one sudden move or sound would spook the horse, Cordell remained still. The horse again snorted and lowered his head to the grain. The bay took a step closer and this time he didn't lift his head as he ate.

Cordell touched the hot and damp skin of the horse's neck and eased his hand forward to secure the loose reins.

Boots pounded on the ground and Cordell shook his head to stop a white-faced youth from rushing over to the horse.

"It's okay," he said gently, "give him a little longer to settle."

The youth nodded and bent to rest his elbows on his knees to catch his breath.

When satisfied the horse wasn't going to bolt, Cordell led him over to the youth who accepted the reins with a shaky smile. "Thanks so much. It's his first rodeo and a kid popped a balloon near him."

"I thought so," Cordell said with a smile, "he's just a young un'. Go easy with him past those flags."

He watched the gelding walk behind his owner as they headed toward two flags attached to the arena fence and that fluttered high above the trailers. As the gelding shied sideways, a tall, well-built cowboy came to the youth's side and took hold of the horse's reins.

Cordell caught the youth's relieved, "Thanks, Levi," before he turned away to carry the feed bucket over to his trailer and continue to saddle Mossy.

PAYTON DIDN'T KNOW where to look. Palms cold, she glanced over to where Cordell was saddling his horse as if nothing had happened. Beside her, Henry stared at the toppled pram, his shoulders bowed and his face pale beneath his tan.

She touched his arm. "Henry, there was no baby in the pram, remember? We thought there was and then we saw the mother carrying the baby behind the trailer."

Henry nodded, but the tension etching his face in sharp and strained lines didn't lessen. Anna and Henry had never been blessed with children and Henry had a soft spot for calves and foals. Seeing the pram tip over and for a brief time assuming a baby had been inside, had scared him. And he wasn't the only one.

She willed her heart to stop racing. It hadn't only been a possible baby in the pram whom she'd felt fear for.

"What was Cordell thinking?" she muttered through clenched teeth.

Henry cleared his throat beside her. "He was always going to be okay. He has a way with horses."

"A way with horses? I'd call it a death wish. I mean who steps out in front of a runaway horse like that?"

"Pay, he wasn't right in front of the horse. It just looked like he was from this angle."

Anger trembled in her hands. "I don't care where he stood. He could have been … hurt."

She stopped talking before she said, and revealed, too much.

"He's survived the rodeo circuit and that black horse of his isn't one I'd turn my back on, he knows what he's doing."

As she watched, Cordell's horse bared its teeth at him as he tightened his girth. Cordell didn't flinch or move away. The horse snapped on air and then faced forward. Cordell gently pulled the horse's front legs to make sure the girth didn't pinch, before gathering the reins and swinging into the saddle.

Her anger drained away like water through the desert-dry earth of her ranch.

Okay. Trinity's and Mandy's admiration wasn't misplaced. She'd now seen Cordell on a horse. And yes, he looked as good on horseback as he did standing on the ground wearing boots, snug jeans and leather chaps.

She glanced at Henry who also was watching Cordell. Color hadn't yet returned to the old rancher's face.

"He might have had everything under control with the horse," she said, "but you can't tell me Cordell doesn't take unnecessary risks."

A twinkle returned to Henry's faded grey gaze. "I know a certain cowgirl who also takes unnecessary risks instead of asking for help and who has adopted a mountain mustang who isn't exactly as quiet as a lamb."

She returned Henry's smile. "*We* adopted the mustang and I'm not even going to start on what risky things you do that your doctor has told you that you shouldn't."

The loudspeaker crackled into life announcing the tie-down roping would soon commence.

She glanced toward the main arena. "I'd best get going

before all the action starts without me."

Henry's expression sobered. "Pay, why aren't you competing? The ladies' barrel-race has always been your event and you missed it last year for the 75th Copper Mountain Rodeo anniversary as well."

She pressed a kiss to his weathered cheek. "Too busy."

The truth was she had even less money this year to enter or to run her trailer into town, but that wasn't Henry's concern.

"Next year," she added with a smile that she hoped covered her fears.

She headed toward the main arena and lifted her hat to drag her hand through her hair. Surely by the 77th Copper Mountain Rodeo it would have rained. Surely by next year she'd be making good on her graveside promise to her parents that their only child would never let them down.

Chapter Five

~

"**S**o ...?"

As she'd been doing since she'd joined her friends on the bleachers, Payton ignored Mandy's loaded question. Before the tie-down roping had started she'd given them enough information about when she'd met Cordell but left out all the parts to do with how he made her feel so out of control. Especially when he took dangerous risks.

She'd even disappeared to buy popcorn, hoping it would keep her friends silent. The loudspeaker boomed introducing the next competitor for the rope and tie event.

"Who hoo, Cordell's on," Mandy said with glee, her cheeks bulging with popcorn. "So ... tell us again, Payton, what were you wearing when you met him."

Payton sighed. The popcorn hadn't worked.

"For the last time ... I was wearing Trinity's pink dress and my old boots.'

Mandy pulled a face. "I can't believe you weren't wearing those to-die-for shoes we found in the thrift store. They'd be any cowboy's fantasy."

"And every cowgirl's nightmare. They were so uncomfortable."

"What's a blister or two when you're wearing killer heels?"

"Killer heels is right. I don't know how you can even walk, let alone dance, without doing yourself an injury."

Mandy laughed. "All it takes is commitment."

"Well, my only commitment is to my cows, not to impractical sky-high shoes."

"Someday you'll eat those words, Payton Hollis."

"Not in this lifetime."

Mandy's smile widened. "Want to make a bet?"

Payton shook her head at her incorrigible friend and waved to the two Bar V5 wranglers she'd spied sitting in an adjacent bleacher. Charlie Randall would be at the rodeo with her dude ranch guests and would have roped Zack Harris into helping her play tour guide. And going off the rigid line of Zack's broad shoulders he'd much rather be back at the ranch.

Payton shifted on the hard seat and dangled her foot through the gap between her and the person sitting in front. Her butt was numb and she needed to go for another walk but she didn't want to miss seeing Cordell in action. She adjusted the angle of her hat. The sun had shifted in the afternoon sky. Too late, she felt the nudge from Trinity in her ribs and heard her muttered, "Heads up."

Boots clattered on metal as a broad-shouldered, masculine body slid into the spare space beside her. A familiar woody aftershave informed her who her new bench-buddy was. Rhett Dixon.

"Ladies," he drawled as he swept off his Stetson and bowed.

"Hey," they all answered, but it was only toward Payton that Rhett looked. She smiled into his handsome face. He'd been pulling her pigtails since first grade and she'd enjoyed his company until he'd begun his crusade to end her single days.

"Payton, you walked right past me with your popcorn. Didn't you hear me call out?"

"Sorry. The crowd must have been cheering."

"New shirt?"

She gritted her teeth as his blue gaze slid over her chest.

"No, same shirt as when I saw you outside the diner two weeks ago." She kicked his boot. "Rhett, eyes above my collarbones. You know what happened last time you forgot your manners."

"How could I forget? My shiner took a week to go away." His smile turned sheepish. "In my defense, I did have a bit of beer on board that night in Grey's Saloon."

"Well, you don't now, so stop looking me over like I'm a breeding cow."

Beside her, Trinity giggled. "You go, girl," she said in an undertone only Payton could hear.

"Sorry."

"No, you're not. Just don't do it again." But her words didn't contain any bite. Good-looking and blond-haired Rhett was harmless. The first son in three generations of ranchers, he'd led an indulged life. After his mother's recent heart attack, he'd started hanging out with the fast-playing and hard-drinking Taylors. With dimples, a movie-star smile and a host of rodeo wins, he had a parade of buckle-bunnies throwing themselves his way. Her disinterest was a respite. As much as he chased her, she had no doubt deep down he knew he would be safe. She'd never see him as anything but the good friend that he was.

Mandy reached past Trinity to tap Payton's knee. "There he is."

"There who is?" Rhett asked, an edge to his tone.

Trinity waggled her eyebrows. "Payton's new cowboy."

Payton turned to Rhett. "Ignore them. He's not my cowboy. He's just someone boarding at Beargrass Hills while he leases Henry's land."

"How long's he staying?"

The hostile note in Rhett's voice was unwelcome. Despite

her clear messages and continued indifference his single-minded pursuit was getting out of hand.

"I'm not sure. He says he doesn't ever stay in any place for long so I've no doubt he'll soon move on."

Rhett didn't answer, all his attention remained focused on the man astride the large black horse waiting for his turn in the tie and rope.

"Well, if his horse's head hung any lower he'd fall asleep."

Payton had seen the speed with which Cordell's horse had whipped his head around to bite him. The black horse was far from sleepy.

"Maybe's he's an old hand and is relaxed," she said.

Rhett lifted a dark-blond brow.

"At least he won't break too early," Trinity piped up, "and earn Cordell a 'cowboy speeding ticket' and ten second time penalty like that last hypo-horse."

Payton smiled. For someone who claimed to go to rodeos for the cowboys Trinity sure knew a lot about tie-down roping.

"Shush, here he goes," Mandy said as Cordell guided his horse into the small square roping area set behind the barrier.

He held a coiled pigging string in his mouth ready for when he'd lassoed the calf and needed to tie three legs together. Her fingers curled into her palms as she waited for the moment when Cordell would nod and the chute operator would release the calf.

Suddenly a brown-and-white calf leapt from the chute and shot toward the middle of the arena. The black hindquarters of Cordell's horse bunched but instead of dashing after the calf, the gelding remained still.

"See," Rhett said with a frown. "What did I tell you? His horse is half asleep."

"No, he isn't. It was a false start. The chute operator pulled the lever too soon and let the calf out. Cordell hadn't nodded."

She didn't meet Rhett's gaze sensing he'd pick up on how closely she watched Cordell. "It happened to me once."

The gate across the arena opened and the calf raced through heading for the company of the other calves in the outside corral.

"Take two," Mandy said as with the arena now clear, Cordell nudged his docile horse a little closer to the barrier.

Cordell nodded to the chute operator and this time when the calf tore from the chute, his horse detonated into action.

Payton barely blinked before Cordell's lariat landed in a neat loop around the calf's neck. He was then off his horse, the calf was on the ground and his legs tied in a half hitchknot. All too soon, Cordell lifted his arms in the air signaling to the field judge to stop the clock.

Cordell then remounted and urged his horse forward to release the tension on the rope anchoring the calf to his saddle. The calf had to stay tied for six seconds. Payton silently counted down from six, her hands unfisted as she reached one. Cordell lifted his hat to the now cheering crowd then smiled and leaned forward to hug his horse's neck.

"I'm no cowgirl," Trinity said in an awed whisper, "but that was fast wasn't it?"

"Yes, dang, it," Rhett said, tone gruff. "That horse sure fooled me. Once he got going, he moved quicker than a firecracker."

Payton nodded, incapable of words. It wasn't Cordell's strength or his expertise with a rope that caused her throat to ache with a strange emotion but the obvious bond between him and his horse.

Rhett turned to look at her and she pulled her hat brim lower to shadow her eyes. Rhett couldn't be privy to her internal disarray. She might not be interested in him but she couldn't have him knowing she was far from indifferent to Cordell.

She was already knee-deep in blue-eyed cowboy trouble.

"I'M SORRY, BUDDY," Cordell said as he lifted the saddle flap to reach the buckle on Mossy's girth. "I shouldn't have pushed you so hard."

Mossy's only answer was a swift flick of his tail.

Cordell tugged at the brass buckle. He shouldn't have let the sight of the blond cowboy sitting too close to Payton short circuit his common-sense. It had nothing to do with him if she had a whole corral full of admirers. But as his adrenalin had surged as the calf had shot from the chute, so had his testosterone. Not that Mossy had needed any encouragement to go faster. His horse always gave his all.

They might have scored a fast roping time but Cordell's restlessness hadn't diminished. He needed to get to the ranch before he saw Payton and to make sure he tied his emotions as firmly as he had the legs of the calf. He lifted the saddle and sweat-dampened saddle cloth from Mossy's back and headed into the trailer.

"Mossy, don't even think about undoing that slip knot," he called out.

He emerged to the sight of Mossy nibbling on the lead rope and Payton standing a body length away watching. For some reason the knowledge she'd left the blond cowboy to find him made him feel far more of a winner than his slick roping time. Careful to not let his feelings show on his face, he went and stood beside her.

She smiled. "So it's okay for you to talk to your horse but it isn't fine for me to talk to my cows?"

He laughed. "You bet."

Her smile grew as Mossy sighed, gave up on the knot and hung his head. "He looks like he's going to sleep. He did that while you were waiting in the roping box."

"He often does. I guess he's seen it all before and doesn't know what all the fuss is about."

"Congratulations on your time. I don't think your roping skills need any polishing. You'll do great tomorrow in the final."

"Thanks, Mossy and I were lucky. And there won't be any final tomorrow."

Surprise creased her brow. "No final?"

"Nope. Mossy and I had fun reliving our rodeo days but we've come to Montana to ranch cattle, not compete. We'll leave the finals to the professionals."

"Fair enough."

He bent to rummage around in the nearby grooming kit for a brush. Mossy didn't need brushing but it was either that or test his theory Payton's soft mouth would taste as sweet as it looked.

Too late he realized Payton had taken a step toward Mossy, her hand outstretched to pat his neck.

"Payton, no." He snagged her waist and spun her into his arms. Mossy's ears flattened, teeth bared and his head swung around. Cordell dragged Payton out of his reach.

Heart pounding, he held her close. Mossy was all show, he wouldn't have bitten Payton, but her fragile bones could have taken a hit from Mossy's hard head.

To his surprise, Payton remained in his hold. The rapid rise and fall of her chest against him let him know that despite her experience with horses she was shocked. Somehow his hand had found the gap between her jeans and her shirt. The bare skin of her satin-smooth back burned his palm. Her hat lay on the ground and he realized the floral scent he'd come to associate with her came from her silken hair. Her neat curves fitted against him like they were made to measure and he forced his arms to relax so he wouldn't draw her that little bit closer.

She leaned back in his hold, gold shimmering in her wide eyes. His gaze dropped to her parted lips as she spoke.

"I ... I ..."

He dropped his arms from around her as though he'd been burned by a brand. He was a whisker away from kissing her. Where the hell was his self-control?

He bent to collect her dusty Stetson. "I know, you don't need any help," he said, voice hoarse as he brushed off the felt and pressed the hat into her hands.

"No," she said turning to look at Mossy who again had his head lowered as though asleep. "I was going to say I didn't see that coming." She settled her hat on her head. "Thank you. I did need your help."

"He wouldn't really have taken a chunk out of you but he could have knocked you with that bony head of his."

She rubbed at her forearms as though chilled. "Why does he do it? I saw you hug him in the arena. You obviously have a close bond with him and yet he still tries to bite you too?"

"He's just ornery. He stays at Ethan's ranch when I'm in Denver and Ethan believes it's Mossy's way of saying he misses me."

Her laugh was hollow. "I'd hate to see him if he really took a set against someone."

"Trust me, it isn't a pretty sight. He used to be a buck jumper and he wasn't too keen on particular cowboys."

"That makes sense. I can see him being a buck jumper as well as a crowd favorite. He wouldn't have quit until he had a cowboy off his back."

"He didn't." Cordell rubbed his stiff shoulder. "My first ride, he busted my shoulder."

"And the second?"

"I lasted under three seconds."

Payton laughed again and this time her laughter contained its usual music. "You either are a slow learner or you like living dangerously."

"Both, seeing as I paid top-dollar to buy him to retrain."

"And how did that go?"

"It was a little like the pecking-order issues you had when milking the cow."

"So you landed on your butt, then?"

He grinned. "More than once. But he's the smartest horse I've ever owned and has the biggest heart. I wouldn't swap him for anything."

Cordell picked up the brush he'd dropped and gave Mossy's hindquarters a wide berth as he walked around to his right side. When he brushed Mossy, he now wouldn't have his back to Payton and they could still talk.

Payton stepped closer, keeping an eye on Mossy's head. "So what's he like with other horses, especially if he doesn't like them?"

"And he won't like them. Even though horses are usually herd animals Mossy prefers to be on his own." Cordell paused in his brushing. "Though I think he will like that spirited little mustang of yours."

"Well, she's more than a match for him so he'd better behave himself when he's out at the ranch."

"He will. Speaking of the ranch, is there a key somewhere I can let myself in with? I'll be heading there soon."

Payton bent to select a brush from the grooming kit. Then watching both Mossy's ears as well as his hindquarters she began to brush his withers. "It's fine, I'll be right behind you."

"There's no need to leave on my account, the rodeo is only getting started."

From over in the main arena country music blared and the buzz of the excited crowd signified the barrel racing was over and the bareback riding event would soon follow the intermission.

Payton's only answer was a shrug.

"I've heard there's dancing later and Jake Kohl will sing." Cordell met her gaze over Mossy's back. "What about your friends and the blond cowboy sitting with you in the stands? They'll want you to stay and join in the Saturday night fun?"

He hoped she didn't notice the tension edging his words when he'd mentioned the blond cowboy.

"I've no doubt you've heard about Jake Kohl singing. Any cowgirl with a pulse will be at the dance tonight. As for my friends, they won't expect me to go. I've already said I'm off home. I've a cow and calf to check."

"Payton, seriously, stay. I can do your chores. You can't work all the time. You need to relax and to kick up your heels. Go to the dance. Listen to Jake Kohl sing." Cordell summoned what he hoped passed as a relaxed grin. "After all, I'm pretty sure you have a pulse."

A smile touched her lips. "When I'm not saving my ranch, I most definitely have a pulse." The laughter in her eyes dimmed and she stepped away from Mossy to return the brush to the grooming kit. "But it's best I go home. Rhett doesn't need any encouragement. Hanging out with him tonight would send the wrong message."

"He's the blond and the one you gave a shiner to?"

She grimaced. "Henry's been talking?"

"He has." Cordell walked around Mossy to also put his brush in the kit.

"It was an accident even though Rhett was out of line. He was sitting next to me in Grey's Saloon and when I stood, he grabbed my butt. My elbow automatically jerked back into his face."

"Ouch. He won't be doing that again."

"I hope not. It's not like him. His family are going through a rough patch and for whatever reason he's gotten himself mixed up with the wrong crowd. I've talked to him and so have his sisters but he won't listen."

"Sisters? Henry said he had a twin?"

"Yes, Kendall. They then have an older sister, Peta."

"That's a name you don't hear often for a girl."

"I know. Her father was so hoping for a boy that when she arrived he changed the spelling of the only name he'd chosen. Even with Rhett being born, Kendall also scored a second-hand boy's name."

"You can bet if Peta and Kendall ever had daughters they'd choose a very girly name."

Payton laughed. "Maybe. I know I would."

"With two sisters and you on his case surely Rhett will come to his senses. And if he doesn't, Mossy and I can sort him out."

"Thanks but I don't need any help handling Rhett. He'll realize soon enough he has zero chance with me."

"How did I know you'd say you didn't need any help?" Cordell said with a grin as he broke eye contact to untie the lead rope and hide his relief she wasn't interested in Rhett.

"I'll see you at the ranch."

He nodded. "Will do."

He watched her go. Mossy rubbed his forehead on the front of his shirt. "I know, Mossy, I like her too." He kept staring at Payton, even though she was now a spot of moving color in the crowd. "And that's exactly why the cattle can't arrive soon enough. We'll be too busy to see her. That's the way it has to be." He looked away from Payton to tug Mossy's black forelock. "We haven't secured Henry's land and come to Marietta to find the answers we need, only to fail now."

Chapter Six

"Mossy, I don't care how big and grouchy you are, you're in huge trouble," Payton said, her hands on her hips. She'd come to check on Gypsy before she did her morning's chores only to find Mossy in with the buckskin. Somehow he'd escaped the corral beside the barn and jumped the wire fence to be with the mare. Payton sighed. Not that Gypsy seemed to mind. Eyes closed, she dozed beside Mossy.

"Does that mean I'm in huge trouble too?" Cordell asked from behind her.

Even before she turned, she knew the only one in trouble was her. The sound of Cordell's slow and deep drawl made her insides curl with warmth. So much for her dawn pep-talk she needed to stay in control if she were to survive living three doors down the hall from him.

"That depends. I heard banging so I assume you've fixed whatever fence Mossy demolished making his great escape."

Head bare, Cordell nodded. "All fixed. Baxter and I will now tackle the far corner of Gypsy's paddock where the fence dips and Mossy would have jumped over. But before we start, I'll get him out of there otherwise you'll never be able to work with her."

"Thanks. Maybe he can go in the next-door paddock. Then

at least my corral will remain intact."

"Good idea."

She bent to rub Baxter's neck as he leaned against her legs. She hadn't seen him since breakfast. Cordell hadn't been there a full day and already the kelpie followed him like a shadow. She glanced at Cordell's tanned profile as he opened the gate. Not that she could blame Baxter.

Cordell's dark hair had grown a smidge longer and was tousled as though he'd dragged his hand through the front. His denim jacket, red plaid shirt and jeans had long ago lost their store-bought creases and now fitted like a second skin. Heat fired in her cheeks as she caught herself admiring his denim-clad rear as he walked toward the horses. She tore her gaze away and whistled to Baxter who'd snuck after Cordell. She was getting as bad as Trinity ogling cowboys.

"Stay with me, Baxter Boy. You'll frighten Gypsy, not to mention Mossy will eat you for breakfast." Payton looked to where Mossy had angled his hindquarters toward Cordell and lashed out with a lightning fast hoof. "That's if he doesn't eat Cordell first."

Unfazed, Cordell ran his hand along Mossy's back to his neck, steadying him even as a nervous Gypsy cantered away. Cordell then turned toward the gate with Mossy following. Payton shook her head. One minute Mossy was set to kick Cordell to California and the next he followed Cordell without a lead rope.

She and Baxter stood a safe distance away as Cordell walked Mossy out of Gypsy's paddock and into his new one.

She then joined Cordell at the gate to watch as Mossy kicked and bucked his way over to where the buckskin mare stood on the other side of the fence.

"Mossy gave me such a look," Payton said, "when he went past that I think if I didn't put him next-door to Gypsy I'd be on the top of his hit list."

Cordell laughed. Without a hat brim shading his face, she had an open view of his expression. Amusement crinkled the corner of his eyes and lightened his irises to a clear blue. Again a memory hovered on the edge of her subconscious. Who did he remind her of? Maybe Rhett, as they both had brilliant blue eyes?

Her gaze lingered. But Cordell's mirth couldn't completely erase the bruise of tiredness that smudged beneath his eyes. She had her suspicions it didn't depend upon where he slept, he always failed to sleep well.

"You know," he said, "Mossy does actually like you. You're the only person, other than Ethan, he's let brush him besides me."

She groaned. "Now you tell me he doesn't like anyone else brushing him."

"Don't worry, I wouldn't have had to tell you, if he'd didn't like you getting up-close-and-personal with him."

Cordell gazed at Mossy with unconcealed affection. Despite Mossy's contrary nature, Cordell loved his horse. And he'd love a woman with that same unconditional depth and conviction.

She swung away from the man beside her. She had to get away from Cordell as well as her thoughts. She had a ranch to save and a drought to survive. Nowhere on her chore-list did it include falling for a cowboy who didn't plan on hanging around.

"Payton?" He caught up with her, his intent gaze examining her face. "Everything okay?"

"Everything's fine. I've got work to do."

His eyes narrowed. "You're not heading into town for the rodeo finals?"

"Nope. I took half of yesterday off."

"So no chance of you coming for a ride to look at the fences on Henry's land and to show me where all the springs and creeks are located?"

"No, sorry. I've got cattle to check."

"Aren't your cattle on the edge of Henry's land near where my leasehold starts?"

She nodded slowly.

"Then come with me. I was going to take the truck but it's a clear day and perfect for riding."

She glanced at the sky Montana was famous for. Brilliant blue, the cloudless canopy stretched above them like an airbrushed canvas. Cordell was right. It was a beautiful fall day. She felt the tug of the natural beauty that she took for granted. She couldn't remember the last time she rode for pleasure or felt the wind on her cheeks and the sun on her back. Tash, her barrel-racing mare, also deserved a ride longer than the quick jaunt to the main gate.

She arched a brow. "Will Mossy behave himself?"

"Absolutely."

It would be madness to spend more time with Cordell. He already affected her in ways she didn't want to contemplate but after today he'd be busy with cattle work. Besides a ride might be what she needed to clear her head. With Cordell away from the ranch and her self-control refreshed and restored she could then refocus on Beargrass Hills.

She drew a quick breath. "Okay."

THE SPRING IN Tash's hooves and the excited bob of her head as she weaved around the cattle told Payton she'd made the right decision. Cordell rode beside her. Mossy appeared to be on his best behavior. Apart from a small buck when Cordell had settled into the saddle, he hadn't put a hoof wrong.

She smiled as a sleeping calf saw them approach, stood and bolted, tail upright, over to his mother.

Cordell chuckled. "I see what you mean. He doesn't even

look like the calf we took to the barn."

"He's such a little glutton but I'm glad he's doing so well." She inclined her head toward a tiny calf who staggered after her mother. "That's the newborn I helped deliver yesterday. She looks so fragile in comparison."

Payton checked the herd for any cows who were on their own and whose udder was swollen. Thankfully there were no further cows that showed signs of calving.

"Fingers crossed," she said to Cordell as he continued to ride beside her, "there's only the three cows to calve as I usually plan to have spring, not fall, calves."

"What happened with those three?"

She pulled Tash to a stop and pointed to where a large black bull emerged out of a gully.

"Trouble, happened."

Cordell stopped and frowned at the bull.

"He has his name for a reason," she continued, "last Christmas he went through four fences to get to the cows and now he's with them again when he shouldn't be."

The bull caught sight of them, stopped and pawed the ground. Cordell flashed her a sharp look.

"I thought you said I was the one living dangerously. Payton, what are you doing with an aggressive bull like him?"

She shrugged. "He was cheap and he has good genetics."

The bull pawed the ground again and his head lowered.

Cordell urged Mossy forward so he stood between her and the bull.

"Payton," he said his voice a low rasp, "turn Tash and go."

She opened her mouth to argue.

"Now," he said in a tone that brooked no argument.

She turned Tash and headed a safe distance away. Hooves pounded behind her and she swung around to see a cloud of dust and the back end of the bull as he retreated to his cows.

Cordell and Mossy approached in a slow canter.

As Cordell drew near, his face was as serious as she'd ever seen him. "That bull isn't just trouble he's dangerous. Promise me, you won't take him on yourself."

"Tash and I'll be fine. Besides I usually check the cattle in the truck and he doesn't seem to have a problem –"

"Payton ..." Cordell's word was almost a growl.

"Oh, all right. Joe has already told me I'm not to go near him unless there are two of us and Henry keeps reminding me to call Brock Sheenan to see if he wants him to breed rodeo bulls from."

The tension ebbed from Cordell's rigid torso. "Just as well Joe and Henry have some sense."

"Hey, I have sense. Bucket loads. Need I remind you I'm not the one riding a horse who will chew my arm off the first chance he gets?" Her words lost their heat as she caught the white flash of Cordell's grin. "Okay, funny-boy," she continued with her own smile. "The cattle are checked, so let's go see some fences."

CORDELL FOLLOWED PAYTON through the various gates that led to the land he'd leased from Henry. He turned for a last look at the bull. The black Angus stood at the fence line, eyes trained on them. Payton might believe she'd be fine handling him, but his gut told him otherwise. He'd ridden enough badass bulls on the rodeo circuit to know the bull might be genetically superior but he was still dangerous.

Fear continued to chill his veins at the thought of Payton possibly being crushed by the bull. He'd already lost a good mate to a brutal rodeo bull. Mossy might appear relaxed but Cordell could tell the veteran horse shared his unease. He could feel his disquiet in every step the horse took.

Cordell rolled his shoulders and focused on the hypnotic swing of Payton's long ponytail across her slender back as she rode in front of him. He should be checking fences and looking for a flat spot to locate portable stockyards not worrying about the self-sufficient cowgirl's welfare. She'd made it more than clear she didn't need his help for anything.

So why then did he feel so compelled to lighten her load and to keep her safe? His attention stemmed from more than his mother having raised him to respect women and to do the right thing. What was it about Payton that undid years of self-restraint? Just when it was crucial that he not feel, his emotions refused to remain banished.

He drew alongside her as she stopped at the top of a rise. Before them snowcapped peaks cast shadows on the lower foothills that rolled into a valley of green. The north wind rippled through the tops of the lush grass that would soon feed Luke's hungry cattle.

"There he is. I can't believe he's still around." Payton shaded her eyes with her hand and gazed into the cloudless sky. A bald eagle floated on a wind current, his white head and tail a dazzling contrast to his dark body.

He stopped watching the eagle to watch Payton instead. He still didn't know what part of his addled brain had asked her to come with him, but he was glad she had. The ride had brought a happy flush to her cheeks and a sparkle to her tired eyes.

He breathed deeply and allowed the crisp air to push aside his tension. He'd never be free but at that moment, riding Mossy in the mountains with Payton, the bonds of his past didn't bind him so tightly.

Payton cast him a contented smile. "I used to love riding here as a child, the hills would be a carpet of yellow, crimson and purples. It's no surprise the nearby Gallatin valley around Bozeman is nicknamed The Valley of the Flowers." She waved an arm to her left. "Over there is a log cabin built by Henry's grandfather. Like my mom, Henry's grandmother loved flowers and with her friends started the local tradition in this part of Paradise Valley of naming ranches after the local wildflowers."

Cordell smiled. "I'd never have guessed of such a tradition, what with Beargrass Hills and Larkspur Ridge Ranch."

"Then there's also Bluebell Falls Ranch, Rose Crown Ranch, Hollyhock Creek Ranch and Fire Weed Ranch." The light in her brown eyes ebbed. "Before my mom got sick we'd come out here when the snow melted and the wildflowers bloomed and think of new ranch names."

"I'm sorry to hear that your mom fell sick."

"Thanks." Payton again stared at the bald eagle. "I don't think she ever got over losing Dad. She hadn't been well for quite a while so when the doctor diagnosed breast cancer in a way, it was a relief to know what was wrong. So I left Montana State, nursed Mom, ran the ranch and finished my liberal studies degree online. The chemotherapy and radiation treatment gave us three more years together and I treasured every day."

Mossy shifted beneath him as the horse sensed his reaction to Payton's quiet words. He loosened his grip on the reins and forced the tension out of his rigid muscles. He knew all about the anguish of losing a beloved mother.

"I'm sure she treasured them too," he said in what he hoped qualified as a casual tone.

"She did. When she was bed-ridden and I'd cut all the flowers in her garden, I'd ride out here and pick the buds from Henry's grandmother's pink rose that still grows at the cabin." Payton's wistful expression contained a host of precious memories. "They'd brighten Mom's room for days."

"So you and Henry have always been close?"

"Yes. My mom and Henry's sister were childhood friends. They used to ride their horses, meet at the log cabin which is about halfway between the two ranches and swim in the spring-fed creek." She glanced across at him. "So if you need fresh water, head to the cabin and then right past the big pine tree."

He nodded. "You need a spring-fed creek near your barn, either that or a working windmill. It isn't just the bunkhouse that has no water, neither does the barn or the horse troughs."

"I know. Sorry. I should have mentioned there was no trough water. I saw Mossy had some last night in the corral so you must have carted it from the hose near the garden shed. As for the horse troughs, I'll fill them tonight by hand."

"It's fine. I'll do it and maybe I could also take a look at the windmill and get it running before Joe gets back."

Payton gathered Tash's reins. "Thanks but it's fine," she said, voice tight. "Fixing the windmill can wait."

She nudged the mare forward and he lost sight of Payton's face but not the impression his offer to help had ended their ride.

"Okay, I think we've seen enough now," she said, her still clipped tone, confirming his thoughts. "The fences all look good and you know where the water is, let's go home."

CORDELL GAZED DOWN from his position halfway up the ladder he'd carried from the workshop and rested against the windmill. "If Payton comes out of the house you'll let me know, won't you, Baxter?"

The kelpie wagged his tail.

Payton had said fixing the windmill could wait but it could just be a simple fix that would restore water to the bunkhouse and troughs. The sooner the water supply was returned the sooner Payton could stop carting heavy water buckets to her mustang and the sooner Cordell could move out of the main house. After the morning's ride, he needed to put some physical distance between them. Between worrying about Payton facing off with the bull and grieving for his own mother, he'd lost focus. There was too much at stake for him to allow his feelings to distract him.

Even without reaching the top of the ladder, he could see the problem. The windmill blades tilted at an odd angle. The bolts must have pulled out of the top mount. He'd straighten the mount and then insert new bolts. He'd seen some in a container on a workshop shelf. Easy.

Payton's angry words cut through the silence.

"Cordell, *get down*."

Cordell glanced to his right where the kelpie had been lounging but the dog was nowhere to be seen. So much for Baxter's watch-dog ability. No doubt a rabbit trail had proved more interesting.

"Okay," he said as he took another look at the windmill bolts to see what size he'd need. "I'll grab some new bolts and then fix the mount."

"No, you won't."

He sighed. She sounded wilder than a coyote who'd missed dinner. "Yes, I am. You need to have water."

"Cordell, *please*," her voice broke, "get off the ladder."

He glanced down. Something was going on, more than her being furious at him for helping her. She stood at the bottom of the ladder, her face chalk-white and arms wrapped round her chest.

He scooted down the ladder steps and jumped the last yards to the ground.

He took a step toward her and held out a hand. "What's wrong?"

Mouth pressed into a firm line, she shook her head and swung away, heading for the house.

"Payton, talk to me." Despite the concern deepening his

voice he kept his words gentle and calm.

For a moment he thought she wouldn't answer and then she spun around.

Her eyes were dark pools of pain. "Promise me, Cordell, you won't go up the windmill again." She dashed at her cheeks as though suddenly discovering they were wet. "Promise. Me."

"Okay. I give you my word. I won't go up the windmill again." He rubbed a hand across his chin. "What's going on?"

The smooth skin of her throat rippled as she swallowed. She glanced toward the house and then back at him. Her small chin lifted but when she spoke her words were as unsteady as an earth tremor. "T ... that's how my father died. He f ... fell from the windmill."

Without thought, Cordell covered the ground between them and gathered her into his arms to pull her close. "I'm so sorry."

She stiffened but after a long second relaxed and laid her cheek against his shirt. "I was there." Her words were muffled and he had to strain to hear them. "But I couldn't do anything when his foot slipped ... and then I couldn't save him when he lay on the ground."

Cordell tightened his hold, rested his chin on the top of her silken head and held her until her shaking lessened. Words would prove powerless against her despair. Overhead a black-billed magpie called but Cordell didn't take his attention off the grieving woman who fitted so perfectly in his arms.

The sound of the magpie roused Payton. She eased away a little. Anguish pinched her pale face. For a beat she stared at him and then her pupils dilated as though she realized he still held her. She pulled herself out of his arms and dragging her hair off her face, took two steps backwards.

He forced his arms to remain by his side and not again tug her close. "Many ranches now use solar power; you could do away with the windmill," he said, tone quiet.

She turned toward the ranch house. "I know but replacing it costs money. When it breaks, Joe fixes it but he always does it when I'm not there."

Cordell walked close beside her and made a mental note to make sure she was well away from Beargrass Hills when Joe tackled the windmill. He'd also make sure she would be inside when he removed the ladder and replaced it in the workshop.

"I came to ask what you wanted for lunch," she said without looking at him.

"To tell you the truth, I'm not hungry."

"Me, either."

He glanced toward his truck and spoke before his self-preservation could deliver a mental head-slap. "Perhaps we both need a change of scenery? Shall we go to Marietta? I need some cattle licks and a few other things if anything is open with the rodeo finals on. We could also have a late lunch somewhere?"

She stopped walking. "We went for a ride this morning, I can't now take the afternoon off."

"You won't really be taking it off. I'm sure there are some things you could do in town?"

"I suppose so." Her brow furrowed. "I do have some shoes to offload. I could also see Trinity and Mandy and maybe catch the last of the rodeo action." She hesitated. "Okay. Let's do it."

Chapter Seven

"NICE SHOES," CORDELL commented as Payton slid into the passenger seat of his pickup truck. He'd keep everything light and breezy between them and try and chase the sadness from her eyes.

"Well, if you were a ladies size six, you could have them," she said, tossing the pink sandals at her feet before securing her seat belt. "They are going straight into the charity bin around the side of the thrift store before Mandy can talk me into keeping them."

She sat back in her seat and threw him an exasperated glance tinged with a hint of a smile. "Apparently heels like these are every guy's fantasy, which makes you all very strange in my book."

He grinned and started the truck engine. "They're not my fantasy. I'm more of a boots man."

He glanced at her scuffed boots. And since meeting her, it was boots worn with a very short pink dress.

Payton suddenly leaned forward and the belt pulled tight between her breasts. Scratch the pink dress. Make that boots teamed with fitted jeans and a white and turquoise western shirt. Payton had no idea how gorgeous she was. Even with no heels or boots, she'd be any hot-blooded man's fantasy.

"Look." She pointed to a wooden corral post. "It's a blue-bird and probably the last one you'll see until summer."

He looked over to where she indicated and caught the flash of vivid blue before the bird took flight.

"Did you see it?" she asked.

He nodded. "It's such a beautiful bright blue."

"It sure is."

She again sat back in the seat and shot him a smile that this time reached her eyes.

The ball of tension within his chest unraveled. Payton was now doing okay. She had herself back under control.

He sent the truck rattling toward the main gate. Which was more than he could say about himself. Suggesting they travel to Marietta together wasn't exactly his brightest idea. In the close confines of the truck he registered every breath she took and every sweep of her dark lashes as she blinked. Her fresh floral scent filled the cabin and made him yearn for a wildflower-filled summer.

She stretched and dug in her jeans pocket. Again the seat belt pulled tight across her chest. A muscle twitched in his jaw as he concentrated on the road.

"What's your cell number?" she asked. "I'll put it in my phone. Then I can message you if we get separated."

He rattled off his number and focused on the Montana scenery and not on the cowgirl beside him.

The further they drove from Beargrass Hills the greener and thicker the pastures became. To his left a grove of aspens fringed a meadow, their amber leaves quaking in the sun. Movement caught his eye, and he saw two elk disappear into the trees. He looked in his rear view mirror back toward the stark brown hills of Payton's home. Beargrass Hills had the misfortune to exist in a tiny dry microclimate that had led to its "pocket drought." The rain clouds had to blow Payton's way soon.

Her phone chimed. She pulled it out of her jeans pocket and read the text message. "Mandy wants to know if we would like to go to Grey's Saloon later for beers and burgers?"

"It's up to you, I don't mind. Baxter and the chickens have all been fed and the horses have water so there's no need to rush home."

She pursed her lips. "How about we make it early as I've a busy day tomorrow and your cattle will be arriving?"

"Sounds good."

She typed off a quick message. The phone chimed again. "Now Mandy wants to know if we'll come to the rodeo to see the bronc riding finals?"

"No, you go. I need to buy the cattle licks. I can meet you later at Grey's Saloon."

"Is that okay?"

"Yes." He hoped she'd missed the huskiness in his voice. The worry in her brown eyes that he mightn't be fine in town by himself had touched him. Usually he was the one making sure everyone else was all right.

"We'll make a quick stop at the charity bin and then maybe you could drop me at the rodeo grounds? I'll text when we get to Grey's Saloon."

"Deal."

TWO HOURS LATER Cordell wished he hadn't made such a deal. After dropping Payton at the rodeo grounds on the outskirts of Marietta his truck felt strangely empty. If he'd thought being away from Payton would settle his emotions, he was wrong. Each time he returned to his truck from running an errand, her floral scent reminded him of the woman who would be cheering on some other cowboy. He only hoped she was having some long-overdue fun.

He'd collected his cattle licks from the Marietta Feed and Supply store that had remained open for any last-minute rodeo needs. He'd also managed to visit Copper Mountain Chocolates. On the floor of his truck rested a paper bag tied with copper ribbon and filled with cowboy-boot-shaped chocolates. He'd purchased the hand-made chocolates on impulse and now wondered what reason he could use to give them to Payton.

While in the mouth-watering store he'd given into his hunger and bought a chocolate-dipped frozen vanilla yoghurt bar. He'd then strolled the main street enjoying the western-themed window displays with their bales of hay, old wagon wheels and rodeo banners featuring the distinctive shape of Copper Mountain. But, even on a sugar high, a cowboy could only do so much window shopping. So he now sat in his truck waiting for Payton to text.

He checked his phone again. Nothing. He tapped his fingers on the steering wheel and stared through the windshield at the rodeo's namesake. Burnished and bright in the late afternoon sun, Copper Mountain stood like a sentinel watching over the town. The snow-shrouded peak appeared identical to the image that had filled his laptop screen when he'd run an internet search on Marietta. And now, just like then, he wished the granite peak could talk. The timeless mountain would be privy to generations of scandals and secrets.

The phone he'd tossed onto the passenger side seat, whooshed. Payton had texted. He scrolled through her message and replied before firing up the truck engine and driving to the corner of First and Main.

Judging from the pickups already parked out the front of Grey's Saloon and the country music blaring over the twin swinging doors, it was already a happening place. His phone whooshed again. He turned and parked across the road near the bank before checking his message.

Payton had seen him drive by and was waiting for him at the entrance of the saloon. He stifled a surge of pleasure and, jaw set, quit his truck. Today had been filled with high emotion, he couldn't let it end the same way. It was time to rein in his feelings.

But as he strode along the sidewalk and Payton smiled as she caught sight of him, the instant lurch in his gut warned him it may be too late.

"Hey," she said, weaving through the rodeo revelers heading inside the saloon. "How was your afternoon?"

"Great. And yours?"

"Good too." Even before she answered, the rich color in her cheeks informed him she'd had an enjoyable time.

Her smile turned shy. "Thanks for suggesting we come into town, it was just what I needed."

"Anytime." He glanced past her, telling himself he was looking for her friends and not the blond cowboy. "Where are Trinity and Mandy?"

"Already inside." Caution eclipsed the smile in her eyes. "Listen Cordell, Rhett drew a bad bull and his ride was over before it started. He was heading straight here and would have a few beers on board by now."

Cordell folded his arms. "Okay. So he's drowning his sorrows. That's understandable." He dipped his head toward the swing doors. "Shall we head in too?"

She reached out and curled her hand around his bare forearm where he'd rolled up the sleeves of his blue western shirt. He failed to suppress a shudder of longing.

"Rhett really is harmless."

"And ..."

Cordell didn't need her to complete his sentence to know where this conversation headed.

"And ... I can handle him," she said, her fingers still curved around his forearm.

"I have no doubt you can."

She slowly removed her hand. His skin mourned the loss of her warm touch. "So there won't be any problem?"

"Not that I can see."

But as he followed Payton into the saloon and a blond cowboy stopped midway across the room to lock gazes with him, Cordell knew there already was a problem.

Harmless. Yeah right. The flare of possessiveness in Rhett's eyes as he headed straight for Payton tripped every internal alarm Cordell owned.

PAYTON SMILED AS Cordell finished another story about Mossy teaching over-confident cowboys a lesson or two. While Trinity's and Mandy's bursts of uncontrollable laughter filled the small, intimate booth, she examined Cordell in the dim saloon light. Sure his tanned hand might lie relaxed on the table and his other hand grasp a beer, but for the first time she caught a resemblance between him and Mossy. Cordell wasn't a violent man, but there was something about the way he sat that suggested if trouble came his way he would be ready.

Just like Mossy exploding into life in the tie-down roping, Cordell was primed for action. He'd made sure he'd sat on the right side of the booth so he'd have an unhindered view of the saloon. Every so often his eyes would scan the room and linger where the noise and laughter was the loudest. And this was usually where Rhett and his hard-drinking friends played pool. If Payton left the booth for any reason Cordell's gaze remained on her until she was seated again. Instead of making her feel frustrated that he didn't think she could take care of herself, a small part of her appreciated his attention. It felt like a lifetime since she didn't have to shoulder life's burdens on her own.

She stifled a sigh. But there was no point feeling this way. There'd be no happy ending for her like there had been earlier at the rodeo when cowboy, Levi Monroe, had proposed to Selah while being carried away by paramedics on a stretcher.

Cordell took a sip of his beer and as he lowered the bottle, his serious eyes met hers. She felt the jolt to her toes. When Rhett looked at her, she never drowned in the blue of his gaze.

Rhett's laugher sounded in the break between country music songs and she glanced his way. He held up his almost-empty beer glass in a silent toast to her. She shook her head and looked away. She'd made it clear to Cordell she didn't want there to be any problem between him and Rhett. But the way Rhett was drinking it was only a matter of time before he did something reckless. When she'd arrived he'd given her a too tight hug that had lifted her off the ground. Her kick in his shins had then seen him lower her to the floor, his expression apologetic. The whole time she'd felt Cordell's steady presence right behind her.

She faked a yawn. If she didn't want there to be any further issues, they should leave. "Ready to go?" Cordell asked above the din.

"If you are?"

"Yes." He pushed his half-empty beer glass away. It had been his only one for the night. She finished off her iced water. She had a busy day tomorrow too and had only ordered a single beer. She slipped to the end of the booth seat and stood.

Mandy gazed at her with horrified eyes. "No, Payton, you can't go yet. We still have to hear what Mossy did to that arrogant Wyoming cowboy."

Trinity, who was sitting beside Cordell, looped her arm through his, anchoring him in the booth. "We're not letting you leave until you finish your story."

"You guys." Payton laughed. "Cordell can finish his story another day. We have to go."

She turned away to let Cordell extricate himself from Trinity's clutches. Mossy wouldn't be the only one with a repertoire of escape artist skills. Cordell's arm would have been clung onto by many more feminine hands than just her friend's.

By the time she'd reached the wide saloon bar, Cordell would have caught her up and they could leave before any trouble started. But as an arm slipped around her waist and hot beer-breath brushed her cheek, she knew she'd left leaving too late.

"Pay, don't go," Rhett breathed into her ear, "I haven't told you how much I like your shirt."

"You always like my shirt," she said with a smile as she pulled herself from his hold, "and I've got work to do tomorrow."

Rhett grabbed for her waist again. "You always have work to do."

"I know, I'm a busy cowgirl," she said as she again went to pull herself free. This time Rhett didn't let her go.

"Rhett, look at me," she said in her best don't-mess-with-me-voice he'd recognize from first grade. "Let me go."

"Pay, you're so pretty when you're mad." Rhett's mouth lowered. "Just gimme a kiss. I've had such a bad day."

She was about to give him a firm shove, when Rhett's arms dropped from around her. He took a step away, swayed, and expression wary, stared at something over her right shoulder. She swung around. All saloon sounds faded.

Cordell stood still, his arms loose by his side and apparently relaxed. Then she looked into his eyes, eyes that were cold, flat and emotionless. It was as though she was gazing into the face of an old west gunslinger who'd have once frequented the historic saloon. A man who, in that moment, had nothing to lose.

Rhett muttered some words she couldn't catch before she

heard the stumble of his boots as he returned to his friends.

"Cordell, I'm fine," she whispered, taking a step toward him. His narrowed gaze remained zeroed in on Rhett. She slipped her hand in his. "Let's go."

She didn't think he'd heard her and then his fingers wrapped around hers.

"Okay," he said, his single word a hoarse rasp.

During the short and chilly walk to the truck, Payton kept her hand linked with Cordell's. If she let go she wasn't sure she could again pull him back from the inner-darkness she'd just glimpsed. If she opened her mouth to speak she wasn't sure she could control the emotions rioting within her chest. She didn't glance sideways as a truck passed and honked its horn or look up at the fairy lights strung between the lampposts like earth-bound stars. She only nodded when Cordell opened the door for her and didn't say a word when he slid into the driver's side seat. But as they left Marietta, she found her voice.

"Pull over."

In the dim light of the truck cabin, Cordell shot her a quick and dark look.

"Now?"

"Yes. Now. And here," she said, indicating where the road-side verge widened and would allow them to pull off a safe distance from the asphalt.

The truck's indicator provided the only sound in the strain as Cordell pulled onto the verge. He killed his lights and then the engine. The moonlight cast a pale glow in the cabin.

She released her seat belt and turned toward him. "What was that all about?"

Cordell's knuckles shone white on the steering wheel before he too unfastened his seat belt. He shifted in his seat to face her.

"Nothing. There wasn't a problem. I didn't touch him."

She'd been around Cordell for long enough to recognize the

repressed anger clipping his words. "You didn't have to. I saw your ... face."

"And?"

She frowned. In the moonlight his features were all hard planes, shadows and secrets. "And ... I want to know why you have such a death wish?"

He matched her frown. "Death wish?"

"Yes, this isn't the only time I've seen you take an unnecessary risk. You would have taken on Rhett and every cowboy in that saloon in a heartbeat, not giving a damn about your safety."

He shrugged. "I don't take unnecessary risks. I take calculated risks. There's a difference."

"True, but when it comes to calculated risks we have different definitions. I use emotion to weigh up if a risk is worth taking." She lifted a hand as if to touch him but then laced her fingers together. "And you don't."

His frown deepened. "That's right. I don't. Emotion has no place in decision making."

"Why not? I've seen you with Mossy. I hear the love you have for your brother when you talk about him. You do experience deep emotion. So why do you shut down and go into a place where you don't feel and you don't care, even about yourself?"

His mouth tensed. "Life isn't always a perfect eight-second bull ride, Payton."

She flinched as the raw memories from earlier in the day battered her. "Don't you think I don't know that?"

Apology glittered in the depths of his hooded eyes. He brushed her cheek with tender fingers. "I'm sorry, that was harsh and out of line."

She nodded, wishing the slow and comforting glide of his touch hadn't ended so soon.

"Cordell, your emotions make you human. They make you

care that your words were harsh. They anchor you, they protect you. You can't keep on ignoring them, especially when you need them the most."

His expression settled into unreachable lines.

There had to be a way to bypass the emotionless firewall he'd surrounded himself in.

She uncurled her fingers and returned his gesture of comfort by sliding her fingers along the whiskered line of his firm jaw.

"Talk to me," she said, her tone soft as she searched his hewn face for a sign he'd let her in. "Let me help you."

He stiffened but didn't move away from her touch. "So how does that work? You're allowed to help me. First, with prime ribs, then with a coat and cookies and with having a place to stay, and yet I'm not allowed to help you. Period."

She hesitated. The only way Cordell would open up to her was if she gave him a glimpse of the pain darkening her own inner world. Her fingers trembled and she lowered them from his jaw. "It's not that I don't want your help … it's more I can't accept it."

He remained silent as if sensing if he replied she'd lose her nerve and not be able to continue.

She swallowed and then spoke. "I need to stay in control. I couldn't control my father falling, I couldn't control my mother wasting away and I can't control when it will rain, but there are other things I *can* control. If I do everything myself, then I don't feel so powerless or so … hopeless and weak."

Cordell nodded, a muscle working in the taut plane of his cheek. He reached for her left hand, linked his fingers with hers and kissed the sensitive skin on the underside of her wrist.

She shivered at the caress of his lips and the fixed intensity of his eyes.

"Payton," he said, voice husky, "you are the strongest person I know but it's impossible to deal with everything life throws at you on your own. Letting someone share your burdens will only make you stronger, not weaker. There's a reason why all the nearby ranches are named after wildflowers. The pioneers formed a community and together they helped each other carve out a new future."

She gazed at their joined hands. Her fingers looked so fragile and slender against his strength. Was it okay to once again draw upon another's solidity? Before death had stripped the light from her life she'd been better able to accept help. Was he speaking the truth? His considered words were filled with conviction. Could she become stronger by relinquishing control?

"If I consider allowing myself to accept help," she said, her voice an uncertain whisper, "will you allow yourself to feel ... and I mean really feel?"

He too stared at their hands and then he slowly nodded.

"Deal."

But the casualness of his tone didn't match the grooves slashed beside his mouth.

This time Payton remained quiet, giving Cordell the space and time to speak.

"But I already do feel," he said, his pained words a rasp in the night-time stillness. "I just ... stop myself. Emotions have only ever been a liability. My mother and grandmother spent their lives running from an abusive man. I guess I absorbed their fear. I still can't sleep well, even as an adult."

He paused and her fingers tightened on his.

"Ethan and I were always the new kids in school. I soon learned to blank out my emotions and to use my fists to protect us. In my teens I started testing myself by taking risks to make sure I wouldn't feel and I guess I haven't stopped. One of the reasons I took Mossy on was because I can never relax around him."

"Well, you got that one right."

The corners of Cordell's mouth briefly curved.

"You are a good and decent person," she continued, "and it is your emotions that make you this way. You can't keep shutting them out and taking dangerous risks because …" Her voice cracked as the image of him halfway up the windmill replayed in her mind. She placed her palm against his face. "One day your luck might run out."

With her left hand still entwined with his, it was as though by touching his lean cheek with her right hand she'd completed an electric circuit. A current of awareness flowed through her, quickening her breathing. As Cordell's eyes darkened to near black, she knew he'd felt it too.

"Payton." His gaze dropped to her mouth and her name was more a groan than a word.

She leaned forward. It didn't matter if Cordell would soon be gone. Even without his mouth covering hers, she was lost. There was no doubt she was a cowgirl with a pulse. A pulse that only beat for Cordell.

He closed the small space between them. His warm breath washed over her mouth. Her lips parted.

White light speared through the misted truck windows. "Get a room," a man's voice shouted before a car horn wailed.

The moment shattered like her mother's floral bone china on the slate kitchen floor.

She jerked back, pulling her left hand free and her other hand away from Cordell's face. What had she done?

She'd lost control and let down her defences. She'd wanted to gain access into Cordell's world to ease the pain that held him and his emotions hostage. She wasn't supposed to then hand him the password to her soul.

She sat back in her seat and closed her eyes to break the connection with the man beside her who watched her closely, his eyes bleak and his mouth compressed. She hadn't only rendered herself vulnerable, she'd also jumped to the front of the Marietta gossip queue.

Everyone had seen her leave Grey's Saloon hand-in-hand with Cordell. Now his pickup, with its white and green Colorado mountain plates, was seen stationary with steamy windows. They may as well have been caught necking at the teenage make-out spot up at the lookout at Bobcat Hill.

She rubbed her forehead. Dealing with a remorseful and hung-over Rhett tomorrow would be the least of her worries. Trinity and Mandy were going to have a field day.

Chapter Eight

THE FRONT DOOR squeaked as it opened and Payton's heart did a funny little leap. Cordell was back. He'd left the ranch house before she'd woken and for some reason until she saw him her day didn't seem to be able to start. Ever since the cattle trucks had arrived and the black Angus were unloaded she'd hardly seen him. It was as though after their emotion-charged talk and near kiss, they'd made the mutual decision to keep out of each other's way. Every so often their eyes would meet and lock, but then one of them would look away and the no-go safety zone between them be reestablished.

Payton's phone had run red-hot after their ill-fated roadside stop. Town gossip queen, Carol Bingley, had been the first to call. Now, five days later, the town's attention had shifted to another juicy gossip item. According to Mandy, who heard all the up-to-date news working in the local hair salon, some stock had gone missing from Hollyhock Creek Ranch and three pairs of cowboy boot tracks had been found.

Payton tucked a loose strand of hair behind her ear and brushed the dust off her worn jeans. At least with Cordell spending so much time with the Texan cows any would-be cattle rustlers wouldn't have a hope of nabbing them. Boots sounded on the hallway floorboards and she busied herself rinsing the coffee pot. She didn't want Cordell to think she'd been waiting for him.

"Payton?" A man's voice called out. She stifled a pang of disappointment. The voice and footsteps didn't belong to Cordell.

"Hi, Henry," she said, "I'm in the kitchen."

She placed the coffee pot in the draining rack with the mug Cordell had used and washed at whatever hour he'd woken. She dried her hands on the dishcloth hanging from the cupboard handle.

As the old rancher entered the kitchen, she greeted him with a cheery smile.

"You're in time for coffee, cookies and chocolate."

Henry's grey eyes smiled. "As usual my timing is perfect."

"It sure is."

Henry sank into the wooden chair at the kitchen table and she assessed his expression. She'd never seen him look so shocked and so old as when he'd witnessed the horse knock over the pram at the rodeo. But today his face was its normal tanned hue.

"So how's that mustang coming along?"

"Good," she said as she placed a plate of oatmeal raisin cookies in front of him. "You won't believe it but that cranky horse of Cordell's has really calmed her down."

She took Sage's hand-made chocolates from the fridge and untied the bag's copper ribbon.

"Stranger things have happened." Henry looked at the chocolates. "Someone's been shopping?"

"Cordell."

"Well, I'll say one thing, he hasn't wasted any time getting to know Marietta if he's already found Sage's store."

"I know," Payton said, as she placed the sweet-smelling cowboy-boot chocolates in a glass bowl. As she set the bowl beside the plate of cookies Henry traced a pattern on the smooth table surface with his blunt finger.

"Has he been asking questions when he's been making himself at home in town?"

"No, I don't think so. He's only ever asked me about Rhett's sisters." She looked up from where she poured two mugs of coffee. "Why?"

"No reason. Just curious. He just strikes me as a man who likes to know what's going on."

"He does." She carried the coffees to the table and then sat at the table too. "You know, I can't help but think he reminds me of someone but I can't for the life of me work out who."

Henry took a second to answer. "Cowboys nowadays all look the same, not like back in my time. Take Rhett, since he started hanging out with those Taylor boys, he's grown his hair long and wears jeans at least a size too small like every other fancy cowboy." Henry drew his coffee toward him. "You still doing okay for hay?"

Payton didn't miss the quick change of subject. "Yes. But I thought you were sending a few bales over for Gypsy, not a whole truck."

Henry's lips twitched. "There must have been a mistake with the order."

She sent him a mock frown. "I bet there was."

"You'll be right now for hay until it rains. Which might be sooner than you think. The weather channel says a storm will be coming through in the next twenty-four hours."

"I sure hope so. None of the predicted storms ever seem to come my way." She selected a cookie to hide the desperation her face would reveal. "I've forgotten what rain looks like."

"It'll rain. Don't you worry about that. And the way my hip aches, it's going to be some storm."

He stared at the single coffee mug in the draining rack.

"When are Joe and Maria back?"

"Three days and I'm counting. I might love baking cookies but I sure struggle preparing a proper meal."

"I bet they're enjoying seeing their new little granddaughter?"

"They would be." She took a sip of coffee. It was a cruel world that had never allowed Henry to have children.

"I hear you and Cordell caused quite a stir Sunday night."

"I'm sure you did. Was that before or after Grey's Saloon? And is that the version where I did, or didn't, have my shirt on when I gave him a lap dance in his truck?"

Henry chuckled. "The version where you and Cordell talked."

"Oh. Who told you that? I didn't think there was a true version out there?"

"Cordell. He called. He didn't want me to think he wasn't minding his manners."

She laughed. "That's right, you mentioned Rhett's shiner to him. I might have known you'd told him to behave himself. You'll be glad to know I won't ever have to give Cordell a black eye. His manners are flawless and, like me, he's only interested in his cows."

She expected Henry to laugh too but instead his shrewd gaze flickered over her face.

She was never so glad to hear Baxter bark. She pushed back her chair to collect another coffee mug. "Speaking of Cordell, he and Baxter are back."

Boots sounded and then the soft fall of socked feet after Cordell removed his boots in the mudroom. He walked through the doorway, his shirt and jeans covered in dried mud.

He shook Henry's hand and then smiled across at her as she poured him a coffee. "Hey, Payton."

"Hey." She only hoped Henry would associate the flare of

warm color in her cheeks with drinking her too-hot coffee.

Cordell sat at the table, careful not to transfer the dirt from his clothes onto the floor. She gave him his coffee and then returned to her seat before his easy grin of thanks weakened her sensible knees.

"Henry, when were those cattle troughs of yours last cleaned?" Cordell asked as he reached for a chocolate with a clean hand. He must have made a stop at the garden tap before coming inside.

"Good question." He dipped his head toward Cordell's shirt that was more dust-brown than blue. "I take it they're clean now?"

"As a whistle. Which is more than I can say about Baxter and me."

"I thought one of your cattle might have looked poorly yesterday but he seems to have picked up today."

Cordell kinked a brow. "You either have super-human vision, Henry, or that was a pair of binoculars I saw the light shining on the other day."

The two men exchanged broad smiles.

Payton smiled too, her heart full. She'd been right in thinking the afternoon she'd met Cordell that he and Henry might get on. Despite their age, the steadiness of their gazes and their innate decency had suggested to her they would respect each other and could become friends.

Henry's rare laughter boomed as Cordell cracked a joke. She wrapped her fingers around the warm sides of her mug to banish her growing chill. The small kitchen might be filled with companionship and fun this morning but it was only a matter of days before Cordell would move into the bunkhouse and then out of her life for good.

She stood, coffee unfinished. She couldn't stay in the cozy kitchen any longer. She had to get back to work and the things she could control.

"I'll leave you two to enjoy the cookies and chocolates, I've got chores that won't do themselves."

HALF-AN-HOUR LATER, CHEST tight and breaths ragged, she tore into the kitchen. Henry's pickup was gone from out the front of the ranch house and from the sound of running water, Cordell was taking a shower.

She sped along the hallway and hammered on the guest bathroom door.

"Cordell."

The shower stopped and the door flew open even as Cordell secured a low-slung white towel around his lean hips.

All air quit her lungs.

High heels and boots weren't her fantasy, just a water-slicked Cordell smelling of soap and sunshine.

Distracted by a rivulet that seemed to be taking its sweet time sliding over his hard-packed abs, for a split-second she forgot what the emergency was.

"Payton?"

Cordell's hoarse, almost desperate, tone brought her gaze back to his face.

"Mossy's gone."

The strain tensing his mouth eased a notch. "It's fine. He'd have performed another Houdini act."

Cordell looked past her as if wanting her to step away from the door to let him pass.

"No." She grabbed at his arm that held his towel in place. Beneath her fingertips his hot skin seared and his muscles grew rigid. "The gate's wide open. There's boot tracks and hoof marks; however he left, Mossy didn't go willingly."

Anger flashed through the blue of Cordell's eyes. But as

quickly as the emotion appeared it disappeared. His gaze turned icy and impassive. But as she let go of his arm and she stepped aside, he dropped a gentle kiss on her forehead.

"He'll be okay, Pay. I'll throw on some clothes and we can go search for him."

She followed Cordell down the hallway. Despite her fears she might know who had taken Mossy, her hormones appreciated their near-naked and tanned cowboy view before Cordell shut his bedroom door.

"It couldn't have been Rhett," she said through the wood, chewing on the side of a nail.

Silence.

"He wouldn't do such a thing."

The door opened. Cordell emerged, face expressionless. His fingers buttoned his emerald-green shirt but not before she'd seen the beads of water glistening on his collarbones. She folded her arms to stop herself from sliding her palms inside his shirt and over his golden skin to brush them away.

"No comment," Cordell said, jaw set as he strode along the hallway to the mudroom. "You'd better call the hospital."

"It wasn't him," she said but her words contained no conviction. There were three boot tracks found at Hollyhock Creek Ranch where the cows were taken. Rhett had been hanging out with three lots of cowboy trouble in the form of the Taylor boys.

"He'll be there if he tries to ride him," Cordell said as he stopped beside the coat rack and pulled on his boots.

Payton reached for her own boots. "But he's a rodeo rider, he'll be fine riding any horse."

"Not Mossy." Cordell's serious eyes met hers. "Call the hospital. If he's not there, then we'll need to look for Rhett as well as Mossy."

As she headed into the kitchen to use the landline, Henry called from outside.

"Hello, the house. I think you might be missing a certain black horse that nearly took my arm off."

Mossy.

She rushed to the window to see Mossy walking behind Henry, his head hanging low as if he were a placid, bomb-proof child's pony. Her brows lifted. Mossy might have snapped at Henry but his resistance must have been a token one. The lead rope Henry held, and the head collar Mossy wore, were the ones Gypsy had used when she'd arrived. Payton had returned them to Henry and they would have still been in his truck.

Cordell strode out from the front porch and she opened the kitchen window to hear their conversation.

Cordell shook Henry's hand and then stood still as Mossy rubbed his head against his green shirt.

"I didn't think he'd get too far even though he's probably been out since last night," Cordell said, running his hand down the horse's legs, checking him for injuries.

"He got far enough. He was running along the fence line stirring up Payton's temperamental bull. Just as well I'd decided to head into Marietta otherwise I'm sure Trouble would have broken through the fence to get to him."

She turned away from the window to reach for the phone. Now that Mossy was accounted for she needed to check where Rhett was. Surely what Cordell said couldn't be true? Rhett wouldn't be in hospital. Mossy had had human help to escape but her childhood friend wouldn't be crazy enough to ride him, even if egged on.

She dialed the number for the Dixons' Bluebell Falls Ranch. Kendall's smooth voice sounded at the other end. "Kendall Dixon speaking."

Except this time her usual serene tone was tense and distracted.

"Hi Kendall, it's Payton, I'm after Rhett."

"Hi, Pay, I'm so glad you called. Rhett's been in Marietta hospital since the early hours of the morning. Somehow he's broken some ribs and injured his knee. He didn't come home last night, which is normal these days, so who knows what he's been doing."

Payton's fingers tightened around the phone receiver. She knew. "Whatever he was doing, a stay in hospital will make sure he won't be doing it again. Give my love to your mom and tell her I'll check on him."

"Thanks. Peta and Dad have gone in, I'm giving Mom her lunch and then I'll go too."

"Okay. I'll see you there."

She slowly replaced the handset. Wait till she saw Rhett. His father and sisters wouldn't chew him out, but she would. His injuries would soon be the least of his worries. His days of hanging out with the Taylors were over. His sick mother didn't need any more worry.

BOTH MOSSY AND Cordell turned as Payton's truck tires spun on the gravel as she left for Marietta.

"I hope you went easy with him, Mossy, because something tells me Payton's about to tear strips off Rhett."

Mossy's head dipped lower and he closed his eyes as Cordell brushed the stiff sweat from his black coat.

His anger at Mossy possibly being hurt had flared like a struck match and then faded as he'd doused all emotion. But now embers continued to smolder. It wasn't Rhett who needed to be taken to task but the three cowboys he hung around with. From the similarity of their thin faces, he'd quickly identified them as brothers. He'd also noted how they'd plied Rhett with alcohol. When he next saw Rhett, after he'd let him know what a fool he'd been, he'd ask where the brothers could be found. His gut told him they weren't going anywhere in a hurry. But they would when he'd finished with them. No-one messed with his horse.

Mossy sighed as Cordell found his sweet spot below his withers.

He glanced in the direction Payton had driven. The other night in his truck he'd been seconds away from finding Payton's own sweet spot. And even now the thought of kissing her made the blood pound through his veins. There was a reason why every shower he'd had since then had been a cold one. Including the one this morning when she'd bashed on the door.

Even knowing there was a crisis, it had taken all of his will-power to not haul her against him and feel the slide of her hands over his wet body. As it was her wide eyes had travelled over his bare chest with the intensity of a physical touch. A small towel had provided scant protection from what she did to him.

He paused in brushing Mossy's flank. He had to get himself under control. He'd meant what he said to Henry, Payton was off limits. He couldn't start something with her only to then leave. She deserved someone far better.

As for why he and Mossy had really come to Marietta, the day was drawing near when his asking of careful questions had to end. And then there'd be only one thing left to do. To act.

The gathering breeze washed across his face. He looked at the sky that was no longer a calm, pristine blue. Clouds, swollen and heavy, hung over the high-country.

A storm would soon roll in.

PAYTON BREATHED A sigh of relief when she saw Rhett's hospital room free from visitors. She'd stopped to chat to a worried Peta and her taciturn father in the parking lot. Kendall was on her way in from the ranch, so Payton had a small window in which to ensure Rhett's rabble-rousing days with the Taylors ended.

She knocked quietly on his door and as Rhett opened his eyes she went in.

"Hey, cowboy," she said as she kissed his whiskered cheek and put the bag of salted caramels she'd stopped to pick up from Copper Mountain Chocolates on the nightstand.

"Hey," he croaked.

She pulled a chair toward the bed and took his hand.

As his guilty gaze met hers she knew, despite his pain, he was lucid enough for the conversation they had to have.

"What were you thinking?" she asked, without a smile.

He didn't pretend to not know what she was talking about.

"I'm sorry. It seemed like a good idea at the time."

"A good idea after drinking all night with the Taylors?"

"They said it would teach Cordell for messing with my girl."

She squeezed his fingers. "What am I going to do with you? You know I'm not your girl."

He sighed. "I do. Now."

"You do?"

"Yes, after seeing you with Cordell at Grey's."

She frowned. "I'm not Cordell's girl either. Those stories about what happened after we left Grey's are rumors. All we did was talk."

"I know. But you are his girl. I've never seen you look at anyone like you look at him."

"Rhett, it doesn't mean anything. You know I only have time for my ranch. Besides, he'll be gone soon."

"Will he? I saw the way he looked at you too." This time Rhett squeezed her hand. "You're special, Pay. Really special. I want you to be happy, even if it's not me putting the smile on your pretty face. Do you love him?"

She stayed silent. The ache in her chest answered for her.

She hadn't even admitted such a truth to herself, but yes, she loved Cordell. Her easy-smiling and gorgeous cowboy had brought light and laughter into her life and pushed aside the loneliness she'd always hidden. From the start, he'd surprised and intrigued her, but most of all he'd understood her.

She nodded slowly.

"Well then, if Cordell can ride that devil of a horse he's the right man for you."

She gave a small grin. "I'm not sure I like being compared to Mossy let alone to the devil?"

"I'm saying nothing that you don't already know. You need a strong man, Pay, you wouldn't be happy with a lap dog. And this cowboy ... as much as I hate to say it, he's the right person for you."

Her smile faded at the sadness in his voice. "Rhett, you'll find the right person too. There's a girl out there waiting for your paths to cross."

"I won't be walking for a while, let alone crossing any paths."

"Yes, you will and you will cross the right girl's path. You have to stop being someone that you're not. I know it's hard since your mom had her heart attack. But getting drunk every night and hanging out with the Taylors isn't going to make you feel any better or numb your fear that you will lose her." Her thumb brushed his hand. "You are special too. Be true to yourself and the rest will follow."

Rhett's nod and the gravity of his eyes confirmed he'd heeded her words. "Any other things, Miss Bossy Beargrass."

She heard light footsteps in the hospital corridor. Kendall had arrived. Payton stood, still holding onto Rhett's hand. Her work here was done if he was calling her by the pet name he'd favored while they were growing up.

"Yes,' she said with a gentle smile, "get a haircut."

Chapter Nine

THE SOUND OF drumming on the ranch house roof merged with the hoof beats pounding through his dreams. Cordell's eyes snapped open. Mossy. When he registered he was lying on his stomach in a double bed that featured a headboard covered in a white and pink floral fabric he knew where he was. Three doors down from Payton in the main house of Beargrass Hills Ranch. He also knew Mossy was safe.

His mental fog cleared a little more and he realized the storm had arrived and with it rain. Relief swept through him. Payton would be happy. He flipped onto his bare back and allowed the tension to drain from his arms and legs. The mustang mare would be used to being outside in the elements and so too was Mossy. In each horse's paddock there was also a sheltering grove of pines. Likewise the Texan cattle would also have plenty of opportunities for shelter with the abundance of trees and draws.

What time was it? He turned his head to check the luminous dials of the bedside alarm clock and groaned. It was two in the morning. He'd only slept for an hour. He folded his arms behind his head and stared at the pale ceiling as he'd done each night now for almost a week.

Usually he couldn't sleep because of his ingrained need to

know where he was and to be ready for trouble. But now his poor sleep had more to do with a Montana cowgirl than with habit.

When Payton had returned from seeing Rhett it'd been late. Cordell had done the chores and after raiding the refrigerator and larder had fashioned some passable sloppy joes. She'd been unusually quiet during dinner. He was also sure she'd blushed when he'd caught her looking at him, an indefinable expression clouding her eyes. She'd then pleaded tiredness and headed to bed early. At least when she woke in the morning, if the storm hadn't already woken her, it would be to a wet world.

Above the wind and the rain a dog barked. Had he also heard laughter? He pushed himself into a sitting position and listened. Thunder rumbled but not before he'd caught the unmistakable sound of a woman laughing.

He threw off the bed covers. What was Payton doing outside? All hell would soon break loose. The storm was only beginning. He grabbed a black T-shirt and pulled on a pair of grey sweatpants. Then, bare footed, he padded along the cold hallway floorboards, through the open front door and out onto the lighted porch. Rain streamed from the full gutters and fell in thick ropes of water. It was as though Mother Nature delivered a year's worth of rain in a single deluge.

The soft glow of the porch light illuminated the girl and the dog dancing in the rain. Dressed in a soaked pink tank top and clinging pajama shorts she kicked at the puddles. Baxter, his liver-red coat dark with water, jumped around her feet. Unaware of Cordell's presence, she stopped. Arms outstretched, she turned her face to the sky, smiled and closed her eyes.

Something in his chest tightened and then tore.

He'd never seen anyone more beautiful. He'd never met anyone who affected him so much. She'd gazed at him through her open truck window and tilted her chin, daring him to judge her as helpless, and had sent his world into a spin. And it hadn't yet stopped spinning. She made him feel. Need, protectiveness, contentment.

Love.

He couldn't deny it any more. He loved the breathtaking, brave and free-spirited cowgirl before him.

His hands fisted by his side. But he could no more tell her how he felt than he could hurt her. He wasn't programmed to stay around. He should return inside. It wasn't his right to share in her happiness. He went to turn away when lightning zigzagged across the jet-black sky. Payton didn't flinch or open her eyes as rain continued to fall on her upturned face. He hesitated. He also couldn't leave her out here with the center of the storm soon to hit.

He stepped to the edge of the porch and called her name into the wind. Her arms lowered and she swung around.

He motioned at her to join him on the porch. With Baxter at her side, she splashed her way over, dripped water over his feet and took hold of his hand.

"Come on, who says I don't ever have any fun?"

Her eyes shone with such golden life, her smile contained such uninhibited joy, all he could do was nod and follow. Getting wet was a small price to pay for stealing a few brief minutes with her in a swirling and surreal world. When the clouds parted and the rain stopped, reality would return. He'd have a promise to keep and a city existence to return to.

Within seconds, he was saturated. Water seeped through his cotton T-shirt and ran down the back of his neck. But as cold as the water was, the feel of her fingers entwined with his, heated his blood. Thunder boomed followed by an almost instantaneous lightning flash. The storm was almost directly overhead. Knowing the wind would steal his words, he tugged her toward the porch. Again, she shook her head. Baxter, his tail between his legs, fled to the safety of his dry kennel.

Thunder again roared. Cordell snagged Payton's slender waist and slung her over his shoulder. He reached the porch just before a jagged bolt splintered the sky.

Chest heaving, he firmed his hold on the back of her knees as he readied himself to return her to the ground. Cool air brushed his lower back and stomach. Payton must have gripped the bottom of his T-shirt to balance herself and had pulled it midway up his torso. He carefully took her weight and lowered her to the porch floorboards. But as he did so her full breasts pressed against his chest and her bare skin slid against his. He bit back a groan. The wet friction between the cotton of his shirt and her tank top had caused her own shirt hem to ride upward. There was now nothing between their naked midriffs but the wet lick of water.

His hands moved to her waist to steady her as her feet touched the ground. Beneath the pads of his fingers, he could feel the jut of her hips and the ripple of goosebumps over her soft skin. He fought for control. She'd be mad at being slung over his shoulder like a sack of grain. It would be okay. She'd tell him off and step away before he did something they'd both regret.

She didn't move.

The soundtrack of the storm's fury dulled to a whisper.

Every breath she took pushed her chest closer to his. Every breath he took threatened to shatter his self-control. When had she laced her hands around his neck? Another three seconds, and he'd be finishing what they'd started in his parked truck.

He didn't even make it to two.

His mouth covered hers. She tasted of rain and sweetness. Smelt of summer and mountain wildflowers. As she stood on tip-toe to match his hunger, the sky could have caved in over him and he wouldn't have cared.

As much as she took, he gave. And as much as he asked for, she granted.

Her hands unclasped from behind his neck and slid over his water-slicked abs and under his T-shirt. He shuddered, knowing he was exposed but powerless to hide how she moved him and what she made him feel.

"Payton," he groaned as they came up for air. "I can't hurt you. I can't stay."

"I know," she said, before again fusing her mouth with his.

His hands found the neat curve of her butt and pulled her even closer. This time she was the one who spoke as they drew apart to breathe.

"Please, tell me you're feeling."

"Oh, I'm feeling all right," he growled as he plundered the delicate line of her soft throat.

"Good, because if you're feeling, as per our talk the other night, that means I need to learn to accept help." He'd never seen her eyes so luminous or heard her voice so breathless. She jumped and he caught her as she wrapped her slim legs around his waist. "And I think I'll start by you helping me get out of these wet clothes."

FOR THE SECOND time, Cordell awoke to the sound of rain on the ranch house roof. But this time the raindrops were intermittent. This time daylight peeked through the pink floral drapes. He smiled. This time he had a naked Payton in his bed.

"What are you smiling at, cowboy?" Payton said, from beside him, her words husky with sleep.

He tucked her closer against his side and kissed the top of her tousled head.

"Nothing."

The hand that rested on his chest slowly slid down to the

sensitive skin of his stomach. His breath hissed.

"Nothing, huh?"

"Nothing." His own fingers trailed along the curve of her hip. "Well, I guess it has rained."

"It has. Finally. Any other reason?"

"Well … it's wet outside so I can have a lie-in."

Her hand travelled lower.

"Any other reason?"

He caught her fingers and lifted them to his lips. He needed a second to make sure when he spoke he had his emotions firmly in check.

"And I slept well because you were with me."

Her smile shone sunrise bright. "Correct answer, cowboy."

She sat, pulling the sheet with her to cover her chest. But he already knew the perfection that now lay hidden beneath the bed sheet. His hands and mouth had memorized every satin dip, curve and hollow.

"Seriously?" he said with a frown. "You're getting out of bed?"

"Yes, you know a cowgirl's work is never done."

She pressed a lingering kiss to his lips. "I'll check the horses and I also want to check my calves. They haven't ever seen rain and those gullies will be streaming with water. Now shut your eyes."

He did as she asked.

She kissed his closed lids. Her silken hair brushed his chest.

"Get some more sleep because when I return you'll have things to smile about. This cowgirl might have work to do, but she also knows how to play."

AN HOUR LATER, Payton had more things on her mind than showing Cordell her playful side. She pressed her foot on the gas pedal but instead of moving forward the truck remained stationary. Dammit.

She'd driven through the pasture conscious of the truck wheels becoming bogged but she'd thought this flat patch of dirt would have provided good traction. But as her tires spun there was no doubt she'd misjudged the water-logged ground. She blew out a frustrated breath and gazed through the mud-splattered windshield to where the cows and the two calves watched her.

She pressed her foot on the gas again. The truck slid forward a body length; she changed gears to reverse and to rock the car out of the grooves cut in the wet earth. But the wheels couldn't get a proper grip. Small clods of mud kicked up by the churning tires, showered the truck cabin roof. She eased her foot off the gas pedal and the revving of the truck's engine quietened.

A black object moved in her peripheral vision and she looked out the side window. Trouble had left the herd and walked closer. Even with the distance between them, she could see the latent power in the thick slope of his shoulders and his broad forehead. She really should give Brock Sheenan a call and see if he wanted the bull. Cordell was right, he wasn't the safest and most predictable creature to have around. She'd tolerated his bad temper knowing his elite genetics would flow through to his offspring. But the longer he stayed, the more he lived up to his name.

She'd try one more time to go forward and if that didn't work, she'd go to Plan B. Walk home and get the tractor. The phone in her jeans pocket vibrated. She pushed aside the denim jacket she wore and took out the phone. Henry's name illuminated the screen.

"Hi, Henry."

"Hi, Payton. Cordell with you?"

She was glad Henry couldn't see her face because the heat

that flooded into her cheeks at the mention of Cordell's name would have been a dead giveaway of the night they'd shared. Her lips curved. A tender and sleepless night that even now made her breath catch.

"No, he's ... at the ranch."

"Thought so. Otherwise, he'd be out pushing by now."

"Henry, where are you?" She looked around but all she saw was that the bull had moved closer. "How do you know I'm bogged?"

Henry chuckled. "My superhuman vision."

"Ah, your binoculars."

She opened her window and waved in the direction of Larkspur Ridge Ranch where it nestled high against the mountains.

"See that?"

"Sure did. Now can you get out or do you want me to come and give you a tow?"

"No, thanks. You stay inside where it's warm."

"You've been there for a while, you know."

She sighed. "I know."

"It's a fair walk home for the tractor and there's more rain coming."

She glanced at the ominous gun-metal grey clouds that hung low overhead. "I know that too."

"It's either have me come down or I can call Cordell and get him to drive the tractor to you."

She thought of the peacefulness of Cordell's expression as she watched him sleep and the tell-tale dark circles that appeared a permanent fixture beneath his eyes when he was awake. She didn't want to interrupt his lie-in. "No. If it really is okay, maybe you could come down?"

"I'm already in my truck."

"Henry!"

"See you soon."

She killed the pickup's engine and pulled her jacket closer to her chest. The bull now worried her. He'd stood closer to the immobile truck than he ever had before and had turned side on as though trying to intimidate her with his size. She'd never stopped around the cattle before, perhaps it was only moving trucks he kept away from? She honked her horn but he didn't move. As plump raindrops fell on the truck cabin she turned the ignition key so she could use her windshield wipers. She wanted to know where Trouble was at all times.

It wasn't long before she heard the diesel chug of Henry's truck. Behind her it was still bare dirt but in front of her there was a rise with both good vegetation and drainage that would provide enough grip for Henry's tires. He'd have to drive around the bogged truck and position himself so a chain could be hooked between the two vehicles. He would then drive forward and pull the stuck pickup free. The trouble was the path from the gate to the front of her truck was where the now head-shaking bull stood.

But as Henry slowly drove toward the bull, all he did was flick his tail, turn and amble away. She released her held breath. Trouble wasn't going to prove a problem. Henry waved as he drove past and pulled to a stop. She saw him unfasten his seat belt and turn to judge the distance between them before he reversed.

Too late she saw a flash of black as the bull spun around. Head lowered and shoulders hunched he powered toward the driver's side of Henry's truck.

She honked her horn and called out but the impact of the solid bull hitting the truck door drowned out all other sound.

Heart in her throat, she threw open her passenger door and slid through the mud to the front of her truck. She crouched and when the bull retraced his steps, she ran low to the ground to the passenger side of Henry's car. She slipped into the truck, her knees quaking. Henry sat slumped in his seat, blood on his forehead. She needed to get his truck moved outside the bull's flight zone so he'd cease seeing them as a threat. Then she needed to get help.

The bull pawed the muddy ground, readying for another assault. The truck's engine continued to idle. She couldn't move Henry but as the vehicle was an automatic, if she could put the column-shift into drive, gravity would propel the truck forward. She fiddled with the column-shift and the car rolled, quickly gathering momentum. She leaned over and with one hand turned the steering wheel and with the other grabbed and then secured Henry's seat belt.

This time when the bull hit, he made contact with the tailgate. Payton lurched forward. She steadied herself and took advantage of the truck's momentum down the slight slope. She prayed her quick assessment of a gap within a nearby cluster of fir trees would be correct. As the truck glided between two trunks and the vehicle slowed to a stop on the level ground, she put the column-shift into park.

At least now the low branches would protect the truck's sides and leave only the front and the back vulnerable. The sturdy fallen branch out her window would then give her a weapon should they now not be far enough away. She could only hope Trouble would think the threat to himself and his herd had passed and he would turn away.

Shoulders shaking, she turned to see where the Angus bull was. He stood at the top of the rise. Blood dripped from his nose and as he shook his head, the action one of pain and not aggression. For the moment, they were safe.

She whipped out her phone and dialed 911. She then called Cordell. As he picked up, she didn't even wait for him to speak.

"Cordell, please, I need your help."

Chapter Ten

"**M**Y MOTHER ALWAYS said an open fire made everything better," Cordell said as he placed another log on the cheerful blaze burning in the stone hearth of the Beargrass Hills living room.

"She would say that having had two boys," Payton said with a weary smile from where she sat on the sofa with a red floral cushion cuddled to her chest. "What is it with fire and boys? I remember a pyromaniac teenage Rhett lighting a campfire every chance he got."

Cordell reclaimed his spot on the sofa. He lifted his arm and Payton again snuggled into his side.

He threaded his fingers into her fragrant hair and massaged her scalp.

"How's the head?"

"Sore. I don't even remembering hitting it, but I've a killer headache."

He slipped his fingers from her hair and brushed aside the silken strands over her forehead to kiss her warm skin.

Silence fell between them, broken only by the pop of an ember in the fire and the splatter of raindrops on the roof.

"I keep seeing Henry slumped in the truck and Trouble charging," she said in a whisper, tremors wracking her.

"You saved Henry's life." Cordell's arm tightened around her waist. "It mightn't have seemed like it, but you were in control. You moved the truck away from Trouble and somewhere safer and then made sure Henry received help as quickly as possible."

He kept his voice even, pushing back against the surge of his own emotions. He knew firsthand how powerless she'd felt. When he'd answered his cell and heard her desperate words, fear had stripped all warmth from his skin. The time it'd take to grab his bullwhip, saddle Mossy and high tail it to where they were, could mean the difference between finding Payton and Henry safe. Or not.

He locked his jaw to keep both his feelings and thoughts at bay.

"Is he really going to be okay?" she asked, words low and anxious. "He looked so broken lying in the hospital bed."

"He'll be fine. It'll take more than a hit from a bull to keep Henry down. Remember what the doctor said? They've done a CT scan and there's no damage to that hard head of his." He smiled. "I also suspect, from the amount of attention they're paying to his hip, now they have him in hospital they're not letting him go in a hurry."

"Henry does hate hospitals." A small smile curved her lips.

"Is that because he's been in there a lot?"

"No. After his rodeo days ended I think it was thirty years before he set foot inside one again. Anna, his wife, passed away suddenly in her sleep so he didn't spend time in hospitals like I did with Mom."

"You said on the day we met, he hasn't any family? What happened to his sister?"

"Mom said she died when she was in her teens. Anna was an only child and so not only doesn't he have any children but he also has no extended family on her side."

"He has you."

Beneath his arm, Payton stiffened. "Yes and look where that got him. He comes to help and ends up with concussion.'

He hugged her. "It's not your fault."

She didn't answer.

"Rhett looks good for someone who came off second best with Mossy," he said changing the subject.

"He does. Thanks for seeing him and for clearing the air before he left the hospital to go home."

"No problems."

She lifted her head to look at him. "You talked for a long time?"

He kept his expression neutral. Payton didn't need to know their conversation involved where he could find the Taylors. "Did we?"

The ring of the phone in the kitchen saved him from any further explanation.

"Sit tight," he said, as he stood to answer the phone.

Minutes later, he returned. He stoked the fire to prolong the time until he sat beside Payton.

"Who was it?" she asked as he returned to the sofa and she scooted against his side.

He took a moment to speak. "Henry."

"Good. He must be feeling better if he called."

Cordell nodded, forcing his mind clear of all emotion.

"What did he want?"

"He's up to having visitors."

She leaned away from him to look toward the waning light beyond the living room window. "Now?"

"No, tomorrow, early."

He knew his reply had emerged too terse when her eyes widened.

"Cordell, what's going on?"

"Nothing." He came to his feet. The living room went from being warm and cozy to cold and claustrophobic. "Henry wants company."

She stood too. "I'll grab some blueberry cookies out of the freezer. They'll be thawed for when we visit tomorrow."

Cordell caught her elbow as she turned.

"He only wants one visitor, Pay." He steeled himself. "Me."

Confusion parted her lips. "You?"

"Yes. I can still take him the cookies, if you'd like?"

She pulled her elbow from his grasp and went to sit on the sofa to again hug the cushion. Sadness dulled her eyes.

He sat beside her. "It's okay. It's not that he doesn't want to see you, he ... needs to see me."

"What for?"

He scraped a hand around the base of his neck. "He didn't say."

"Would it be because he's mad at me for not calling Brock about the bull like he'd asked me to?"

"No. You're like a daughter to him. He wouldn't be mad or blame you for what happened. He loves you and would be relieved you're okay."

"Then why doesn't he want to see me?"

The deep misery pooling in her gaze moved him far more than if tears had slipped over her cheeks.

He spoke before his emotions could sabotage his thoughts. "I'm certain Henry only wants to see me because somehow he's worked out ... the real reason I came to Marietta."

He briefly closed his eyes. It was time to set his secrets free. But for some reason it didn't make what he was about to say any easier. He'd come to heal the wounds of the past but along the way he'd lost his heart as well as his ability to control his feelings.

"Cordell?"

Payton's fingertips brushed his cheek.

He braced himself. Then, he opened his eyes.

"He wants to see me because ... I'm his son."

PAYTON STARED AT Cordell's impassive face as though she'd never seen him before. His features may appear as though carved from the same stone as the rugged Montana mountains, but the glitter in his eyes indicated his emotions hovered very close to the surface.

"His son?"

He swallowed and nodded.

"How? He loved Anna, he wouldn't ever have been unfaithful to her?"

"He wasn't." Cordell's voice sounded as rusty as the blades of the windmill she refused to look at. "Ethan and I ... happened ... before he was married."

The pieces of the jigsaw slotted into place.

"That's why Mossy let Henry lead him without too much fuss. That's why you reminded me of someone. I see now you have Henry's smile." She traced the line of his mouth with a gentle finger. "And you know what, you look a little like the photo Henry has of his father in his office." Her hand lowered. "But then again maybe you don't. Do you have a picture of your mother?"

"I do." He dragged his billfold out of his jeans pocket, flipped open the leather and pulled out a folded photo. She carefully prized it apart. A smiling, dark-haired woman had her arms around two boys.

"She's beautiful." Payton looked closer at the faded color photo. "Perhaps Henry could have known who you were because you have your mother's blue eyes?"

"Maybe, but lots of people have blue eyes. Look at Rhett, he does too and we're in no way related."

She brushed her thumb across the boy on the left, who with his tousled hair and take-no-prisoners stare was obviously Cordell. "You haven't changed."

"I'm not sure that's a good thing. Look at me and what a little hellion I was. Ethan hasn't changed either." Affection softened his tone as he gazed at his brother. "His hair is still always neat and he'd rather talk his way out of trouble."

She handed Cordell the photo. She stayed silent as he replaced the precious photo into his billfold and returned it to his jeans pocket. Outside darkness pressed against the windows but she didn't move to close the drapes. She didn't want to provide any excuse for Cordell to shut down on her. It would be hard for him to embrace his feelings, let alone to talk about a past that would be steeped in painful emotion.

"Where do you want me to start?" he asked as he settled back onto the sofa, strain gouging grooves beside his mouth.

"At the start," she said as she tucked her legs beneath her and faced him.

"It isn't pretty."

She nodded.

An ember in the fire exploded and he stared into the flames. "My mother's father was killed in a tractor accident when she was ten. My grandmother remarried but the younger man she'd thought she knew and she hoped would take care of her and her daughter turned out to be a drunk and a bully. He isolated my grandmother from her family and friends, pulled my mother out of school to be home-schooled and basically kept them prisoner on his remote ranch."

A muscle worked in his jaw at the effort it took to subdue his anger.

"Money was tight so when Rick discovered my mother had a way with horses, he entered her in rodeo events and pocketed the prize money. At the Casper rodeo she didn't do too well and instead of taking his anger out on her in public, he took a whip to her horse."

Payton compressed her lips to contain her own rage.

"Until Henry stopped him."

"That's my Henry."

A smile eased the bleakness in Cordell's eyes.

"Well, a year later, Mom had turned eighteen, she and Henry again met up at the Casper rodeo. By now Mom was allowed to leave the ranch on her own because Rick knew she'd never abandon her mother. Mom and Henry got together but once the weekend ended she went back to the ranch and never saw him again."

"He didn't try to find her?"

"He did. But my mother made sure he couldn't. She gave him a fake number and address. She was under no illusions what Rick would do to Henry if he discovered they'd been together."

"So what happened when she found out she was pregnant?"

"It was a huge shock. But the pregnancy gave her and my grandmother the strength to leave. It took some planning, and all the while they had to hide my mother's pregnancy, but in the end they got away."

"And were you all then safe?"

The fire burned low in the hearth but Payton didn't leave the sofa. Cordell's desolate expression told her more than words could of the fear that had characterized his childhood. "Not for a very long time. But between my mother and grandmother, we were loved and well cared for and somehow they worked enough odd jobs to keep us fed and warm."

"Did he ever find you?"

Cordell's gaze turned gunslinger-cold. "He caught us one winter in South Dakota. In my young imagination we were running from some fire-breathing monster. So when this thin, grey-haired man, reeking of alcohol and stale sweat, grabbed me when I left our trailer I didn't feel afraid. It was only when I saw all the life drain from my mother's eyes I knew this man was the … monster."

The hand Cordell rested on his thigh, fisted. Payton placed her hand over his. His fingers unclenched. He turned his hand until their palms met and he linked his fingers with hers.

"So I bit him," he continued, tone flat, "and punched and kicked him until he let me go. Somehow we all got away."

She swallowed past the emotion in her throat. "Was that the only time he caught up with you?"

"No, he tracked us to Colorado Springs. But by now we were done running. My mother had taken a waitressing job at the local diner and a widowed rancher had started coming in on the days she worked. He then asked her to be his housekeeper and we all moved to his ranch. The following spring they were married."

Payton's eyes misted. "That's so lovely."

"When Rick arrived at the ranch, he didn't stay standing, let alone in our front yard, for long. Scott escorted him to the sheriff's office. About six months later, Mom was on the computer and for the first time ever I saw her cry. But her tears weren't ones of sorrow, just relief. The front page of the local paper of her hometown featured a story about a drunken Rick not making it out of his car wreck alive."

"And you finally were all safe?"

"Yes, we were." Cordell stared at the now flameless fire.

"I'm so glad." She squeezed his hand and stood. "Is Scott still on the Colorado Springs ranch with Ethan?" she asked as she fed two logs onto the fire and used the poker to stir the hot embers.

"No." Sadness threaded Cordell's tone. "One winter we lost both my grandmother and Scott."

"And your mother?" Payton held her breath as she returned to the sofa.

Eyes hooded, Cordell didn't look away from the now hungry flames. "You might have gained an extra three years with your mother but Ethan and I only got three weeks."

This time the moisture that filled Payton's eyes weren't tears of happiness. "I'm sorry."

She laid her head on his shoulder.

He nodded, still not looking at her. "Six months and three days ago I lost my mother to breast cancer. Six months and five days ago I discovered I had a father called Henry."

Payton lifted her head to look into his drawn face. "You had no idea about Henry?"

"No." Cordell looked away from the fire. "I once asked my mother who my father was and all she said was he was a good man who couldn't be with us. It was only when my mother called Ethan and me to her bedside and handed us a newspaper clipping about Henry winning best all-around cowboy at the Copper Mountain Rodeo, we found out who he really was."

"And Henry never knew about you and Ethan?"

Cordell shook his dark head. "Mom said she didn't tell him at first because it was simply a matter of survival, and then later when she saw a newspaper story about his wedding, she didn't want to ruin his life."

"But now she wanted him to know?"

"She did." He paused, jaw taut. Payton could only imagine how painful his still fresh memories were. "And she said I was the one to do so. But she made me promise I wouldn't waltz in and disrupt his life. I had to make sure it was the right decision to tell him."

"So leasing his land was the perfect chance to get to know him?"

"Yes." A faint smile played across Cordell's lips. "Leasing

land closer to Texas for Luke's cattle would have been a whole lot easier. But I still don't know how Henry beat me to it and figured it all out."

"I think I know. You said your mother had a way with horses. That day you stopped the runaway rodeo horse, Henry told me not to be angry with you for taking such a risk because you had a way with horses. I thought he looked shaken because the pram fell over and he'd assumed a baby was inside, but he really looked shaken because he must have known who you really were."

"Maybe. And now he wants to talk to me."

She leaned forward to kiss Cordell and erase the uncertainty from his tense mouth. Tonight's emotions would be nothing compared to talking to the father he'd never known.

"Yes, he does and knowing Henry he'll ask you what took you so long to find him."

She pulled back a little and smiled into Cordell's shadowed eyes. "You have a big day tomorrow and my head is still killing me; I think we both need an early night."

Her smile widened as laughter kindled in his gaze and his face relaxed.

"We do. And with that bad head of yours, I'm going to have to help you out of your clothes all over again."

Chapter Eleven

PAYTON POURED THE last of the water into Mossy's water trough. She sat the empty bucket on the ground and took a second to catch her breath. She really shouldn't carry two buckets at the same time even if it did mean fewer trips. Usually Cordell helped to replenish the horses' water, but it was no surprise he'd headed into Marietta early.

In light of yesterday's drama, it also was no surprise Henry wanted to talk to Cordell. He wouldn't want to waste another day not having things settled between him and his son. She smiled and watched as a magpie landed on the nearby gate. She still couldn't believe Henry was a father. And not to just Cordell, but also to Ethan.

Cordell had briefly left the guest room bed last night to make a call to his brother. He'd then returned with a relieved grin to say Ethan would soon be on the road and would reach Marietta by mid-morning.

Mossy approached and the magpie flew away. The horse hung his head over the fence, and snorted.

She laughed. "Is that your way of saying pretty-please, Mossy?"

She reached into her jacket pocket. As she usually did when the troughs were full, she fed each horse an apple. Every day

Gypsy grew more accustomed to her presence and would shyly extend her nose for a pat. Every day Mossy simply took the apple, glared at Baxter who always stayed close to Payton's legs, and walked away.

Today, Mossy chewed his apple and leaned forward to sniff and then nibble Payton's loose hair. Baxter edged a safe distance away. She touched Mossy's thick neck. When he didn't move, she slid her hand over his velvet-soft coat.

That would be right. She finally won him over and he'd soon be gone. Tension barreled through her and Mossy tossed his head.

"Easy Mossy," she crooned but the moment was lost and he whirled and took off to the far side of his paddock. Gypsy whinnied and followed, galloping along the fence line between them.

Payton looked at Baxter. "You're my witness. Mossy did let me pat him for all of two seconds."

Her light-hearted words didn't fool the kelpie. He whined and wriggled forward to lick her hand. Just like Mossy, the kelpie registered her distress that it wasn't only Mossy who'd soon be gone.

Cordell had been honest from the beginning when he'd said he couldn't stay. A childhood spent moving around had conditioned him to never remain in one spot. He also had a business in Denver to return to. She had no doubt he'd be back; he had a father to get to know and cattle to look after, but he wouldn't be back to be with her. The clock was ticking on her time with him and the day drew nearer when she'd have to pick up the pieces of her life. But it wouldn't be today. Or tomorrow. She took a deep breath and pushed away her sadness.

"It's okay, Baxter Boy. We don't have to say good-bye to Cordell and Mossy just yet." She rubbed behind the kelpie's ears. "Let's go and tackle that muddy pickup. It'll take until lunch to get it clean."

As predicted, cleaning the truck outside, as well as the inside, took an age. She leaned out the open driver's side door to toss a pile of small clods she'd collected from the truck floor when Baxter ran past and barked in the direction of the main gate. She glanced up and saw Cordell's white truck heading their way.

He soon pulled to a stop beside her.

"Having fun?" he asked with a brief grin as he approached. His gaze swept over her as she sat in driver's seat of her truck.

"I'm not sure fun is the right word. Remind me never to get bogged again."

He moved closer to brush his thumb across her jaw. "The truck might be looking clean but you're not."

She leaned forward, expecting him to kiss her. But instead his hand lowered. Cool air replaced the heat of his touch. Eyes fathomless, he moved away to walk around the truck as if to inspect it.

"I think you missed a spot over here."

She slipped from the driver's side seat to follow him. Uncertainty fluttered within her. Something wasn't right. She could only hope his talk with Henry hadn't been a disaster.

She kept her tone light. "Are you volunteering to help? Because I'm getting so much better at letting people help me, you know."

"I do know." He returned her smile but his guarded gaze gave no indication he remembered the ways he'd more than helped her over the past nights. He folded his arms. "But, as much as I'd like to play in the mud, I've come for Mossy."

"Mossy?"

"Yes. I dropped Ethan at Larkspur Ridge to shower and to take a power-nap before we deliver Trouble to his new home. Henry spoke to Brock Sheenan and he's happy to take him on. He also has a quiet bull he wants to talk to you about having in

Trouble's place."

"Thanks. Brock has good bulls, I'd definitely be interested in a swap." She examined Cordell's impassive face. "Do you want a quick coffee? I take it all went well with Henry if Ethan is at Larkspur Ridge?"

"Yes, it did. But I'd better not stop for a coffee. I want to ride around the Texan cattle before I collect Ethan." Cordell's arms unfolded. "But you could help me convince Mossy to leave that mustang of yours."

She fell into step beside him and tucked her hand into the back pocket of his Wrangler jeans. His arm looped round her waist. But even with their thighs touching as they walked she couldn't banish the impression a chasm was opening up between them. If all went well with Henry, something else had to be going on?

She assessed his set profile. "So is Henry happy being an instant father?"

"Yes. And you were right. He wanted to know why I took so long to find him, let alone to tell him."

"How did Ethan take him? He can be a little ... gruff."

"Not with Ethan, he isn't. Henry was as sweet as those cookies I left behind on the kitchen bench and he wants you to bring him in this afternoon."

She nodded. "Will do. When you took Ethan to Larkspur Ridge did you notice anything?"

"If you mean the *empty* guest wing Rosa always keeps ready, yes, I did."

"I told you he was a rogue when you turned up for cookies and a place to stay." She toyed with a button on his shirt. "I'm glad he didn't offer you bed."

An unexpected bleakness washed across his blue gaze before his mouth lowered to hers.

His kiss ended all too soon.

"At this rate," he said, breaking eye contact and taking a step away, "I won't get Mossy caught let alone saddled. So Miss Muddy Cowgirl, I'll take it from here, and let you get back to cleaning that pickup of yours."

PAYTON RETURNED CORDELL'S wave as he drove his truck and trailer past her on his way out. Uneasiness settled into the pit of her stomach. She wiped the last smear of mud from the truck door and dropped the rag into the sudsy bucket of water at her feet. She couldn't shake the feeling Cordell wasn't just driving out of Beargrass Hills, he was also driving out of her life.

She watched until she could no longer see the back of the trailer, then busied herself putting away the hose and the buckets. But the more she occupied her hands, the more her thoughts raced. As much as she didn't want to admit it, instinct and the emotional distance she'd just sensed between them, told her their time together had expired. Cordell had fulfilled his promise to his mother and now was getting ready to leave.

Throat aching, she looked at Baxter. "You're in charge, Baxter Boy. I can't stand around here moping, I'm taking a road trip to deliver Henry his cookies."

She'd relinquished control and allowed Cordell into her world. It was her own fault she'd now have her heart broken. He hadn't expressed himself with words but the tenderness of his touch let her know she was more than a casual fling. She wasn't just another risk he'd taken to challenge himself that he couldn't feel.

She turned for a last look at the undulating foothills where Cordell would now be checking the Texan cattle. The scenery blurred into a swathe of green.

But Rhett hadn't been right. She wasn't Cordell's girl. And he wasn't her cowboy. Her heart bled. No matter how much she wanted him to be.

CORDELL LIFTED HIS right hand from the steering wheel and flexed his bruised knuckles.

He shot Ethan a quick look. "When we see Payton, we don't need to go into too much detail about where we just were."

The smile Ethan flashed him in the dim light of the truck cabin could have been his own. "I can't wait to meet the cowgirl who has tamed my big bad brother."

"When you do, remember I'm supposed to be taking fewer risks and living less dangerously. And tackling the Taylors doesn't exactly fall into those two categories."

Ethan chuckled. "Tell Payton the truth, you talked first and they listened. Which they did until the older Taylor decided he was done with your jabbering."

"What was wrong with my jabbering? You were the one who told me to not go in with all guns blazing."

"I did but next time you talk your way out of trouble, at least try and look a little friendlier. That death-glare of yours would snap-freeze a lake."

"Next time, you can do the talking and I'll be the back-up."

Ethan flexed his own bruised hand. "After our 'conversation' there won't be a next time. I've no doubt the Taylors are on their way to Reno like they said they would be."

"It was thanks to Payton's cowboy friend, Rhett, we found them. He had no idea they were into anything illegal until the night they stole Mossy for him to ride. The youngest brother let slip their trailer hadn't only ever carried a stolen horse."

"Well, their thieving days are over. The relief on their widowed aunt's face was worth taking all three of them on. The sheriff will visit in the morning to sort out who owns the cattle we found corralled for re-branding. He said he'd make a few calls so when the Taylors reach Reno they'll have some charges to face."

Cordell lowered his headlights as a car passed. They'd soon be at Larkspur Ridge where he'd leave Ethan for the night. He glanced at his brother who smothered a yawn.

"Thanks for your help today. I know how tired you are after driving all night."

He rolled his shoulders against his own weariness. He hadn't slept well. Not because he was worried about his morning talk with Henry but because every time he closed his eyes he saw Payton being crushed by Trouble.

"It's been a day I won't forget in a hurry," Ethan replied. "Meeting Henry. Taking that bad-tempered bull to Brock's. And talking to the Taylors. I haven't had this much fun since you moved to Denver and life become dull and boring."

Cordell laughed but when Ethan glanced at him, he knew his twin had sensed the strain beneath his amusement.

"You okay with how things have worked out?" Ethan asked.

He nodded. "Henry is a tough but a good man. Even without knowing about us, he spent years looking for Mom. He'd realized she hadn't been in a safe place. He was glad to hear she'd found happiness with Scott and that he'd loved us and raised us as if we were his own."

In front of them the ranch house lights twinkled in the darkness from the top of an invisible hill.

"So are you staying?" Ethan asked, voice quiet.

He didn't even try to misunderstand what Ethan had asked. He took his time to speak. "One minute, I am. And the next, I'm not so sure. She could do so much better than me."

"According to Henry, she doesn't want anyone but you."

"I have no idea how Henry knows such a thing."

"Maybe he just knows Payton?"

He grunted. "Maybe."

Ethan laughed softy. "You are so Henry's son. You're even

grunting like him now."

But Cordell didn't join in with his brother's mirth. His heart felt like it was about to rip in two.

BAXTER BARKED FROM within the warmth of his kennel nestled beneath the pine tree as Cordell parked his truck beside the barn. He made no effort to move. Payton had left the porch light on and its soft pool of light beckoned him inside. Still he didn't leave the truck. His bruised hand tightened around the steering wheel until his breath hissed.

Physical pain was nothing compared to his internal torment. All his life he'd blanked out his emotions and now they appeared hell bent on revenge. Twisting and bucking, they gave him no peace or respite. Payton said his emotions made him human but all they did was cause him anguish. They rendered him vulnerable and they made him feel inadequacy and fear.

He'd been lucky Mossy had his wits about him when they'd driven Trouble away from Payton and Henry because he sure didn't have his. When they'd arrived to find Payton outside the truck, branch in hand waiting for the bull to charge, he hadn't been able to breathe, let alone focus.

What would happen if Trouble got past Mossy? What would happen if he failed to protect Payton? What would happen if he lost the woman he loved?

And ever since his fear hadn't left him.

He sighed and he released his clamped grip on the steering wheel. His heart told him to stay, he did deserve a special woman like Payton. But his mind told him the only way to remain safe and to not feel was to keep moving.

He made his way inside. In the kitchen he saw a foil-covered plate on the bench. His chest tightened. Payton had kept dinner for him. The living room fire crackled and he headed into the warm room. She lay asleep on the sofa, feet bare and a handmade red floral quilt covering her.

Breathing ragged, he bent to caress her smooth cheek.

The only place he'd ever want to be was by his beautiful and brave cowgirl's side.

She murmured his name and he bent to kiss her. She twined her hands around his neck and kissed him. A slow, sweet kiss that he never wanted to end.

He could do this. He could silence the demons inside. He could learn to live with his emotions, no matter how defenseless they made him.

He gathered Payton in his arms and she snuggled into his neck. He filled his lungs with her floral scent. He could never look at a perfumed beargrass wildflower again without thinking of her.

He carried her along the hallway heading for his bed, but as he drew near to her bedroom door. He stopped.

He'd ridden badass bulls. He'd braved Mossy's wrath. He could do this. He could take the ultimate risk and tell her he loved her. He could stay. He took a step toward his own room. Blood pounded in his ears. Fear choked him. He again stopped.

Legs leaden, he turned to walk through Payton's doorway. He gently laid her on the bed and pulled the covers to her chin. Head bowed, he quit the room, without once looking back.

Chapter Twelve

PAYTON AWOKE TO two thoughts. She was in her own bed. Alone. And that she wasn't going to lose Cordell. She mightn't have any control over him leaving but that didn't mean she couldn't fight for her cowboy. She needed to tell him how she felt and then she needed to ask him to stay.

She scrambled out of bed. She still wore her clean jeans and pink western shirt she'd put on to visit Henry after lunch yesterday. Trinity would cringe at her wardrobe selection but the creased and unromantic outfit would have to do. It wasn't what she wore that was important, just the three simple words she had to say.

But when she saw Cordell's door open, the bed made and a packed duffle on the floor, her stomach plummeted to her bare toes. She drew a calming breath. Maria and Joe were returning that night, Cordell was simply getting ready to move into the bunkhouse.

But as she sped along the hallway to see if he was in the kitchen, the tremble in her hands said she didn't believe such an explanation. She pushed open the kitchen door but the room was also empty save for a small note on the table. The line of her rigid shoulders relaxed as she scanned Cordell's message. He wasn't leaving.

He'd left early to collect Ethan to have breakfast with Henry. He'd then spend the morning showing Ethan around Marietta and would bring Henry home to Larkspur Ridge after lunch. He'd see her then.

She bit the inside of her cheek. She now had over half a day until she would have a chance to talk to him. She needed a plan and failing that she needed to bake cookies. She reached for her cell phone that sat next to the microwave oven. Instinct cautioned her she'd only have one chance to convince Cordell to stay. Now there wasn't such a rush to speak to him, her jeans and western shirt had to go. She needed all the ammunition she could get. What she really needed was a makeover.

She dialed Mandy's number.

"Hi, Payton," Mandy answered.

"Hi, Mandy. Is today still your day off?"

"Yes, it's Monday. Why?"

"Are you sitting down?"

"No, but I am now."

"Good. Can you please style my hair?"

Payton held the phone away from her ear as Mandy squealed. "You bet. Cut and blow-dry?"

"Anything."

"Anything?" Mandy's voice grew incredulous. "Who are you and where is the real Beargrass Hills cowgirl called Payton Hollis?"

She chuckled. "Anything goes as long as I don't have a pixie cut. Do you remember we all got them in high school? My neck has never felt so cold."

Mandy laughed. "Now there's my practical girl."

"Are you still sitting?"

"Yes."

"I also need to … shop for a … dress."

Silence. Then, "Pay, is everything okay?" Seriousness wiped

all amusement from Mandy's words.

"It will be."

"You know Cordell will love you just the way you are?"

A lump formed in her throat at her friend's concern. "I'm hoping so. I don't want to change who I am, I just need some sort of ... secret weapon."

"Secret weapons are good, especially if they come with sky-high stilettos. I always said you'd change your mind about wearing heels."

"No heels."

"Okay then, we'll pin that one for later. You know Trinity will hate to miss all the action. She has had a client cancel, the little girl has chicken pox, so she might have some time. I'll text her. I think we're going to need sugar, and it's a nice day outside, so how about I meet you at the ice cream store and we formulate our game plan? Text me when you leave."

"Will do. And Mandy, thanks."

"You're welcome." She laughed. "And don't think you've gotten out of giving me a proper explanation for all of this."

"Not for a minute. Is now a good time to change the subject and say Cordell's twin brother is in town?"

Again she held the phone away from her ear as Mandy squealed. "Do hurry up, Payton, we have so much to talk about."

BUT AS PAYTON sat in Crawford Park outside the domed courthouse playing with her uneaten vanilla ice cream she thankfully couldn't get a word in. While Mandy and Trinity debated the color of her soon-to-be inflicted foils, she watched the golden autumn leaves drift to the ground from the park's flame-bright trees. Normally the sight filled her with a sense of peace, but not today. Until she convinced Cordell to stay, a hard ball of concern was permanently lodged in her midriff.

Trinity checked her watch and pushed her cookies n' cream ice cream over to Payton. She usually finished Trinity's leftovers and to Mandy and Trinity's disgust she then never had trouble fitting into her jeans. But this time she couldn't even finish her own serving.

"Yes, okay," Trinity said as she stood, "go with caramel highlights but only subtle ones." She pulled her fitted jacket over the waist of her charcoal-grey pencil skirt. "I've got to run. My next appointment is in fifteen minutes. But I'll be right to come shopping for a dress in my lunch break."

"Good luck," she said as she hugged Payton, whispering in her ear, "*subtle* caramel highlights, okay?"

Payton waved as Trinity then headed toward her speech pathologist office across town at the east end of Bramble Lane in time for her next small client.

Mandy picked up her mocha toffee ice cream and as she ate her gaze remained fixed on Payton's unruly, over-long hair.

Payton shifted on the park bench. "No pixie cut, remember?"

Mandy's gleeful smile failed to offer any reassurance. "But otherwise anything else is fine?"

She sighed. "Do your worst."

WHAT FELT LIKE a lifetime later, Payton prized herself out of the hair salon chair and dutifully followed Mandy over to where Trinity sat flicking through a thick magazine. Trinity sprang to her feet, her smile wide.

"Look at you, Pay. Cordell doesn't stand a chance." She touched the glossy, loose curls that fell onto Payton's right shoulder. "Mandy, you are genius."

Mandy gave a small bow. "Thank you." She smoothed away

a lock of hair that had fallen onto Payton's forehead. "It does help having such a beautiful blank canvas to work with."

Heat filled Payton's cheeks. "Thanks but this is all your work, Mandy. Come tomorrow and you'll be seeing the real Payton again."

Mandy winked. "After what I've done to your hair I guarantee we won't be seeing you or Cordell for days."

She chewed on her lip. She could only hope so.

Mandy frowned. "Payton ..."

Payton released her lip. "Sorry. I know you told me not to do that. I'll ruin my lipstick."

Trinity grinned. "Nice make-up job, too, Mandy. Not too heavy but just enough. I never knew your eyes were so golden, Pay, or your lashes so long."

"That's because," Mandy said, "she has a record for applying *all* her make-up in under five minutes and she doesn't ever blend."

Trinity's brows lifted. "What are we going to do with you, Pay?"

Payton linked arms with her best friends. "Take me shopping."

Trinity laughed. "Yes, that will do as we know how much you hate trying on clothes."

As they left the hair salon, Payton stopped and looked left along Main Street toward the Java Café. "Trinity, hadn't we better get you something to eat before we shop? This is your lunch break."

"No, I'm right. I grabbed some yoghurt and fruit from the fridge at work before I left. Do you and Mandy want anything?"

They both shook their heads.

"I'm still full from the ice cream," Mandy said, "that will teach me to get a large serving."

"So am I," Payton lied, gazing past the café to where she

could make out the sign for Marietta Western Wear in the next block.

"Don't even think about it," Trinity scolded. "We're shopping for a dress not for jeans and western shirts."

"This way," Mandy said pulling Payton along to the boutique one store down from the hair salon.

She walked through the doorway. A bell tingled, announcing their arrival. An elegant sales associate smiled as she looked up from the paperwork she was completing on the counter. The boutique smelt of jasmine and the soft music piped around the brightly lit store completed the impression of luxurious extravagance.

Payton hesitated. What was she doing? She shouldn't be splurging money on a dress? She still had her favorite boots to fix.

Trinity gave her a little push from behind. "Pay, it's my treat. You never let me buy anything for your birthday or Christmas and you are always baking me cookies or bringing me vegetables."

The sales clerk shuffled her paperwork together and beamed at them. "Anything I can help you with, ladies?"

Mandy stepped forward. "Yes, please. We need a dress. And not just any dress. One that will make a cowboy's jaw drop."

"Pay," Trinity said softly from beside her, "it really is okay. Mandy has done your hair and make-up. Please let me do this for you."

"You really don't have to."

"I know. I want to."

"Thank you"

Trinity hugged her. "That's what friends are for. Now let's get shopping."

Payton's head spun after the first two dresses were held up against her. After five, the colors and expensive fabrics all merged into a rainbow of chaos.

"Too short. Too dowdy. Too sexy. Not sexy enough."

Mandy and Trinity's words swirled around her in an ever-increasing crescendo of sound.

She sank into the chair that would usually be reserved for long-suffering males lured into the boutique by a woman's smile and bedroom promises. She was never going shopping again.

Then she spied a white dress. Against the sea of color and movement it spoke of peace and simplicity. She came to her feet and collected the dress from the rack. Falling to above the knee with a nipped-in waist, the skirt featured a white lace overlay. She hesitated and then returned the dress to the rack. The bodice was far too plunging.

Trinity whisked it off the rack. "Don't you dare put this back. This is perfect."

Payton stopped herself from chewing on her lip. She recognized the resolute note in Trinity's voice. When Trinity put her mind to something she usually got her way.

"Trin, wearing your pink strapless dress to Eliza's wedding just about killed me. It felt like it would slip off whenever I breathed. Who knows what Cordell got an eyeful of when I helped him with the calf? I just wouldn't be comfortable wearing a dress that shows more than it hides."

Mandy nodded. "Even though I'm sure red-blooded Cordell wouldn't mind an eyeful, let alone, the low bodice, I agree, it's not who you are, Payton. But I do have a solution." She went to a shelf and unfolded a white lace camisole. "You'd have something like this at home that you could wear underneath. It would have to have a touch of lace on it though to match the dress."

"Sorry, there's no camisole, let alone any lace, in my closet."

Mandy groaned. "No lace at all?"

"Nope."

"Poor Cordell. Next shopping trip we are not going to buy a dress."

Trinity held the white dress against Payton. "Try it on."

Payton glanced at the sales clerk who'd returned to her paperwork after it'd become obvious Payton had two enthusiastic fashion gurus helping her.

She smiled. "Do try it on. Your friends are right, the lace camisole underneath will work really well."

Payton touched the soft lace of the overskirt. "The dress would look good with boots."

"No," both Trinity and Mandy chorused.

"Yes. I'm sorry, Mandy, I'm not coming over to the dark side and wearing heels. Besides Cordell says his fantasy is boots not heels, anyway."

Trinity's and Mandy's eyes grew round.

"Tell us more," said Mandy, her voice slightly breathless.

Payton chuckled. "And spoil the fun of your fertile imaginations? I don't think so. But, I will try on the dress."

When she emerged long minutes later, she knew she'd found the right outfit. With the fitted camisole underneath, the plunging neckline wasn't an issue. The dress was perfect. The fine weave of the fabric caressed her legs and she did a little twirl.

Tears glistened in Mandy's eyes. "Cordell won't be able to leave."

Trinity nodded, her smile wistful. "It's a wrap. That's the one."

Payton hugged Trinity and then Mandy. "I expect to repay the secret weapon favor for each of you when the time is right."

"It's a deal." Mandy hugged her back. "Now go get your cowboy, Pay."

Chapter Thirteen

THE BUTTERFLIES MAKING their home in her middle threatened to take flight as Payton saw Cordell's pickup beside the barn.

Just. Breathe.

She parked her own truck in its usual position adjacent to the corral. Smoothing her hair like Mandy had showed her, she slicked her lips in the sweet-tasting pink gloss Mandy had slipped into her bag.

She swallowed and opened the door. Her secret weapon had to work. If her plan failed, the days of knowing Cordell waited inside the ranch house for her, were numbered.

But as she left her truck, she turned right instead of heading toward the front porch. From over near the horses she'd caught a flash of red plaid and denim. She walked around the barn and for the first time in what felt like a lifetime, she looked at the windmill. She kept her chin high to stop her tears falling.

Not a day passed when she didn't miss the infectious chuckle of her father's laughter and the warmth of her mother's gentle smile. But Cordell was right. Letting go of the control she clung to both empowered and made her stronger. Knowing that he would soon be there to help with an unconscious Henry had given her the extra strength she'd needed to hold off Trouble until Cordell and Mossy arrived. Just like her pioneering forebears, she didn't have to fight every battle on her own. It wasn't a sign of weakness to ask for, and accept, help.

Her steps slowed. From the back, the cowboy talking to Mossy looked familiar but something was off. The man gazed across the valley and she glimpsed a profile that wasn't Cordell's.

Ethan.

She must have spoken his name because he swung around. His tanned face broke into a smile that resembled both Cordell's and Henry's.

She walked forward. "Hi, you must be Ethan."

Ethan took off his hat and extended a hand. "And you must be Payton?"

"Yes, I am." She returned his handshake. "Welcome to Montana."

"Thanks."

Up close she could see subtle differences between the twin brothers. Ethan's eyes might be the same clear blue, but whereas Cordell's were as turbulent as a storm-fed creek, his were as calm and as steady as a still pond. The strong line of his jaw hinted at a strength equal to Cordell's, but a strength that would be quiet and considered.

Realizing she was staring, she quickly slipped her fingers from his.

The breeze teased her hair and fine windblown strands clung to the gloss on her lips. She brushed them away with a quick hand. So much for making a good first impression on the brother of the man she loved. She was wearing makeup and a dress and looked nothing like a working cowgirl who wanted to be taken seriously.

"Your mustang mare is a little beauty," Ethan said with a wide smile. And in his smile she saw all the lightness and laughter Cordell had gifted to his brother by shouldering the darkness of their childhood.

"She is. I was hoping she'd teach bossy Mossy some manners."

Ethan chuckled. "I'm afraid it's too late for that."

Mossy bared his teeth and leaned over the fence to swipe at Ethan's arm. Ethan casually moved away.

"Mossy, that wasn't very nice," Payton said with a frown.

"It's okay, it's not personal," Ethan said, taking a step closer to the fence. As Mossy again bared his teeth, Ethan reached out to rub the horse's neck. To her surprise Mossy's ears flickered forward and he lowered his head.

"I don't blame him for being ornery. He associates seeing me with Cordell leaving as I'm the one who then looks after him."

A chill replaced the warmth of the autumn sun on her bare arms.

She took a second to speak. "And this time?"

"The same deal," Ethan said not meeting her eyes.

All sound faded. All sensation ebbed. All she could hear was the desperate pounding of her heart. She'd left it too late to fight for her cowboy. Cordell's duffle hadn't been packed to move into the bunkhouse.

"When?" she managed.

"This afternoon. He used my sedan to bring Henry home as it would be more comfortable than his truck. So after he's checked his cattle, he'll swap vehicles, load his gear and then I imagine he'll hit the road. Knowing him he'll want to get into the office early tomorrow."

"What about Mossy and the Texan cattle?"

"I'm staying for a couple of weeks to spend time with Henry, so I'll check the cattle and also feed Mossy while I'm here. I'll talk to Cordell, and then when I go I might take Mossy and the trailer home with me to Colorado Springs."

She barely nodded. Her life was unraveling way too fast. Just like that, Cordell would be gone. And from Ethan's solemn tone she had no doubt when he did return it wouldn't be for long. He'd see Henry, check the cattle and then be off again. She squared her shoulders. She wasn't done fighting. Until Cordell drove his truck through the main gate she wasn't giving up stopping him from leaving.

Ethan rubbed his jaw. "I heard the sedan pull up, if you want to go and catch him before he swaps vehicles."

"Thanks." She angled her chin. "I do."

Payton strode from the horse paddocks to the barn in record time. Cordell had parked Ethan's conservative white sedan beside his truck. Back to her, he lowered the tailgate of his pickup. The driver's side door was already open as if he needed a fast get-away. She slowed her breathing and strove for calm. This couldn't be the last time she saw his Wrangler clad-butt and the snug stretch of his western shirt across his broad shoulders.

She knew the moment he realized she approached. He stiffened and slowly turned.

Her hair and dress had the desired effect.

His jaw didn't drop. His face was a carved and immobile mask. But everything she needed and hoped to see was in his eyes. Hunger, longing, pain all flashed across his gaze in quick succession before a shutter descended over his emotions. The hope within her wavered. Her secret weapon hadn't succeeded.

"So when were you going to tell me?" Her question emerged far more shaky than strong.

"Tell you what?" Wariness slowed his words as he glanced at the knuckles on his right hand.

"That you were leaving for good."

He frowned even as his mouth tensed. "My brother tell you that?"

"He did." She looked toward where Ethan still remained

near the horses.

Cordell crossed his arms as his stare travelled slowly from the top of her blow-dried head to the tips of her scuffed boots. When he'd finished his thorough examination, her breaths were shallow and her hormones were over-heating. Her body might have only one thing on its to-do list but her mind had a plan to follow.

"You look ... incredible," he said, words husky. His darkened gaze returned to the tight white lace of the camisole that filled the gap left by the dress's plunging neckline.

"Don't try and change the subject."

He sighed. "I'm not. Here ..." He unfolded his arms and turned to reach into the pickup tray. He pulled out her favorite broken boots and the ripped horse rug she'd wrapped the abandoned calf in. "I'll give you these before I get too ... distracted. They've all been fixed."

"Thanks."

Never had a word been so hard to say. It was as though even speaking posed a threat to the tight grip she held on her tenuous self-control. Cordell might be leaving and yet he still looked out for her. He'd known the boots and the rug had needed mending without her saying anything and had taken them to Marietta to be repaired. He felt something for her even if he wasn't prepared to act upon it and stay. It was all the encouragement she needed to change his mind.

"Payton —"

She closed the distance between them and pressed a finger to his lips. "I need to say something first," she said in a firm voice, "and I hope it will change your mind about leaving. If it doesn't then I hope one day you'll find somewhere you feel safe enough to never leave." She paused and fought to speak past the emotions stealing her composure. "I love —"

The rest of her words were lost in a gasp as Cordell's warm

hands secured her waist and he lifted her onto the tailgate. Even before her butt landed on the cold metal, his urgent mouth claimed hers. He kissed her like a man who had found a place to call home. A man who wasn't ever going to leave.

She locked her arms around his neck to let him know she was never letting him go. Even if this was their good-bye kiss.

The clearing of a throat broke them apart. Chest heaving, she looked across to where Ethan rested his hip against his sedan. She saw the brothers exchange a long and serious look before Cordell rasped, "You say too much."

Ethan grinned and winked. "You can thank me later."

Cordell rested his forehead on hers and they remained silent, letting their ragged breaths do the talking, while Ethan reversed and drove away.

Still uncertain, despite their kiss and the possessive way he held her, of where the conversation was heading, she remained silent.

"You don't know it," Cordell said, drawing back a little and touching her cheekbone. Against her skin she could feel the shake in his fingers. "But my non-risk taking brother just lived dangerously. Did he say anything else when he told you I was leaving?"

Her hands slid from around his neck to grip his shoulders. "He said he might take Mossy home with him."

Cordell chuckled. "And you think Henry is a rogue. Mossy isn't going anywhere. And neither am I. What Ethan didn't say was that I'd be back in a week ... for good."

"For good?" she said, a catch in her voice.

"Yes." Emotion fired in his eyes, emotion he didn't try and repress. "I've found somewhere I feel safe." His lips touched her temple. "And that's wherever you are."

"Are you sure?"

She wasn't even certain she'd asked the question, let alone

that it had been coherent and audible.

"I had to think my way through it, but I've never been surer of anything in my life. Just like I've never been as scared as when I had to protect you from Trouble. I didn't think I could deal with the fear of anything happening to you but the alternative is to not be with the woman that I ... love." He pulled her even closer. "And that isn't an option." The white flash of his smile brought tears to her eyes. "I love you too, Pay."

The tenderness of his slow and thorough kiss silenced the last of her inner doubts that being by her side was where her cowboy wanted to stay.

"A week will be an eternity," she said as they drew apart.

"I know, but it will give me time to complete the sale of my consultancy business to my manager and to pack up my condo." Happiness intensified the blue of his eyes as he glanced toward the rugged mountain backdrop behind her. "I can't say I'll be sad to leave Denver."

He tangled his fingers through her hair and lowered his mouth to speak against her lips. "Once Luke's cattle have returned to Texas I'll buy some of my own. Then there could be a few things for a cowboy to do around here if a certain stubborn cowgirl will let him help out."

She nodded, incapable of words. It had rained and now Beargrass Hills would also have a team at the helm, just like in the days when her parents had run the ranch. The responsibility of preserving her home wouldn't rest solely on her shoulders. She lifted her mouth to his, accepting all the help he'd ever offer.

When their kiss ended, Cordell took a step back. "I've got something else for you."

She reluctantly let him go. He moved to the driver's side seat, leaned in and pulled out a bunch of pink roses.

Her heart swelled. They were from the old pioneer rose bush at the cabin that she'd always picked blooms from with her mother.

He handed them to her with a gravity that promised her a lifetime of love and flowers.

"Luckily, I took these out of the sedan before that meddling brother of mine left. Little did he know, I wasn't going to leave without telling you how I felt and that I'd be back to stay."

She breathed in the faint perfume of the delicate pink buds and then placed the roses onto the tailgate beside her. She clasped the front of Cordell's shirt to pull him against her.

"Just as well, cowboy, because on page one of the sassy and modern cowgirls' manual it says to never let go of your man."

He smiled a crooked grin. "I hope there's also something in there about how to say goodbye to your cowboy who you won't be seeing for a long and lonely week?"

"There could be." She hooked her legs around him, her fingers skimming the hot, smooth skin where his shirt opened. He shuddered beneath her caress. "Help me get out of this dress and you'll find out."

"I thought you'd never ask." His mouth found the sweet spot at the base of her throat before he lifted her from the tailgate and held her tight. "But the lace and the boots stay on."

THE END

Kiss Me, Cowboy

A Montana Born Rodeo Novella

Melissa McClone

DEDICATION

In memory of Sierra,
a beautiful and beloved horse,
who belonged to my friend Shalimar.

Special thanks to Alissa Callen, Megan Crane, and
Rachel Johns.
Working on this series with them was so much fun!
And extra thanks to Sinclair Sawhney for being an
editor extraordinaire!

Prologue

D^{AVEY.}
Gone.

Crap.

No more fart joke texts, or bathroom selfies, or a *wish you were here* postcard from some hellhole COP in Afghanistan.

Zack Harris sat against a tree, his legs stretched out. The sound of the river, flowing three feet away, brought back memories of trainings and deployments. Brothers, not by birth, but by orders and circumstance.

Non-hostile – helicopter crash.

Twenty-nine was too young to die.

Zack downed another beer then tossed the empty can next to the first one he'd drunk. He cradled his head in hands, torn between needing to forget and wanting to feel alive.

Nothing had helped since he got the call this afternoon. Nothing would. He'd been through this before and knew the routine. Things would never be the same.

Not fair, Davey. You deserved better.

"Zack."

He looked up to see Charlie, the lone female wrangler at the Bar V5 dude ranch, who prided herself on being one of the boys. She was twenty-five, but looked younger with her hair pulled back in a single braid. The setting sun brought out the copper strands. She wore a short sleeved shirt, faded jeans, and boots. Pretty, if one liked the fresh-face, no make-up type, but off-limits, so what he liked didn't matter.

She rode horses better than any guy and used to compete in vaulting—gymnastics on horseback. A smile twitched at the corners of his mouth. Davey would have had a field day with that tidbit.

Davey. Damn.

"Not a good time." Zack picked at a twig sticking out of the dirt. "Go away."

"Nope."

He didn't look at her. Maybe she'd get the hint.

"Think I'll stay." She sat next to him, in his personal space close, pissing him off worse than a fire ant colony that invaded a picnic. She placed a lantern on the ground. "Looks like you could use a friend."

He shrugged. "I'm…"

Aw, hell. He couldn't say he was fine. He wasn't.

She touched his arm, the skin-to-skin contact and caring gesture exactly what he needed.

A lump burned in his throat. His eyes watered. He blinked.

Her hand remained in place. "You don't have to say anything, but I'm here, and I'm not going anywhere."

The warmth in her eyes and the sweet tone of her voice awakened a place in his heart he thought long dead. Words he'd bottled up poured out, one after another, stories about Davey and others lost, secrets he'd never told a soul.

The sun disappeared beneath the horizon. Darkness surrounded them. Zack didn't care. Charlie didn't seem to either.

A good thing. She was his lifeline, his way back to the civilian world, a place he felt disconnected from at the moment. He talked, and she held his hand. He cried, and she comforted him.

She wiped away his tears with her fingertips.

Embarrassed, he looked away.

"It's okay," she whispered.

No, it wasn't, but if she could pretend, so could he.

Charlie sighed. "I wish…"

Her compassionate tone made Zack look up. The lantern glowed softly, giving off enough light so he could see her face.

She leaned forward, toward him. The connection between them intensified. He came closer, driven by an urge he shouldn't be feeling. Not with Charlie.

Zack stared into blue eyes filled with empathy, wanted to know what she wished and was about to ask…

She kissed him.

A kiss so tender and sweet, Zack knew she'd been heaven-sent to get him through this night. He didn't plan on kissing her back—that would be against his rule—but she wasn't stopping. Why not kiss her? It was only one kiss…

Chapter One

September, a year later…

"HAVE YOU MADE your decision, Charlie?"

Sweat dampened the back of Charlotte Randall's neck. Too bad she couldn't blame the perspiration on the warm September temperature and the trail ride back to the Bar V5 dude ranch, but the fault lay in a combo of nerves and procrastination. Two things she hoped to overcome in the next, oh, ten seconds, so she could figure out what to say to ranch foreman and co-owner Tyler Murphy, riding on her right.

"No." She looked at her boss, keeping a smile on her face and the reins loose in hands.

Without shifting in the saddle, she pressed her boots harder against the stirrups. Two nudges on Sierra's flank would send her horse cantering down the dusty path in the Gallatin Range foothills to the barn. But doing so might tip off the other wranglers that Charlie was upset. She didn't want them to know, especially with three ranch guests on horseback behind her. Visitors came first, no matter what.

"I haven't," she said. "But I'm getting closer."

Not the total truth, but not a strike-her-down lie. Still Charlie glanced at the clear, blue, big Montana sky overhead to see if

God was sending a lightning bolt her way.

Nope. Good for now.

Which wasn't saying much.

"Colorado your only other choice?" Ty asked.

She nodded, not trusting her voice.

"The same place you worked last winter?"

"Yes," she forced the word from her dry throat. "The horse ranch."

"I know horses are your first love. There are plenty of them here. All over Montana for that matter."

"I know."

For the past two months, a trifecta of uncertainty, longing and reluctance over whether to remain at the dude ranch or accept a seasonal position again in Colorado had kept her awake at night. She was no closer to deciding than on that hot July day when she'd discovered the Bar V5 would be welcoming guests year-round instead of closing to visitors from mid-September through early May.

Normally, a skeleton crew worked all year to care for the livestock and do ranch maintenance. Until this past winter, that group had included her. But with the new schedule coming into effect, the ranch wanted to hire more year-round staff and fewer seasonal employees.

If she could get over her infatuation with fellow wrangler Zack Harris, once and for all, having to decide what to do would be a moot point. She could stay on the ranch, close to her friends in Marietta and not too far away from her mother, who had relocated to Billings with her newest boyfriend. But not for a lack of trying, Charlie had had zero luck getting Zack out of her system, let alone her heart.

She blew out an exasperated breath. A case of unrequited love shouldn't affect her life like this. She was twenty-six, not thirteen. But then again, Charlie had been waiting for Mr. Right to show up for years. She didn't want to end up like her mother, who chose one wrong guy after another and was heading toward marriage number five with a much younger man.

Ty wiped his arm across his face. He was attractive in a too-bad-he's-the-boss kind of way, but at thirty-five, he seemed older. Not his looks. His actions.

Maybe because he'd raised his sister, Rachel, and was used to playing the father figure to those around him. As foreman, he handled the daily operations of the ranch. He also took good care of the wranglers, cattle, barn cats, and Dusty, their loyal Australian cattle dog. If she'd had a big brother, she would have wanted him to be like Ty Murphy.

"You can't put off making a decision much longer," he said. "The rodeo is this weekend."

"I know."

The welcome fundraising dinner was two days away on Friday night. The ranch staff and guests would attend the dinner, then the wranglers would rotate chaperoning and playing tour guide to guests over the next two days. Except Charlie. The rodeo was her baby and she would be there all three days, but another wrangler, Dustin, would be in charge Friday night.

"I've been redoing the itinerary since they moved the dance to Saturday night to accommodate Jake Kohl's schedule," she continued. "He's supposed to perform his newest country and western hit."

The 76th Annual Copper Mountain Rodeo used to mark the end of the Bar V5's tourist season. But since Nate Vaughn, the ranch's other co-owner and Ty's new brother-in-law, decided to stay open, only the seasonal employees would be leaving.

Would that include her? She wished she knew the answer.

Winter guests would bring a new vibe to the Bar V5, Nate had told her. More like a new pain in the neck. Charlie needed to spend this winter away from the ranch again for the sake of her sanity and, most importantly, her heart. Unless she could figure out a way to get over Zack without quitting the job she loved and moving out of state. If only she knew how to do that.

"I'm not meaning to hold you up or be difficult." She patted Sierra's neck—her horse loved rubs—not wanting to meet Ty's watchful gaze. "But I want to be sure."

"Understood. It's a big decision. You're Montana born. You've been working at the Bar V5 since you were in high school. I see the appeal of spending time someplace else, but I don't want to lose a hard worker like you." Ty didn't give out compliments lightly, and she straightened in her saddle. "I have others interested in your position. Like I told you before, if business is good, we may have to hire seasonal employees early. If you're not back from Colorado, I might not be able to hold a fulltime spot for you."

Working part-time wasn't an option, nor was leaving the other job early. If she chose Colorado, she would be saying goodbye to the Bar V5 for good.

Darn Nate Vaughn. She liked and respected the guy. He'd quit his venture capital job to turn his dad's near bankrupt cattle ranch into a thriving, working dude ranch, but the changes *he was making* to the ranch's schedule were messing up *her* life by taking away *her* options.

Sierra arced to the left to miss a three-inch divot in the trail. The horse would never be called petite. For such a large girl, who looked strong and fearless and never got spooked, she went out of her way to avoid holes or divots, no matter how small, unless the trail was too narrow to go around, then she'd cross as if no big deal.

So brave and affectionate with a wild mane and tail that could never be tamed. But that didn't lessen the horse's beauty. Gorgeous was the only way to describe her. Charlie gave the mare another pat.

Sierra was the best horse ever. Wherever Charlie ended up, staying here or moving to Colorado, her horse would be going, too, even if the ranch had been their home for years.

"I'll let you know after the rodeo," she said. "On Monday."

"Great."

Her gaze flew to Ty's. He'd never seemed impatient before, but the clock was winding down. Of course he needed the position filled. Nothing personal, right?

Her chest tightened, making breathing difficult. She cleared her throat. "You said you had people interested in my job. Do you have someone waiting for my decision?"

"Yes."

His flat tone brought tears to her eyes. Frustration was natural. He and Nate had been more than patient waiting for her decision all season. Why couldn't she make up her mind?

She blinked away the unfamiliar stinging. Cowboys didn't cry. If she hadn't cried when her third stepfather had sold the ranch after his and her mother's divorce, she didn't need to cry now. Not over her job at the Bar V5 and not over Zack Harris.

Anger at herself heated her skin. The situation should have never come to this.

Charlie fanned her face, as if shooing flies. The airflow helped the tears vanish. The other wranglers had never seen her being "girly," and she wasn't about to start. The only thing she'd ever wanted was to fit in. Something she'd struggled with, due to her mother dragging her from one town in Montana to another with each new relationship. Charlie had learned to adapt, changing like a chameleon with each new place and school.

She'd worked hard from the time she'd stepped foot on the Bar V5 so the guys would accept her and not treat her differently—one of the boys—but keeping her feminine side hidden was getting harder the older she got. Painting her toenails fun colors and wearing lacy underwear only went so far. No one knew when she was PMSing, or ate ice cream from the container when sad, or that she was ready to start a family of her own. And they wouldn't know, unless she let them peek underneath the mask. She always won at poker. No one could read her game face.

The one time she'd let down her guard had been with Zack down by the river. She'd kissed him to make him feel better, an act of empathy after the death of his army friend. Even before that night, she'd found him attractive, heroic, and kind. But the situation had blown up in her face and, a year later, continued wreaking havoc in her heart. Her life.

Ty's watchful gaze made her squirm. She tightened her hold Sierra's reins.

The beautiful mare—a mixture of mustang, draft, and quarter horse—turned her head and gave Charlie a what-are-you-doing look.

That was the problem. She had no idea what she was doing. Each time she'd decided to go to Colorado, something made her reconsider. Well, someone. Zack. The reason she'd left Montana this past winter.

Her brain wanted to tell the army vet turned cowboy and shooting instructor good riddance. But her heart wasn't ready to give up on them being a couple, even if Zack had told her they could only be coworkers, nothing more. She hated that he hadn't called them friends.

Zack rode up on her left side atop his horse Blackbeard, as if on cue. The sky provided the perfect backdrop for the dark handsome horse and his gorgeous rider.

Stubble covered Zack's chin and brown hair stuck out from his hat. His features weren't model-perfect, but his rugged good looks and slightly crooked nose gave him character. His lips made her think of hot kisses shared on the riverbank.

Forget about that night.

The last thing she needed was to swoon with an audience.

Particularly this one. Not that she would, but she'd come close in the past. Twice.

"Admit it," Zack joked. "You're dragging this out so we'll beg you to stay. A woman wants a man on his knees saying he can't live without her."

"Not all women." Charlie didn't allow hope the chance to bloom. The next words out of his mouth would likely be about the hot chick he met at Grey's Saloon last Saturday night. *Flirt* should be Zack's middle name. Of course, he never flirted with Charlie, making her feel... asexual. Undesirable. Unattractive. "I'll bet you can live without me just fine."

That was the problem. Dating someone he worked with was against the rules. Not the Bar V5's, but Zack's. Nothing would convince him otherwise, or so he claimed.

Time to get out of here. Charlie clicked her tongue.

Sierra increased her gait, moving in front of the others slightly. Not enough distance to warrant questions, but enough to give Charlie space from Zack. Something she'd wanted this entire summer.

Pathetic.

Her, not him.

A year after kissing him she was still crushing on him like a lovelorn teenager. She'd tried moving past her attraction and the memories of the night spent talking and kissing until the sun rose, but so far no luck. She'd fallen cowboy hat over spurs, fallen hard like a hoof to the chest. No Cupid's arrow needed.

L-O-V-E.

She'd gone all-in that night, as if she'd held a royal flush instead of a pair of threes. She'd made the first move by kissing him, driven by empathy that quickly changed to desire. One touch of her lips against his had sealed the fuzzy warmth of affection growing that night as she learned more about him, wrapping around her heart and making her see a future with

Zack.

Not just any future. The one she'd been dreaming about for... years.

Questions such as what boots would look best with a wedding dress had popped into her mind. She'd picked what old ranch cabin they could renovate and live in as husband and wife. She'd pictured mini-Zack-lookalikes running around the Bar V5 with child-size cowboy hats on their heads and Dusty nipping at their heels to keep track of them as a herding dog would.

Lovely fantasies.

Her problem? Zack didn't feel the same.

Following their hot and heavy goodbye, she'd expected him to ask her out on an official date. He'd apologized instead, asking forgiveness for kissing her back and explaining how dating coworkers was against his rules.

When she joked how rules were meant to be broken, he hadn't been amused. If anything, he'd looked upset, muttered something about a bad experience and gave another apology. She had been, in a word, mortified and embarrassed. That was two words, but who was counting?

She'd never mentioned liking him, or wanting to date, or anything about that night. She'd wanted to put the evening behind her, except she... couldn't.

His lack of feelings toward Charlie hadn't changed her wanting to be with him. Oh, no. Shrugging off what could have been with Zack would have been too smart and logical. Instead she focused on what they could have together if he changed his mind.

Heat rose up her neck. Breaking a wild mustang with her hands tied and wearing a blindfolded would be easier than getting Zack to like her.

She'd escaped to Colorado this past winter for needed space and perspective. Time away to cool her feelings and decide what she wanted when she returned to Montana. She'd loved the horse ranch. For the first time, she hadn't tried to be a cowboy. She'd been one hundred percent cowgirl, found herself accepted as-is, and asked out on dates. She'd returned to the Bar V5, ready to put her crush and their kisses in the past so she could find a new guy to date, one who would like her back. But within two weeks, her feelings for Zack returned, stronger than before.

His had remained the same—nonexistent.

She'd tried to see if he'd changed his mind about dating someone from the ranch. He hadn't.

Insecurities, however, had kept her locked in the "one of the guys" mold. Best not to "rock the ranch" as Zack had answered when she asked about the possibility of dating a hypothetical coworker. So she didn't.

Talk about screwed. Tortuous didn't begin to describe this summer. She daydreamed of his kisses and a western themed wedding while he dated one beautiful woman after another.

Look where she was now. An entire year wasted wishing and hoping and praying, for what?

Absolutely nothing.

If not for her bunkmate, Caitlin Rodger, a close friend from high school and a preschool teacher in Marietta who ran the children's summer program for the ranch, and her cat Mistletoe, Charlie would have quit in July. Which made her wonder why making the decision to leave the ranch was so difficult.

Don't give up yet, her heart whispered.

Shut up. Charlie grimaced, angry for not being able to change the way she felt.

Zack and Blackbeard caught up to her and Sierra. "What if we don't want to live without you?"

His "we" wasn't lost on her.

She leveled her gaze at him. "We don't always get what we want."

He pressed his lips together. A muscle ticked at his jaw. "That's—"

"Charlie will make the decision that's right for her." Ty rode up along her right side, but his gaze focused on Zack. "Got it?"

"No, I don't get it." The intensity in Zack's green-gold eyes sent her blood rushing to the tips of her Ariat boots then boomeranging up again. "Doing something you love, with people you like, near your hometown is a no-brainer. Hell, your mom lives in Billings. Why move all the way to Colorado?"

"You," the word burst from her lips.

Zack's brows drew together. "Huh?"

Oh, crap. She swallowed around the rodeo belt buckle sized lump in her throat.

"You… wouldn't understand."

Please buy that. Please, oh, please, oh, please.

His lopsided grin took ten years off his face and tripped her heart.

"Try me," he said.

Charlie couldn't blame him for her feelings or be upset he wasn't interested in her romantically. She was the one who kissed him first. Of course, he had kissed her back. That didn't make her special. Any guy in his situation would have done the same. But she was tired of getting upset at herself over this— over him.

"I don't think so."

Zack would never understand. That much she knew. As long as he was around her, no man could compete with the way she'd built him up in her mind, magnified his kisses in her memory and set her heart on him, only him. All the wranglers were good guys, but Zack's kindness and thoughtfulness set him apart from the other cowboys. He would go out of his way for anybody, and had, but until that night she'd never seen such a display of openness or display of emotion or love for his fallen friend. He'd touched her heart in a way she'd never expected.

But now…

Her future held nothing but frustration if she continued on a path of unrequited love. But the thought of leaving the ranch made her feel as if she'd been caught in the middle of a stampede and trampled, but her need to end the romance wasteland she'd been living in buoyed her with a new resolve.

She raised her chin. "But you're right about one thing."

"What's that?"

"This should be an easier decision to make. Thanks for getting me back on track."

Colorado was her only choice if she wanted to step out of the box she'd put herself into and have a romance with someone special. Charlie did. She had so much love to give, and wanted to give, but she needed to find a man who would love her back. For herself. Not some cowboy whose personal rules couldn't be broken or amended. At first, she wondered if she might have a chance with him if they didn't work together, but as time went on, she questioned whether he'd used his rule as an excuse to let her down gently. Whichever, she needed to fix this mess.

A sighed welled up inside her. Yeah, and once she was no longer crazy for him, she needed to find someone else. He didn't have to be a wrangler. But whoever that guy turned out to be, she hoped he was a lot like Zack Harris.

BACK AT THE Bar V5, horses put away in their stalls, Zack leaned against the doorway to the barn. A warm breeze carried the familiar smell of cow, horses, and dirt. Paradise Valley was God's country, a land like no other he'd seen. And he'd seen many during his time in the army. He couldn't imagine anyone wanting to leave this place permanently.

Especially Charlie.

She'd worked at the Bar V5 longer than him. She considered this ranch home the same as him. But something in her tone on the ride back told Zack she'd made a decision.

The wrong one.

Not going to happen.

He rested a booted foot against the door jamb. Sweat soaked through his T-shirt and dampened his hairline. Dirt covered his jeans. A cold drink and a shower sounded like heaven. But he couldn't head to the bunkhouse without talking with Charlie first.

He hadn't understood her going to Colorado this past winter, but she hadn't traveled much and he knew she was coming back to the Bar V5 so he hadn't worried. This time would be different.

Ty exited the barn with Dusty at his heels and Onyx, a black barn cat, at his side. He looped a thumb into his jean pocket. "Thought you'd be at the bunkhouse."

"Something I want to take care of first."

His friend, who happened to be his boss, gave him a hard, knowing look. "If this has anything to do with Charlie—"

"She belongs here."

"Something's calling her to Colorado or pushing her away from here."

"Not me." Zack raised his hands, palms forward. "We... I haven't—"

Damn, he couldn't bring himself to say the words. A mixture of embarrassment and something he couldn't name.

Ty grinned wryly. "Didn't think so. Divorced couples get along better than you two."

"That's her doing, not mine. I've been treating her the same as I did... before."

Before Charlie kissed him, and he kissed her back.

Zack didn't regret many things in his life, but he regretted that night with her at the river. He'd been overwrought by grief following Davey's death. Words coupled with emotion had poured out. He'd opened up like never before.

Charlie had been there to listen and comfort. A touch on the arm led to holding hands. Her kissing him turned into a make-out session. More than one. Unexpected, but what he'd needed. She'd been so caring and kind and loving. So soft and feminine, something he hadn't expected from the cowgirl who acted like a cowboy most of the time.

He'd wanted more. Her. Until sunrise made him see the light and realize the mistake he'd made by thinking about what he wanted, not his fellow wranglers and what was best for the Bar V5.

Relationships changed group dynamics. Zack had seen that happen during deployments where friendships became stressed and people got hurt. One woman had caused his squad to implode. He didn't want that to happen at the Bar V5, his home now, his… family. A romance would affect the wranglers in a negative way.

He'd also heard Charlie's friends talk about her search for the perfect guy. Perfect didn't describe him. Far from it. She deserved more than a guy like him could give her.

He wasn't capable of making a commitment to a woman because of his parents. Charlie was a forever type of girl. Any fool could see that. He'd been a fool to think he could have her, even for one night. "If I could take back what happened…"

"So you've said."

"But that was over a year ago and can't be the reason she wants to leave now. All we did was talk and kiss. Hell, she made the first move. No big deal." But they could have easily made the night into something more, something special. He shook the thought from his head.

"Yeah, you're right. It's not like Charlie to hold a grudge,"

Ty said. "The horse ranch may have made her a better job offer. Or she could have met a guy in Colorado. Wants to be with him."

Zack's stomach clenched. Charlie was pretty, even when she tried downplaying her looks. But she seemed more interested in the livestock than men. He'd heard talk of dates, random gossip at Grey's Saloon, but he hadn't seen her out with a guy. "You think?"

"That would explain her wanting to move there."

Yeah, more so than anything else, but… "Why wouldn't she tell us? And why all the waffling?"

"She's a woman." Ty reached down and scratched under Onyx's neck. The cat purred like a John Deere tractor. "One thing I learned raising Rachel is a female's thought process is different from ours."

This should be an easier decision to make. Thanks for getting me back on track.

Maybe, but Zack needed to know what Charlie meant by those words. None of his business. He'd been telling himself that for two months, ever since Ty mentioned Charlie might not stay at the Bar V5. "I'll keep that in mind."

"Remember what I said. The decision is hers. Don't try to change her mind if her heart's set on leaving."

As if anything Zack did or said could do that, but in good conscience, he had to try. He'd lost track of his parents, who hadn't contacted him in over a decade. In jail or dead? Those were the likeliest options for the woman and man he'd called mom and dad. He'd never searched for his parents, afraid of what he might learn. What remained of his army family kept in contact, but spending time together hadn't happened with them so spread out. He needed to keep his ranch family together. Sure, people came and went, but the wranglers had stuck together for the past two and a half years, ever since he'd arrived. And Charlie...

She cared about him, about all of them. Wranglers cared about each other, the way he did for Charlie. She would be happiest at the Bar V5, not with some guy she barely knew in another state.

Now to convince her.

Chapter Two

~

A MINUTE LATER, Zack watched Ty walk toward the bunkhouse, the animals following as if he were the Pied Piper. Horses loved him, too, and would be in line if they weren't locked in their paddocks. The guy had a gift.

Like Charlie.

Zack had to convince her to stay. He hopped onto the top rail of the nearby fence. He'd sit while he waited.

A few minutes later, Charlie stepped out of the barn. Two copper braids hung down from her hat. The only time he'd seen her wear make-up had been at Nate and Rachel's wedding. Charlie had worn a dress showing off long, toned legs no one expected, least of all him. He'd had to keep his distance that night and keep the other wranglers away from her, too.

She might act like a cowboy, rough and tumble, ready to jump into a fight if called upon, but she was girl-next-door pretty, with blue eyes that sparkled and a generous mouth that readily curved into a smile. He didn't let himself think of her as a woman often. Treating her like a guy kept him from focusing on her soft lips, sweet scent, and sexy curves.

She rubbed the back of her neck. "Thought you'd be at the bunkhouse by now."

He shrugged. "Was waiting for you."

She inhaled sharply.

Ty was right about them not getting along. She seemed more pissed off today. He jumped off the fence and closed the distance between them. "Got a few minutes?"

"For?"

The blues of her eyes reminded him of two tempting, deep pools of water. Perfect to jump into when he was hot and sweating. Truth was, drowning in her didn't sound like a bad way to go. The reason that would be a mistake poked at him like hungry mosquitos.

"I want to talk," he said.

She glanced toward the main house, a worried expression on her face. "We're expected to mingle with the guests. Nate and Ty will be fuming if we show up for dinner smelly and dirty."

"Won't take long."

For a minute, he thought she might say no, then she crossed her arms over her chest. "Shoot."

"You said I wouldn't understand about Colorado. Maybe not, but give me the chance." He kept his tone light.

She looked as skittish as a newborn colt.

"I might surprise you."

"You always surprise me," she muttered.

"What was that?" he asked even though he'd heard her.

Charlie's discerning gaze ran the length of him. "My choice doesn't affect you."

"Not true," the words came out stronger than he intended.

Her lips parted slightly. "Yeah, right."

"We have a good crew of wranglers. Sure, Ty can hire someone to take your place, but you work hard. You're the only one who can keep Bluebelle from conking her head against the gate. You'll be hard to replace."

Charlie did more than most men around here, and she never complained about the work, the dirt, or any of the more prickly guests who arrived thinking they knew everything about ranch life.

He continued. "You can sweet-talk the cattle, horses, and guests like no one else. Don't waste your gift. Stay at the Bar V5."

"The ranch in Colorado might not have cattle, but they've got plenty of horses for me to work with over the winter. Colorado sure is pretty with all the snow."

"So is Montana. Trust me. You don't want to miss Rachel's gingerbread or the Christmas dinner she'll cook."

Zack looked around at the fences, outbuildings, and the red barn, the oldest building at the ranch. A feeling of warmth settled over his chest. The way he'd felt the first time he'd trekked down the Bar V5's long driveway after hearing in town the dude ranch might have an opening.

"Colorado is too far away," he said. "I haven't been here nearly as long as you, but the Bar V5 is my home. You and the other wranglers are my family. The ranch is all I've got. I don't want that to change."

"No one is irreplaceable," Charlie said. "Anyone of us could get injured or quit."

"True that, but you're the only one thinking about leaving right now." Her nonchalance over taking another job bugged him. She'd told him she considered the wranglers her family, too. "Our crew's mish-mash personalities and skills remind me of being in the military. Don't have all the regulations to follow, paperwork to deal with, or the hurry up and wait scenarios, but until I found this place, I was lost, struggling to find my way back in the civilian world. Ty took a chance on me. The way he does with most of us. Is leaving how you want to repay him?"

She flinched. "Don't try to guilt trip me into staying. If you remember, I helped train you. I have my reasons for leaving."

"Some guy."

Lines creased her forehead. "Excuse me?"

"There has to be a guy involved. That's the only reason that makes sense." He waited for her to deny his assumption, but she didn't. "Who is he?"

She flushed, then lowered her gaze. "Doesn't matter."

Ty had been correct, but Zack didn't feel any relief. He kicked the tip of his boot into the dirt. "If I'm going to have to train someone to take your place, I want to know who's taking you away from the Bar V5."

She started to speak then stopped herself. "Just a guy I like. We're not dating or anything."

He wondered about her definition of anything. "Yet you're thinking about moving because of him?"

"I-I... yes."

Something felt off. "You don't sound sure."

Her jaw tensed. "I will be certain by the time I tell Ty my decision on Monday."

So much for thinking she'd made her choice. "You're still deciding?"

She nodded once, a pained expression on her face.

He didn't like seeing her in such turmoil. Kissing her would make her felt better, but his rule existed for a reason. One he would be hard-pressed to forget. "Might be easier if you found a guy closer to home."

"Hard to do when I'm working all the time."

"So how'd you meet this guy?"

Charlie twirled the end of a braid with her finger. "Work."

"He's a cowboy?" Zack asked.

Another nod. She wouldn't meet his gaze.

Interesting. His rule kept him from kissing her again, but maybe some other guy's kisses would be enough to make her stay put. "Forget going to Colorado. There are lots of cowboys in Montana. Hell, Marietta for that matter."

She didn't look up. "Told ya. Work gets in the way."

Yeah, Charlie wasn't one to hang out at bars trying to be picked up. But if she fell for someone local, she would forget about the other guy and keep working at the Bar V5 at least for a while longer.

A brilliant plan to keep her in the area. "I could help you."

Her gaze jerked up to his. "Help?"

"Find you a man."

Her kisses tempted Zack, but she needed someone better, someone who could give her more than a life of bunkhouses and barns and heartache, someone who didn't come from a line of petty crooks and jailbirds.

But who? No one not from the Bar V5. A workplace romance would mess up everything. That left...

The rodeo.

Oh, yeah. He grinned, tapped his finger against the side of this cheek. "I know exactly how to go about this."

Her face paled. "Please tell me you're kidding."

"I'm dead serious," he said. "The rodeo's coming to town. The streets of Marietta will be filled with cowboys and tourists. Hell, you could lasso yourself a rich guy. Chelsea Crawford Collier seems happy with Jasper Flint. Maybe the guy has a brother."

If a man caught Charlie's eye—didn't matter if he was a cowboy or not—life at the Bar V5 would remain the same. Zack's family would stay together.

Fixing her up with someone wouldn't be hard. Until Rachel and Nate's wedding at the Bar V5 this summer, he'd never seen Charlie in dress, but Zack had to admit the cowgirl cleaned up well.

Off limits.

She eyed him warily. "Thanks for the offer, but I can find my own dates."

"You said you couldn't due to work."

"I'm good."

"Not if you're thinking about leaving." Charlie might not think she needed help, but she did. "I'm going to help find you a reason to stay."

Surely, out of all the people in town for the rodeo, he could find one man she would like. Even if a small part of Zack wished he could be that guy.

DARN ZACK HARRIS. Charlie trudged to the women's bunkhouse, her boots kicking up a wake of dirt, her heart a tangled mess, and her resolve all but gone. She rubbed her eyes, wishing she could blame the dust for making them water.

Forget about being a suck-it-up cowboy. She was a girly girl, too, one who wanted to stomp her feet, pout, and dive into a container of Ben and Jerry's Chunky Monkey. Spoon optional.

Find you a man.

Of all the things Zack could say to her, that had been the most surreal. Language Arts had never been her best subject in high school, but she knew the meaning of irony. No doubt her teacher Mrs. Cooper would have a hard time finding a better example.

Charlie didn't know whether to be touched Zack wanted her to stay at the Bar V5 or whack him alongside the head for being so freakin' blind to her wanting *him*, not some other cowboy or what was the other word he used? Oh, yeah, tourist. As if some guy with a fat wallet in new boots giving him blisters would equal the worth of the man she'd worked side by side with for the past two and a half years. No one had the same heart, the same kindness to guests, young and old, and quiet strength she'd come to rely upon even if he had no idea what she was doing.

This was insane. She didn't need Zack to find her a man.

She'd found one. Him.

But he was treating her like a heifer to be auctioned off to the nearest guy he could find. Talk about embarrassing and frustrating. She bit the inside of her mouth, tasted blood.

Their kisses hadn't rocked Zack's world the way they had Charlie's. She got that, but she thought he'd felt a twinge of attraction or a spark of heat. Clearly he hadn't. His so-called rule had been nothing more than an excuse, probably so working together wouldn't be awkward. And maybe that would be true if she hadn't fallen in love with him.

Darn Zack Harris.

Wanting to fix her up like she was a drinking buddy, not a red-blooded woman who had once kissed him—over and over again. She could make her own decisions about men, or rather; she could once she stopped seeing Zack as so darn sweet and cute. Okay, hot.

She balled her hands then flexed her fingers. Overreacting to everything he did or said was not healthy. But this reaffirmed what she knew in her heart—she couldn't keep living like this. Her throat tightened at the direction her decision was heading.

But what else could she do?

A familiar red, all-wheel-drive hatchback was parked outside the women's bunkhouse. Caitlin's car. Charlie accelerated her pace, eager to see her friend, and at the front door, brushed off the dirt from her boots.

Inside, a meow greeted her, followed by a cat rubbing against her leg. She bent to pet the no-longer-so-little tabby. "Hello, Mistletoe. You keep growing. I've missed you."

"She's missed you." Caitlin's straight, brown hair fell past her shoulders. She wore a short-sleeved flowered print dress with sensible flat shoes, the kind made for chasing preschoolers and standing most of the day except during circle time. She hugged Charlie. "Me, too. How are you?"

"Great."

No one knew about her and Zack. At first she'd wanted to keep what happened a secret, afraid what the other wranglers and her friends might say if they found out. But as the days, weeks, then months passed, she'd been too embarrassed, given her feelings weren't reciprocated. Charlie's insides twisted like a rusted hinge in need of a spray of WD-40, but she kept a smile pasted on her lips.

"I'm excited about the rodeo."

Caitlin nodded. "I can't believe Jake Kohl is the honorary rodeo chair. I love his music."

"So do I. I heard Selah Davis is flying back from Seattle to interview him for that magazine she writes for. She's so lucky. Jake is one easy on the eyes singer."

"There should be other good looking cowboys hanging around town this weekend."

"Don't let Noah hear you say that." Charlie envied her friend, who had a job, a cat, and a man she loved.

Caitlin had reunited with her former college boyfriend, now a vet at the Copper Mountain Animal Hospital in Marietta, on Christmas Eve, thanks to Mistletoe.

Caitlin grinned. "Hey, there's nothing wrong with looking. We've been doing that during rodeo weekends since we discovered boys don't have cooties."

"Very true."

Charlie smiled at the memories of rodeos past and some of the more appealing eye candy. Caitlin was a year older, and their friendship had been cemented after volunteering to help a group of yearlings rescued from a Canadian ranch and brought to Marietta.

"How's the new apartment working out?" Charlie asked.

"Okay. Being walking distance to Main Street is convenient. I don't miss the long drive from the ranch into town, but I prefer living out in the country. I think Mistletoe does, too." The cat rubbed her head against Caitlin's leg. "Marietta might be small, but the town is noisier than I remember. This ranch is a slice of Montana heaven. A peaceful, quiet one at that. You're so lucky to live here."

Not the words Charlie wanted to hear, especially since they were true. Her chest tightened. As Zack had said, the Bar V5 was home, not the dingy place she'd shared with her mom through high school. Charlie wanted to focus on the things wrong with the ranch so leaving would be easier.

"Your apartment is closer to where Noah lives."

Caitlin nodded. "But between his shifts at the animal hospital and making house calls, I don't see him as much as I'd like. One of the hazards of dating a dedicated veterinarian, but I wouldn't want him to be any other way."

The affection in Caitlin's voice intensified Charlie's longing for the same kind of a relationship, full of respect and kindness and love. Someday....

"Glad you feel that way," Charlie said. "Animals don't like being transported. Noah coming to the ranch has made things easier on the livestock and us."

"That's what he tells me. He loves his job." Caitlin picked up Mistletoe. "Though I'll be honest, I've been tempted to wear a kitty ear headband and draw whiskers on my face to see if I could get more time with him."

Charlie laughed, but she understood her friend's dilemma. She'd have more luck getting Zack to like her if she were a horse. "If you dress up, take pictures. But you have to know, Noah is totally into you."

"He keeps saying that, and I'm crazy about the guy." Caitlin nuzzled her chin against Mistletoe. "Hard to believe we've been together almost nine months. Even with his schedule, this time has been better than when we dated in college. Amazing what one kitten can do."

"Maybe I should get a cat and see if I can find a guy like you did."

Caitlin stared over the top of Mistletoe's head. "In the market for a relationship?"

Her friend's curious tone set off warning bells. Charlie raised her chin. "Nothing wrong with going out occasionally."

"I agree. I'm happy you're considering the possibility. You haven't shown much interest in dating for a while."

Because of Zack. She could give the exact date if she wanted. "It's time."

"With the rodeo in town, you're not going to need a kitten to find a guy. Your pretty smile will work fine."

Charlie's cheeks heated. Smiling hadn't worked for her in the past. Making the first move, either. She wasn't sure what was left.

"Just be careful not to shoot down every guy who approaches you," Caitlin said. "No mortal man can live up to your high standards and quest for perfection."

"No one is perfect." Especially Zack, who didn't love her back.

Caitlin gave her a look. "Then don't expect them to be."

"I don't."

"Josiah."

Oh, yeah. Charlie remembered Josiah Whittaker. Three years older. Cute. Nice. Good roping skills, but... she crinkled her nose.

"He didn't shower much and smelled. One of those guys who think soap and deodorant are optional," she explained. "Expecting proper hygiene is not a high standard."

"Dane."

Sex in cowboy boots. That was how she would describe Dane Wilcox. Smokin' hot, too. He hung around Marietta when not rodeoing. Too bad he was also a total player.

"I was not going to be another notch on his belt. That's having self-respect."

"I have more names," Caitlin said.

"Not necessary."

"Just be mindful. This is something you've done for a long time. Remember how no one was good enough for you to ask to the Sadie Hawkins dance in ninth grade?"

Freshman year, when her former favorite stepdad had an affair, divorced her mother and kicked them off the ranch before selling the place. The shock and hurt had left Charlie reeling for months.

"I'll be open-minded. Thanks."

"No, thank you. I want to hear about the cowboys you meet and kiss."

Her friend would be disappointed. She wouldn't be kissing them unless they kissed her first. Lesson learned. She swallowed a sigh.

Caitlin glanced at the clock hanging on the far wall. "I only have a few more minutes. I'm meeting the other preschool teachers at the Main Street Diner for a working dinner and need to drop off Mistletoe before that. I stopped by to see if my jean jacket was here."

Charlie pointed to the wall by the front door. The jacket hung on the third hook from the left. "I would have brought it to town this weekend."

"I'm happy I got to see you sooner than that." Caitlin placed Mistletoe into a soft-sided carrier then grabbed her jacket. "Going to the welcome dinner on Friday?"

"I'm doing everything rodeo-related this weekend with our guests." Jenna ticked off events with her fingers. "The dinner on Friday, pancake feed, parade, rodeo, community steak feed, and the street dance. Not to mention seeing as many events as we can. We'll try to squeeze in a tasting at the FlintWorks Brewery and a little shopping, too."

"Busy schedule."

"The guests will be exhausted, but they're paying to see the rodeo so we make sure they experience all Marietta has to offer." Charlie rubbed the back of her neck. "But this should be the last year a wrangler makes the itinerary and is in charge. I spoke with Nate and Ty. Told them it's time the ranch hires a concierge or event planner. Ever since Rachel and Nate had their reception here, we've been getting calls about weddings and parties. With guests here in winter, someone's going to need to answer questions about ski resorts and other winter sports."

"What did they say?"

"Good idea. Did I know someone for the job?" She grinned. "You'd be perfect."

"I'm a preschool teacher. I like working with kids not their parents. Same with the summer program here. If you didn't love the animals so much, I'd say you'd be great at the job."

"Not interested."

"Too bad, because what you've got planned for this weekend sounds like fun."

"You going to the rodeo?"

"Of course, I am. I've only missed one. My freshman year at MSU. I might be solo this year if Noah has to work."

"Hang out with us. Nate sponsored five tables at Friday night's dinner. We have more than enough room."

"Thanks. I'll text you to work out the details. And keep me posted on any hot cowboys developments."

"Not holding my breath."

A wistful expression formed on Caitlin's face. "I used to say that. And look what happened. The right guy is out there for you. I found mine, when and where I least expected."

Charlie knew exactly where her guy was... in the men's

bunkhouse about a hundred feet away. Probably in the shower, hot water pouring down and steam rising. She shook away the image of a naked Zack.

Falling for another man might be her only hope to get over Zack without leaving Montana. Charlie had lost her heart. Her mind might be next.

She'd considered taking another job at a local ranch, and was going to visit Payton Hollis at Beargrass Hills Ranch to see if the cowgirl knew of any job openings in the area, but Zack would still be too close. Charlie didn't think she would get over him. "Drive safe."

"I will. Keep an eye out for sexy cowboys."

"You got it."

Hot cowboys in town or not, the chances of anything changing between now and Monday morning when she gave Ty her decision were slim to none.

A lump burned in her throat. What was she going to do?

Sunshine and warm temperatures meant eating dinner at long, custom-made tables on the lawn behind the lodge. The smoked brisket, baked sweet potatoes, kale salad, and fresh rolls filled Zack's stomach. Tasty food and good company. Didn't get much better than this. He sipped his strawberry lemonade.

A breeze rustled through the trees. He stretched his legs beneath the table, relaxing until he checked the livestock before bedtime. Routines made life more comfortable. Chores gave him a sense of purpose. Down time left him bored.

The conversation faded, allowing the faint sound of the river on the far side of the meadow to be heard for the first time all evening. Charlie would have her hands full herding this talkative bunch at the rodeo. But given how much she enjoyed interacting with guests, he didn't think she'd mind.

"Wait until you taste the welcome dinner." Standing at the end of his table, Charlie bounced from toe to toe, her excitement for the upcoming rodeo contagious. Guests Dan and Allie Hathaway beamed, eager to hear more about the plans for the upcoming weekend after grilling Charlie about her love for horses and experience in Colorado last winter.

"There's a choice between chicken, trout, and beef that comes from local ranches," she explained. "The chef never says where to cut down on the natural competition."

Dan's buzz cut made Zack remember his days at basic with a zero-size clipper blade taken to his whole head. "The chef sounds smart."

"Very," Charlie agreed. "And talented."

"I can't wait." Allie, a forty-something, stay-at-home mom with blond shoulder-length hair, touched her husband's arm. A boulder-sized diamond sparkled on her ring finger. "I may take a walk on the wild side this weekend and order my meat medium-rare."

Dan kissed his wife's forehead. "That's my girl. No more charred offering for you."

"Lots of folks like well-done. Order however you like. You'll see slabs of beef that look like their ready to walk off the plate and others cooked thoroughly." Charlie's words flowed with the ease of a seasoned politician trying to earn a constituent's vote, but her tone was as genuine as her smile. "We aim to please all tastes in Montana."

"That's for sure." Dan patted his stomach. "I'm going to have to hit the gym when we get home."

"Take a hike in the morning before your shooting lesson." Charlie looked at Zack. "You can help them burn off calories and get their blood pumping, can't you?"

"Of course." Zack winked, wanting Charlie's smile to reach her eyes.

Deciding between Montana and Colorado was not good for her. She should forget about the horse ranch and stay where she belonged. Everyone could see the strain—dark circles under tired eyes, tight lines around her mouth, headaches she downplayed—except her.

"Cowboys know many ways to work off calories and get the ticker moving," he added in a playful, almost sexy tone.

Charlie flushed, making him wonder why. She wasn't the kind of woman who embarrassed easily.

"Zack's the expert."

"I am." Maybe he hadn't noticed the color on her cheek earlier, but he doubted she was sunburned. She was too careful with sunscreen for herself and their guests. "Been known to run morning workout sessions for guests who want more exercise."

"Just what you need, dear," Dan said. "Morning hikes and exercise sound better than that hot rock yoga class you do."

Allie elbowed him. "Or your sunrise spin session in a sweaty studio with half-dressed hard bodies."

Charlie leaned between them, like a camp counselor breaking up two kids who were agitating each other. Bar V5 cowboys had to know how to work with animals and people. Sometimes dealing with the livestock was easier.

Her V neckline gapped. White lace peeked through the opening. Camisole or bra, Zack couldn't tell, but he wanted another look to find out. He remembered touching those breasts over her shirt, but that had almost got him into trouble last time. He couldn't go there again.

No workplace romance allowed, even if Charlie was hardworking, sexy with a killer body. He had scars, physical and mental ones, to show what could go wrong when people were… distracted.

She smiled at the Hathaways. "You'll be in good hands with Zack."

So would Charlie.

He swallowed.

Chapter Three

WHAT THE HELL was Zack thinking? Doing?

Stop. Regain control. Charlie would not be in his hands again.

He straightened, pulling his legs in and fighting the urge to bolt from the table and take cover. "We can go for a trail run if you want a real workout."

Dan held up his hands, laughter in his eyes. "Let's not go crazy. We're on vacation. A hike will be fine. Preferably after a couple of those delicious cinnamon rolls."

Zack and Charlie nodded at the same time.

She stopped first and looked at Dan. "Those are well worth the calories. I don't know if you've heard, but Nate's wife Rachel runs The Copper Mountain Gingerbread and Dessert Factory, so the Bar V5 gets the choice items. We can stop by the bakery as well as the chocolate shop run by a local named Sage Carrigan when we go to town."

"Can't wait." Dan set his glass of red wine on the table. He glanced at his watch, an expensive, hi-tech piece. He stood. "Come on, Al. Time for our couples' massage."

Allie rubbed her hands together. "We usually take our four kids with us on vacation. This trip is our first without them in…"

"Much too long." Dan held his wife's hand and pulled her to her feet, then looked at Zack. "See you after breakfast for the hike."

"Looking forward to it," he said.

The two walked away, giddy as teenagers.

Charlie's gaze followed them. "They're nice."

"They seemed interested in you working with horses."

"They were being polite," she said. "Must be hard to find your way as a couple without kids in tow."

"Not the first husband and wife we've had like that."

"Nope." She looked at Zack. "And they usually return the next year with the entire family."

"I'm sure that'll be the case after you show them the finest Marietta has to offer."

She gave a mock bow. "I'll do my best."

"You always do." His gaze locked on hers. Those blue eyes would be the death of him, but he didn't look away. He... couldn't.

The connection between them had to be a shared love of this ranch, of the livestock, of the wrangler lifestyle, nothing more. If he kept telling himself that, he might believe the words. Better happen soon because he had no choice but to believe them.

"What?" she asked.

He blinked. "Didn't say anything."

"Oh."

Ellie, one of the housekeeping staff, cleared the tables. A handful of guests walked to the river with Ty. Dusty darted back and forth making sure no one got left behind. Three others talked with Dustin Decker, a former rodeo cowboy turned dude ranch wrangler, who readied a bonfire.

Sparks flew out of the pit.

Zack rose, his hand on Charlie's shoulder to stop her from

taking action. "Dustin has this."

The wrangler stomped on the ground, then returned to adding more wood.

Zack realized he was still touching her. He let go of her, immediately missing her warmth. Not that he was cold.

He motioned to Dustin. "Check it out."

She nodded. "I am."

Her looking at the wrangler bothered Zack like a burr between his sock and boot. "See something?"

Her head whipped toward him. "What? Oh, no. Nothing's wrong. You were right letting Dustin handle the sparks. He knows what he's doing. An expert marshmallow roaster, too."

Crap. Zack's gut tightened. What if she liked Dustin? That would mess things up as bad as if Zack liked her.

Time to put an end to any possible Bar V5 wrangler romance. "Dustin's been texting with a riding instructor in Livingston. She wants him to talk to her equestrian students."

"He told me. He tells a good tale. I hope something works out between them." Charlie's eyes brightened to match her smile.

That wasn't the reaction Zack expected. Hmmm. "Yeah, great."

"Much better than a sleazy buckle bunny wanting only to sleep with a former rodeo champion," she said. "He deserves better."

Charlie didn't sound like a jealous woman. Zack scratched his chin. He must be wrong about her liking Dustin. That was a relief. "Sure does."

"What about you?" she asked.

"I don't tell stories."

She made a face. "Have you been seeing anyone?"

The question was one they'd talked about before. Especially on Monday mornings to whoever had the weekend off. No reason talking about other women should feel weird, but this did.

"No one in particular." Nor would there be. Zack touched his shoulder, rubbing the spot where a bullet had gone straight through. He had two more bullet scars, a Purple Heart, and a Bronze Star Medal. But shiny awards could never make up for the losses the squad faced because one of them had fallen in love with a member of their support team. "I'm not about to be tied down by one woman."

"So you've said."

"Still stands."

She studied him. "You and Ty are two peas in a pod."

"That's us," he said. "Two grizzly cowboys content to live in a bunkhouse until they bury us with our boots on."

Charlie opened her mouth, then pressed her lips together.

"What?" Zack asked.

"Don't you think you'll get lonely?"

Zack shrugged, not wanting to think about that too much. He noticed the smattering of freckles across the bridge of her nose had darkened. She must have forgotten sunscreen this afternoon. "You can always find company when you need it."

Her eyes dimmed, as if turned off by a switch. She blinked, and they returned to the normal color, but she wasn't smiling. "I'm sure you can. Ty, too."

He knew that look. "Go ahead and say what's on your mind."

"You don't want to get married, have kids, a family?"

"I have a family." He motioned with his hand. "All of you are my family."

"You could have one of your own, too."

Zack knew that was true, but thoughts of his poor excuse for parents were a constant reminder that he was better off alone. He didn't want to disappoint someone he cared about.

"Marriage is too much trouble and work. Not many women would be happy living on a wrangler's salary or out in the country."

She raised her chin. "Some women would be."

"You, but you're not like other women."

"Gee, thanks."

"That's meant as a compliment."

"What about children? You're great with the ones that visit the ranch."

"Other people's kids. I'd only screw up being a parent."

The way his mom and dad had messed up with him. That was all he knew. Not worth the risk.

"You're selling yourself short."

"Some of us aren't cut out for the picket fence life. I'm not. Ty, either. Dustin isn't sure yet. The others…"

"Will be married before they hit thirty, maybe thirty-five, if they can't get their crap together."

"You sound certain."

"I am."

"How do you know?" Zack asked.

"I listen," she said. "I know they say men don't talk much, but if you pay attention you figure out what you need to know."

"I'll have to remember that." He looked at the sun sinking toward the horizon. "Time to check the animals. All the guests are taken care of. Want to help?"

Her lips parted. "Uh… sure."

For a second, he'd thought she was going to say no. That would have been odd. Charlie spent more time in the barn than anyone except Ty. Zack stood. "Good. Sierra will want her goodnight kisses and rubs."

While Charlie lavished attention on the animals, he was going to figure out what type of guy she wanted to spoil her with love, attention, and fun. Because she deserved to be spoiled, more than any woman he'd ever met. If he were that guy, he'd know right where to start.

But he wasn't. And would never be.

Unfortunately.

OVER THE NEXT two days, Zack asked Charlie what kind of guy she liked. For two days, she replied the same way. No answer. Anytime dating came up, Charlie told him she didn't want his help finding a man.

In the upper horse meadow, where Nate's horse Arrow pastured, Zack snipped extra wire from the fence post with a diagonal cutter, then shoved the dikes into his pants leg pocket. He secured the wooden rail.

His fault Charlie wouldn't tell him what he needed to know.

Zack tested the fence, shaking and pressing against his repair.

He should have been subtler with Charlie. Gone about getting info the roundabout way. Tried to see if her friends would help him out.

Except the clock was winding down. Her decision deadline was Monday, and what would he say to her friends anyway?

Playing matchmaker was out of his comfort zone. He hadn't a clue what to do. That frustrated the hell out him when this was so important.

Truth was, he didn't like trying to figure out the right person for her. Each time he imagined Charlie with a guy, a funny feeling settled in the pit of Zack's stomach, reminding him of Christmastime when he'd helped Rachel with her gingerbread stand at the Scott Tree Farm and ate too many cookies.

What if he fixed Charlie up with the wrong guy? Some jerk who made her cry? Or made her ecstatic she wanted to be with him 24/7? He frowned, not liking either option.

But his alternative was letting her leave. No way.

He rechecked the double fence repair. Sturdy. Arrow wouldn't be able to escape the meadow in search of a mare again.

The horse should have been named Houdini. Casanova wouldn't have been a bad name, either. Only Nate and Charlie could control the beast. One more reason she shouldn't leave. Nate didn't have as much time to ride now that he was married and taking the Bar V5 to the "next level" as he called the changes to the ranch. Ty was the resident horse whisperer, but he had trouble with Arrow. The horse, however, acted like an angel whenever Charlie was around.

Nate called Arrow lovesick. The guys joked about the way the horse followed Charlie like she kept carrots in her back pockets. Well, she did, but Arrow's devotion went deeper. He'd follow her anyway.

Damn, the fence might not hold after all.

Zack headed across the long grass toward the two gates installed to keep Arrow where he belonged. Down below, out of sight of this pasture, the horses not on today's trail ride grazed. He would take them treats. They deserved special attention after how hard they worked during the summer months.

Winter was when the horses rested, and he shared Charlie's concern about the horses needing a lull. Both Nate and Ty promised guests staying at the ranch wouldn't change the horses' schedule. Zack believed them, but wouldn't have analyzed the implications unless she'd brought them up first. Charlie seemed to know what each animal needed and when. They'd missed her last winter and would miss her if she left for good.

She wouldn't. He would make sure.

His stomach grumbled. Almost lunchtime.

Maybe Rachel's macaroni and cheese with bacon would inspire him to figure out the right man for Charlie. He felt trapped. He needed something to get him out of this box canyon. The welcome dinner was tonight, and he had zero intel to go on.

No worries. He'd been faced with difficult and more complex situations. This one should be a breeze. Would, not should.

Hooves sounded behind him. Zack didn't have to look over his shoulder to know Arrow followed him. Stealth-like movements weren't the horse's strongpoint. He relied on brute force to escape rather than the ninja skills the barn cats used.

Arrow wanted something. That much was clear. The horse was as predictable as the Taylor brothers who would be getting into trouble during rodeo weekend.

Zack would be facing his own trouble if he didn't figure out a plan for this weekend. Every year, Nate invited the Bar V5 guests and staff to the welcome dinner, his treat. The event, held in the park, would be the perfect time to scope out possible dates for Charlie and arrange an introduction or two.

If only Zack could figure out who to start with...

Some of families in the area with unmarried sons came to mind. Sheehan. MacCreadie. Douglas.

But Charlie had known those guys since high school. If she hadn't dated them before, she might not go out with them now. Or maybe she had dated them.

Aw, hell. Zack didn't want to set her up with an ex. He raised his hat and scratched his head.

Why couldn't she be one of those women who went on and on about themselves, the men they liked or didn't like, and what they expected life to hand over in a nice, pretty package? Of course, if she did that, she wouldn't be his Charlie.

Not his. The Bar V5's Charlie.

Big difference. One he couldn't afford to forget.

Zack opened the first gate, stepped through, then closed the gate behind him. He locked then double-checked the latches, not wanting to take any chances with Arrow getting out again.

There had to be someone for Charlie, but who?

Zack tugged off his gloves and stuck them in his jacket pocket.

The gate clanged. An annoying sound which earned the desired result. Smart horse.

He turned to see Arrow pushing against the gate. "What's wrong, boy?"

The horse whinnied.

"Nope, you can't go find some sweet filly."

Arrow snorted.

"Stop with the attitude. We don't all get the girl." Wasn't that the truth? An image of Charlie, so kind and loving while she consoled him by the river, popped into his mind. Caught up in the moment. That was the only explanation to what happened between them. The only sensible explanation, he amended.

Arrow tossed his head.

"If you think I'm going to let you out so you can lead us on another chase, forget it. I've got too many chores and lunch is waiting." Zack pulled out an apple. "How about this?"

The horse's tail lifted. His ears pricked forward.

"Hungry, tough guy?"

The horse pawed at the gate with his front legs.

"I'll take that as a yes." Zack fed the stallion, careful to make sure the stud couldn't bite him. Arrow was ornery that way. "A shame you aren't human. Bet Charlie would fall for you. Though you wouldn't think twice about leaving her for the next girl who came along, would you?"

Unfortunately that described many of the cowboys he knew. Ty. Dustin. Himself.

Arrow munched on the red apple, oblivious or ignoring Zack. Knowing the horse, the latter.

"I need to find a guy who's going to treat her right. Go the distance." He rested his arm on the gate rail. "I don't want to have to hurt anybody, and that's what I'd have to do if they hurt Charlie."

The horse stared at him, as if he understood.

"I keep trying to make lists of names, but I get stuck." Zack shook his head. "Too bad you can't tell me who would be good with Charlie."

Arrow nudged his arm.

"Sorry, that was my only apple." Zack brushed his hands together. "Guess I'll have to see who she pays attention to at the dinner and start there."

Arrow sounded like he was making a raspberry.

"Don't worry. I'll figure out someone. No way will I let Charlie leave."

No way at all.

FRIDAY NIGHT UNDER a big white tent in the park, the 76th Copper Mountain Rodeo Welcome Fundraiser Dinner was underway. Based on the organizers' beaming smiles, Charlie assumed the night had been a smashing success. She wasn't surprised given the turnout.

Hundreds of people sat at round tables covered with red gingham cloths. Centerpieces—tin buckets filled with freshly cut flowers and tied with red bandanas—had been made by Risa the florist at Sweetpea Flowers and auctioned off to the highest bidder at each table. A cowboy band played, complete with a yodeler, but the conversations and laughter from the attendees nearly drowned out the music. No one seemed to mind, including the musicians whose smiles never wavered.

A wonderful evening. Mother Nature cooperated, keeping the temperature warm, but pleasant. The area could use rain, but everyone wanted dry weather for the weekend. A downpour on

Monday would be welcomed.

Yet for everything going right, Charlie felt as if she carried fifty-pound bags of feed on each shoulder. Tick-tock. In sixty or so hours, she needed to tell Ty her decision. She could almost hear the countdown in her head.

She glanced at Zack, so handsome in his ironed Western shirt, jeans, and buffed boots. She could only imagine what he must have looked like in his army uniform. Her pulse accelerated, a familiar reaction where he was concerned. She swallowed a sigh. Something she did a lot around him, too.

Colorado, a voice shouted. She had to admit that appeared to be the best option.

Charlie's short, chipped fingernails dug into her sweaty palms. She searched for Caitlin, the one person who could make her concentrate on the cowboys here. Other cowboys.

Where was she?

No text had arrived this afternoon. No reply after texting her back. That was very unlike her quiet and predictable friend.

Noah's influence?

Probably.

He'd convinced Caitlin to take the summer job at the Bar V5, thinking she'd love being outdoors so much. He'd been right. Still, she should be here tonight.

The welcome dinner was their first look at the out-of-town rodeo attendees, especially the cowboys. This had been a do-not-miss event, and as teenagers, they'd saved money from their summer jobs to afford tickets.

"Looking for someone?" Zack asked from two seats away.

Her gaze sought his like a heat-seeking missile, locked on target and ready to make contact, something she'd avoided doing all evening. "Caitlin."

"I haven't seen her." He stood. "Don't see her. Sure she's attending the dinner?"

"I thought so."

Women seated at nearby tables eyed the handsome wrangler with interest, He wasn't a rodeo cowboy, but Zack would have no trouble finding a hook-up tonight. Charlie's stomach roiled. She wished she could blame the reaction on too much apple pie for dessert, but she knew that wasn't the case. She focused on her absent friend.

"Caitlin said she was coming when I saw her two days ago," Charlie added.

"Text her."

"I have. Several times. No reply."

Zack studied her, making her wipe her mouth with the back of her hand, thinking she had pie crumbs on her face.

"Did you try Noah?" Zack asked.

"No. He's working tonight." Charlie dragged her teeth over her lower lip. "Caitlin's on her own."

"You're worried."

Charlie nodded once.

"Give me a couple of minutes." Zack rose then walked to the table where Nate and Ty sat. The three men spoke. Ty pulled out his cellphone and made a call. Sixty seconds later, Zack returned to his spot. "Ty spoke with Noah. Caitlin's with him. They're on their way back from Bozeman. Should arrive shortly."

Charlie leaned forward until her ribcage hit the table. She straightened. "What are they doing in Bozeman?"

"No idea. But Ty assured me Caitlin is fine. Her phone died and she doesn't have her charger. That's why you haven't heard from her."

"Okay, thanks." Charlie appreciated the answers but had questions. Noah was supposed to be working, and a trip to Bozeman had never been mentioned. Okay, the town wasn't that far. Still... something felt off. "I wouldn't have thought to call

Noah. So glad you did."

Zack's smile crinkled the corners of his eyes making him look model gorgeous. Her stomach did somersaults, maybe a cartwheel and handstand, reminding her of her vaulting days on the back of a horse.

He winked. "That's what family does for one another."

Her heart pounded like the hooves of a stampeding herd. Too bad she wanted a different kind of family with Zack, one with gold wedding bands on their fingers and cooing babies in their arms.

She cleared her dry throat. "Appreciate it."

Why did Zack have to be so nice? Why couldn't he be a jerk like so many other guys in town? That would put an end to her crush ASAP.

Dan and Allie approached the table, walking hand in hand. "My stomach's fuller. My wallet's lighter. And my suitcase is going to be a whole lot heavier. Not sure a whole cow's going to fit in there for the flight home."

Allie shook his head. "Bidding on a cow? We hardly eat red meat. What were you thinking?"

Dan kissed her hand. "No worries. The money goes to a good cause. Someone we know will want the beef if we don't."

"Well, the kids like hamburger meat," Allie said.

"They'll have plenty of that." Charlie appreciated Dan's generosity tonight. He'd paid double what his two items were worth. "During the bidding, Brock Sheehan mentioned something about flash freezing the meat."

Allie smiled warmly. "He's such a nice man."

The wranglers at the nearby tables nodded, including Charlie. Brock was not only a respected rancher, but also a special kind of guy. He'd helped Ty keep the Bar V5 from going under before Nate returned to take over. Brock deserved the good things happening to him. The widower and father of twins had remarried recently and his new wife, Harley, was expecting a baby in a few months.

"At least the Bar V5 gift certificate won't take up space," Dan said. "We'll turn in the coupon before we leave and reserve a family vacation for next summer. The kids are going to love coming here."

Zack shared a knowing look with Charlie. She knew what her fellow wrangler was thinking. The Hathaways would have returned whether they'd won the gift certificate or not. That was why the ranch often sold out for the summer by April. The same guests returned year after year.

Allie smiled. "I heard you have a great kids' program."

"We do," Charlie offered. "During the summer months, children can participate in structured activities, rides, swimming and supervised play. That gives families options when they want to hang out together and when adults want to do something on their own."

"Sounds like heaven. For the adults at least," Allie clarified.

"Kids usually hate to leave," Zack added.

A memory made Charlie smile. "Remember when that boy, Aidan, hid so his family would miss their flight and have to stay another night."

Zack chuckled. "Took hours to find him in the barn."

"The barn?" Allie asked.

"Dusty found Aidan in a small space where the cats sleep." Zack shook his head. "Not sure how the kid crawled in there, but we had to remove planks to get him out.

"Did they miss their flight?" Dan asked.

"Oh, yes. His parents were not amused," Charlie said.

"Good to know children have such a good time here," Dan said. "But our kiddos better not pull a stunt like that."

"They won't," Allie mouthed.

Servers removed dessert plates and empty glasses. People

stood, ready to head to their trailers, home, Main Street shops, or the bars.

Cowboys rode hard and partied harder. Charlie didn't go to Grey's Saloon often, and she avoided the Wolf's Den altogether—Ty's advice when she turned twenty-one.

"We have vans heading back to the ranch on the hour from nine until midnight. If you have any questions or get lost, just call. We'll find you," Dustin announced with Zack and Ty at his sides. Several other wranglers and staff members joined them so the guests would know who to look for, but Charlie hung back because she would be on cleanup duty tonight and bringing up the rear. "Don't worry if you want to go back to ranch early. You'll have more time to shop and look around Main Street this weekend. Now, if you'll follow me, I'll point out the pickup location and show you Marietta's Main Street."

The guests rose from the tables. Ellie, the newest and youngest member of the staff, placed the five centerpieces won at the Bar V5 tables into boxes. Charlie checked to make sure no one had left a jacket, reading glasses, a purse, or cell phone.

"Find anything?" Zack asked.

Charlie jumped, not expecting to hear his voice. She placed her hand over her racing heart. At least she could chalk this reaction up to surprise, not attraction. Progress? Not really, but she'd take it. "I thought you were going with Ty."

"Wanted to see if you need help."

"No one left anything. That's a good sign for this weekend." She looked at the guests filing out of the tent. During past rodeos, she'd hunted for forgotten items at the rodeo arena and other places. But this group seemed like a with-it crew. "You off now?"

Zack nodded. "Ready to go?"

She gave one last look on the floor around the tables, nodded, then headed toward the tent's exit. "I'm sure Grey's is the place to be tonight."

He fell in step with her. "You should stop by."

Her heart leapt, only to have common sense tie down the organ with a stern "Get real." Telling her to stop by wasn't an invitation out. Zack was being polite, as usual. No reason to think anything else was going on. "Thanks, but I'm not much of a partier, and tomorrow's going to start early and last way too late."

"Lots of new faces in town."

"And some old ones."

"Like?" he asked.

"You want me to name names?"

He shrugged, but she could tell by the gleam in his eye he was up to something. "If you're thinking about setting me up…"

He held up his hands, palms facing her. "I haven't lived here as long as you. Remember I grew up in Butte. Still trying to get to know people."

What he said was true, but she wasn't sure if she trusted him. Oh, her heart did, but her head… not so much. "You really want to know?"

Chapter Four

~

CHARLIE WALKED OUT of the tent and into the park, the path lit by portable streetlamps brought in by the town. Zack had wanted to know. His interest surprised her, but no reason not to tell him.

"Well, I didn't expect to see Jude Guthrie tonight," she admitted. "After his parents died, he and his brothers sold their parents' ranch. Never thought he'd be back, but Jesse's here, so maybe he's visiting."

"Know Jude well?"

"No."

"Want to get to know him better?"

Darn Zack. Not-trustworthy. Should have listened to her head. Heaven knew he'd led her heart astray, chasing a pipe dream for the past year. Her shoulder muscles bunched, tired from carrying that imaginary load.

She flashed him a not-going-to-answer look. Sticking out her tongue at him would have been better.

Zack held up his hands. "What?"

"Nothing." Dropping this was best for both of them. She stepped onto Main Street. People covered the sidewalks and streets, not only the ones who attended the fundraising dinner. The town and folks in surrounding areas turned out in big numbers for the Marietta—rodeo weekend and the stroll, a Christmas celebration held in December.

"The town sure knows how to celebrate," Zack said.

"Merchants will be smiling until Black Friday." Storefronts twinkled with white lights. Front windows celebrated the 76th Copper Mountain Rodeo with decorations ranging from hay and boots at Main Street Shoes to Rachel's gingerbread replica of the rodeo grounds at her bakery. "Let's run by Sage's shop. A salted caramel sounds good. Unless you want to go straight to Grey's."

"I'm in no rush. I'll go with you."

People filled the streets; safe from traffic thanks to barricades she'd seen being put up when they arrived earlier by sheriff deputies Dawson O'Dell and Scott Bliven. "Do you see Dustin or any guests?"

Zack looked around. "Nope. The stragglers will have to manage without you."

"Not quite." She raised her cellphone. "I programmed in everyone's cell number and gave them mine."

"You're going to contact each one?"

"If they don't make a van, yes."

"That's a lot of calling."

"When has talking ever been a problem?" The second the words were out of her mouth she wanted to take them back. She and Zack hadn't spoken much, except about the ranch or her leaving, since that night by the river. Embarrassment and self-preservation had been her excuses. She could only imagine his. On second thought, she didn't want to. "I mean..."

"Charlie!"

The sound of Caitlin's voice carried through the crowd. Charlie had never been so thankful to see her friend as she was now. She stepped out of the flow of traffic. Noah and Caitlin made their way through the people to them.

"What were you doing in Bozeman?" Charlie asked.

Caitlin beamed. "Noah got off early and surprised me."

"You missed the dinner."

"Any hot cowboys?"

"A couple may have caught my eye. No idea of their names."

"That's what the rodeo program is for." Caitlin bounced from foot to foot. If not for holding Noah's hand, she looked as if she might float way like a bouquet of helium filled balloons. "Before you tell me about the cowboys, I have something to show you."

She stuck out her left hand. A solitary diamond ring in a gold setting graced her ring finger.

Charlie gasped.

"Squee!" Caitlin jumped up and down. "I'm engaged. I mean, we're engaged."

Charlie squealed, hugged Caitlin. "Oh my goodness. Congrats."

Noah cleared his throat.

Charlie glanced his way. "You too. The ring is gorgeous. Good job, Noah."

Zack shook the veterinarian's hand. "Congrats, man."

"Thanks." Noah smiled. "Managed to surprise my girl. Not easy to do."

Caitlin shimmied her shoulders. "Easy when I completely forgot today was the day we met until Noah reminded me."

"And they say women have the best memories," Noah teased. "We guys don't do so badly."

The pieces of the puzzle clicked together in Charlie's mind. "You were at Montana State. That's why you went to Bozeman."

Noah nodded. "I figured I could propose at MSU in the exact spot where we met years ago or at the vet clinic where we found each other again in December."

"I love the Cooper Mountain Animal Hospital, but trust

me," Caitlin said. "You made the right choice."

"I need details," Charlie said.

"Well, we were outside the library. He asked me if I remembered what happened here. I said this was where we met." A dreamy expression formed on Caitlin's face. "He wished me happy anniversary, then dropped down on one knee."

Charlie rubbed her arms. "I just got a chill."

"I know, right?" Caitlin glowed. "I was shaking. I was so surprised, I could barely breathe."

"She's not exaggerating," Noah added.

Caitlin nodded. "And when he showed me this gorgeous ring…"

Her voice cracked with emotion, the same way Charlie felt inside. She was thrilled for her friend. Caitlin had been lonely for so long and deserved this, but Charlie wished Zack could take a lesson from Noah.

Her heart pounded with longing. She touched her chest. "So romantic."

Caitlin sighed. "I know."

The two men shared a glance, then a shrug.

"Well done." Zack patted Noah on the back.

Noah grinned. "Thanks. Came off as planned. Well, except for the temperature being too warm to bring Mistletoe along for the ride. Couldn't leave her in the car and she's still not too happy wearing a harness and leash."

"She's doing better," Caitlin said.

"I am so, so happy for you. Both of you." The words flew from Charlie's mouth like a bucking bronco out of the chute. "Way to kick off the rodeo with incredible news."

Caitlin touched Charlie's arm. "I want you to be my maid of honor."

"Yes." Charlie didn't hesitant. She hugged her friend. "Of course, I'm honored, but you might have to explain to Jay why he's not your man of honor."

Jay Patterson was one of Caitlin's best guy friends from high school, who was married to a great woman named Jen. They had two kids, Justin and Jasmine.

Noah laughed. "I'm asking Jay to be my best man so we're good."

"We don't know much about the wedding yet," Caitlin explained. "But we want a December date."

Charlie's heart dropped, plummeting like a rock off the top of Copper Mountain. "Three months away December or next year?"

"This December."

Crap. Charlie's stomach clenched, making her wish she hadn't eaten her entire slice of pie. "That's quick."

"Yes. And no, I'm not pregnant," Caitlin said matter-of-factly. "But we reconnected on Christmas Eve so want a Christmas wedding."

"We don't want to wait another year to get married," Noah added. "And since Caitlin's parents are planning to be in Marietta for the holidays. This works well."

"Oh, that's great they're coming back." Caitlin's parents hadn't returned home since they left over five years ago to RV across America. Good for her friend, but Charlie's skin itched, her head, arms, and legs. She fought the urge to scratch. "A short engagement makes total sense under the circumstances."

For them.

But this was a big complication for Charlie.

"It really does." Caitlin bounced from foot-to-foot, her excitement overflowing. "After the excitement and fuss surrounding the Great Wedding Giveaway this spring, I know I want something small and intimate."

"Rachel and Nate's reception at the Bar V5 was nice," Zack said, surprising Charlie that he remembered the wedding. "The ranch looks pretty in the winter decked out in lights and decorations."

Caitlin's lips parted. She looked up at Noah. "Oh, a wedding at the lodge. What do you think?"

"Sounds perfect, just like you. I'll speak with Nate and Ty," Noah said.

The two were so good together. Happy tears stung Charlie's eyes. "I can't imagine a better place than the main house to get married. Mistletoe will be able to attend."

"She can carry the rings if we get her more used to her leash," Caitlin said.

Charlie rubbed the tears slipping from her eyes. "You're going to be a beautiful bride."

Zack handed her a bandana. "Here."

Oh, no. Zack was seeing her cry. But he'd also kissed her and felt her up, something no other wrangler had done. Let him deal with a few tears. She took the cloth and dabbed her eyes. "Thank you."

"We have calls to make. And I need to charge my phone." Caitlin gave Charlie another hug. "We'll talk more after the rodeo. I know three months is a tight timeframe, but with your help, we can pull off a wedding."

Charlie nodded, but all she could think about was how could she help her friend if she moved to Colorado. She wouldn't be around to do anything. Long distance wedding planning? Plane tickets to and from Bozeman were expensive, and flights limited. The drive would be weather dependent in the wintertime, and hard to make with her limited days off from the horse ranch.

What was she going to do?

"Have fun tonight." Caitlin and Noah walked away, their gazes locked on each other, as if the crowd around them didn't exist.

"You okay?" Zack asked.

Charlie nodded, not trusting her voice. She returned his handkerchief. "Thanks."

"If you're living in Colorado, being Caitlin's maid of honor is going to be tough and expensive."

Impossible. She nodded again. Caitlin was the first person Charlie had befriended when she moved to Marietta. She couldn't let her down. She had to figure out a way to make being a bridesmaid work.

Think, think, think.

Moving to Colorado didn't seem like the best option now, but staying at Bar V5 with the status quo? Continuing to crush on and compare every guy she met to Zack didn't hold much appeal. She needed to do something, but what?

Find you a man.

Zack's words echoed through her mind.

A man. Another man.

Charlie couldn't, could she? She swallowed around the engagement ring sized lump in her throat. If she found someone else to focus her energies on, someone else to push out thoughts of and her attraction for Zack, then maybe... maybe staying wouldn't be so bad. She could move on with her life and be a dutiful maid of honor and friend, helping Caitlin with her wedding.

Sounded good in theory.

All Charlie had to do was swallow her pride, and ask for help. Something she never did, but this was an unusual situation.

She had no one else to ask. Not really.

Caitlin would be caught up being newly engaged, thinking about her wedding and buying bridal magazines. Charlie would be the same way if she were wearing a diamond ring on her finger. She wasn't about to get in the way of her friend's special time.

Rachel's bakery would be crowded with customers this

weekend. She'd mentioned hiring extra staff to handle the demand and hours. Charlie wasn't about to interfere with Rachel's business.

Ellie was too sweet and naïve to track down a man for Charlie. The housekeeper wasn't that much younger, but seemed more like a teenager with her wide-eyed innocence and friendliness. Plus, Ellie would have her hands full cleaning this weekend with the back-and-forth of guests between town and the ranch.

Zack was Charlie's only choice.

Again.

Shoulders squared and chin up, she took a deep breath. "I've changed my mind."

"About?"

"You finding me a date." She swallowed. "I, um, could use your help. I'm thinking we could start tonight."

HOT DAMN. ZACK stood on Main Street wondering what had made Charlie change her mind in the last fifteen minutes and want his help. Sure, Caitlin and Noah had gotten engaged, but what did that have to do with Charlie's dating status?

She didn't seem the jealous type. But she sounded almost desperate. Ty's words from two day ago sprang to mind.

One thing I learned raising Rachel is a female's thought process is different from ours.

Forget the why, and concentrate on the how—how to find the right guy for Charlie. With her input, the matchmaking process just got easier. And they were in the perfect place to start the search. Main Street was hopping.

"Come on." Charlie wove her way through the crowd, chin up and her gaze scanning the faces they passed.

Zack had no idea where she was going. He caught up with

her, touched her bare arm. Her skin was soft beneath his calloused hand. "Hold up, partner. Let me in on the plan."

She stopped, glanced at his hand, then met his gaze. "No plan. Just trying to find him."

Heat emanated from the spot where his palm rested on her arm. Not quite tingling, but close. He liked the feeling. And if he wasn't careful, he could be easily distracted, but a few more seconds couldn't hurt anything. "Him?"

"A guy for me to date."

She hadn't been kidding about getting started right away. Zack realized he was still touching Charlie. Doing so felt good, natural. He remembered touching her before...

Uh oh. He raised his hand and pressed his arms at his side, reminding himself of the mission—keep Charlie at the Bar V5. Might be a good idea not to touch her. Physical contact could lead to more kisses and complicate things between them.

"Might help if I knew what you're looking for in a man," he said.

"Let's see." A serious expression crossed her face.

She didn't seem to be taking this endeavor lightly. He didn't know why that made his gut clench.

"Under forty, in shape, employed, likes animals and kids," she said in a serious tone. "Oh, and not in jail."

Hmmm. Jail. Better cross Trey Sheehan off the list, but his brother Dillon qualified. Many other men in Marietta did, too, including Zack. *Oops. Not going there.* "That's a broad list. Might be better to narrow down your criteria."

"I want to be open-minded about this. Not box myself in."

"Sounds good." The less qualities she had, the easier the job, except... "I'm assuming chemistry is important."

She nodded. "Very."

The way she'd kissed him had been explosive. His lips twitched as if remembering the attraction between them. Boy howdy, that had taken him by surprise.

"But you never know ahead of time if they'll be sparks or not," she added.

He hadn't expected the chemistry they'd shared, and given his reaction to touching her, still shared. Something was there. Something more than sexual attraction. Something he needed to ignore.

"Hey guys." RJ McCreadie barely slowed. "See you at Grey's, Zack?"

"Maybe later," Zack said. "Have fun."

"Planning on it." RJ waved and kept walking.

Hmmm. The MacCreadie family was well established in the area. RJ was a good guy, someone Zack considered a friend and met Charlie's criteria. Too easy? Not if Zack approached this using KISS—Keep it simple, stupid. He smiled smugly. "I've got this figured out."

"What?"

"Who you should date."

She stopped. "Who?"

"RJ."

Charlie kept walking. "No."

"I thought you were going to be open-minded about this."

"I am. I am openly-minded closing that door."

"Why?"

"Think about what RJ said," she explained. "He greeted us as 'guys' and asked if you were going to Grey's, not me."

"He's used to seeing you as a wrangler. One of us."

She shook her head.

"Then what?"

"No sparks. Not on my end. And his actions tonight confirm none on his. Otherwise, he would have taken the extra second or two to make sure I was included."

A million and one questions ran through Zack's head about

how Charlie knew this without a hint of uncertainty in her voice. None of his business, but maybe he could get RJ to tell him one of these days. "Fair enough. On to the next candidate."

"Candidate?"

"Unless you want to call them potential boyfriends or lovers."

"Candidate works."

Three cowboys sauntered past. Not from around here. One, a straw-haired cowboy who looked like he could be a model in a glossy magazine, gave Charlie the once over, grinned and then nudged his friends.

"I wonder if the chocolate shop will be crowded," she said, her gaze focused on the people around them, not noticing the three men.

Interesting. Charlie didn't realize the guy and his friends were leering at her chest. He knew their look. They were interested in one thing and not her pretty smile. "Too hard to tell with all these people in the way, but Sage's confections are worth the wait."

She quickened her pace. "For sure."

Good, Zack thought. The sooner they got away from these clowns, the better.

"I hope the line's not too long," she said. "I doubt I'll find any… candidates at the chocolate shop."

He wouldn't mind her being seen as eye candy if guys appreciated the whole sweet package, not only her sexy lady parts. "Maybe not, but the sugar will fortify us for our search."

She looked up at him with her big, baby blues.

The ends of her copper hair swayed. Pretty, yes, but sexy, too. He liked how she wasn't wearing a ponytail or braids as usual. The long, loose strands flattered her high cheekbones, made him think of the hair spread over his chest. He swallowed.

A wide grin spread across her face. "I like how you think."

A good thing she couldn't read his mind or she might not be so happy. But he did like her. As a friend. Make that a coworker. He forced himself to remember what could go wrong with a workplace romance. No war this time, but an unpredictable horse or bull, coupled with distractions, could cause injury. He wasn't going to take any chances with the people he cared about and called family. Maybe if he tried to think of Charlie as a little sister...

He noticed the three cowboys behind them. The group had changed directions. Coincidence or Charlie? Zack assumed the later. He had no idea if they were from Montana or a different state. Didn't matter. Having her fall for someone far away defeated the purpose of finding her a man to keep her at the Bar V5. Better rethink how to pick a candidate. Once these three went away.

Up ahead, a woman pushed a baby stroller. She maneuvered in and around people with the ease of a NASCAR driver. This was his opportunity to send the cowboys following Charlie away and also help out the stroller mom.

"Watch out. Baby stroller headed our way." He slipped his arm around Charlie's waist and pulled her close.

Her muscles tensed beneath his hand. "The stroller's not going that fast."

"Not taking any chances." Zack grinned. His tactics were working—the guys veered off—except... heat and tingles shot up his hand and arm. Touching Charlie felt so good. Her body fit nicely against him. Soft and curvy in all the right places. If he weren't trying to make a statement to the three cowboys, Zack would have lowered his hand. A self-preservation move, but continuing to touch her might keep a territorial pissing match at bay. He hoped so. Zack hadn't gotten into a fight since leaving the service. He had no doubt he could flatten the guys in less than seven seconds, but he didn't want Charlie jumping into the fight, if there was one. He wanted to protect her not let her get hurt.

Zack glanced over his shoulder. The three cowboys were headed in the opposite direction. He balled his hand, then pumped his fist. "Yes."

"What?" she asked.

"Just thinking aloud." The line at the chocolate shop was out the door. He stood at the end. "Sage must be thrilled."

"She's worked hard and earned the success. And that means more chocolates for us in the future."

Up ahead in line was Beau Bennett, a local. They'd shared stories about being deployed in Iraq over beers one night. "You might have been premature to say you wouldn't meet a guy at the chocolate shop."

Her brows furrowed. "What are you talking about?"

"Up ahead. Leaning against the doorway to the shop."

"Don't know him."

"Beau Bennett. Owns Copper Mountain Security. He's been trying to get the business off the ground for a couple years. Works nonstop."

She raised her hands. "Good choice, I mean candidate. He's attractive, but I'm not interested in dating a workaholic."

"Does this mean you have more criteria to add to your list?"

Her mouth slanted. "Sorry. This is all new to me."

"No worries." But seeing Beau gave Zack an idea. "Would you date a military veteran?"

"Yes." No hesitation, no wishy-washiness. "In a heartbeat."

He knew the guy for her, a former Marine and double-amputee. "What about Lane Scott?"

She moved forward in the line. "Lane is a great guy. Truly amazing. Hot, too. The martial arts place he's started with his brother is cool."

"Sounds like a 'but' is coming."

"But... a friend liked him. She's moved on, but I would feel weird going out with him."

"You live in a small town. The dating pool isn't large." They moved to the doorway of the chocolate shop. "There's going to be overlap."

"True, but she was crazy about him, have his babies crazy. I wouldn't feel comfortable."

Zack would never understand women. Time to stop trying as Ty recommended?

"Besides," Charlie continued. "I doubt I'm his type or he would have asked me out before."

Point taken. Still... "People change. Especially guys. They get tired of playing the field and decide to settle down. Maybe Lane—"

"No." She lowered her voice. "I don't want to be with a guy because he's finished sowing his wild oats and I'm what happened along at the right time. I deserve more. I want—"

The passion in her voice was a real turn-on. He leaned toward her, catching a whiff of her shampoo, fruity, like berries, tasty enough to eat. His gaze dropped to her mouth. "What?"

"This is going to sound silly."

Her lips were perfectly shaped. Just right for kissing. "Maybe to you. Let me decide for myself."

She started to speak, then stopped. Her lips pressed together so hard, they nearly disappeared.

Good thing. Another second and he would have indulged in something he had no business tasting.

"I won't say a word." He crossed his heart like a guest's kid kept doing during a late August stay. "Promise."

"I want a guy who wants to be with me because he can't imagine being with anyone else but me. That's how I want to feel about him, too." She looked at the display of candies, a worried expression on her face. "Silly, right?"

"Not silly." But he didn't want her disappointed. "Finding someone who feels the same might take a while. Longer than this weekend. That kind of love isn't automatic, okay?

"I'll be more patient. It's my future after all."

Her smile suggested relief. She didn't act upset at him. A surprising elation over Charlie seeming to want to stay at the ranch combined with a sense of nausea over her being here to chase down a man. His stomach churned. The people in front of them paid for their candy.

"Looks like our turn," she said. "What do you want? It's my treat for you helping me."

"I haven't done anything."

"Saying yes was huge. Staying with me now is nice. The rest will come."

Charlie was so sweet, caring, and kind. If he could date her... stop. Now. "I'd like a salted caramel and a dark chocolate almond cluster."

"Your wish is my command."

Too bad that wasn't the case. He knew what he'd wish for... a kiss. Not a chocolate kiss. A Charlie kiss.

Bad idea. Bad, bad, bad.

Zack had better find her a man soon before he did something that would ruin... everything.

Chapter Five

❀

SOLDIER, WRANGLER, MATCHMAKER, *perfect guy.* Charlie covered her face with her pillow, then groaned. The mantra about Zack wouldn't stop. All night the words circled Charlie's mind, making her chase sleep like Mistletoe trying to catch her tail.

Sunlight peeked around the edges of the bunkhouse's window shades and red gingham valance. She lay in bed, not ready to start the long day ahead.

Pancake breakfast. Opening ceremony. Preliminary rodeo events. Community steak dinner.

Saturday at the Copper Mountain Rodeo was one of her favorite days of the year, but not this morning. She'd rather hang out with Zack, the two of them, like last night when he'd touched her. Twice. If she closed her eyes, she could almost feel the heat of his skin against hers.

She wiggled her toes.

Talk about sparks. Highly combustible.

After he pulled her out of the way of the oncoming stroller, she'd sidled up to him like a vertical saddle blanket. She hadn't wanted to move.

Ever.

But standing there any longer would have been awkward.

Not to mention damaging to her psyche and unhealthy. She'd forced herself away, using Sage's treats as a reward for not melting into a pile of goo at Zack's boots. Yeah, Charlie could justify anything for a salted caramel, but this time she'd earned a piece of candy. Well, three. That was how many she'd eaten by the night's end.

But she wasn't delusional. A few minutes spent together on Main Street in a crowd meant nothing.

So what if conversation flowed? They'd been discussing what kind of guy she wanted to date. So what if she had to bite her tongue and not answer "you" to many of Zack's questions? He wasn't into her. So what if she'd shot down the candidates he'd brought up? None had measured up, and honesty was one of her virtues. At least that was how she saw it. She couldn't answer for Zack.

Stop thinking about him.

Or about what might happen if she couldn't find a guy and turn this crush thing around. Waiting until Monday to talk to Ty about staying still seemed like the best choice.

Charlie climbed out of bed. Her bare feet padded across a colorful wool braided rug.

She was trying to be open-minded. Her reasons for not wanting to pursue his suggestions weren't pulled from the air. They were real. Honest. Non-negotiable.

She slid on a pair of lacy, lavender panties and a matching bra. No shower was necessary when she'd be spending the day at the rodeo and would need one before the dinner and dance tonight.

But she couldn't deny her perception was slanted. The one man who appealed to her, the one man who fit her criteria and then some, was the one trying to find her a date. Zack didn't want her.

She rubbed her tired eyes.

Get over him.

That should be the mantra. She needed to let go of her infatuation. Forget about him. Find someone else.

This wasn't only about her now. This was for Caitlin, too.

Sure, friends would help with the wedding planning, including experienced brides like Jen Patterson, Rachel Vaughn, and Jenny Wright, whose wedding plans had fallen apart, but she'd found love with bull-riding champ, Colton Thorpe. Everyone loved weddings and Marietta was the kind of place where neighbors and friends pitched in.

But Charlie didn't want to push off her responsibilities. She wanted to be with Caitlin every step of the way—looking for a dress, making plans, throwing a bridal shower, having fun at a bachelorette party.

Nothing should get in the way of that. Especially a guy. A thick-headed one she worked with.

Charlie wiggled into a pair of Wrangler jeans, pulled on a camisole then a button down long-sleeved cotton shirt. She added a leather belt with a sparkly buckle, something she'd won years ago.

Last night, as soon as they'd bumped into folks from the Bar V5 outside the chocolate shop, Zack had said goodnight and headed toward Grey's Saloon. Charlie doubted he was scoping out candidates for her. More likely finding a woman for him.

Way to start the day off right with thoughts like that.

A glance in the mirror brought a cringe. Her horse Sierra's mane looked better than Charlie's hair. Two braids would work, but then she remembered the old flat iron one of the summer housekeeping staff had donated to the communal bathroom after she'd purchased a new one.

Why not? As the straightener heated, she brushed her teeth and applied sunscreen.

Twenty-minutes and one small burn on her hand later, she

hadn't done too badly. Having those clips Caitlin used to separate her hair might have helped, but Charlie liked this better than braids or a ponytail. Except...

Something was missing.

She dug through a small box she kept in her underwear drawer and found the pair of horseshoe-shaped earrings she'd picked up in Livingston a few months ago. Ones she'd never worn. She removed the small, round silver posts she normally wore, placed them in the box then inserted the dangling horseshoes.

There.

Charlie did a double-take at her reflection. She looked pretty, if she dared say so, ready to attend the rodeo and meet a handsome cowboy.

A new her?

More like the real her. And this cowgirl was more than ready for whatever the day held. She slipped on socks and her well-worn, comfy cowboy boots then grabbed her hat off the hook.

No matter what guy—make that candidate—turned up next, she would give him a chance even if her heart disagreed and her brain offered a list of Zack-centric objections.

She owed that to Caitlin.

But most importantly, Charlie owed that to herself.

Because if she ever wanted to be a blushing bride and have a family of her own, she couldn't waste another single moment thinking about Zack Harris.

AN HOUR LATER, Charlie found herself back under the white tent in the park. The smell of buttermilk pancakes and syrup filled the air. People laughed. A child squealed. A baby cried in the distance.

This was Marietta, the town she loved, where neighbors and

strangers came together to celebrate something All-American, The Copper Mountain Rodeo. Maybe Colorado wasn't such a good idea, even if Caitlin hadn't gotten engaged. Running from a source of heartache wasn't Charlie's style, and look at what she'd be leaving behind.

She carried her paper plate past the row of griddles situated behind the serving line.

"Hey, Charlie." A smiling Chelsea Crawford Collier wore a denim apron and held a spatula. Her thick, blonde hair was coiled on her head in a sexy up-do no other pancake flipper could pull off. She stood next to her mother, who, as one of Marietta's First Families, had been working the pancake breakfast since she was a child. "Love the new hairstyle."

"Thanks. Amazing what a flat iron can do."

Charlie found the Bar V5 folks seated at a few nearby tables. Zack wasn't here. Not surprising. He only participated in Friday's events. A good thing, she told herself. Having him out of sight might limit the comparisons between him and every other guy here.

The round tables from last night had been replaced with long rectangular ones this morning. She sat with Allie and Dan, and Tess and Paula, two thirty-something women from Las Vegas who'd arrived at the Bar V5 for a rodeo weekend stay.

"Has everyone had a chance to look over today's schedule?" Charlie asked.

The four nodded. Tess placed her Styrofoam coffee cup on the table. "I noticed a break between the rodeo and dinner. Will there be a chance to return to the ranch to freshen up?"

"Yes." Charlie poured syrup on her pancakes. "After walking around and sitting in the stands all day, you may feel like you're wearing a coat of dirt and want a shower."

"Or you can tough it out like a real cowboy," Dan said. "A little dirt never hurt anyone?"

"Says the man who had a shower with a propane water heater delivered when we went camping." Allie grinned. "My husband will be wanting a shower before half-time or whatever the rodeo calls a break."

"Intermission," Charlie offered. "We have vans running all day between town, the rodeo grounds, and the Bar V5, so wherever you want to go let me know, and we'll get you there ASAP."

"You're always on top of everything, Charlie." Dan sounded serious for the first time since they'd met earlier in the week. "I hope you're compensated well."

"Nate treats us real good."

"If you get tired of cows and want to concentrate on just horses—"

"Not now, dear." Allie swatted at her husband's hand, and he looked duly chastised. "Breakfast is not the time for business."

"Mind if I join you folks?" a male voice asked before Charlie could respond.

She looked up to see local rodeo champ Rhett Dixon, a blue-eyed, blond-haired cowboy with to die for dimples and an equally killer smile. She motioned to an empty seat at the table. "It's all yours, cowboy. But I thought you'd be getting ready for today."

He sat. "I've got tie-roping up first and bulls last. I need my pancake fuel."

"Based on the crowd this morning, so do the spectators."

She introduced those at the table to the cowboy whose string of rodeo wins matched the trail of broken hearts he'd blazed, waiting for Payton Hollis to finally date him. Charlie could sympathize with him, given her feelings for Zack.

Tess smiled warmly. "Looks like we'll have to stick around until the end to watch Rhett compete."

Rhett tipped his head, grinned wryly, then winked. "I can't guarantee what the bull will do, but I'll be sure not to disappoint."

Charlie could almost hear the other women sighing, including Allie.

Leave it to Rhett. The guy was a charmer. Rumor was he'd been going through a tough time with his mother's heart attack, and he was spending too much time with the troublemaking Taylors. But the Rhett that Charlie had known as a teenager was a good guy and skilled cowboy.

He wiped his mouth with a napkin. "Happy Zack told me to stop by this morning and say hi."

Charlie's throat tightened. "When did you see him?"

"Last night at Grey's."

Her stomach churned. She didn't need a PhD in sociology—or would that be psychology?—to know Zack had sent Rhett as the next candidate. Darn, and she'd vowed this morning to give this a try.

Except Rhett's heart was unavailable.

Like hers, a voice mocked.

Shut up.

She didn't understand. How could Zack think Rhett was the right guy when he'd drop any woman in a New York minute if Payton snapped her finger?

Well, Charlie wasn't about to be rude. "Glad you could stop by."

The others at the table nodded and asked Rhett about competing. She stared at her nearly full breakfast plate. No longer hungry, she stabbed at a pancake.

"Tenderizing your breakfast?"

That voice didn't belong to Rhett. That was Zack. Her gaze jerked upward to see him standing at the table, looking amused. Well, her plate did look pitchforked. "Practicing for the future so

I'm ready when you boys annoy me."

"Better watch out," Rhett joked. "Payton's the same way."

Zack frowned, lines deepening on his face. "Payton Hollis?"

Rhett smiled. "Just need to convince her to leave her precious cows for a couple hours so we can dance the night away on Main Street."

"Good luck," Charlie said the words with the upmost sincerity. Liking someone who didn't like you back was the definition of purgatory. She couldn't wait to escape. "I hope the dance works out as you planned."

"Me, too." Rhett glanced at his clock. "I need to run. Nice to meet you all."

With that, the cowboy took off.

"Almost time for the parade," she said. "Then we'll head to the rodeo grounds."

Zack dangled the keys. "Let me know when you're ready."

Her heart bumped at the thought of spending more time with him. "I thought Nate was driving. Along with Ty."

"Change of plans. Drivers will rotate, but I'm going to be with you guys at the rodeo today."

Charlie stiffened, surprised by the news, but she wanted to be careful what she said in front of the guests, even if they didn't seem to be paying attention. She knew Zack wasn't a big fan of rodeos. He preferred riding to watching others. "Filling in for someone?"

"My choice."

That was... odd. Zack stuck close to the ranch during rodeo weekends. Unless...

"Searching for candidates," she said in a soft voice, so only he could hear.

Zack nodded once.

Her heart melted. He really was a good guy. "Not necessary."

"But it is."

He leaned next to her, his breath warm against her ear.

"Sorry about Rhett," he whispered. "Figured he'd be over Payton by now."

The brush of his whisker stubble against her neck prickled. Goosebumps appeared.

"No worries," Charlie said softly, wishing Zack would back away. If she turned her head slightly to the right, his lips would be against hers.

The pounding of her heart turned into a syncopated beat. She forced herself to breathe. Being so close to him was doing crazy things to her body. Things she liked. No, she didn't.

"You look nice today." His words were practically a caress. "Never seen your hair straight like that or the lucky earrings."

Her lips parted in surprise. She pressed them together, stunned. A kiss would have had less impact than Zack's words. He didn't give compliments. Not to her anyway. Why should he? He never noticed her clothes, hair, or jewelry.

Charlie's throat was as dry as the Badlands, but she forced out a word. "Thanks."

She fought the urge to smooth her hair, or touch her earrings, or kiss him. Heaven help her, but she wanted to plant her mouth against his.

Her insides trembled, a mix of need and fear. She scooted away from him, putting distance between them.

What was going on?

The only time he'd acted like this had been the night by the river. But that had been different. He hadn't been himself. Why was he doing this now?

Charlie wasn't sure she wanted to know the answer. She couldn't allow herself to focus on Zack. This weekend was her chance to break free of the crush that threatened to ruin her life. She couldn't mess this up.

Forget Zack.

Forget his help.

Forget ever kissing him again.

She could find her own candidate—make that own man who might like her back—and she would.

Charlie stood, forced a smile. "Come on, everybody. Let's head to the parade."

THE PARADE DOWN Main Street celebrated small town America and cowboys. Zack had never attended until today, but found himself cheering along with Charlie who waved at every group that went past. And there were plenty of them, including a decorated fire engine, horse-drawn hay wagon, local horse groups, a Native American dance troop, a marching band, children riding decorated bikes and wagons, and 4-H and Future Farmer of America—FFA—floats.

The rodeo's opening ceremony was another piece of Americana. The festivities opened with a Grand Entry where riders carrying American, Montana State, and sponsor flags galloped around the arena. Competitors were introduced along with officials. The presentation of the rodeo queen and her court followed. A touching rendition of *The Star-Spangled Banner* sung by a boy and girl brought a lump to Zack's throat.

He wiped his eyes. Darn dust was making them water.

Down in the arena, the rodeo crew prepared for the first event. Zack sat next to Dustin in the stands. The Bar V5 guests were seated in the rows below, while Charlie stood in the aisle, beside her charges, resting one booted foot on a bleacher.

"No one was injured when the horse got loose," she explained to douse the rumors spreading through the stands like wildfire. "He ran into a stroller, but no baby was inside. The horse was caught and everything's fine."

"Lucky kid," Dustin murmured to Zack.

"Luckier horse."

This was an unfamiliar world to Zack. He had never been part of the rodeo scene growing up in Butte. His parents had been involved in one get-rich scheme after another, a handful legal, most not. Their marriage had been one of convenience at times, survival at others. Love hadn't played a role. His birth had been an accident, something his mom and dad had reminded Zack of daily.

Anything fun, such as sports or horses, was considered a waste. He'd learned to ride thanks to his one and only school friend. Not many folks let their kids play with the son of two-bit criminals who were in and out of jail.

Instead of showing off in the arena, he preferred riding Blackbeard to the high elevation cow camp during rodeo weekend, where the herd summered and guests, who wanted a more authentic cowboy experience, spent time. Except this weekend, Charlie wouldn't be up there. So he'd offered to take Ty's place here.

Stupid? Yeah, since Zack imagined being bored out of his mind. Watching hotshots outgun each other wasn't his idea of fun. But he justified the actions because of wanting to help Charlie.

He didn't understand why some cowboy hadn't roped her yet. Not just last night, but at all. Pretty, sharp, strong, funny. Those words described Charlie, but he'd never put them together until now. If he were looking for a wife—which he wasn't—and if they didn't work together—which they did—he would call her a catch.

She stood in front of the guests dressed like a cowgirl, with dangling earrings and a blinged-out buckle, a way he'd never seen her but liked. Her attitude was cheerleader rah-rah. Warm and appealing like the apple pie served at the dinner last night.

She could give the rodeo queen and her court a run for their money.

Going through the rodeo program, Charlie pointed out the local cowboys and cowgirls competing in the preliminary events, as well as the champions who'd come to town. Her smile never wavered. Enthusiasm sounded in her voice.

Watching her reminded him of a baby bird taking flight for the first time and soaring. He couldn't imagine the rodeo next year without her. She belonged at the Bar V5 and here in Marietta.

"This never gets old," Dustin said, as if talking aloud.

"Do you miss competing?" Zack asked.

"Hell, yes. Nothing beats rodoeing." The former champion touched his right knee, one that was healing from his most recent operation. "But I'm grateful I can walk, and ride, as well as I can, given the pins and screws inside me. No reason to push it."

Zack laughed. The guy was too much. But that was what had made him a champion. "Save the act for the people who sign your paycheck."

Dustin's brows drew together. "Don't know what you mean."

Zack leaned closer. "I saw you steer wrestling Diablo."

"Crap." Dustin mouthed a few other choice words, but Nate had a rule about swearing within earshot of guests. He rubbed the back of his neck. "Anybody else with you?"

"Blackbeard."

"At least he won't tell. You gonna?" Dustin sounded like a kid who'd been caught firing his air-soft rifle without safety goggles. "Charlie would kill me if she finds out. Not to mention Ty, since I've been blowing off my physical therapy this summer. And Nate due to insurance."

"I won't say a word as long as you promise not to do that

again," Zack said. "I'm all for men being men, but they don't call that bull Diablo for his sweet temperament. He's one mean SOB. He could kill you if given the chance."

"I was careful."

Based on what he'd seen, Zack withheld judgment. The guy had been stupid and brave. "You were alone. Ever heard of the buddy system? Pull that solo crap again, and if you're lucky enough to survive one more time, I will announce your little secret from the mega-horn."

Still standing below, halfway in the aisle, Charlie clapped her hands. "Okay now. Game time. Tell me your favorite rodeo event and win a prize."

"Bulls."

"Barrel racing."

"Calf roping."

With each event called out, some multiple times, she rewarded the guest who answered with a coupon to a store on Main Street—a free drink at the Java Café, a candy from the chocolate shop, a cookie from Rachel's bakery.

But who needed to go anywhere else when Charlie looked good enough to eat? Zack found himself staring and glanced at the program he held.

"Steer wrestling," someone added.

Dan placed his hands on either side of his mouth. "Don't forget bronco riding."

"Dancing," yelled Allie.

Charlie burst out laughing, and unexpected warmth spread through Zack. A charming pink colored her cheeks. Her blue eyes twinkled and brightened her face. She really was something.

"We'll be dancing tonight on Main Street." She handed out the remaining coupons. "It's one of my favorite events, too."

"Charlie sure does a good job with the guests." Dustin sounded impressed. "Do you think she's going to leave?"

"Hope not."

Zack had better get back to looking for more candidates if he wanted her to stay. But he'd been having too much fun with her at the parade and opening ceremonies to think about finding her a guy.

"Me, too." Dustin stared at her, reviewing the rodeo program with the guests while a rodeo clown performed in the arena. "She looks different with her hair straight. Nice style on her."

That was the last thing Zack expected the wrangler to say. He shot him a sideways glance. "Most women look good when they take time to fuss with their hair."

"Charlie looks really good. She's wearing jewelry, too."

Aw, hell. Dustin stared at Charlie, like a dog that found a bone and wanted the first bite. Not if Zack had any say. "Thought you were interested in that riding instructor in Livingston."

"I am. Going out next week." Dustin's gaze remained locked on Charlie. "Just never realized how pretty Charlie was. She looked nice at Nate and Rachel's wedding, but so did the other women. You gotta admit Charlie's sweet."

Sweet, sexy, and everything in between. A part of Zack wanted to call dibs. He couldn't do that, but he could rein Dustin in before the guy decided to put a move on Charlie and cause the same trouble Zack had been trying to avoid for all of them.

"Be careful. Dealt with workplace romances when I was in the army. Not smart to play where you get paid."

"What happened?"

"Things fell apart at the worst possible time. Three of us got shot. Two didn't come home."

"Damn, man." Dustin looked at him. "Was she your girl?"

"No. Another guy's, but we all suffered for his romantic

urges."

Zack stared at Charlie, knowing she could make him feel better. Laughter lit her eyes, and ignited something deep, unexpected within him. "Take it from someone who's been there. Leave Charlie alone. Stick to the riding instructor. We'll all be better off."

"Drop the BS and come clean." Dustin's gaze bounced from Charlie to Zack. "You like her."

Crap. Zack straightened. "Never said that."

Dustin flashed a lopsided grin. "Didn't have to."

Okay, Zack was attracted to her. He wasn't about to deny that fact. Any red-blooded man with a heartbeat probably felt the same way about Charlie Randall. But he'd learned from his staff sergeant that in certain situations, the less said the better. Zack pressed his lips together.

"I see." Mischief gleamed in Dustin's eyes. "Having trouble taking your own advice? Must be why you both act like you don't get along. But how do you get away with dating other women? Some kind of open relationship or is it kinky foreplay?"

Zack's muscles bunched so tightly a silver dollar would bounce off them. His hands balled. He counted to twenty in Spanish to keep his blood pressure from soaring into the danger zone and his adrenaline from pushing him into action. That didn't work. The urge to punch Dustin kept growing. Zack counted in Arabic.

Family, he reminded himself. Sometimes family members got on each other's nerves.

He unclenched his fists, then he took a deep breath, followed by another. "Nothing's going on, but if there was, do you think I'd tell you?"

"Maybe."

Zack gave Dustin a time-to-cleanse-the-gene-pool look. "You think?"

"Nah, you wouldn't say a word."

"Neither should you." Zack kept his voice low and his tone steady. "Imagine how Charlie would feel if she overheard you. Or worse, if someone in the stands repeated what you said."

Dustin's cheeks turned fire engine red. "She'd kick my ass."

"And rightly so."

"Sorry." A contrite expression crossed Dustin's face. "You don't think she heard do you?"

Zack surveyed the scene. Some habits died hard. People around them chatted, read the program, texted on their phones and snapped pictures. "No, I think you're safe."

Dustin blew out a breath. "Great. I wouldn't want Charlie mad at me. You never know what might happen between us someday."

Zack watched Charlie open a water bottle for a guest. So helpful and kind. A special kind of woman. His kind…?

"Someday ain't happening," Zack said in a low, but firm voice to Dustin. "If anyone one at the Bar V5 is going to be with her, it'll be me."

His words shocked the hell out of Zack. He'd thrown the gauntlet, but he'd only meant to deter Dustin, right? Zack wished he knew.

However appealing the idea of being with Charlie might be, if Zack accepted the challenge, he would break the one rule he swore he never would.

Chapter Six

O N SATURDAY NIGHT, Charlie and the Bar V5 guests traveled from the community steak dinner to the stage area on Main Street like a herd of cattle. Anticipation for the dance and seeing Jake Kohl kept people from minding.

She hurried everyone along the outside edges of the crowd, eager to reach the stage before the non-Bar V5 attendees. Dustin had texted he and Zack had saved spots for the guests. A few minutes later he waved at her from a location with easy access to the dance floor in front of the stage.

Charlie looked around in awe. "I can't believe you snagged these prime viewing spots."

"Zack managed this," Dustin said. "Spoke with a former Marine."

"Well, you were here to help. Great job. Nate should give you a bonus."

Dustin's cheeks flushed. "Thanks."

Ty looked around as if counting off guests the way he would cows. "This crowd's bigger than last night. Going to make keeping track of our people difficult."

"They'll be fine." Something Charlie couldn't always say about those attending the rodeo with the Bar V5. "This group doesn't need babysitters."

But the wranglers might. She noticed Zack speaking with Tess and Paula. He wore a plaid western shirt with a white T-shirt underneath, jeans, and boots. Handsome, as usual, and being polite to their guests.

Not that Charlie was jealous. This was part of their jobs, and she liked the two women, who genuinely enjoyed attending rodeos. They were walking encyclopedias about rodeo trivia and traveled to a new one each year. They didn't act like buckle bunnies, but had mentioned wanting to go to Grey's after the dance.

The friendship between the two made her think about Caitlin, who was skipping the concert while Noah worked swing shift. She wanted to look through bridal magazines and pin wedding ideas on Pinterest, rather than deal with a big crowd. Charlie didn't blame her friend, except she'd miss Jake Kohl's performance.

The country and western singer would be the only man she'd be able to see tonight. Forget about finding a potential boyfriend unless she bumped into one, literally. Walking anywhere, except to the dance floor, would be too much of a chore.

Earlier today, her search had come up empty. Taking care of guests had been her priority. All she'd managed to do was check out names in the program. Locals like Levi Monroe who traveled the circuit and out-of-towners like Cordell Morgan whose name she hadn't recognized.

Maybe she would have better luck tomorrow. Charlie crossed her fingers. Finding a guy to could make Zack—well, thoughts of him—disappear from her mind and heart was her only way to stay sane.

Jake Kohl walked out on stage. Screams and applause filled Main Street. The handsome singer wore jeans, a black western shirt, boots, and a straw cowboy hat. He stood in front of a microphone and smiled.

"Hello. I want to welcome everyone to the 76th Copper Mountain Rodeo," he said with a butter-melting Southern drawl. "I'm thrilled to be this year's honorary chair. Thank you for moving the dance to tonight, so I could attend and perform a couple songs for y'all."

The crowd went crazy, cheering and whistling, stomping and shouting.

Jake's grin widened, sending female hearts aflutter. He tipped his hat to more cheers. "I'd like to kick off the evening with a new song about what happens when love doesn't work out as you planned."

Charlie nearly laughed. Bet she could have written the lyrics herself.

Jake strummed his guitar. His voice was strong, one that could easily crossover to the pop charts, but his heart seemed rooted in Nashville and country music. He sang lyrics about sunsets, pickup trucks, and broken hearts.

Fitting, Charlie thought, ignoring the lump in her throat. The urge to glance at Zack was strong, but she wasn't going to do it. Nope. No way.

So what if the song perfectly summed up her longing and frustration, in less than a verse? She tapped her toe to the beat, watching people step onto the dance floor.

"Hey, Charlie." Dane Wilcox, aka sex in cowboy boots, stood next to her, his jean-clad thigh touching her leg. His hair was mussed, his eyes dilated, and his skin flushed. "You're looking hot tonight."

She focused on the stage. "I'm sure you say that to all the women you meet."

"Only the pretty ones." He stumbled into her. She smelled beer on this breath. "I made the calf roping finals. Been celebrating. Want to take this party back to your bunkhouse?"

Charlie looked at him to see if he was serious. He seemed to be, although he was drunk. "Sorry, Dane. I'm working tonight."

"Don't know what you're missing girl." Before she could reply, he was moving on to another woman.

"You handled that well." Zack spoke loudly to be heard over the music. He must have finished talking with Tess and Paula. Charlie was surprised he wasn't dancing with the female guests. Most of the wranglers did. Maybe he would later.

"Thanks." His gaze was intent, focused only on her. She liked feeling like the only woman in his world. At least until he turned his head. "I've had practice over the years."

"Nice song."

She nodded. "Jake Kohl is one of my favorites."

"Good singer."

"Yes." But the sound of Zack's voice gave her a thrill no singer could. Her pulse accelerated and her palms felt clammy. She nodded, hating the way her body betrayed her.

He extended his arm. "Care to dance?"

Her heart slammed against her chest, an uncertain and dangerous rhythm taking hold. He wanted to dance with her? She wasn't sure what to think, what to say. Then she realized this was part of getting over him. She could dance with him and not act like a schoolgirl with a crush. She took the hand he offered.

He led her the short distance to the dance floor then placed his free arm around her waist. "Do you want to lead or should I?"

Her cheeks warmed. Someone must have told him about her dancing at Nate and Rachel's wedding. He'd been there, but never came close to her. No wrangler had. Must have been the dress she'd worn. None of the guys knew how to deal with the unexpected where she was concerned, including Zack.

Time to move on, she reminded herself. "You, please."

"We can take turns if you'd like."

Her cheeks burned hotter. Strange, she rarely blushed. Well, except around Zack. But that was over. Or would be soon.

"That's okay," she said. "Maybe next time."

"Sounds good."

Did that mean he wanted to dance with her again? Hope uncurled inside her. She could barely breathe.

Uh oh. Passing out on the dance floor would not be good or tripping over his or her feet, either. *No swooning, remember.*

He squeezed her hand. "Relax. You're so tense."

Easy for him to say. This was a moment she'd dreamed about so many times she'd lost count and was turning out better than what her subconscious had imagined. But she couldn't forget this was just a dance. No reason to indulge in more fantasies that wouldn't come true. "Sorry, I enjoy dancing, but I don't get the chance except at weddings."

"You're doing fine." He danced gracefully, doing a two-step, with no clunky movements or stepping on toes. "There are places to dance in Marietta."

"You need to have someone to dance with."

He pulled back slightly to look at her. "What am I?"

The perfect guy. Crap. She hoped she didn't say that aloud. "You and Ty aren't about to take me along when you hit the town on a Saturday night."

"I'm not minding this."

"That's because you aren't here to pick up chicks." At least she didn't think so because Zack was dancing with her, and they were working. Unless she was the chick he wanted.

Hope flared once again then crashed to the asphalt, breaking open like an egg. She couldn't let herself get carried away. Dancing was a way to wean herself off him.

"I'm here to have a good time," he said.

She gazed into his eyes. "I'm having the time of my life."

What was she saying? Nerves were getting the best of her,

making her resolve waver. She should press her lips together to keep quiet.

"Glad to hear it." His smile took her breath away. "Me, too."

The way he looked at Charlie made her believe him. She had no idea why he'd asked her to dance or why he was being so... attentive, as if she was more than one of his fellow wranglers from the ranch, but she no longer cared about his reasons, or hers for agreeing to dance.

His hand rested low on her back, his hold possessive and protective. Every nerve ending tingled. She wanted to pinch herself to make sure she was awake.

A hundred thoughts whirled through her brain, but she was afraid to say anything that might ruin the dream come true moment. Too bad she wasn't wearing a tiara, not that she owned one, but she felt like Cinderella at the ball sans fairy godmother, magic wand, high-heeled glass slippers, rodents turned attendants, and a giant pumpkin.

One dance meant nothing in the grand scheme of life, in Marietta for that matter. No happily ever after was waiting for her, and that was okay.

This time—shared with friends, neighbors, ranch guests, and people they would never see again—was something she would cherish. In this instant, dancing with Zack gave her the freedom to be herself. She loved the feeling, more than she thought possible.

She was no longer hiding behind familiar labels—wrangler, one of the boys, coworker. She was a woman in the arms of a handsome man, and relishing every single second. Maybe what she wanted was as simple as someone seeing her as Charlie when she worked at the ranch and Charlotte when she didn't.

Zack pulled her closer, spinning her until she was dizzy. She clung to him. Laughed. Leaned back her head.

"You're so light on your feet," he said.

"Are my feet touching the ground?" She sounded breathless, the way she felt. "I feel like I could float away."

"I've got hold of you. I promise I won't let go."

If only he wouldn't let go. Not when the music ended. Not ever.

She had to stop focusing on what she couldn't have. This song needed to be enough. "Thank you for asking me to dance."

His gaze locked on hers, as if transfixed by an invisible force. She felt connected to him, the way she had that night at the river. She couldn't have looked away if she tried. And like then, this didn't feel like infatuation or lust. This was love. He was a sexy cowboy, heroic veteran, and a caring friend all rolled up into one. How could she not love him?

"Thank you for saying yes," he said.

Charlie would say yes. Again and again. All he had to do was ask. The way he looked at her, she could almost believe...

She wet her lips.

Only a dance. Don't get carried away.

Jake Kohl went straight into a new song. Dancers remained on the floor. Zack didn't let go of her, so she kept dancing.

Other ranch guests joined them. Allie and Dan. The women from Las Vegas. A couple from Boise. Charlie lost count, but everyone was moving to the music and smiling.

Especially her. Her entire body seemed to be smiling.

The band played, but Jake Kohl stopped singing.

"This is what I love to see," the singer said into his microphone. "Happy people having a great time. Are you having fun at the 76th Copper Mountain Rodeo?"

Cheers and screams hurt Charlie's ears, but she didn't join in. Her gaze locked on Zack, afraid if she looked away the moment—everything—would not only end, but also disappear.

More people screeched and clapped. Jake must have said

something, but she'd missed his words. Hundreds of dance attendees surrounded her and Zack, but Charlie felt as if they were dancing alone for the attention she'd paid others.

"Hold your dance partner close," Jake said in a playful tone. "Now come on. I know you cowboys can hold women closer than that."

Zack released her hand then wrapped his arms around her. She went willingly. Her fingers splayed across his back. She pressed against his solid chest, soaking up his warmth and his strength.

Was this really happening?

"Gaze into your partner's eyes..." Jake laughed. "We're getting to the good stuff."

Yeah, Charlie agreed. Good stuff.

"Now cowboys." Jake's voice deepened. "Kiss your partner."

Desire flashed in Zack's eyes, desire for her. Her lips parted, a mix of anticipation and uncertainty. He lowered his mouth and kissed her like a man who'd been in the desert without water. She knew exactly how he felt.

Unexpected, but oh-so-welcome.

His lips moved over hers, making her knees feel like soggy hay. She clung to him, not wanting to let reality intrude on this fantasy come to life.

His taste and scent brought a rush of memories from the night that changed everything. Only tonight something was different. He'd kissed her first.

Her lips tingled, and the sensation spread through her body. With each kiss she fell deeper into him.

Deeper and deeper.

A warning bell sounded faint, but there nonetheless.

If she weren't careful, nothing would be left. She didn't dare take the chance.

Charlie drew back. But Zack wouldn't let her go. He followed her, keeping his lips against her mouth. She could easily give in to the moment, to the sensations pulsing through her and the tingles she never wanted to end. But self-preservation made her let go of him.

"What are we doing?" she asked.

He touched her face. "Following orders."

The caress of his fingers against her skin made her feel special, but she couldn't be distracted. "You're not in the army any longer."

"You complaining?"

"No."

That was the problem. Charlie should be. She wanted more of his kisses. Like Sage's salted caramels or Rachel's cookies, one was never enough. But if Charlie gave in to temptation, if she went after what she wanted, she worried Zack would bring up his stupid rule or give some other excuse to downplay what happened between them. Foolishness wasn't fatal, but could make her feel like dirt. Been there, didn't want to do that again.

"But we work together," she said finally.

"We weren't the only ones kissing."

"I wasn't paying attention to anyone else."

He hesitated, as if thinking. "A kiss doesn't change anything. It didn't before."

Oh, boy. The heat rushing through her veins turned to ice. He couldn't be more wrong. A kiss had changed everything. For her, at least. More of his kisses would have the same effect. Thank goodness she'd stopped.

Yet her heart panged. Nothing new where he was concerned, but she wasn't about to sigh. She held her head high. "Dancing was… um, nice, but I need to return to the guests."

Jake Kohl sang another song.

Zack held her hand, pulled her toward him. "Another dance

first?"

Temptation flared, but dancing, even more kisses, wouldn't change anything. Only one thing would, the one thing he would never give her—his love. "Thanks, but I don't want to monopolize your dance card. I'm sure Tess and Paula will want their turns."

"Plenty of dancing left tonight. Another band takes the stage after Jake Kohl." Zack gazed into her eyes. "We're sort of dancing now anyway."

They were, because of the crowded dance floor. But Charlie couldn't pretend this moment together meant nothing to her. Sure, she might be fine tonight, but what about tomorrow and the days that followed? She had Caitlin to consider, too.

"I'm supposed to be looking for a guy. I can't do that if we're"—Charlie pointed to him, then herself—"dancing."

Leaving off the kissing seemed to be best.

He flashed a cocky grin. "I'm a guy."

Her breath caught in her throat, and her pulse skittered. "Does that mean you've thrown your no dating people you work with rule out the window?"

Please tell me you have. Please, oh, please. She crossed her fingers behind her back.

"I haven't." A muscle twitched at his jaw. "I'm sorry. You're right. This was—"

"If you say this was a mistake and apologize, I will hurt you bad."

Amusement gleamed in his eyes, along with something else. A challenge, perhaps. "Think you could?"

She raised her chin. "I'd give it my best shot."

"I'd like to see that, sweetheart, but I wasn't going to say either of those things."

"Oh." Had he just called her sweetheart? Or maybe she was hearing things. "What were you going to say then?"

"I've enjoyed this, but we should get back to the guests."

A familiar lump of disappointment burned in her throat, but Charlie kept her shoulders back and her head up. She wove her way through the people on the dance floor. She shouldn't be surprised by anything Zack said. If anything, he was helping her see that she was ready for more.

More kisses. More affection. More... love.

But not with him. He didn't want those things from her. The way he kissed her suggested he cared and was attracted, but something held him back. His rule or was there more? Either way, she couldn't change his mind or fix what kept him from dating her.

Zack followed her. "You okay?"

"I'm fine." When had she become so good at lying?

"I've been told by trusty sources those two words mean the opposite of what they imply."

Busted. But she wouldn't admit a thing. She glanced his way. "Your trusty source should have warned you that's something not to be spoken in front of the opposite sex. Or did they forget that part?"

A beat passed. "Should I be quiet?"

"Yes."

Enticing kisses or not, she couldn't keep putting herself through this yo-yo of emotions. The rodeo had been going on for nearly twenty-four hours and the only hot cowboy she'd kissed was Zack.

Worse, one question kept running through her mind...

If she hadn't stopped kissing first, would he have?

Desire brushed across her skin like a breeze off the river. Probably best if she didn't know the answer. Because even if she knew kissing him was a bad idea, she wanted to feel his lips against hers again.

Her back pocket buzzed. Charlie pulled out her cellphone

and glanced at the text on the screen. Her chest tightened. "Oh, no."

"A guest?"

"No, Nate." She gripped the phone. "Arrow escaped again."

"I just repaired the fence."

She read the second text. "He got out the gate."

"You mean the double gate."

"Who knows what goes through that stallion's mind?"

"Sex."

She stumbled.

Zack reached out and grabbed her arm. "Careful."

She straightened, regained her balance. "I'm good."

The word "sex" had thrown her. Maybe she wasn't quite over his kisses as she hoped to be.

Time. She needed time and distance. She lengthened her strides, not easy to do trying to get through the dancers. "I need to get back to the ranch to help Nate."

"I've got keys to one of the vans." Zack whipped out his phone. "We can let the others know, then take off."

"Nate's sending Rachel and Ellie here to help with the guests. He's heading out to search with Dusty now." Charlie stared at the sun sinking into the horizon. "We don't have much daylight left."

"No worries." Zack laced his fingers with hers and squeezed. "Arrow has an MO he follows. Seek out a mare first. If one's not available, lead Nate on a wild good chase until he's cursing like a sailor, then find you so he can get treats and rubs."

She was grateful for Zack holding her hand and his words. He knew her well and what she needed. "For someone who says he prefers cattle, you know a lot about horses."

"Remember what you said to me about listening to us wranglers?"

She nodded.

"I do the same thing with you and Ty."

Zack's admission surprised and impressed her. He'd paid more attention to her than she realized. "Arrow could be anywhere."

"True, but Arrow's a smart horse. He's not going to go wild, not until he can find a stable of mares."

"I hope you're right."

Zack squeezed her hand again. "That horse loves you. If Nate can't track him down, I know you can."

Charlie stared at their linked hands, wishing she didn't want his support but knowing that deep in her heart of hearts, she did and wanted...more.

Too bad he wouldn't pursue anything more than a dance or kiss with her. She had a feeling they would have been good together.

Really, really good.

TRACKING DOWN A horny stallion was not how Zack expected to be spending Saturday night during the 76th Copper Mountain Rodeo. Punishment for tossing the gauntlet earlier? More likely penance for getting caught up in the moment, doing what he'd been told and kissing Charlie, completely forgetting the rule he'd built his working life around.

What the hell was he doing?

Sending mixed signals wasn't fair to her. But damn, the woman made thinking straight difficult. Especially when she kissed like a dream and made him forget both common sense and reason.

Zack parked the four-wheeler outside the lower meadow where the mares often grazed, entered, then closed and latched the gate behind him.

Considering he couldn't take his gaze off Charlie in her

flowered print top and faded jeans earlier, he should have known this wouldn't be a typical evening. She'd looked so darn pretty, how could he not ask her to dance, and then with her hips moving against his, not kiss her?

But his attraction for Charlie was more than lust. The realization worried him.

Feelings toward her had bubbled up at the dance and now simmered beneath the surface, waiting for another chance to appear. Not the brotherly or family kind of caring, either. Far from it.

Damn. He needed to get these feelings under control before strong emotions led to a disaster. Zack wanted to keep everything the same. Finding Charlie a man was the best way to make that happen, and she was correct. He wasn't helping matters by dancing with and kissing her the way he had.

Zack turned up the collar on his jacket to ward off the dropping temperature. He carried a bag of apples and carrots. If Charlie couldn't entice the horse into the field, then maybe Arrow's favorite treats would draw him out.

"At the lower meadow." He spoke into a walkie-talkie. They were easier to use when cell coverage was spotty at best. "Charlie's here. No sign of Arrow."

His headlamp lit a path through the grass. The sun had slipped below the horizon fifteen minutes ago, taking what warmth remained in the air.

"No sighting in the cow pasture," Nate's voice came over the walkie-talkie. "Checking along the river."

One of them had better find that damn horse soon.

Zack strode across the meadow where the mares grazed toward the beam from Charlie's headlamp. She sat on the grass, holding a lead rope. A fleece blanket and coffee thermos were at her side. Not her first time at this rodeo.

"See him?" Zack asked.

"Yeah, Arrow's out there, but he's spooked." Her voice stayed calm. She stared off into the darkness. "Did you close the gate?

"Yes."

"He's trapped now."

Zack squinted. A pair of night vision goggles would come in handy, but tactical gear wasn't on the dude ranch's "To Buy" list. Though if Arrow kept this up... "I don't see him."

"Listen."

He did. "I've got nothing but crickets."

She closed her eyes, using what he called her horse intuition. He didn't know what else to call her and Ty's connection to these animals.

"He's by the trees," she said, opening her eyes. The moon was a crescent sliver surrounded by a million stars, but nothing amazed him more than her.

Zack had watched her manage off-the-wall situations with horses no one else could handle. "Should I let the others know?"

"Let's see how we do on our own. I don't want to freak out Arrow any further."

"You're the boss." He held up the bag. "I've got the treats."

"Give me a carrot. You eat an apple."

"Huh?"

"Arrow has to be hungry. He loves treats." She stared off in the direction of the trees, focused on the escape artist. "He'll hear and smell us eating and want to join the party."

Made sense. A part of him wished she would show the same concern about him as she did Arrow, but that wouldn't do him any good. They weren't going to be dating. He handed her a carrot, took an apple and set the bag on the ground.

Her carrot crunched with her bite.

He bit into the apple. "Juicy."

She finished her carrot. "Arrow's favorite."

"Mine, too. This one's sweet." Like Charlie's kisses. Kissing would be a good way to warm up. She had to be cold sitting there, but Arrow might not like Zack messing with his girl. That gave him an idea. "Horses don't get jealous, do they?"

"Not in the way humans do. Or dogs and cats for that matter," she said. "But horses can be defensive about their rank in a herd or their amount of space in a pasture or the attention given from a horse or person."

"No one wants to be left out."

"That's for sure."

Her wistful tone intrigued him. "Sounds like there's a story there."

The air was so quiet he could almost hear her consider the question.

"There is," she admitted. "Years of being dragged from one Montana town to another by my mom was hard. I'd want to fit in at a new school, so I learned to be a chameleon and adapt quickly. Making friends and joining groups was easier that way."

Made sense. "My parents didn't care if I went to school or not, but when I did go, it was the same one. Still hard to make friends when you're never there."

"Sounds like we both had challenges at school."

"But we made it through."

She nodded. "Moving to Marietta and staying here until I graduated high school made a big difference."

"Joining the army saved me. Otherwise..."

He would be in jail, or trying to avoid arrest, or working some scam to cheat hard-working folks out of their money. Because that was what his parents did. They'd been showing him how to do the same when he left. He pushed the memories aside. Not his life anymore.

"I wouldn't be here," he said. "And I can't imagine being anywhere else."

"Even now?"

"A clear, star-filled night sky overhead. A pretty woman…"

"A rebellious horse." She clicked her tongue. "Come on, Arrow. I have apples and carrots. You know you want a treat."

Zack watched, waited, nothing. "Arrow's too smart to fall for the treat ruse."

"Sometimes you have to be patient. Try again." She pulled an apple from the sack. "Want another one?"

Zack had a better idea. "How about a kiss?"

Chapter Seven

THE CIRCLE OF light from Charlie's headlamp shone on the grass, moving back and forth. Okay, Zack's plan didn't impress her. He understood because he would be the first to admit he didn't know as much about horses as the other wranglers at the Bar V5, especially her and Ty, but Zack's gut instinct was strong enough he would stick with his hunch. "Don't let the kissing part throw you."

She frowned. "You're exact words were 'how about a kiss'. What part are you talking about?"

"My fault. A slight failure to communicate. I'm not talking about us kissing."

She gave him a look. One he deserved. He was playing with fire. They didn't have to kiss. A hug might work. Except he wasn't going to mention that.

"Let me try again. We would kiss, but we'd be kissing for Arrow's sake. To get him to come out from the trees," he explained, feeling like an idiot. His feelings for her were making him act irrational. "Horses may not get jealous, but I've seen how they act, especially our wants-some-action Houdini. Arrow loves you. If you give me attention, he might get defensive—protective even—and come over."

Charlie didn't jump to her feet and kiss him. That was too

much to expect under the circumstances. But she hadn't said no to his idea. That pleased him.

"Might work," she said finally. "If Arrow doesn't get mad and try to hurt you."

"Get that rope lead on him, and I'll be fine."

She stood, brushed her backside with her free hand, something he wouldn't mind doing to her if she needed help. "Worth a shot, I suppose."

Her lack of enthusiasm bothered him, but this was about the horse, not them kissing. A totally selfless gesture. *Yeah, right.*

"I don't want to have to stay out here all night," she added.

But he knew she would. She or Ty would sleep with sick or injured animals. Arrow on the loose was no different. Truth was, spending the night out here wouldn't be so bad, even in the cold, as long as Zack and Charlie were together. Cuddling and sharing body warmth didn't suck. "We've done it before."

"Mabel," they said at the same time.

Bluebelle's calf, Mabel, had gone missing in June. They'd found her right before sunrise, trapped in a trench. He and Charlie had each put a rope on Mabel to pull her out.

"That was some good teamwork," she said. "But exhausting."

Zack nodded. "Like with Mabel, we have nothing to lose if this doesn't work with Arrow. And if it does, our comfy beds await and we can get a full night's sleep."

She pursed her lips. "What about your rule?"

Charlie seemed fixated on his no-work romance rule tonight. Funny, that hadn't come up in months, not since she returned from Colorado this spring. But he understood, given the way he'd kissed her.

"The rule doesn't apply here," he said. "We're doing this for our jobs and Arrow. Not us."

As soon as he'd spoken the words, Zack knew Arrow wasn't

the only reason he wanted to kiss Charlie. He prided himself on being honest, but being around her short-circuited his brain. If he kept saying things like this, he might have to rethink his definition of honesty.

He was going to steal a kiss. His suggestion was as simple and complicated as that.

She stretched her arms and wiggled her gloved hands, making him think of the warm-ups swimmers do before a race. Was this how she prepared for a kiss? He bit back a smile. Kind of cute.

Her arms went to her sides. She held the lead rope in her right hand.

"Ready?" he asked.

"As I'll ever be." She looked up at him. "Kiss me, cowboy."

"You can kiss me, cowgirl."

Charlie lifted her chin. "Your idea."

Fine. She wasn't going to have to twist his arm. He would kiss her. Gladly.

For Arrow.

Better not forget that key point.

Zack lowered his mouth to hers, touching her lips gently.

Soft, warm, sweet.

The words described Charlie's lips, her kiss, the woman. He wrapped his arms around her, pulling her closer, but the jacket she wore—more life vest than piece of clothing—and his kept them more separated then he'd like.

Still no complaints. Not when he could run his fingers through her long hair and kiss her.

Intoxicating.

More potent than whiskey, her kisses tasted better, too.

Her hands moved up his back until her fingers curled in Zack's hair. She trailed kisses along his jawline until reaching his ear where she nibbled and licked...

Oh, yeah. A fire burned in his belly. He loved what she was doing to him. He wanted another kiss.

Zack turned his head, searching for her lips.

He found them. Parted. Jackpot.

His tongue explored and danced.

Addictive was the only way to describe her taste. Her kisses. Her.

She moaned. The sexy sound sent his control slipping another notch. But this wasn't only about kisses. Something deeper was happening here. His heart wanted... more.

Fingers pressed into his jacket. "Zack."

He wasn't sure what he was feeling, but he knew he wanted all of Charlie—her body, her heart, and her soul.

Something hit his shoulder. Knocked him back. He landed flat on his ass, gasping for air.

Oh, crap. Arrow. Zack had forgotten about the horse completely.

Charlie.

Adrenaline shot through him. He sprung to his feet, took a step toward her, froze, staring in amazement.

Somehow Charlie had managed to get the lead rope around Arrow's neck. She shot Zack a concerned glance. "You okay?"

Her voice was barely above a whisper. For Arrow's sake, so she wouldn't spook him.

Zack nodded. He'd bruised his ego, nothing else. Charlie was safe, so was the horse. That was all that mattered. "You?"

"Good."

Arrow's head went over Charlie's shoulder and tilted toward her face. The horse looked at Zack as if to say 'mine, don't come any closer.' Not jealous, but that horse was one possessive devil.

All the things that could have gone wrong sent Zack's stomach churning. He'd forgotten about Arrow. Put them in danger. One or both of them could have been injured. Over a kiss. Talk about stupid.

What about your rule?

The rule doesn't apply here.

It should. At all times. Tonight was proof.

Yet his lips tingled, ached for more kisses. And his heart yearned for her affection.

"You are such a handsome boy," Charlie said in a quiet voice, letting the horse take the lead of what kind of attention he wanted from her.

Her patience and nurturing tone touched Zack. The horse was big and powerful, a mass of muscle and strength, uncontrollable and unpredictable, yet she cooed to Arrow with love and tenderness, as if he were a helpless foal, not a dangerous stud.

A ball of heat burned in the center of Zack's chest, warming him from the inside out. So amazing. Charlie would make a great mom.

Where had that come from? The random thought sent shockwaves through Zack, but that didn't stop an unexpected image of her holding a baby from forming in his mind.

Not good. Yes, he had feelings for Charlie, more than a coworker caring for another. How could he not? She was skilled and attractive and sexy. Amazing. But he couldn't go there, not even if his heart wanted to. Off-limits. He had to make these feelings stop.

Forget about marriage, a wife, kids. That was something other people did, people who didn't come from a past and parents like his.

You'll never amount to anything.

Loser.

I wish you'd never been born.

His parents' words erased the appealing image of Charlie. He was so afraid of turning into his mom and dad, or worse, proving what they'd said about him was true that he'd decided not to risk having a family of his own, even if he longed for one. He would make do with the family he'd created with the people in his life, like the one with Charlie and the other wranglers. That would have to be enough.

Arrow nickered. The low, soft sound made the horse seem more like a giant, lovable puppy rather than a total pain in the ass. He rubbed his head against Charlie, totally besotted with the cowgirl.

Zack wouldn't mind trading places with the horse for a few minutes. He was besotted, too. Only he had to keep that at bay, under wraps because of... his rule.

"That's my boy." With a slow, precise movement, she removed a carrot from her jacket pocket—when had she put that in there?—and fed the horse. "Here's your treat. You know how to be a good boy. I know you do. And there's more breeding we want to do with you, but not if you keep getting into trouble. Okay, sweetie?"

The horse chewed on the carrot, soaking up Charlie's attention like the lovesick, testosterone driven teenager he was.

She looked over at Zack. "Nice job with the kissing part."

No mistaking the humor in her voice or her praise, but he couldn't pretend the situation could have gone very wrong. "Good teamwork once again, but we got lucky. I forgot about the horse when I was kissing you. Either or both of us could have been hurt. Just proves why getting involved with a coworker is a bad idea."

"No one got hurt. We're fine," Charlie countered. "Be happy we caught Arrow."

Zack would be happy with more kisses. That only made him angry. "I'm glad we got the horse, but—"

"No buts. I wouldn't have been able to do this without you, Zack," She smiled. "Thank you."

Her words made him feel like he could run up Cooper

Mountain in bare feet. He didn't need a mirror to know he'd flipped the switch on his emotions and was grinning like a fool.

Truth was, he wanted to be here to help her. Tonight, tomorrow, whenever she might need him. He wanted to prove he wasn't like his parents and destined to repeat his family's past. He wanted her respect. That was all he dared hope for.

So what if Zack thought he was Charlie's type? Hell, a part—a growing one—wanted to be her guy. But being coworkers wasn't the only obstacle in the way. The other was harder to swallow, but one he couldn't forget.

Zack wasn't capable of giving Charlie Randall the love and the family she wanted. He wouldn't want to even try because he would only end up hurting her.

And that was the last thing he wanted to do.

INSIDE THE BAR V5's state of the art horse barn, Charlie hung back, leaning against an empty stall door, letting Nate, Ty, and Zack place Arrow into his paddock. Her on-edge nerves threatened to get the best of her, not to mention her still throbbing lips from kissing earlier. Best if she stayed out of the way.

A few feet away, Zack stood by the stall door, waiting for Nate's signal to slide the panel into place. The worry in Zack's eyes when Arrow had interrupted their kissing remained front and center in her mind. His reaction had been so immediate, the concern in his voice so real, her insides melted.

His actions were those of a man who cared about her, not as a coworker or friend, but as a woman, a special one in his life. So why wouldn't he see where this could lead? Sure, he had his rule, and tonight she saw how romantic distractions could get in way. But something else seemed to be holding him back.

She remembered the things he'd said about not wanting a

girlfriend now, let alone a wife and family in the future. Not once in the past two and a half years since he arrived had he dated anyone seriously. The "Move On," "Walk Away Now," and "Don't waste any more time" signs flashed brightly. She knew the odds of anything happening between them were slim to none. Still her respect and affection—okay, love—for the man had grown tonight. How was she going to find someone else to date when her heart wanted only him?

Arrow backed out of the stall. Again.

Nate swore. "If you didn't produce such pretty foals, I would make a gelding out of you."

"Honey, not vinegar," Charlie said.

"This horse pisses vinegar. On purpose." Nate nodded at Zack who slid the stall door into place then had Ty secure three locks. "He's my pride and joy, but I don't know what to do. Triple fence and gate his pasture."

"Talk to Noah," Zack said, making her think they'd make a horseman out of him yet. "He's a vet. He might have ideas."

Ty nodded. "If all else fails, we can send Arrow to a horse ranch. Do some breeding and training. Couldn't hurt."

"Something has to be done," Nate said. "We've been lucky each time he's gotten loose."

Charlie didn't have to look Zack's way to know his gaze was on her. He knew what the horse meant to her, and that they'd been lucky in the meadow. "None of us want anything to happen to Arrow."

"I'll call Noah on Monday," Nate said. "See what he says before we make any decisions."

Ty nodded, then looked at Charlie and Zack. "Been a long day. Sleep in tomorrow. Just be at the rodeo grounds before the finals starts."

"Thanks, but I'll be ready to go in the morning with the first van," Charlie said.

Zack stood next to her, as if in solidarity. "Me, too."

"Non-negotiable," Nate answered for Ty. "We've discussed this. We're weaning calves this coming week. Not taking chances you get rundown. You can attend the finals, since all you do is sit and watch, but the others will take the guests into Marietta and spend the morning shopping and sightseeing."

"Fine." She knew better than to talk back to Nate. She didn't have the same reservations speaking up to Ty, but he nodded his agreement with his partner. "Looks like Zack and I get a lazy morning in bed."

Zack winked. "You bringing breakfast? Oh, wait, you don't cook. Guess it'll be up to me."

Ty and Nate laughed.

She bit the inside of her mouth. Her fault for not thinking about what she was going to say, but she blamed Zack for messing with her heart, her brain, and now words. "With that, I'll say goodnight, un-gentlemen."

She exited the building and headed toward the old red barn. On her way inside, she touched one of the outer boards. So much history between these four walls.

Overhead lights allowed her to see the cats playing, running, and scratching. The atmosphere comforted her like a handmade quilt wrapped around her shoulders. She loved the amenities the horse barn offered, but this old building was her favorite place at the Bar V5. Here, she'd learned about horses from Nate's dad, Ralph, and from Ty.

"Charlie, wait."

Zack. She didn't know how he was going to act—like a man who cared about her or a coworker giving her a hard time. She wished he would choose one. This back and forth was hard on her heart. She kept getting her hopes up only to have them dashed.

She looked at him. "Want to tease me some more?"

His assessing gaze studied her, as if trying to see if she'd been exposed to some contagious illness. He probably wouldn't like hearing he was the virus, and she was searching for the cure.

"When have we not teased around like that?" he asked. "No reason to take the kidding personally."

"I'm not."

He raised a brow. "Sure about that? You called us ungentlemen. That's a first. Normally you'd swear and tell us off."

"I..." Oh, no. She scraped the toe of her boot against the dirt floor. He was right. This was no different than before, except she was taking what they said personally. "You're right. I don't know why I didn't take the ribbing as a joke."

Or maybe she did know. The thought of spending a morning in bed with Zack wasn't a joking matter.

He pushed a strand of hair off her face, the gesture sweet yet intimate. Her throat tightened. Why couldn't he see what they could have together?

"You're tired." He lowered his hand. "It was a long day before we left the concert. Arrow made everything longer tonight."

She nodded. "Sleeping in might be good."

"I'll wake up early anyway."

"Me, too." She remembered the looks on Ty's and Nate's faces. "We still won't be allowed to go to the rodeo."

Zack shrugged. "We can go for a ride."

"You mean, one were we don't have to work?"

"Exactly. Sound good?"

She forced herself not to nod enthusiastically. "Yeah. Better than sleeping in."

"You're a true cowgirl."

"If the boots fit..." She straightened a rope hanging on the wall. "I was sixteen when Ralph Vaughn offered me a free horse stall in exchange for ten hours of labor a week. I ended up working twenty and received a paycheck a month later. Been here ever since."

"You'll be here much longer."

Would she? Charlie had always thought so, but now…

Two cats peeked out of Ty's office. Their slow movements made her think they'd been asleep. Maybe the mousing hour had arrived.

"I always thought I'd be here forever," she admitted.

His eyes narrowed. "You don't sound so certain now."

"I'm not." There. She'd said it. Her world didn't cave in or implode. "What if there's another place I belong?"

"You belong here."

"Maybe."

"We're a family."

"I know, but…" She took a do-I-dare breath. "You boys have me pigeon-holed. You see me one way. You don't know what to do when I change things up. Wearing jewelry and styling my hair turns into a big deal. Everyone avoids me like a leper if I'm wearing a dress."

Zack shrugged. "That's because we see you as one of the boys."

"All I ever wanted was to be included. You wranglers have. But I'm getting tired of being one of the guys."

His forehead wrinkled. "Then stop being one."

"I did when I was in Colorado."

He stiffened. "How was it?"

She sighed. "Wonderful. I didn't have to pretend there. I could be myself."

He reached for her, touched her shoulder, his gaze intent upon hers. "Be yourself here."

"I'm trying." She touched her horseshoe earrings. "Do you know my real name?"

"Charlie."

"That's my nickname. Charlotte is my real name. Pretty and feminine, don't you think?"

Another shrug. "Nice, but you're more a Charlie."

"You proved my point."

"A name doesn't matter. Neither does wearing bling and make-up. The person you are is in here." He pointed to her heart. "Remember that and all will be good."

She sighed. "You make it sound so simple."

"Don't complicate things. Women do that sometimes."

"Is that what your trusty source told you?"

"Damn straight," he said. "But see, you didn't even notice I called you a woman."

She flinched, unsure how she'd missed that. Tired, maybe. "I didn't."

Wicked laughter lit his eyes. "I'm looking forward to our lazy morning ride."

Anticipation gave her a second wind. "Me, too."

Even if a lazy morning in bed with a particular cowboy with the initials ZH held a certain appeal, too.

HEAVEN. THE BAR V5 was Zack's slice of heaven on earth. Riding with Charlie this Sunday morning only made the place sweeter. He turned Blackbeard toward the river, following Charlie and Sierra. The sound of rushing water grew louder.

Almost there.

Contentment flowed through him.

This was his favorite trail ride, one guests of all riding abilities enjoyed, but being out here with only Charlie was special, like the woman herself.

Charlotte.

Zack couldn't wrap his head around her real name. The woman riding ahead was Charlie, a wrangler and horse trainer at the Bar V5. Okay, he noticed a red ribbon braided in Sierra's mane, something he'd never seen before. But she was still Charlie.

So what if ponytails and braids hadn't made an appearance all weekend and she'd worn her hair loose again? He liked how the breeze teased the ends of her locks. That didn't make her Charlotte.

The way her jeans cupped her bottom looked hot no matter what name he used. Zack never thought he'd be jealous of a saddle, but today he was.

Charlie glanced over her shoulder. Her smile, warm and bright, reached her eyes. The blue color matched the clear sky overhead and made him think of pools of water again.

He wanted a drink.

Nope, he corrected. Not thirsty. He couldn't immerse himself nor dip a toe in. But he could look, admire, enjoy. She was beautiful. And his. At least for the length of the ride.

"Want to stop down by the water and give the horses a rest?" she asked.

He knew Blackbeard's pace and how far they'd ridden. "Sure. We have time."

Later this morning, they would drive vans into Marietta with guests who'd slept in. Before that, he wanted to give Arrow an extra, special juicy apple—repayment for last night's kiss and today's "sleep in" assignment. The stallion may have been naughty, but his bad behavior worked out well for Zack.

At the trail's end, within view of the river, he climbed off Blackbeard and attached the reins to a post. Charlie did the same with Sierra, giving the pretty mare a hug.

"Too bad we didn't bring a picnic," he said.

"A little early for lunch. We just ate breakfast."

His stomach was full from the stuffed French toast, maple sausage, fruit medley, and smoothies. "I was thinking more along the lines of dessert. It's never too early for a sweet treat."

Especially if Charlie's lips were involved.

Okay, bad idea. But when Zack had returned to the bunk-house last night, he'd kept thinking about her. He'd dreamed about her kisses and woke up with her on his mind. He needed to control his feelings. Suggesting a ride with only the two of them hadn't been his smartest idea, because his imagination was running wild with what they could do together here.

Charlie stood at the river's edge. She wore a fleece jacket over a pink Henley. Funny, but he'd never seen her wear pink before. More Charlotte influence?

She picked up a rock. "I love this place."

This wasn't the first time they'd been here alone. The last time... *Don't go there.* "Me, too."

"We kissed for the first time here."

His gaze traveled to the tree where they'd sat and later lay on the ground, only to end up covered in twigs and leaves. "I was thinking about that."

She wiped her hands on the thighs of her jeans. "The water level's low."

"Just wait." He hooked a thumb into a jean pocket, trying to tell himself he hadn't wanted to ride here for a repeat perfor-mance of what had happened over a year ago. "The rain is coming."

"So the old timers say."

He moved toward her, slowly to see if she moved away. She remained in the same spot.

"Why are we talking about the weather?" he asked.

"Better than talking about the past."

"I'll concede that point."

Her eyes widened. She wrung her hands. "Will you concede on your workplace romance rule?"

The hope in her voice poked at him like small branding irons, burning her initials into his heart. "You know what could have happened with the horse last night."

"But nothing did. You, me, and Arrow are fine. Just because something went wrong before—"

"Tragically wrong." He moved toward a nearby tree. "Avoidable. That's why I have the rule."

"I'm trying to understand. But it's hard when you keep kissing me."

Crap. The atmosphere had changed from comfortable to tense in an instant. A ruck in full gear and combat boots during a rainstorm would be more fun than the conversation that was coming.

Lines creased Charlie's forehead. Of course, she must feel the strain, too.

Damage control time. Zack exhaled.

"I messed up, okay." He rocked back on his heels. "I shouldn't kiss you."

She looked up at him. "I like kissing you."

"Me, too. I mean you." Damn. He was screwing up. Again. His lips wanted another taste of Charlie's sweetness to the point of not caring what that might do to him or her or the other wranglers at the Bar V5. "There's something between us."

He'd said the words he'd been ignoring for over a year. Blood roared through his veins. He waited, wondered what she would say.

The relief in her eyes knocked him back a step. His butt bumped into the tree's trunk.

"Thank you for admitting that," she said sincerely. A smile spread across her face. "I thought I was the only one who noticed a... connection."

"Hell, no." He hadn't known what she'd say, but he hadn't expected her gratitude. "There's an invisible cable connecting you to me. Unbreakable. I've tried."

"Me, too." She rubbed her lips together. "So what do we do about it?"

Chapter Eight

WHAT WERE THEY going to do about the connection between them? Zack rested the heel of his left boot against the tree. "No idea. But I'm hoping we can figure out something. This isn't good for either of us."

Charlie rubbed a rock, looking from the river to him. Her gaze narrowed. "That's honest."

"I try to be." He started to speak then stopped, unsure if he should tell her the reason why. At this point, she knew most everything else about him. What did he have to lose? "I've learned being honest is the only way. If I'd... if we'd all been honest..."

She dropped the rock and moved closer. "Who are you talking about?"

He brushed his hand through his hair, but that didn't lessen his agitation. "My squad."

"Davey?"

Her remembering the name of his friend who'd been killed in action surprised Zack. Then again Charlie was like that, able to recall facts that made one feel she not only listened, but also cared. "Yes. He was there, part of the squad. Another guy named Hood, a gung-ho corporal, lived and breathed the US Army. We kidded him about becoming an officer. He probably would have risen up the ranks if…"

Charlie touched Zack's arm, the gesture meant everything to him and that scared him. He couldn't get attached to her. Not in that way.

Her eyes clouded with concern. "If what?"

"If he hadn't fallen for a pretty specialist named Remington, who was assigned to support us."

"A workplace romance."

"In the middle of a warzone." Zack stared at Charlie's hand on his arm. "Hood was a damn good soldier, but he became distracted, counting the hours on watch or patrol until he could be with his girlfriend."

"He was in love." Charlie sounded wistful, more like a Charlotte than a wrangler who'd made a name for herself training horses. "That's what happens."

Zack wouldn't know. He'd never been in love. But he didn't blame guys for finding comfort and company where they could. But Hood… "We teased him. Most of us were jealous though we never admitted the truth. Who wouldn't want a girlfriend when you're far away from home?"

"You must have been lonely."

"Deployments don't last forever. We've got each other. Brothers." He remembered Davey's care package with a whoopee cushion inside. Man, they'd fun with that. "But Hood started showing up late, skipping out early. No one reported him. We covered his ass, figuring he'd be over *her* soon enough."

"Was he?"

Remorse over not speaking up clawed at Zack. He hadn't been the only one to keep quiet, and they all shared the blame. "No. He proposed."

"That's serious."

Nodding, Zack struggled to remain in the present and not fall into the nightmare of the past. "There was this one time. We were attacked. We got caught in a firefight, and others were taking mortar hits. Hood..." Zack closed his eyes wishing he or Davey could have had an extra second or two to react, to reach out and stop the guy. "He deserted his post, left us, to find his fiancée. He wanted to protect her."

Charlie didn't say anything, but kept her hand on his arm. That gesture earned his gratitude and... more.

"Knowing he left you in the middle of a battle must have been hard," she said finally.

"Damn straight. Hurt like hell." Zack's gut twisted. The bullet scars sometimes burned, all in his head according to a therapist, but he no longer tasted the metallic bitterness in his mouth so that was an improvement, right? But he didn't want the same thing to reoccur. He couldn't let that happen to anyone else. "Hood got shot. A couple of us did."

Charlie squeezed Zack's arm. "I'm so sorry."

"Me, too."

He would never condone Hood's actions or what his dereliction of duty cost the squad or the price paid by two families back home, but Zack understood a little better now. Attraction—or whatever he felt for Charlie—had a mind of its own. Made you stupid.

"Hood died that night. Never made it to his fiancée. Remington had followed orders and remained safe." Zack's heart ached at the tragic loss. "But she was so distraught over Hood's death, she took her own life."

Charlie's gaze filled with compassion. She removed her hand from his arm. "I'm sorry. I didn't understand your rule before or why you were so concerned. I do now. Makes sense after what you've been through."

Man, he needed a beer or a shot of whiskey to settle his nerves, because nothing made sense now, especially his wanting to bury his head against Charlie's chest and have her hold him.

Too bad alcohol wasn't allowed during working hours. Not that a drink or ten would make a difference in the long run. Thankfully he learned that lesson early and knew his limit.

"Does it make sense?" he asked, torn between the past and the present, not sure what to think.

"Totally." An unexpected smile erased the lines of concern on her face. Her face brightened. "This is going to be so easy to fix."

He drew back, confused by the change in her. "Fix?"

She nodded. "I don't need to find a man. I need a new job. Winter's coming, but with a recommendation from Nate and Ty finding one shouldn't be that hard."

Zack's world tilted. He lost his balance, caught himself, cursed. He'd been trying to keep her at the Bar V5. Having her leave was the last thing he wanted. "Stop with the quitting nonsense. You're not going anywhere."

"Yes, I am. This is the perfect solution," she countered with a firm tone. "You don't date coworkers. If I'm not a coworker, there's nothing standing in our way of going out."

He understood her logic even if he didn't agree. "Leaving a stable job you love is a big step to take when we haven't had a date."

"No dates, but plenty of kisses." She spoke as if this were a done deal. The decision made. "You admitted there's something between us."

"Yes, but—"

"What?" A hint of panic edged the word.

He took a breath. Telling her was the only way to keep from making a big mistake. "I'm not looking for a girlfriend."

She blinked. Once. Twice. "One you work with or—"

"Not at all," he finished for her. The words sounded cold. He wanted to make sure she didn't feel bad. "This isn't personal," he clarified.

Charlie inhaled deeply, then exhaled slowly.

A breath was better than yelling. Not that Charlie did that. She never raised her voice.

"You're okay with this?" he asked, eying her warily.

She shrugged. "You've mentioned you're not looking for a relationship, but you might change your mind one of these days. My not working here will make things easier if that happens."

What the... this didn't sound like the no-nonsense Charlie he knew. He leveled his gaze at her. "You're willing to bank your future on 'one of these days'?"

She nodded. "That's better odds than never which was all I had until a few minutes ago."

The obvious relief in her voice made his heart hurt, but he felt as if his head was bumping into a two-by-four with each of her words. "I have no idea what you're talking about."

Zack didn't want to disappoint her, but he wasn't going to lie. What he was about to say was for Charlie's own good.

"I know I've talked about not wanting a family. That wasn't BS, I mean it," he said. "Marriage isn't for me. Hell, the longest I've ever dated a woman is two weeks."

Her lower lip quivered.

Crap. He reminded himself she would be better off with someone else. Might as well say what else needed to be said. "So even if you quit..."

"We'll never be a couple."

Charlie's sad tone made him like a class-A jerk. "I'm sorry."

"Sorry," she repeated, as if trying out the word for the first time. "You're sorry."

"Yes, I am."

She stared at him. Her gaze narrowed, hardened along with her jaw, as if she'd put on a bulletproof mask. "Are you sorry?"

He flinched. She'd never used such a harsh voice with him. "What's that supposed to mean?"

"You kiss me. Not once, but multiple times." She spoke faster and louder. "As soon as things seem like they could go somewhere, you bring up your no romance at work rule."

"You said you understood about that."

"I do, but not when you're using a tragedy to your advantage."

He crossed his arms over his chest. "I'm not doing that."

"You are. You've done it every single time." She drew her lips into a thin line. "You bring up the past as if that decides not only the present, but also the future. You need to get over whatever is keeping you from moving forward."

"I'm fine."

She gave him a look. "So much for being honest."

Zack started to speak, then stopped. Uncertainty pressed against his breastbone. "I'm not lying. I'm... confused."

"So am I. I get I kissed you the first time. I take full responsibility for that." Her eyes darkened. Her voice grew stronger. "But the other times... the hot and cold action. Do one thing, then say another. That's on you, bub."

"It's not like that."

She looked upward at the sky and exhaled slowly.

"I care about you." He scratched his cheek. "But you want something I can't give."

"That's because you choose not to give it."

"This is for your own good. You deserve better."

She shook her head. "Don't pretend you weren't aware of what you were doing. You led me on. More than once. Whenever it was convenient or you wanted a kiss. And you're right, I do deserve better."

Ashamed he wasn't able to deny her words, he hung his head. "Maybe I could have done things better, but I was doing the best I could. For you. All I wanted... still want... is for you to stay at the Bar V5."

"Why?"

"I told you. We're a family. I don't know if my parents are alive or dead. You and the wranglers are all I have. I was trying to keep my family together. Maybe that's selfish. I won't disagree with what you said. But doesn't family matter to you?"

"Yes, but what you're doing isn't how family treats one another."

His chest tightened. "I don't know how families are supposed to work. My parents are... were the poster children for dysfunction."

"Here's the deal." Her steady gaze remained on his. "Family is supposed to want what's best for the other person, even if that means being apart. Look at my mom and me. Distance doesn't change how you feel about each other."

"You'll forget—"

"Not forget. Miss. Big difference," she explained. "Doing what's best for oneself and holding everyone else back so they can't pursue their dreams is not being a family."

"I haven't—"

"You've thought only about yourself, what you want and need. Not anyone else."

Zack tried to come up with a defense, but couldn't think of one. He rubbed his aching temples. Did that make him guilty?

"You had a rough time growing up, but having jerk parents doesn't give you the right to manipulate people so they do what you want. Stop hiding behind the past and deal with your feelings." She squared her shoulders. "It's advice I need to follow. I haven't been honest about my feelings. There's something you should know."

The hairs on the back of his neck prickled. "What?"

Charlie's eyes dulled. "That night you found out Davey had been killed and we kissed, I fell head over heels in love with you."

The words echoed through Zack's brain. He tried to make sense of what she said, but failed. "You fell in love with me?"

"Here comes the bride, naming our kids, crazy in love with you."

Damn. He swallowed. Rocked back on his heels. Thought about bolting. He scratched the stubble on his chin. "Why didn't you say something?"

"What could I say after learning about your rule? Crazy. Insane, I know." She half-laughed, then clasped her hands together. "Worse, I couldn't figure a way to get over you. So I went to Colorado for the winter."

He cursed. "You should have told me."

"Would anything have changed?"

A beat passed. And another. "No."

Her mouth twisted. "Then why have you kissed me when you have your rule and don't want a relationship?"

Zack felt heavy, as if he was wearing body armor. A part of him didn't want to answer, but she needed to hear this and he wanted to say the words aloud. "You're an amazing woman. Beautiful."

Charlie's facial expression didn't change. "There are lots of women like that."

Not like her. A lump burned in his throat. He'd screwed up. If he wasn't careful, he was going to lose... everything. "At the concert, I lost control. That's why I kissed you. In the meadow, I wanted to catch Arrow, but I wanted a kiss as much or more. I was thinking about what I wanted, being selfish, when I kissed you."

She stared at the river. "Did what I want or need ever enter in the equation?"

"No."

"Not surprised," she mumbled.

"I'm being honest."

"Me, too." She moistened her lips. "When I left last winter I wanted to see if distance would get me over you."

"Did it?"

"Yes. Until a couple weeks after I came back." Her gaze met his. "It's been hell ever since."

The anguish in her voice was a slap to his face. She'd been the one person who'd been there whenever he needed someone, and he'd hurt her. Unknowingly. But that didn't matter. He'd toyed with her emotions and her heart, all for his own selfish needs. Inexcusable.

"I had no idea. But what I did was wrong. I am sorry. Truly, I am."

He meant each word, but she didn't show any reaction. Her face remained blank, no emotion visible. His insides knotted.

"I don't know how I'll make this up to you, but I will. I promise." He reached for her.

She jerked away. "I can't do this anymore."

"Do what?"

She blinked. Once. Twice. "When Caitlin got engaged, I realized I didn't want to move to Colorado. But I was stuck here at the Bar V5 in a miserable state. I thought another man could get me over you, and lucky me, you had offered to help."

Damn. He couldn't imagine how that must have made her feel. "Charlie."

"Charlotte," she corrected with zero hesitation. "When you kissed me, I thought things might work out, but I see now that's not possible. You're the one who's stuck. Let's hope a new job gets me over you once and for all."

"No. I'm not stuck." The words shot out of his mouth like machine gun fire. He needed to make her understand what he was doing. "I've been trying to protect you."

From me.

A collage of his parents' mug shots, friendships with bail

bondsmen, never knowing what would happen and who might not come home played in his mind like a slideshow.

"I never meant to hurt you or put you through hell." His heart wanted to explode out of his chest. He forced himself to breath. "Don't leave the Bar V5 because of me."

"I'm not." Her gaze never wavered as she moved toward her horse. Charlie grabbed the reins and mounted Sierra. "I'm leaving for me."

SUNDAY AFTERNOON, THE awards had been presented to the champions, and the closing ceremony finished. The 76th Copper Mountain Rodeo had come to an end. Cowboys loaded trailers. Vendors packed up their booths. Tourists hit Main Street.

Waiting for Dan and Allie, Charlie stood next to one of the Bar V5's vans. She noticed the couples walking hand in hand. Was she the only single person in Marietta?

The ache inside her grew.

She was likely the only non-engaged woman in town with a stack of bridal magazines to review. Caitlin had given them to her earlier with Charlie's first maid of honor assignment—make notes and flag pages with western and Christmas themed wedding ideas.

This wasn't going to be an easy task. Every romantic image or song made her eyes burn. But for her friend, Charlie would do her best and get the job done. She had to admit she was relieved to be driving the Hathaways to their friend's house for dinner tonight. Not only could she avoid the magazines tonight, she wouldn't have to see Zack.

Out of sight, out of mind. She crossed her fingers.

Charlie hadn't been able to stop thinking about him. She didn't know who'd won during the finals, or made a crappy time, or been carted off on stretcher. But she could describe Zack's look of hurt that turned into shame while they'd spoken. She rubbed the back of her neck.

Nothing stood in their way of being together, nothing except Zack. She'd taken a chance today, been willing to sacrifice her job to be with him, but he wasn't willing to take that chance.

Her eyes stung, and she blinked until the sensation disappeared. No more tears. Time to face the truth. She'd had a problem herself with being honest—about her girly side, what she wanted in life, her feelings for Zack. But she'd overcome her fears and told the truth. But he couldn't do that—for whatever reason.

Someday, she would find what she was looking for—a love that was mutual, unconditional, everlasting—once she moved beyond the heartache and loss. Not that they'd been together, but she grieved the possibilities of what might have been. When she found someone else, she had a feeling he would be the exact opposite of Zack Harris.

"Charlie." Dan carried shopping bags in both hands. "We're so glad you were free tonight."

Allie held as many bags as her husband. "You specifically requested Charlie."

"That didn't mean we'd get her."

A smile tugged on Charlie's lips. At least the Hathaways would keep the mood light during the drive. Maybe they could distract her so she didn't think about Zack. "Let me help you."

She took their bags, placed their purchases in the back of the van, and then she climbed into the driver's seat. "Buckle up."

"You are so helpful, a horsewoman and an excellent tour guide," Allie said from the seat behind Charlie. "Is there anything you can't do?"

"Bake," Charlie said, half-jokingly. She turned the key in the ignition. "I mix up baking powder and baking soda, much to Rachel's chagrin. I won't be getting a job offer from her bakery anytime soon."

In the rearview mirror, she noticed the couple sharing a glance. Someday she would have that. Someday...

"This is going to sound like a non sequitur, but would you be interested in a new job opportunity?" Dan asked.

Charlie's pulse raced. She gripped the leather-covered steering wheel and focused on the road. "Depends on what it is."

She sounded calm, but her insides trembled.

"Yesterday morning at the pancake feed, I mentioned something about business."

She remembered him saying that. "Right before Rhett joined us."

Dan nodded. "Our visit to the Bar V5 this week is twofold. Pleasure but also scouting."

"Are you here to scout that football player from Marietta High? I can't remember his name but I hear he's got pro potential," Charlie said.

Allie grinned. "We're scouting you, dear."

"Me?" Charlie glanced at them in the rearview mirror. "You're from Silicon Valley. What do you need with a cowgirl?"

"Not us, but a close friend," Dan said. "He wants to hire someone to shadow his current horse manager who plans to retire in two years."

"Horses?"

"Heard of High Country Mustang Ranch?"

Charlie's mouth gaped. She lifted her foot off the accelerator to make sure she wasn't going over the speed limit. "That's one of the most reputable horse ranches in Montana."

Less than an hour from Marietta and Caitlin. Closer to the Bar V5, but as long as Charlie didn't have to see Zack... "What's the catch? Is it an internship?"

"No catch. The position is full-time. You will receive a salary, benefits, horse stall and cottage." Dan beamed. "Paddy

Killarney has been researching candidates for over a year. Someone in Colorado recommended you. Your foreman at the Bar V5, too."

Her heart slammed against her chest. "Ty?"

"Yes."

Wow. Charlie couldn't believe he'd done that. Ty had mentioned other places in Montana when they talked about her leaving. Had this been what he'd meant? She wondered if Zack knew, not that she cared. Or should care.

"Paddy wanted an independent assessment before meeting you. So he sent us," Dan said. "We go way back."

"I don't know what to say," she admitted. "I'm stunned."

"You'll love Paddy. Salt of the earth. Likes horses better than people."

Charlie couldn't believe this was happening. "Sounds like my kind of guy."

"He says you remind him of one of his granddaughters," Allie said.

"I can't wait to meet him." Charlie meant the words. This might be what she needed.

"You won't have to wait long," Allie said.

"About forty-five more minutes." Dan laughed. "We're having dinner at the High Country Mustang Ranch."

Ty had said he'd programmed the directions into the GPS. He must be for this job change if he'd given his recommendation and agreed to let her drive the couple to dinner.

"Okay, but..." Charlie's muscles tensed. "I'm not dressed for an interview."

"That's how Paddy wants it. To see you as you are."

An image of Zack appeared in her mind. Charlie swallowed around the lump in her throat. He'd never seen her. Not really. "This is..."

"Don't worry," Dan said. "See what you think of Paddy, the

facility, and job offer, then you can decide. There's no rush."

"Be happy. Smile," Allie advised. "This is a wonderful opportunity."

At the horse ranch forty-five minutes later, Charlie exited the van. She wasn't sure what impressed her more—the gorgeous mountain lodge or the tall, thin man with long, white hair and leathered skin standing on the massive front porch. Allie and Dan disappeared into the house, acting as if they'd been here before.

Charlie took a breath, straightened, then flexed her fingers.

The man—she assumed Paddy Killarney—walked down the steps to greet her. "Welcome to the High Country Mustang Ranch, Charlotte."

Unfamiliar contentment flowed through her. Strange, given she'd never been here before. But his knowing her real name impressed her. "Hello, Mr. Killarney."

"Please call me Paddy."

His handshake was strong and firm. No doubt like the man himself. His smile made her feel comfortable and welcome. "It's so nice to meet you, Paddy. Thanks for letting me visit your ranch."

"The pleasure is mine." His gray eyes twinkled. "Do you prefer to go by Charlotte or Lottie?"

His choice of names delighted Charlie. Tension seeped away. "Charlotte is fine."

He motioned to a stone path leading off to the left. "Would you like to see the horses?"

Anticipation soared. Maybe things happened for a reason, even if those things... hurt. She raised her chin and smiled. "I'd love to."

Chapter Nine

THE EVENING AIR up at cow camp nipped at Zack's face. He'd skipped the rodeo finals, afraid he might snap at some poor unsuspecting soul or one of the ranch guests. Instead, he offered to take a shift up at cabin and stay the night. He wore a headlamp though the sun hadn't fully set. But he didn't want to be caught in the dark. Not much moonlight tonight.

He stood at a watering station, checking the level after the hot day; thankful he had chores to do before bedtime. Sitting around the bunkhouse, drinking, punching his pillow, and missing Charlie would not be productive.

But damn, he missed her.

Hard to believe things had been going well between them until this morning. If her harsh words and glares were anything to go by, she hated him now.

That was his fault. Talk about clueless. Looking back he could see a couple signs—her asking about his rule, the looks she gave him. But in love with him?

Here comes the bride, naming our kids, crazy in love with you.

After what he'd pulled, he didn't blame her for no longer liking him. He walked back to the cabin, really a basic four-walled structure to keep the elements out.

Far below, a pair of headlights appeared on the ranch's

driveway. Guests or a wrangler? Zack would hear the stories tomorrow at lunch, on the porch, during a ride. Many stories were told at the Bar V5.

He only hoped Charlie was okay and still mad at him. Anger was easier to deal with than sadness. At least that had been his experience.

A calf ran after his momma.

Poor little guy didn't have any idea what was happening this week. Weaning time at the Bar V5.

Zack and the wranglers would move the herd on Tuesday, separating the calves from the cows. Some, like Mabel, would remain at the Bar V5. Others would be sold and transported away. The circle of life or, in this case, beef. This was the "working" part of the dude ranch not all guests understood or cared to know.

"Zack," Ty walked toward him. "Have a good day?"

Good wasn't how Zack would describe today, far from it. "What are you doing up here?"

"Checking in. Thought you might want some company tonight. You didn't seem yourself earlier."

"I'm…" He thought about holding Charlie in his arms and kissing her last night, then hearing her accusations this morning and seeing her disgust. "Been a bad day."

"Has to be woman trouble."

Frustration gnawed at Zack. "Charlie."

Ty cursed, something he did only on special occasions. "You said nothing was going on."

"It wasn't when we talked. This is… new. Well, old. Over before it began."

"So that's why you're moping like a weaned calf?"

"I'm… aw, hell. Yeah, I am."

A beat passed. And another. Ty's eyes darkened. "She drove Allie and Dan to the High Country Mustang Ranch for dinner.

Paddy Killarney is thinking about hiring Charlie."

Zack cursed. Twin calves ran to the opposite side of their momma. Any horsewoman would be tempted to take a position at a ranch with such a stellar reputation. "She probably has an offer in hand."

"Hope so, since that's the plan." Ty grinned proudly. "I'm expecting her to give two weeks' notice tomorrow."

Crap. Zack's heart lodged in his throat. He splashed water from the drinking container. "What the hell are you thinking?"

"That Charlie deserves better. She's an amazing horse trainer stuck in a dead-end job."

"The Bar V5 is not dead-end. Hell, you're part owner."

"Exactly," Ty agreed. "That's why she's stuck. No better job for her here. She'll never be foreman. My sister married my business partner. I'm not going anywhere."

Didn't matter. Zack was not letting her leave. "Charlie belongs here."

"She did, but her skills have increased and keep improving. Hell, she's teaching me things now. Time to put her knowledge to use. She's moved beyond wrangling cattle and guests on horseback. She should be running a horse barn, getting involved in breeding, and if Paddy Killarney is as smart a man as he seems to be, he'll offer her a job tonight."

Charlie would say yes. Dammit.

"You look like a bear woken in the middle of winter. What gives?" Ty sounded genuinely confused, matching the way Zack felt. "Be happy for Charlie. This is a once in a lifetime opportunity. Her future will be set."

A future without him. Zack struggled to breathe.

That night you found out Davey had been killed and we kissed, I fell head over heels in love with you.

Here comes the bride, naming our kids, crazy in love with you.

Her words rang through his head once again, as clear as

Philadelphia's Liberty Bell in 1776. Charlie had wanted to give him a once in a lifetime opportunity—her love unconditionally—and he'd turned her down, hadn't listened. Not really. He'd been too caught up in his own selfish needs.

Aw, hell. "I thought I'd screwed up, but I just realized how much."

Ty's looked at him. "With Charlie?"

"Big time. Epic."

A bell clanked in distance. A cow mooed. Dusty barked. The dog's job was to keep the herd from wandering off.

"What did you do?" Ty asked.

Maybe a better question would be what didn't Zack do. "I broke Charlie's heart. At least three times. I was never good at math so she might have a different count."

"Once wasn't enough?"

"Overachiever." Sweat coated Zack's scalp. He itched under his hat. "I messed with her heart and her life. Didn't know it at the time, but now… I think I love her." Something sliced deep within. "No, I'm positive I love her."

"Have you told Charlie how you feel?"

"I just figured it out myself, so the answer is no. But if she takes the job—"

"She won't be that far away." Ty frowned. "She deserves this opportunity, but don't make excuses or let a few miles keep you from going after what you want."

Too bad excuses weren't the only thing standing in Zack's way. "She hates me. No way she'll forgive or love me again."

"Let's go inside."

Zack followed Ty into the cabin. Lanterns hung from hooks. No electricity at cow camp, but the rustic bathroom had a shower with a propane water heater. Paying guests didn't mind roughing it a day or two for the experience. Most could live without cellular service. Few could live without daily hot showers.

The smell from the canned turkey chili lingered. Food was better—a real meal with courses including dessert—when guests were here. He sat at the dining table, a glorified picnic table. The fireplace was unlit. Zack would stay warm without a fire. No reason adding to the list of cleaning that needed to be done since cow camp was closing for the winter. Guests wouldn't be back until late spring.

"Here's the deal." Ty sat then handed Zack a bottle of water. No alcohol was allowed at the cabin. "Love isn't a switch you turn off and on, though I'm sure a few people wish it was. Even if you're mad at someone, you can still love them."

"She rode off and left me alone at the river. Pretty sure she wanted to punch me."

"Did you deserve it?"

Zack stared down at the table, feeling as if he were back in middle school and discovering girls for the first time. "Yeah, I did. Deserved to be knocked out."

"So apologize."

"I tried."

Ty's jaw jutted forward. "Try harder."

"She might not talk to me."

"What if she does?" Ty countered. "Do you want to live not knowing what might have been if you hadn't been afraid?"

"I'm not afraid." The words burst from Zack's mouth. "Okay, maybe I am."

"Only you can figure out what happens next, unless you're willing to give up and live with any regret you might have."

"I don't want more regrets where Charlie is concerned." Zack rubbed his thumb against his fingertips. She was the best thing that had happened to him, but he'd been too afraid of the past repeating itself to take a chance. "I have nothing else to lose and everything to gain."

"Go for it then."

A mishmash of thoughts circled through his brain. "Any idea how?"

Wind rattled the windows, but Ty didn't flinch. "You've worked with Charlie for two and a half years. Use what you know about her."

Zack downed his water. He'd known Charlie for that long, but he'd only met Charlotte. "That sounds... hard."

Ty's eyes gleamed with amusement. "Nothing worthwhile in life comes easy. That's what Nate's dad, Ralph, used to tell us. And so far, his words have proven true."

MONDAY MORNING ARRIVED with a burst of sunshine. Darn, Charlie squinted. She'd forgotten to close the blinds when she went to bed. She showered, then dressed, forcing herself to go through the motions. Last night, not wanting to appear impolite, she'd forced herself to eat dinner, but she had zero appetite for breakfast now.

Because of Zack.

Self-preservation?

Staying out of the dining room and kitchen lessened her chance of bumping into him. But she knew she couldn't avoid him forever. A couple more hours would be good, a couple days even better.

On the walk to the old red barn, her boots kicked up puffs of dirt. She yawned, stretching her arms overhead. She hadn't slept much due to a mixture of excitement, exhaustion, and a broken heart. But she wanted to keep her word and tell Ty her decision, even if she never had anticipated making this one.

A dream comes true?

Not the one she'd hoped for with Zack, but a dream job was still good. No, great. As Allie had said, this was a wonderful opportunity. Charlie agreed, even if her heart was torn on the point.

Inside the barn, two tabbies rescued from a hoarder situation near Bozeman darted between Charlie legs. She nearly tripped. The barn cats loved to chase one another. A good thing she hadn't fallen on her butt. That wouldn't have been the way to start her day. But then her backside would match her bruised heart.

The foreman's office door was open, as usual. The small room functioned more as a cattery than a working space. Ty's love of livestock extended to felines, and Nate was the same way, carrying cat treats in his pockets. A seven-foot tall cat tree occupied one corner. More than one sleeping cat occupied each perch. An electric fountain-drinking bowl, a new addition purchased by Rachel, would keep water from freezing in the wintertime.

Charlie hoped the barn cats—feral, non-indoor, and other non-adoptable ones—knew they'd hit the rescue lottery being taken in by the Bar V5. Between Ty, Nate, and the wranglers, the cats were well fed, healthy, and if they wanted human affection, given attention and love. She'd noticed a couple cats at the High Country Mustang Ranch last night. Another sign she was making the right move? She hoped so.

Ty sat behind his desk. A laptop was open and positioned around two cats sleeping. A stack of papers had been pushed off to the side.

She knocked on the door jamb.

Dusty peeked around the corner of the desk. He trotted over to greet her.

Ty looked up, smiled. "Didn't expect you so early since you were with Allie and Dan last night."

Charlie shrugged, but didn't feel indifferent. She curled and uncurled her toes. "I'm not used to sleeping in once a week, let alone two days in a row. Do you have a minute?"

Ty motioned her inside his office.

Charlie entered, stood behind a chair and held onto the back for support. Nerves threatened to get the best of her. She ignored the trembling sensations. She had no idea why her body was reacting this way when she knew in her heart of hearts this was the right decision.

"Something on your mind?" Ty asked.

Her heart pounded, loud and booming, like the fireworks shot off in Livingston on the 4th of July. "I've made my decision."

He leaned over the desk toward her. "And?"

"I'm staying in Montana, but leaving the Bar V5."

Ty's grin was a mile wide and as bright as the Las Vegas strip. "You're going to work for Paddy."

She nodded. "I wasn't sure how much you knew."

"Enough, and I'm happy for you. Nate is too." Ty's sincerity warmed her heart. "This is a fantastic opportunity. But you'll be missed. I hope you know that."

"I do. I'm going to miss everyone here." Especially Zack. Charlie stared at her hands on the back of the chair. She'd chipped her nail polish. "Thanks for the recommendation. Means a lot."

"You're a hard worker. Skilled. You earned the recommendation."

She beamed.

"You made the right decision," Ty continued. "You'll do great. And with you at the horse ranch, Nate might send Arrow."

"Oh, gee, thanks," she joked. "Instead of chasing him here, I'll get to there."

Laughing, Ty leaned back in his chair. A gray cat jumped on his lap. "Standard two week notice?"

She nodded, pulled out a resignation letter from her back pocket. "This makes my leaving official."

"Not necessary, but thanks." His gaze narrowed. "Are you wearing fingernail polish?"

She nodded, pleased he noticed. She'd painted her nails when she couldn't sleep last night. Normally she removed the polish from her hands and only left the toes.

He shook his head, a reaction that didn't surprise her. "I've known you since you were in high school. You've always seemed more comfortable hanging with the boys than any women, except Caitlin."

"That's true." Charlie accepted the blame for trying to fit in rather than be herself. "But it's time to let my inner cowgirl loose into the world."

"The world better watch out."

She grinned. "If you don't mind, I'd like to borrow a horse trailer to move Sierra over when the time comes."

"We'll help you move everything," Ty said warmly. "You and Sierra are part of the Bar V5 family. Always will be."

If only Zack understood that. A familiar sting burned Charlie's eyes. She blinked. "Thank you. For everything."

Each morning, Ty wrote a list of chores and projects needing to be done on a white board behind his desk. He pointed to number six. "Can you ride to the picnic area and see if there's a navy wind breaker? A guest lost one last night during a twilight ride after the rodeo."

"Sure thing." Charlie rubbed Onyx's side, happy to have something to do. If she didn't keep busy, her thoughts would be focused on Zack. She couldn't let that happen, not when she wanted to get over him. "I'll saddle up Sierra and head over there."

At the river, she secured Sierra to a post. Emotions churned within Charlie. She hugged her horse. The Bar V5 was home. No matter what she did or where she went, nothing would change that. She thought of this ranch as home and the people her family.

Including Zack.

Leaving wouldn't be easy. She'd moved in the day after high school graduation, and she'd been living in the women's bunkhouse since. She'd grown up here, but she couldn't stay.

This wasn't only about Zack. The High Country Mustang Ranch was a dream-come-true job. The facilities, including two covered, heated arenas, were hard to ignore. Not to mention the beautiful horses and the advancement potential. Turning down the offer had never entered her head.

Even if Zack had.

Don't think about him.

She searched the picnic area and edge along the river. No navy windbreaker. She would have to keep an eye out on the ride back.

Music.

Charlie listened closer, thinking she might be hearing the river. No, music played. The first song Jake Kohl had sung while she and Zack danced on Main Street.

Her chest tightened. Not with regret, but sadness over things between them ending so badly.

As if on cue, once again, Zack rode up on Blackbeard, wearing leather chaps over his jeans and a long duster. He looked like he'd ridden off an old western movie set, similar to a poster hanging next to her bed.

So hot. Her mouth went dry. Not the reaction she should be having to a guy who stomped on her heart… more than once.

A wireless speaker was attached to Blackbeard's saddle. Jake Kohl continued singing. She had no idea what Zack was doing.

But she never could figure him out. No reason to try now.

"Good morning." He extended his hand. "Care to dance?"

"Too little, too late, cowboy." She forced herself not to look him in the eye. "Dance by yourself. I'm leaving."

"Wait." He hopped off his horse then secured Blackbeard. "We need to talk."

She clung to Sierra. "We talked enough yesterday. Nothing more I need to hear you say."

"One minute." His contrite look made her place a hand over her heart. "Might take me five. Then you can leave. I promise."

His promises couldn't support the weight of a feather, but he rubbed his fingers together, the action he did when nervous.

She weighed the pros and the cons. Five minutes? She could stand here for that long without losing it completely.

Charlie crossed her arms over her chest. "Go."

He flinched, as if not expecting her to agree. One deep breath followed another, but he said nothing.

She tapped her toe, not caring if she were being mean or impatient. He'd hurt her. "Tick tock. You'll be down to four minutes soon."

"I love you."

She shook her head, blinked, unsure if she'd heard him correctly. "What did you say?"

"I love you." He blew out a puff of air. "I think I fell in love with the day I walked up the driveway looking for work."

Charlie's breath caught in her throat. She forced air in and out, afraid she might pass out or cry. "But you said…"

"I have no idea what I was talking about," Zack admitted. "That first day at the Bar V5, I hadn't been hired yet, but Ty took me for a tour of the ranch. We ended up in a pasture where you worked with a foal, Arrow."

His words touched her heart, something she believed was immune to his charm. "I don't remember that."

"You were completely focused on the foal." His smile transformed his face, erasing the lines of tension. "You kept laughing and smiling at Arrow. But you were the burst of sunshine I desperately needed. Since that day, you've continued to be that to me."

Her pulse sped faster than a champion barrel racer. "You never said anything."

"I had my rule, but there you were, and I never stopped feeling that way about you. I just got good at pretending. And hiding. Like you, Charlotte."

Her hands trembled. "I…"

"I'm the one who screwed up." He reached for one of her hands tentatively, as if waiting for her to pull her arm away. She didn't, and he laced his fingers with hers. "Forgive me. I know I don't deserve another chance, but I'd love one. If only to show you I'm not a complete idiot and that I mean what I say."

Each nerve ending tingled. She hadn't competed in vaulting or rodeo events in years, but she recognized the anticipation. She felt as if she was about to begin the next chapter of her life.

"I forgive you," she said.

"Thank you." He brushed his lips across hers in a tender kiss. "I won't let you down."

"No one is perfect. Just do your best. That's all any of us can hope for."

"You come pretty darn close to perfection."

"Not even," she admitted. "I've been so scared I'd end up multi-divorced because I was dating the wrong guy, I was afraid to date any potential Mr. Right, too."

"You fell for me."

"A guy with a rule about not dating coworkers. Not exactly setting myself up for dating success. We're an odd pair when it comes to relationship."

He embraced her. "We are. But that's what makes us good

for each other. How does being a couple sound?"

"Awesome." She couldn't believe this was happening. "My whole life I've wanted to fit in. But I know where I belong, next to you."

His smile brightened his face. "Ty told me about your job. Congrats."

She studied him. "You mean that."

"I do." He sounded sincere. "You'll make one helluva horse barn manager."

"It's a lovely place. You'd like it." She wet her lips. "I have my own cottage."

"I can't wait to check it out. See you in action. Go out on a few official dates."

She lifted a brow. "A few."

"Many."

"Better."

He hesitated, rubbed her hand with his thumb. "What I said about not wanting a family?"

Charlie held her breath.

"I've changed my mind," he continued. "I wanted a family so badly I built one here at the ranch. I've tried to protect and care for that family, but not in a good way. You were right. I've realized I can't hold on too tight. Sometimes you have to let go and love people, no matter what. I'm not my parents. I don't have to be like them. I can have the life I want."

She blew out a rush of air, and then embraced him. Joy overflowed from her heart, making the rush of river water in the distance sound that much sweeter. "I love you."

"I love you, too."

"Everything she'd dreamed about for the past year was hers for the taking. No more fantasies, only reality now. And the future...

The future had never looked brighter. Her mother had been

correct when she'd told Charlie never give up because dreams could come true.

"Remember who said it first today," he added.

She winked. "Remember who kissed you first."

"Oh, I won't ever be able to forget. The time, the place, you." His charming grin made her want to fall into his arms and stay there. "Kiss me, cowgirl."

And she did.

THE END

Please Me, Cowboy

A Montana Born Rodeo Novella

Megan Crane

Chapter One

~

H E WAS MUCH, much worse up close.

Gracelyn Packard had worked for noted billionaire Jonah Flint for a year now, going about her business happily unnoticed in the swathe of lower level employees who made up his entrepreneurial think tank in Dallas. But this peremptory summons to appear before him, deep in his lion's den of an office, was different.

This verged on terrifying—and Gracelyn was not easily intimidated. She'd ejected that from her system years ago. If she hadn't, she never would have made it out of her dead-end prairie town and her family with no aspirations extending beyond the greater limits of Custer County, Montana. To say nothing of its crowning joke of a would-be metropolis, tiny little Miles City.

But something about Jonah Flint set her teeth on edge, made her skin seem to shrink tight against her bones, made her nearly shiver in unexpected reaction to his proximity. Made her the kind of restless she associated with the sudden, shocking summer thunderstorms of her childhood out there on the Great Plains, hot and electric and *lethal*. She tried to stand a little bit straighter, wishing she hadn't worn the most perilous pair of stilettos she owned today, even as she ordered herself to keep from fidgeting.

She would *not* smooth her hands down over the deceptively simple shift dress she wore. She knew it was exquisitely tailored to look both feminine and professional at once; that's why she'd bought it in the first place. She would *not* check to make sure her long, dark hair was still neatly arranged in its slicked back, high ponytail. She paid a lot of her hard-earned salary for the high-end products that ensured not a single strand of her thick hair dared defy her, no matter the Texas humidity outside on a late summer day like this one, still broiling and sweaty hot in September.

She would not act like this man's prey, here in this frigidly cold office that catered to the suit he wore and only added to her unease. Not that it mattered how she felt inside. She would not act, ever again, like she was *less than* anyone, despite a long, poor childhood that had taught her she'd never be anything but.

No matter, if that was exactly how it felt to stand there in the center of Jonah Flint's loft-like, steel-accented and sunlit office as he sprawled behind his massive desk like the king she supposed he was, all of his formidable and breathtaking and notoriously dangerous attention trained directly on her.

He was more than six feet of lean, lethal muscle packed into a very, very rich man's suit. He had dark blonde hair cut short to accentuate the poetic asceticism of his narrow, intelligent face. And his mouth was a grim, hard line that made her insides quake and roll as he trained his dark, brooding hazel gaze directly on her.

He's beautiful, she thought, almost dreamily, as if she couldn't help herself.

Gracelyn was instantly horrified with herself.

He was her boss. He was her boss's boss's boss. He was *Jonah Flint,* for God's sake! She might as well find the sheer, dizzying face of a remote mountain attractive, and he was about as approachable besides.

And his shocking male beauty was the last thing anyone was likely to notice about him, anyway. That air of barely-leashed ferocity, of all that power and influence he wielded precisely as he pleased and in that particularly grim way of his, was the first and last thing that Gracelyn had ever noted about him before now from the great distance of her low-level analyst's position.

He was her boss, but he was so much more than that, she could see now that she was much too close to him. He was dangerous beyond measure, which she could *feel* in her bones like some kind of sudden-onset arthritic ache. And he was looking at her as if she was very small and very, very breakable. She knew she was neither, but then, who knew what could happen should he choose to wield even the smallest bit of all the power she could practically *see* surrounding him? He was like a storm cloud.

Or a premonition, the fanciful part of her that she'd been so certain she'd left behind in that barely-there town far outside Miles City more than a decade ago whispered, horrifying her even further.

Making her feel like an alien in her own body—or maybe that was just the way her heart hit at her ribs, low and slow and nearly as overwhelming as he was.

"You're from Montana," the great Jonah Flint said, Texas in his voice and an assessing gleam in his gaze. He didn't stand. He didn't sit any straighter in his throne-like CEO's chair. He didn't give an inch, as unyielding as the great granite desk he sat behind. And of all the things Gracelyn had imagined this lion of the business world might say to her one day when her business acumen and dedication gained his notice, as she'd been determined it would, *that* was not it.

That had not even been on the list.

"I am, yes." Gracelyn's voice sounded strange in the great room then, too prim and too forced. Clear indications of the nerves she knew better than to let a man like this see. She would *not* pretend to clear her throat when it was only her sudden, unmanageable embarrassment that needed clearing. She would *not* avert her gaze from his, look meekly at the floor like some submissive thing desperate for his approval, or show him in any way how much he got to her. She knew better than that. Powerful men respected power above all things. Gracelyn knew that the way she knew her lungs would fill with her next breath.

"Good." *His* voice was like the rest of him. *Unyielding,* she thought, and granite besides. His sharp hazel gaze was the same as it swept over her, from head to toe and then back, while she told herself she had no reaction to that. None at all. "You'll do."

"I'll do?" she repeated, like an idiot. But she couldn't seem to help herself—something she'd have to think about later, when she had the space to analyze whatever the hell this was. "I'll do what?"

Some kind of awareness sharpened in the air between them then. Something thick and hot, though Jonah still didn't so much as move a muscle. Only those gleaming eyes of his changed; darkened. And suddenly, Gracelyn felt as if there was no space between them at all, and certainly not the great heft of that dark, imposing desk of his that should have felt like half the state of Texas or more.

It didn't feel like any kind of barrier at all. It might as well have been a sunbeam, for all the protection it granted her. She couldn't breathe.

And Gracelyn had never been any good with feeling trapped. It had always made her angry, as her entire childhood and teenaged years as one of those low-class, ill-bred Packards could testify. At length. Worse than angry. The feeling of claustrophobia—of too many low expectations and no hope she'd ever exceed them—had always made her mouthy. That particular combination had been the impetus for, among other things, her hasty departure from her middle-of-nowhere hometown about four seconds after she'd graduated from high school. It had gotten her into more trouble than she cared to recall.

Today, in this man's office, even feeling that old sensation return in the way her hands itched to curve into fists, was damn near suicidal. She knew that. Of course she *knew* that.

"You'll do whatever I want," he drawled, and his voice was like a touch, seductive and demanding at once. She would *not* react to it. "Isn't that what I pay you for?"

"You pay me for my willingness to work well over eighty hours a week and forgo any semblance of a normal life," Gracelyn retorted, unwisely. She knew it was ill-advised even as she said it, but that didn't help her stop. It never had. "Somehow, I don't think that's what we're talking about here."

She had the sensation of the world shifting beneath her, and she knew what it was: the glorious future, far away from her mess of a family, that she'd busted her ass to create as it spiraled off into nothing because she couldn't keep her big mouth shut.

You're going to get yourself into trouble with that mouth, her grandmother Betty had told her a thousand times if she'd told her once. *Maybe, one day, the kind of trouble you can't turn off, either.*

Jonah rose then, more than six feet of trouble in a sleek black suit, and she wished he hadn't. God help her, him *sitting* was bad enough. She watched, fascinated and apprehensive at once, as he uncurled his long, hard body from that chair and got to his feet in a simple sort of *uncoiling* that shouldn't have made her pulse skyrocket. He smoothed his hand down the front of his suit jacket and *he* did not look the least little bit like prey when he did it.

Beautiful, she thought again, and it was worse this time because she *felt* it—him—everywhere. Like he'd run that hard palm of his down the length of her spine.

"I've read your file," he told her after a moment of shrewd hazel consideration that made her think he'd felt it too, that spark of sensation that still bloomed a path down her back. But that was crazy. "You're ambitious."

"I prefer the term 'dedicated,'" Gracelyn demurred, though a wise woman would have long since shut the hell up. Well. She'd never claimed to be wise. Just much too stubborn for her own good. A trait she'd heard called *hard-headed* more than once.

"I like ambition. And I like that you have balls." Jonah eyed her, that mouth of his far more intriguing than it should have been, when he hardly let it move outside that same set, unimpressed and impatient line. It warmed her almost as much as his praise did. "Most employees at your level who get called in here fall apart right where you're standing. Stammering, flushing, apologizing all over themselves before I say a single word."

He liked that she hadn't done any of that. She didn't know how she knew that, but she did. Like pure, incontrovertible fact. Like that same warm spark, still spreading its lick of flame and bad decision-making all through her.

"Is that why you like to wait a minute or so before you speak?" she asked, and her voice wasn't *tart*, exactly. It wasn't that she was *teasing* him, which would have been crazy. But she didn't sound particularly deferential, either. "To see if you might have to call in the paramedics?"

She still hadn't looked away from him. And she'd have sworn on a stack of her grandmother's collection of family bibles that what moved over his face then, a mere shine in his eyes and a ghost on his lips, was a smile. And there was absolutely no reason why she should feel that the way she did, like a flare of dark heat. Like fire, everywhere, especially in the places it shouldn't have been.

Like a whole lot of trouble, a wise woman would run away from.

But Gracelyn dug her heels into the floor beneath her, because she'd been a lot of things in her twenty-nine years, but *wise* had never been one of them. Clearly.

"I need to spend some time in Wherever-the-Fuck, Montana," Jonah told her in the next moment, that hint of a smile gone as if it had never been.

Yet, Gracelyn could still feel that intense heat. There was that earthquake rolling, deep within her, every time his gaze met hers, and it didn't appear to be going anywhere. *Nothing but trouble,* she reminded herself—but then again, that might as well have been the Packard family's call to arms. Maybe she'd been kidding herself all this time, thinking she was any different from the rest of them.

She smiled politely rather than turning and running from the room, which would have been the smart thing to do. "I don't think I've heard of it."

A glint of gold in those brooding hazel depths. "It's a family matter that requires my personal attention and a week or two of my time." He waited a moment, his gaze never shifting from hers. "That's where you come in."

Gracelyn blinked. "And you need me, a random employee you've never met before, to help you handle a personal family matter because . . .?"

"I don't need you. I need a Montana native who knows how to work a small Montana town in general and one small town Montana woman in particular." That gaze of his swept over her, leaving brushfires everywhere it touched. It was a warning and a punishment, a terrible temptation all at once, and that was before his mouth crooked and wrecked her completely. "I need a girlfriend."

JONAH FLINT WAS pissed before he left the Dallas city limits.

He'd been irritated ever since his twin brother Jasper's phone call—or really, if he was honest, ever since Jasper had left Dallas and their old, insanely profitable well stimulation and hydraulic fracturing services company behind for no good reason a couple of years back.

By the time he hauled himself all the way to Marietta, Montana, slap down on the outskirts of absolutely nowhere he'd ever want to go willingly—much less settle down permanently, as his twin had unaccountably done—Jonah had moved far beyond *pissed* into brand new territory.

And the woman beside him wasn't helping his mood any. She'd flown with him from Dallas and now rode with him in the back of the Range Rover in what looked like a perfectly composed, perfectly calm silence she could maintain until the seas rose. Damn her.

If he was bothered—and since Jonah tried to be honest with himself, he could admit that he was a whole lot more than *bothered* by this woman with all that heat in her eyes and that enigmatically cool smile on her lips—he thought she should be, too. It only seemed fair.

Beside him, she shifted slightly on the leather seat, her eyes on what even Jonah could grudgingly admit was a pretty view of the nearest mountain range, and he really didn't need to be any *more* aware of her. But just like that, he was.

Of all his employees, only three had fit his criteria: female, raised in small town Montana, and within a reasonable age range of his thirty-six years. The first had been much too young for him. Worse, she'd been completely overawed in his presence, meaning Jasper would have spotted her as a bright red-faced ringer from a mile away. The second had been great on paper, but hadn't fit the sort of physical requirements Jonah had always historically had for the women he slept with. That meant that since Jonah wasn't actually head over heels for her, his damned brother would see right through that, too.

Which had left only this one. The most intriguing and disconcerting woman he'd encountered in ages, and also the perfect person for the job.

Jonah had spent the past few days telling himself that Gracelyn, from God Only Knew Where, Montana, merely fit his requirements. On paper, as well as in person. That *fitting the requirements* was enough. That this little adventure would take the two weeks he'd allocated to sort out his twin brother's monumental stupidity. And that she fit into his plans smoothly and easily, which was all he'd wanted.

I don't expect you to understand emotion, Jonah, his brother had drawled in that all-too-amused way of his that Jonah had detested since they'd been kids. Because neither one of them had ever been that amused about anything. *But I do expect you to show up and pay your respects anyway. If you think you can handle that kind of human interaction.*

Jonah could damn well handle anything. That was why he'd tripled his already excessive fortune in the last two years, while his twin brother was off playing Messiah of the Microbreweries in his little small town hiding place. But he was good at leverage. And it had occurred to him that a girlfriend on his arm would prove things to Jasper in a way his bank balance could not. Especially since Jasper apparently no longer saw the point of money, and had decided he was more into marrying more gold-diggers instead.

His mercenary first wife—who now lived in Jasper's old Preston Hollow house in Dallas with Jasper's replacement—had been bad enough.

Jonah didn't understand any of this. But, he knew his twin. And he knew what he had to do to rescue the idiot from his mid-life crisis. So what, if Jasper honestly believed his slide into irrelevance was "happiness?" It was pathetic, was what it was.

He was *Jasper Flint*, not merely Jonah's brother, but his identical twin. He was meant for better things than some nowhere town and a *schoolteacher*.

But the pleasant anticipation of the good deed he planned to do for his befuddled twin didn't quite explain the hum of something a little too much like excitement he'd felt when his secretary had buzzed this woman into his office. Gracelyn Baylee Packard of the country-fried name and exemplary resume.

A whole lot like Jonah himself, not that he was making comparisons with underlings he planned to use for his own purposes. He'd been rocked when she'd strode into his office that afternoon, all long legs in killer heels and that sulky mouth he'd been unable to stop imagining under his. That smooth, silken fall of dark hair that she was still wearing in a precise and perfect ponytail today, which gave him the nearly ungovernable urge to bury his fingers in it and see what kind of mess he could make of her. She'd almost made him laugh and God knew, Jonah didn't laugh about much these days.

He'd thought of nothing but the flash of temper in her dark brown eyes when he'd issued his orders. He'd had piles of work to get through on the trip here but had spent far more time than he cared to acknowledge studying the way her jeans clung to the sweet, taut curve of her hip. And he seemed to be the only person in the vehicle who was bothered by anything, which, in turn, bothered him that much more.

Jonah couldn't explain any of it.

He glared out the window at the wide place in the road his twin unaccountably called home, and focused on that indignity instead.

"Look at this place," he muttered. "What the hell is he thinking?"

"Paradise Valley is widely held to be one of the most beautiful places in the world," his fake girlfriend replied. "Maybe that's what he's thinking."

Her voice didn't sound rusty from disuse, though she hadn't done anything but smile politely since she'd met him at his airfield in Dallas. Her voice sounded the way it had in his office that day. Smooth, with hints of the personality she wasn't quite sharing with him. And he had the strangest sense that if he wasn't careful she could slide in and around all the barriers he kept around him to keep other people at arm's—

Hang on. What was wrong with him? He wasn't *dating* Gracelyn. He'd hired her to perform a task with very clear parameters.

You are to act as my girlfriend and I'll pay you triple your salary to make it worth your while, but you need to remember at all times that you're my employee, he'd told her curtly when she'd sat down across from him the seating area in his office. When she hadn't turned and run out of the room, or started talking about lawsuits and/or psychiatric help after he'd told her he needed a girlfriend. *That means I make the rules.*

I'm unlikely to forget that, Mr. Flint, she'd replied, with that flash in her dark eyes he'd been unable to get out of his head since. Yet her voice had remained perfectly courteous and damn her, he'd been fascinated. He still didn't know why.

For starters, you need to call me Jonah. He'd imagined he'd seen a kind of heat in that level gaze of hers then, though she'd blinked it away.

And what are the physical requirements? she'd asked in the same cool tone. *Because I'm willing to do many things to succeed in business, Jonah, but the boss isn't one of them.*

He hadn't known what he'd enjoyed more in that moment. The way she'd emphasized his name—an obvious poke at him, when he couldn't remember the last time someone other than Jasper had dared—or the fact she'd thrown that card on the table first and fast?

Some people in this company and hell, all over this country, spend a whole lot of time contorting themselves to try to get in my pants, he'd murmured instead of answering her. *I think I might be insulted.*

I have this thing about not wanting to sleep with someone who signs my paychecks, she'd replied, that sulky mouth tipping over into a little smile that he could feel in his pulse, in his blood, everywhere. He still could. *I call it 'aversion to prostitution.' I know, I know. I'm weird.*

Later, Jonah would reflect on the sad fact that this bizarre conversation was the most fun he'd had with a woman in years. And he hadn't exactly spent that time working on his chastity belt. He liked sex. But it had all started to blend together, like so many of the workouts he seemed to do on autopilot these days.

Gracelyn wouldn't blend, he'd understood immediately, right there in his office. She didn't. Gracelyn felt like a burst of electricity and Jonah had gotten much too used to the dark.

But then, back in their first meeting, he'd only considered her for a long moment.

It has to be convincing, he'd finally said. *I'd imagine all that really means is potentially kissing me in public, at its most extreme. Can you handle that?*

She'd studied him instead of answering. Then, as the moment stretched out, it had occurred to Jonah that she might actually turn him down. He hadn't had the vocabulary to describe the half-baffled, half-furious thing that had rolled through him at the notion. Nor could he recall the last time he'd worried that someone might reject him. In work or play.

Yes, she'd said. Eventually. Succinct and to the point, her expression unreadable. *I think I can handle that.*

He stared at her across the backseat of the Range Rover now, the little western town Jasper had claimed was *the jewel of Montana* forgotten as he focused on her instead.

It was a little too easy to focus on her.

"You're playing my girlfriend," he told her, with perhaps

unnecessary roughness, but he decided she could take it. That she would. "That means you don't disagree with me."

"Have you ever had a girlfriend before?" she asked dryly, but sat a bit straighter when his eyebrows rose. "I'm sorry. I meant, yes, Jonah. This is a terrible place. Awful. The Rocky Mountains are hideous in all directions and that river was much too wide and picturesque in all of this annoying September sunshine. What a nightmare."

"Better," he murmured, his attention moving to that too-smart, too-sulky mouth. "But without the attitude, please. My brother knows I would never date a woman who argues too much."

"Why not? Afraid she'll win?"

She looked faintly astonished at herself, as if her mouth was working of its own accord, and maybe that was why he reached over and took that pretty little chin of hers in his hand. He told himself he was teaching her something when he held it fast.

That the fire that roared through him at even that little bit of contact was a mild thing. A tiny flame. Barely more than a spark and hardly worth noting.

And that he was a freaking saint for not touching that damned mouth of hers.

Or tasting it. At length.

"I don't want a debate." He said it slow and even rougher, so there could be no mistake. "I want a date."

"But the debate part is why a date is fun," she argued, and her voice went a little hoarse. There was a hectic thing in her dark eyes that he could feel clawing into him, as well.

Jonah knew he should let her go. He knew he was letting the emotions only his twin ever stirred up get to him. That this was stupid and worse, breaking the guidelines he'd laid down himself. They weren't where anyone could see them tucked up in the back of his Range Rover with its tinted windows. This wasn't public, or for Jasper's benefit.

But he only shifted closer to her. He could smell the faint hint of perfumed almonds that he assumed was her shampoo and it should have worried him, the deep, hard punch of lust that slammed through him at the delicate scent.

"Debating is what complicated women do when what they really want is to get naked," he told her instead, lazily, and he still held her in his grip while he did it. "They want a man who can keep up with them verbally. They think it means he can do the same in bed. They want to be convinced." He forced his attention away from that *mouth*, but those eyes of hers weren't much of an improvement. Too dark, too clever. A little too hot on his. "I'm more straightforward."

"Are you?" she asked softly. "Or is it that you're one of the ones who can't keep up?"

And if he didn't know better, because it would mean she had some kind of death wish, Jonah would have said she was teasing him. Maybe even flirting with him.

The only thing more insane was that he was doing the same damn thing.

"I either get naked or I don't," he corrected her, and he was still holding onto that delicate jaw of hers while he said it. He was still much too close. "And I don't talk around it."

"I'm trying to imagine that. The famous Jonah Flint flinging off his clothes in a romantic restaurant, rather than having the usual charged, innuendo-laden conversation the rest of us mere mortals like to call *banter* and sometimes even *foreplay*. I feel certain that kind of display would have made it into the papers, don't you?"

He didn't understand what moved in him then, or why he still hadn't let go of her, or why, if he was as straightforward as he'd just claimed he was, he didn't do something about the need that clawed at him. He could think of three things he'd like to do, then and there, that would take the edge off. But he didn't.

"I don't date much—"

"What a shock."

He ignored her dry tone. "I have mutually beneficial evenings, most of which take place in private."

"Be still my heart."

"I don't play games, Gracelyn." Was that the first time he'd called her by her name? It was the first time he'd said it, while he was touching her, and that jolted through him. He saw it in her, too. The awareness he'd felt in his office shimmered between them. It filled the Range Rover, blocking out the little town on the other side of the windows, and that needy thing dug into him, deeper and harsher. "Want to revise the parameters we set?"

Our physical relationship will be a performance, she'd clarified primly, sitting across from him on the leather couch where his accountants talked numbers and he'd conducted all manner of boring business meetings. *Is that correct? Something for your brother's benefit, to convince him you're capable of relationships even while you disapprove of his. To summarize.*

He hadn't liked the way she'd put that. But. *Yes,* he'd gritted out.

So, in private, we will remain perfectly professional with each other. Business colleagues, nothing more.

You will remain my subordinate, yes, he'd said. Maybe he'd needed the reminder.

In a professional sense, she'd retorted. *Of course.*

And they'd agreed.

She looked dazed now, as if she'd forgotten all of that until he'd mentioned revising it, and then she tugged her head back. Jonah let go of her chin a second later, and he told himself he was glad. That he'd been pushing her, hoping she'd balk. That this had to work within the boundaries they'd set in Dallas, or it wouldn't work at all.

That the need and the fire in him had nothing to do with anything, and should be ignored.

"No," she said, too quickly, which he shouldn't feel like a victory. "I don't want to revise anything."

The Range Rover pulled up to the curb of an old train depot, tricked out into something much newer and more appealing, with the name FLINTWORKS stamped into its side. Jonah scowled at it. Then back at her. His for the next two weeks, and he liked the feel of that a little too much. *His.*

"Fine," he said shortly. "Then, resign yourself to your role as my significantly less argumentative girlfriend. Do you remember why we're here in this ridiculous place?"

There was something like mutiny in her dark gaze then, and he expected her to balk, but she nodded instead. "Tell me."

She glanced away and pulled in a breath, but she was composed and distant all over again when she looked back at him a moment later. She even smiled that same polite, professional smile he'd seen in his office when she'd shaken his hand and thanked him for considering her for this project, like it was freaking corporate contract.

And Jonah told himself that was just as well. That she *should* hide behind her professional mask, if she had one. That it was better. He decided he could blame Jasper for that, too.

"We're here to break up your brother's inappropriate engagement," she said, her tone completely unobjectionable. Jonah might think it was for the best, but that didn't stop him loathing it. "In the tradition of many a concerned relative, I'd imagine."

"Correction. To stop his engagement before it starts. Jasper plans to propose two weeks from now at some cavity-inducing small town rodeo event, which apparently holds some emotional significance for the two of them. I shudder to think why. I, therefore, plan to have him safely back in Texas and deprogrammed before he can make that kind of mistake. He already married one cold, money-grubbing bitch. I can't stand by and watch him do it all over again."

Jonah stared at her until Gracelyn nodded her assent, almost as if he wasn't paying her for her obedience, and when she did he jerked his chin toward the car door.

"Come on, honey," he murmured, the endearment coming out of nowhere and nearly making him smile, especially when she flinched in surprise at the sound of it. "Let's do this."

Chapter Two

GRACELYN DIDN'T THINK Marietta was ridiculous.
She dutifully climbed from the SUV, then stood there
on the sidewalk in the September sunshine with the mountains
scraping into the bright blue sky and the pretty little town a
happy, vibrant thing all around her. If she'd grown up in a place
like this, maybe it would have encouraged different behavior on
the part of her immediate relatives and maybe she wouldn't have
left them in such a hurry, she thought. Maybe she would have
gone back since. Maybe everything would be different.

Maybe she wouldn't be swamped with an emotion she didn't
recognize, deep and dark and melancholy, as she took in the big,
big sky that stretched out above her. She felt wondrously small
and precious beneath it, in a way she hadn't in over a decade.
The sensation washed through her and she swayed slightly on
her feet.

It filled her up. It was as big as all that arching blue, vast and
breathtaking. It felt like grief.

Homesick, a voice inside of her stated, plain and matter-of-
fact, the way her grandmother Betty might have if she'd been
standing at Gracelyn's side. *That's what you call it. That's what it is,
love.*

Homesick, of all things, when Gracelyn had never looked

back. Not once, in all these years. When she'd never missed a single thing about the place she'd come from. When the only things she'd kept with her from those dusty, heartbreaking years were the old boots on her feet right now and a few of her grandmother's fattiest and best recipes.

She couldn't be homesick. It didn't make sense. She'd never liked her parents' home very much, for one thing, which was why she'd gone to live with her grandmother when she'd been ten. That and her parents' arrests. This was nothing but an unexpected reaction to being back in Montana after so long. It had to be that, however surprising. Because Marietta was nothing like the battered old town—in truth, a wide, unmarked area on the map at the end of a country road featuring little more than a collection of failed farms and ruined lives—she'd been forced to call home.

The houses and storefronts weren't all boarded up, for one thing. There was the grand old hotel they'd be staying in just down the street. And there'd been enough cars parked as they'd driven down Main Street to suggest actual commerce, rather than a handful of sad, broken old men telling each other lies about their prospects outside the local bar. She'd seen mowed green grass and the kinds of flowers in the fronts of the buildings that spoke of care, of dedication, of pride. Marietta wasn't a ghost town. It wasn't dead. If Gracelyn listened closely, she could almost *hear* it thriving. The only thing she'd ever heard in the place she'd grown up was that bitter wind, blowing in cold from the northern Plains and leaving nothing but emptiness and regret behind.

She pressed the heel of her hand against her chest and told herself she didn't remember a thing.

Not those endless Sundays, filled with the mandatory church service that was the family requirement for sampling her grandmother's cooking in that careworn farmhouse a hundred miles from nothing. Not the long, lazy summer afternoons bleeding into endless evenings while she waited for something, anything, to change, to get better. Not all those years running half-wild with her cousins in the fields and down to the creek. Or the silly songs her cousin and best friend Bex had created to make the barn chores bearable. Or that particularly sweet scent of the changing season that hung in the air over the prairie after a long, hard winter, when spring still seemed like a far-off fairy tale wise folks knew better than to believe in.

Gracelyn didn't remember, damn it. She refused.

But then Jonah climbed out behind her and Gracelyn stopped thinking about her painful past and all the people she'd left behind her on a ramshackle plain far to the east. Because Jonah Flint was formidably attractive and deeply problematic, but still a far more appealing prospect than her personal history. And she'd agreed to touch him and kiss him in certain public scenarios before she'd known that a simple touch of his hard fingers to her chin could send her spinning.

Her *chin*. And he wasn't touching her any longer, yet she was still spinning.

Gracelyn made herself smile up at him. It was much harder than it should have been through the big sky cartwheels and old regrets inside her head, and he didn't make it any easier when he only stared back down at her, intense and grim. And, there was no getting around it, too damned beautiful to bear.

She'd assured herself that he was one of those executive types who'd look stiff and vaguely silly in casual clothes. Too much the corporate shark to take to faded jeans and cowboy boots, or the soft button down shirt he wore that strained against the smooth muscles of his biceps and clung to the hard planes of his chest. But instead, he looked . . . good. Entirely too good. His hazel eyes were hot, his mouth was firm, and everything else was hard and muscled and mouthwatering.

And she had the great hardship of having to pretend she was his girlfriend and getting paid for her sacrifice besides. *Boo freaking hoo.*

She told herself *that* was why she felt so overheated, despite the hint of crispness in the air, far more fall than leftover summer this far north of Dallas. That it was her upcoming performance that was getting to her, not her panicked worry that she might slip and forget she was supposed to be *pretending.*

Jonah reached over and took her hand in his. And this was an act, she reminded herself as their palms scraped together and sent wildfires storming through her, burning away all the shadows of her past, as if they were little more than mist and he the heat of a red-hot, high summer day. He watched her as if she fascinated him, as if he could see every single thing she'd hidden away inside her, if he studied her long enough.

And some part of her believed that he could. That he already did.

Gracelyn couldn't allow that. She'd left those lost country roads and the terrible disappointments of her family behind her for a reason, no matter her reaction to being back in the same state as all of them now.

"I don't like *honey*," she said. Because she had to speak then, or she'd tip forward into him and then maybe lose herself off of the side of the planet, and that was what came out. It had the added benefit of being true.

His dark hazel eyes glinted. "I take it you aren't offering me your thoughts on natural sweeteners."

"It sounds old-fashioned. Forced." Unlike the way his hand folded over hers, as if they'd been crafted to come together like that, but she wasn't thinking anything so insane. Of course she wasn't. "Two septuagenarians pretending to be hip for the young folks."

"What about *babe?*"

She mock-shuddered. "Chauvinistic at best."

"*Darlin*?" She shook her head and she saw that ghost of a smile on his hard mouth, there and then gone again in an instant. "Then you should probably brace yourself. I'm Texan born and raised. *Darlin's* going to come on out from time to time whether you like it or not. *Sweetheart*?"

"That might as well be an ad for a terrible Valentine's Day movie desperate singletons drag their bored dates to, little realizing the men are only putting up with the make believe holiday in the first place, because they don't want to be That Guy Who Broke Up with Her on Valentine's Day, like some Taylor Swift song."

"Not that you've given it any thought."

She eyed him, and that bland look he trained on her. "I'm an analyst. I analyze."

"You sure do. How about *baby*?"

"That's demeaning, obviously." Gracelyn started to scowl at him, then remembered her role here was to be obliging and sweet and yielding, not scowly, especially where someone could see them. Which was why she smiled sunnily when she continued. "Maybe you should ask yourself why you'd *want* to use an icky diminutive for a grown woman?"

Another twitch of that harsh mouth, a gleam of dark gold in his eyes, and he used his free hand to wrap hers tighter in his. "Because it's an endearment, not a rant. It's about sex and affection, Gracelyn. Not politics."

Gracelyn had never before had occasion to think too closely about the use of endearments, much less her feelings on the topic. So she couldn't have said why the subject was suddenly of such critical importance to her. It blocked out everything else. The past she'd left behind so deliberately, cutting off everything she'd known before she was eighteen with surgical precision. Her current geographic location a mere two hundred and fifty miles or so west of what had once been her family's farm and how edgy that made her. The brilliant sensation of his warm, hard fingers threaded through hers, indistinguishable from all that Montana sky so blue and bright above them.

Her voice was a little more husky than it should have been, then. "What's wrong with my name?"

"Couples have secret languages."

Jonah tugged on her fingers, raised them up to his mouth and then, horribly and inevitably and marvelously, set his mouth against her knuckles. It wasn't a kiss. It was a press of her knuckles against the hard line of his mouth, as if in thought. As if her hand was an extension of his. It spoke of an intimacy her body rushed to accept, to make real. It soared through her, leaving a hollowness, a deep and atavistic longing, in its wake. And it was another kind of grief, because, of course, it wasn't real. It couldn't be real.

"Endearments are a part of that," he said, his mouth moving against her skin. "An easy part."

"Endearments are organic," Gracelyn retorted, shaken and off-kilter and not sure how to go about getting her balance again. "They can't be flung around like this, hoping one sticks, three seconds before we walk into bar and try to play off this completely fake relationship for an audience."

She was careful to keep her expression far blander than what was happening inside of her—one of the finest lessons her childhood had taught her, now she thought about it. They'd never expected her to up and leave, no matter the scholarship she'd worked so hard to secure, making no secret of her aspirations. They'd dared her to try, then laughed at her as she did.

No one leaves this place alive, they'd assured her as if the run-down old farm was Appalachian, out of that old song about Harlan, and it might as well have been. *You dream big, but you'll be right here with the rest of us when the dust clears.*

They'd been so damned sure she was the same as all the rest of the Packards with their clipped wings, bad reputations, and limited horizons—and part of their certainty came from the fact she'd stopped showing them anything she didn't want them to see. Right about the time it was clear they didn't actually want what was best for her. Also when she'd been ten, as she recalled. It was one of her finest talents—that and her mulish determination to do the very thing people told her she couldn't.

And there was no reason her age-old mask should feel like it was choking her today, with Jonah Flint staring down at her as if he could read the things she'd etched into her very soul. As if the mask that had saved her once was no protection from him at all.

As if this wasn't a game they were playing. As if what happened here, between them, mattered.

Speaking of fanciful, she snapped at herself. *That's bordering on straight up crazy.*

"It doesn't have to fit," Jonah pointed out. His voice was a gentle rumble, too deep and male to be soft. But still, it shivered through her. It felt like another one of those almost-kisses, that hard mouth against her skin as if it belonged there. "It has to sound like it fits, which isn't the same thing."

Gracelyn saw the moment he remembered himself, and his purpose here. The dark gold in his gaze disappeared as if it had never been, and he went colder, harder, without seeming to move a muscle. He kept hold of her hand, though he dropped it from his mouth, and he started toward the building in front of them. Gracelyn told herself she barely noticed how easily they walked together, how in sync they were, and so quickly, as if they really had walked hand in hand a thousand times before.

He chose you because you suit his image of the girlfriend he doesn't actually want, she reminded herself harshly. *And you're doing this because who the hell else gets to say they spent two weeks this up, close, and personal with* Jonah Flint? *This could be a major stepping-stone in your career—but not if you're all fluttery about* holding hands *with him!*

Jonah tugged open the depot's front door and a cheerful burst of noise floated out to greet them as he ushered her inside. Gracelyn had spent some time researching the other half of the once unbreakable Flint brothers team in the past few days. She knew that Jasper Flint had opened this microbrewery only a few months back, after painstakingly renovating the old train depot here in Marietta. But research and even detailed pictures on the internet hadn't entirely prepared her for the appealingly clean lines and little touches that were obvious at first glance. From the big, bright paintings on the walls to the airy, open balcony seating area up above, every little detail was well thought out and gave the place a wide open, effortless feel.

Perfectly Montana, she thought.

There were great steel vats behind high glass walls and a busy bar counter staffed by cheerful-looking bartenders in bright blue shirts. She saw a busy, open kitchen in the back and a menu written in a bold, welcoming hand across a chalkboard on the wall beside it. And then, when a family group claimed a table and sat down, she saw him.

A man who laughed with his whole body and looked like something she'd made up, in all those fantasies she'd deny she'd had, ever since that afternoon in Jonah's office.

A man who looked so much like Jonah it made her heart stutter in her chest, because he simultaneously looked nothing like Jonah at all.

"Holy crap," she whispered, not realizing she'd come to a stop until Jonah frowned down at her. "That's what you'd look like if you were happy."

She couldn't have described the look that moved over Jonah's face then, only that it hurt her. Him, too, she knew—and she didn't know how she knew. But then, that quickly, something dark and fierce replaced it, and his hand tightened slightly—only slightly—around hers.

"That's what I would look like if I'd suffered a mental break and possibly had a frontal lobotomy to match," he told her, his voice as precise as a man with that much Texas in his voice could hope to get, and she felt the lash of it as surely as if he'd broken her skin with its sharpness.

Then he was moving, and the other man—*Jasper*, she told herself, because of course it was Jasper, the younger Flint twin by barely a minute, identical in almost every physical way except for his longer, carelessly dark blonde hair that he wore so haphazardly and that utterly non-Jonah expression of lazy amusement on his face—glanced up and went still.

And for a moment that Gracelyn felt thud in her like a deep and terrible drum, they could have been interchangeable.

"Sweet Jesus," came an older female voice from one of the tables nearby, complete with a lascivious cackle, "did you know there were *two* of them?"

"I bet Chelsea did," came the muttered reply. "That wench."

Is this Chelsea woman a bad influence on your brother? Gracelyn had asked back in Dallas, trying to understand why this situation called for such dramatic measures on the part of a man like Jonah, who she rather doubted usually needed to produce fake girlfriends for family occasions. *Drugs? Alcohol? Gambling?*

Because she certainly knew more than anyone should about the way those nasty little vices cut out souls and left walking, talking, utterly empty shells behind in their wake.

She's a schoolteacher, Jonah had replied from the leather sofa across from her in his office, spitting out the word like it was a vicious curse. Like he'd said *Voldemort* in a roomful of Harry Potter's wizards.

She'd gazed back at him. *An* evil *schoolteacher?*

He is Jasper Flint, Jonah had bit out, his outrage evident in every syllable, and something far darker beneath the words. *He is my brother. He is better than a goddamned* history teacher.

Gracelyn couldn't have said what came over her as they walked across the floor of the microbrewery toward a man who looked entirely too familiar, eerily the same, yet wasn't. Jonah was among the wealthiest men in the world, a fact no one in Dallas, a place fairly bursting with wealthy men, could fail to notice. They'd flown here today on one of his fleet of private jets. He owned more property than some small countries. He was as respected as he was feared, which Gracelyn knew very well, since she worked for him. She was close enough to him at the moment that she could tell, as a person who'd grown up around folks who'd never met a difference of opinion they couldn't escalate into an assault charge, that the particular hardness of his lean muscles meant he could probably knock some heads together if he wanted. He was, by any measure and according to documented fact, a tough, hard, deeply formidable man who could take care of himself in any and all situations.

Clearly.

But she moved closer to him anyway, as if he needed that. As if he needed her support, when she was well aware he'd only come here in the first place to break up his brother's relationship. And if she knew Jonah at all, maybe it was his brother who needed the help.

If he needed it, she acknowledged as that thing like grief swelled in her again, she would fight off all his demons herself. One after the next.

If he'd let her.

"Jonah," said his twin, his voice warm despite the wariness in his own hazel gaze, so much the same it was almost alarming. "You came. I didn't think you would."

"Of course I came," Jonah bit out, sounding colder than usual. "It's not every day my twin brother—"

He shifted, or Jasper did, and Gracelyn saw the pretty blonde woman standing there, just behind Jasper. She thought Jonah must have, too, though he gave no outward sign of it.

"—opens up his own brewery and starts talking about rode-os like a born again cowboy," Jonah finished smoothly. "How could I resist?"

For no good reason, Gracelyn pulled her hand from his and then slid her arm around his waist instead, her fingers pressing into his lean hip. She didn't know which one of them that was meant to reassure. The dark, brooding look Jonah slid down at her in response didn't make anything better or more clear, it only made that odd hollow thing inside of her deepen. Then twist.

But she had a job to do, and this wasn't it.

"Hi," she said, breaking into whatever silent communication was happening between the brothers before her heart split wide open in her chest.

She stuck out her hand toward the woman she assumed was the potentially evil schoolteacher like any friendly, folksy Montana woman would, and she should know. She'd been one, once upon a different life. That was why she was here, she reminded herself. Not all this *touching* that was turning her into someone she hardly recognized, and they'd only just got here.

She turned her smile up a notch as the other woman took her hand. "I'm Gracelyn. Jonah's girlfriend."

"YOU DIDN'T MENTION you were coming up when we spoke," Jasper said once he and Jonah had moved to the bar, ostensibly grabbing a few drinks to toast his surprise arrival and their happy brotherly reunion.

If Jonah had any reservations about leaving Gracelyn to handle the schoolteacher on her own, well, it was too late now. Besides, he needed to get a sense of where his brother's head was, and he didn't need anyone to tell him that would be a whole lot easier without the local barnacle attached to him. *Divide and conquer*, he thought, as if he and Gracelyn were really a team.

It was like Jasper was psychic. "Just like you didn't mention this girlfriend of yours."

Jonah checked a sigh just audible enough to be sure Jasper heard him, in the time-honored fashion of every older sibling, everywhere.

"I thought that phone call was all about your big announcement." Jonah leaned against the bar and eyed his brother. He focused on Jasper and not the overly-enthusiastic bar staff who milled around him and laughingly called him *boss*, all clad in too-bright t-shirts with the FlintWorks logo stamped across the front. "It was also the first time we've spoken in a year. Or maybe you think I should have thrown her in your face right about the time you insinuated human emotion wasn't exactly in my wheelhouse?"

Jasper had the grace to look faintly abashed, but that was the thing about Jasper: he wasn't one to hold a grudge. It either made him an idiot or a saint, and Jonah's money had always been on *idiot*.

"Given that the last time you used the term 'girlfriend' to describe a female in your life we were eighteen and you were angling for a major post-Prom payoff, yeah," Jasper pointed out, grinning as if no time had passed and it was fine to bring up ancient history. "Maybe you should have."

"I wasn't aware I had to run my relationships past you for review," Jonah replied coolly, because he wasn't his brother. He made his grudges into sky-high monuments, painted them bright colors so they'd never be forgotten, and lived in them like they were his home. "My apologies. I thought we were grown-ass men."

Jasper's trademark shit-eating grin was familiar, certainly, if strained just slightly around the edges, showing that he wasn't as at ease with this reunion of theirs as he was trying to appear. Which had the immediate effect of making Jonah feel better about the whole thing.

"Relationships?" Jasper asked. Of course he did. "Plural? *You?* Jonah Flint, the Man Who Walks Alone?"

Jonah inclined his head slightly, and almost let himself smile. Almost. Jasper laughed, as if he had.

Still *almost* smiling, Jonah turned back to the noisy, Saturday afternoon bar crowd as Jasper prepared their drinks.

Oh, babe, *you know what I like,* Gracelyn had murmured when he'd asked for her drink order. The laughter in her dark eyes as she'd called him a name she'd rejected had been a little punch to his gut, but that had seemed better than the great mess of things that battered at him when he thought about his messed-up relationship with Jasper.

Ignoring both thorny topics, Jonah forced himself to look around at this place his twin had made. With his own two hands, more or less, if the relentlessly positive emails Jonah had done his best to ignore over the last year were to be believed.

"Not so bad, is it?" Jasper drawled, thunking pint glasses of beer down on the counter between them one by one. "Definitely not the end of the world, as I believe some people might have thought when I came up with this plan."

Not the end of the world, sure. Just the end of everything they'd built together. Just the end of *them*. Jonah hadn't been surprised, really, when Jasper had flounced off into the ether two years ago, demanding they sell everything and reinvent themselves. He'd always been the emotional one.

But he'd always thought his brother would come back, because Jasper always had before, no matter where his spontaneous bursts of restlessness had taken him. They'd always reinvented themselves *together*. From their earliest days, when their angry, brutish father had driven them around Dallas in a cloak of righteousness to show them what they couldn't have, Jonah and Jasper had been united in proving him—and the world—wrong. Even Jasper's marriage to the toothy and faithless Marlene hadn't changed things between the brothers, because Marlene—and the house and the cars and the *life*—had never been anything more than an accessory. A billionaire's shiny bauble, like so many of the brittle women they knew in Dallas, interchangeable from all the rest and wholly unlamented once she'd gone.

This was different. Jasper was a sophisticated man. He'd moved in dizzyingly high circles in Dallas with that easy grin of his, making everyone he'd encountered think he was their new best friend. He was good at it, damn it. What the hell was he doing, tying himself down in a place like this?

The microbrewery wasn't the problem, Jonah acknowledged as he looked around. He was impressed despite himself, because of course anything Jasper did would be impressive. That was the Flint way. Jonah wouldn't mind investing in the place, taking a look into regional expansion. He could see opening another FlintWorks near his vast ranch holdings north of Flathead Lake, on the other side of the Rockies. It would thrive near the winter skiing and summer lakefront communities, he was sure, as most Flint projects did.

But he certainly wouldn't set himself up as a bartender there. Just as he wouldn't disappear into the soft gaze of some local girl who must have thought she'd won the freaking lottery the day Jasper had rolled into town. Jonah had hardly looked at the blonde woman his brother had introduced as *Triple C*. He'd worried his feelings about her would have been written all over his face, and he knew exactly how his brother was likely to react to that kind of insult. Especially as he was probably expecting it.

No need to race toward his endgame when an amble would

do the same trick.

"I can see that you like it, you know."

There was laughter in his brother's voice, still. There always was, and Jonah found it as infuriating as ever. How different would their lives have been if Jonah had decided to take after their reckless, vow-breaking mother too? Instead of their grimly righteous father who'd ruled over his home and the two sons his wife had left behind her with all the fury of the Old Testament?

"I can already hear the expansion proposal," Jasper said, making no attempt to conceal his amusement. "You can't help yourself."

When Jonah turned back to face his twin, he trotted out a grudging smile. He told himself he was only playing his role as he did it. But he knew better. This was Jasper. This was his brother, his twin. The only person on the face of the earth he'd ever trusted, and one of the very select few he'd ever loved. His father had been a terror. His mother had taken off when the twins had been five, the better to craft herself a merry family of little girls Jonah didn't care to acknowledge, with a significantly more manageable man off in Virginia.

He'd long since forgiven his mother for leaving his father. It was the fact she'd never come back to rescue her sons from the same fate that he'd held on to for the past thirty-one years. She was his first, best, and deepest grudge, and he had no intention of letting go of it any time soon.

Which meant Jasper was the only family Jonah had. Being back in the same room with him, even if that room was in this pissant town on a lonely road no one would want to travel on the first place, mattered. He felt it seep into him, like a kind of light. Or like the heat of Gracelyn's smooth arm around his back, which promised nothing but the ruin of him, he was well aware.

Like all those things he told himself he didn't want, because he couldn't have them. Because he would destroy them all himself, given time. He was a man who knew his limitations. He always had. Because he'd always had a mirror image right there in front of him to show him what his life might have looked like if he'd been a little bit limitless instead.

If he'd been someone else entirely, free and unfettered and all the rest of that crap. If he allowed himself to be irresponsible. If he'd been a little bit less like the father he hated and feared he resembled in equal measure.

"Don't count your chickens just yet, little brother," Jonah replied lazily when Jasper smiled back at him, as if everything between them was right again—as it would be again, one way or another, if he had anything to do with it. "I haven't tasted the beer. It could suck."

Chapter Three

GRACELYN TOOK ONE look at Chelsea Crawford Collier— inspiration for the microbrewery's most popular beer, according to a sign near the bar with a picture of her smiling face attached—and knew everything she needed to know about her.

The smooth blonde hair that fell around her shoulders, the open face with a hint of freckles. A friendly smile that Gracelyn could tell was entirely genuine. Nice clothes that flattered her figure but weren't overly suggestive, indicating she took care with her appearance and pride in herself besides, complete with the kind of quiet confidence that made her seem even prettier than she was. She looked like a woman who knew exactly who she was and where she belonged. It was evident as much in her easy handshake as it was in the number of people who called her name, or caught her eye as they happened past the table they'd claimed near the currently empty little stage.

Gracelyn had grown up poor white trash in a place where there wasn't a whole lot *but* poor white trash, and still the Packards had been the trashiest of them all. Criminals, convicts, drunks, drug addicts and gamblers, and that was just Gracelyn's parents. She'd spent her childhood set apart from the good kids, the ones whose parents hadn't descended into meth use or too many drunk driving or domestic violence arrests. She'd come to think that had been another twisted sort of gift—because she wasn't often fooled by people after growing up so hard. People, good and bad and everything in between, tended to wear their intentions on their faces or deep in their eyes, no matter what lies they told with their mouths.

And Chelsea Collier looked like what she was supposed to be: a perfectly nice schoolteacher in a pretty small town, who happened to be dating one of the Flint brothers.

What she did not look like—at all—was a gold digger.

These days Gracelyn lived in a big city filled with a lot of oil money, which meant there were a whole lot of women attracted to the lifestyle that went along with that money. Dallas gold diggers were a breed apart. Big hair, big jewelry, big smiles on their ruthlessly maintained little bodies. The faintest hint of cheap sex like a perfume hanging around them, making it clear how far they'd be willing to go to get their hands on one of the fortunes lying around for the taking. They were claim-jumpers, every one of them, from the diamonds they flaunted that could never be big enough to please them, to their extravagant shoes.

That was not this woman.

But Gracelyn was not here because Jonah valued her opinions or sought her counsel, something she would do well to remember. Nor was she here to make friends with Chelsea Collier. *Antagonize her,* Jonah had murmured in her ear when he'd bent down to her, supposedly to get her drink order. *See what happens.*

Which was her fault, Gracelyn supposed, for having assured him she could do exactly that.

Can you be a bitch? was what he'd asked, bluntly. The way she'd been asked, in other interviews for far less questionable jobs, what she thought her skill set might contribute to the company in question.

What kind of question is that? she'd asked him mildly. *I lived through middle school, if that's what you mean.*

Dark brows had risen above those shrewd hazel eyes. *Is that a yes?*

Don't worry, she'd told him, smiling slightly. *I can be wildly antagonistic, while pretending to be polite. It's one of the only skills my mother ever taught me.*

Which was true, as far as it went.

"I know this is a ridiculous thing to say," Chelsea was saying now, right here in Montana where asides about Gracelyn's mother felt a whole lot less amusing than they had in Texas, "but while I knew they were twins, I didn't expect them to be *quite so* identical."

Gracelyn laughed her agreement. She looked across the happily crowded floor of the brewery, where families were having a late Saturday afternoon lunch and friends grabbed appetizers and a few beers, toward the two men who stood on opposite sides of the blonde wood bar, as if they were a mirror split in two.

One laughing with his head thrown back, open and easy as if he did it all the time, because he probably did. And one smiling back at him, crooked and slow, as if he was thinking about learning how to do it himself.

Jonah was *smiling.*

Gracelyn caught herself staring. She jerked her attention back to this woman Jonah was so dead set against and reminded herself that this was a *job.* It was an opportunity to observe how one of the finest business minds in the country operated, if only in the realm of his personal life. It was not an opportunity to ogle her boss. Or his equally good-looking, apparently far sunnier-tempered twin.

"It's a little disconcerting, I grant you," she managed to say in reply.

Chelsea leaned forward, propping her elbows on the table

between them, and if there was a single gold digging bone in her body, Gracelyn would swallow her own tongue. Assuming the sight of Jonah grinning didn't make her do that anyway, of course. But she gritted her teeth against the urge to do something really stupid, like say so.

"I doubt Jasper would want me to say this, but I know he's really, really moved that Jonah's here, that he surprised him like this." Chelsea's smile dimmed slightly, but stayed put. "I know things have been a bit strained between them since Jasper left Texas, but I really hope this visit of yours helps mend that." Her gaze was so sincere it made Gracelyn want to look at anything else—yet she made herself hold it, and the other woman brightened in response. "I'm assuming this is your influence?"

It didn't say anything good about Gracelyn that she wished that was true. That she really did have any influence over Jonah, though the very idea was laughable. Or, hell, that she was really in his life in the first place.

"Can a Flint man *be* influenced?" she asked lightly.

"Not often," Chelsea replied, a warm sort of humor in her voice. "It kind of depends how you go about the influencing, I think."

There was a pause, as if she was waiting for Gracelyn to say something about the brothers' relationship or about Jonah, to pick up the thread she'd put out there like anyone else would, to build a bridge between them as the first step towards friendliness. But Gracelyn only gazed back at her, giving her what she and her cousin Bex had always called the Pamela Packard Special—Gracelyn's mother's trademark blank gaze that had reduced grown men, officers of the law, and even hardened criminals to impotent displays of discomfort and, usually, babbling.

Funny how easy it still came, like it was right there in her blood.

Chelsea blinked. "Uh . . . are you from Texas too?"

"I'm from right here in Montana, as a matter of fact," Gracelyn said. And of course, Chelsea liked that. Visibly. This was the entire point of Graclyn's being here, wasn't it? The supposed connection she was meant to use and exploit with this woman—as if being from the same very big state meant anything. Why did the whole thing make her feel faintly sick, suddenly? "A little bit north of Miles City."

"I love the prairie," Chelsea said, with a reverent sort of sigh. "Nothing like the birds singing, the grass rustling, and only the horizon and the sky as far as the eye can see."

"You obviously haven't spent a lot of time on the prairie, then," Gracelyn said dryly, as if Chelsea was both naïve and faintly amusing. "Or you'd describe all of that as *empty*."

Chelsea's laugh was definitely strained, then. *Point to me,* Gracelyn thought, and hated herself.

"No," Chelsea said after a moment, shifting in her chair to put a little more space between them. "My family's been in Marietta pretty much forever. Some would call it having roots. I'm engaged in an eternal debate about whether or not it's more a noose than roots." When Gracelyn let another pause drag out too long rather than answering, she straightened and got more brisk. Put on her teacher face, if Gracelyn had to guess. "So you grew up in Miles City, then?"

"Not exactly." Gracelyn leaned back in her chair, crossing her legs and propping one elbow on the chair's back, well aware that particular pose made her look aloof and unapproachable at once. It didn't matter if her lips were curved. "You have to drive north out of Miles City until you hit Deadman's Road. Take that until it runs into a big old butte, then turn left. Go, oh, fifty miles or so, and make sure you don't blink when you see a few rickety buildings huddled together against all that sky. A church, a bar, and a general store, in the middle of nothing but prickly grass. A few of the more optimistic folks like to call it ranch land. It's really not." Her smile was sharp then, she could feel it, and she could see it reflected in the stiffness of the other woman's face. She recognized that expression. She'd felt it on her own face a thousand times when she'd still been a kid in her mother's clutches. "That's where I come from. Hooray."

"It doesn't sound like you're planning a visit home while you're in Montana, then," Chelsea said, carefully. Very carefully. Her hands clasped together tightly, and Gracelyn really couldn't think of a time in recent memory she'd felt worse about herself.

"Definitely not." Gracelyn forced a little laugh that seemed to stick into the glossy table top between them, brittle and pointed. "I couldn't wait to leave the moment I left high school and I've certainly never been back since. Small town, small people, small lives. You know."

She smiled then, knowing that wouldn't cover the slap of her words, and she told herself it wasn't her business to feel badly about the way Chelsea's open expression shut down at that. Hard. It wasn't her place. *You will remain my subordinate,* Jonah had said back in his office. Back in Dallas, where everything had made sense and all the parts of her life had stayed right where she'd put them, out of sight and as out of mind as possible. And that meant that her place was to do her job, whether she liked it or not, or quit.

She chose her job. She would always choose her job. It was all she had—she'd made sure of that.

And she was good at her job, because it was that or go crawling back home and she *refused,* so Gracelyn tilted her head slightly to one side. Then she stuck the knife in, deep. "Didn't Jonah tell me you were born here?"

THE SUITE JONAH had taken in the Graff Hotel just down the

block from FlintWorks was an old, painstakingly restored and renovated affair. There were burnished plaques on the wall naming a local copper king as the suite's initial, historic resident, and nods everywhere toward the many Wild West ghosts that were said to still haunt the place. There was a graceful, Victorian living area with windows that looked out toward Copper Mountain in the golden evening light. There were nooks and crannies, unexpected closets, and near-secret rooms, as befitted a lovely hotel from a bygone era. It all should have delighted Gracelyn.

Jonah had stalked off into the master bedroom when they'd entered the suite, jerking his head toward one of the smaller side rooms to indicate where he expected her to sleep and then leaving her to it with a thud of his bedroom door. She could have explored. She could have lost herself in all the delicious splendor of the place, that local hero and San Francisco tech tycoon Troy Sheenan had restored with little more than gritty determination to succeed where everyone predicted he'd fail, according to all reports—the kind of story Gracelyn loved above all others. She so wanted it to be hers someday.

But instead, she stood in the center of her room's polished bit of floor, hardly noticing the stout four poster bed or the old daguerreotype photographs that lined the walls, harkening back to Marietta's earliest Old West days. There were any number of things she could do and should do, she knew. Unpack, for one. Attend to the long list of messages that were clogging up her phone, because her immediate supervisor was less than impressed—or just straight up jealous—that one of his analysts had taken off for parts unknown with The Man Himself. Or she could try to shake all of this off and take herself out for a run, the best way to lance this sort of emotional poison that she knew would otherwise take root and expand within her.

But she didn't do any of those things, because all Gracelyn

could think about was the tight, frozen expression she'd left on poor Chelsea Collier's face when the other woman had only been trying to be nice. Or the too-straight way the other woman had been standing when they'd exchanged a deeply insincere goodbye, as if she'd been trying very hard to hold herself still. As if otherwise, she would ache.

Gracelyn had never seen that particular set of reactions on another person, but she'd certainly felt them all. Every time her mother had eviscerated her. Pamela had torn into her for sport, or because Pamela was hurting herself and didn't know what else to do with it, or because she was drunk and mean, or just because she could. It had never occurred to Gracelyn that it was possible she could make someone else feel that way, for any reason, and her stomach lurched at the sad knowledge that she had.

Because it was her *job*.

"Gracelyn."

Or, possibly, because it was him.

The impatient note in Jonah's voice clued her in to the fact he'd said her name more than once. Still, it took her another beat to focus on him, standing there in the open doorway to her room.

And then a whole other beat besides, because he was wet.

Not actually wet, of course. Just . . . showered. Though it took her entirely too long to work that out as she gazed at him. His hair looked much darker when it was damp and slicked back against his head, and that in turn, made those eyes of his glow dark gold despite the cranky look in them. But the key point was that he was shrugging his way into a t-shirt, which meant that for a brief and glorious moment, she was staring directly at his ridged abdomen. The play of his skin against the fine muscles beneath. The trail of dark hair that dipped below the waistband of his jeans.

This was the reason, if she was honest with herself, that she'd been so deeply concerned with her job performance that she'd happily acted like such a jerk. Because Jonah had told her she should.

"What are you doing?" he asked when his t-shirt was in place, which wasn't really as helpful as it should have been, because Gracelyn knew, now.

She knew. The sad truth about herself. And the more pressing and immediate truth about the state of his very fine body.

And that t-shirt was tight, hugging his chest in a way that made her whole body seem to *prickle* to attention. Jonah's mouth shifted into something softer then. Something almost warm, like he was playing with her. Like he *could* play. The notion made her blood feel like molasses, heavy and sweet in her veins.

"Am I paying you to stand in the middle of your hotel room, staring off into space like a slack-jawed yokel?" he asked quietly, nothing but gold in those eyes of his. "I don't recall putting that in my budget."

"No sir," she replied, as stunned at the notion that Jonah Flint was teasing her as she'd been by the sight of his mouth-wateringly hard abdomen. But then the afternoon rushed back at her. And all she could see was Chelsea Collier and the look she'd put on her face, in her blue eyes. A look she recognized from a life she thought she'd put behind her. "My job is to attack and undermine nice women who have the temerity to be dating your twin brother without your permission."

Jonah studied her for a moment, his gaze narrow. He put out a hand to hold the doorjamb in a way that wasn't erotic at all, despite the shivering thing that rolled over and then stretched out deep inside of her. It told her that anything he did was erotic. To her.

"Do you know her?" His tone was polite, the gold gone from his gaze.

"No. Nor, after today, will I ever."

"Are you planning to relocate to the Marietta area?" He sounded distant and much too cool. It put her on alert. "Perhaps take a position in the same high school where that *nice woman* teaches history classes?"

"I'm not much of a teacher, no," Gracelyn said tightly.

"Then what the hell do you care if you hurt the feelings of a complete stranger you'll never see again?" His voice was still polite, but there was no pretending she didn't feel the flare of power in it then, or see it right there on his clever face. It reminded her who he was. Who *she* was, more importantly. "I asked if you could do this and you assured me you could. Did you lie to me, Gracelyn?"

There was a cold glint in his hazel gaze then that made Gracelyn think that lying to this man was one of the more foolish things a person could do, with consequences she'd rather not face, thank you. She swallowed. She resisted the urge to fold her arms across her chest, which she knew he would read— correctly—as a protective gesture on her part.

"I didn't lie to you," she managed to say, to push out through her throat which was suddenly and unaccountably too tight. "But it's been a long while since the middle school social scene. I think I forgot that being that mean takes its own toll."

"Your job is to worry about the toll I'll take," he said with a quiet ruthlessness that crowded out everything else in the suite. In the whole state and that great big sky above it. "You're not here to care about anyone else."

He was right, of course. What *did* she care? This wasn't her family. This wasn't her fight and she wasn't her mother. She was a hired gun with no stake in what happened—and her feelings were her own problem.

This isn't real, she told herself then. *This is an emotional reaction to the fact you're back here—because you know that if you wanted to, you could jump in a car and drive home in a few short hours. You could see Bex and Grandma Betty. You could—*

She didn't want to think about that. Or them.

"I think I understand the job just fine," she replied instead, aware that her hands were in fists only when he focused all that brooding attention of his on them. She shoved them in the pockets of her jeans instead. "It's the execution that I'm finding a bit harder to cope with. You'll forgive me, I hope. I've never pretended to be anyone's bitchy girlfriend before."

Jonah looked at her then for what felt like a long time and Gracelyn didn't have the slightest idea what he saw. Something told her she didn't want to know, but even so, she couldn't bring herself to break his gaze.

"You're different here." His voice was low. Rough. "Maybe it's the clothes."

She felt that like a touch. The way that hazel gaze gleamed gold as it moved over her, tracing the soft t-shirt she wore under her travel blazer and the way her jeans slicked over her hips. He lingered at her silver belt buckle and then shifted up again, to the breasts that were a lot more visible in clingy cotton than they'd ever been in one of her workplace appropriate dresses. She ordered herself to ignore that swooping feeling inside of her, as if she'd just stepped over the edge of a very high cliff.

Not stepped. Jumped.

"It's a well known fact that all women are bitchier in stilettos," she agreed. She'd meant to sound light. A little bit arch, a little bit amused. What came out was much huskier, threaded through with a thousand layers of all the things she didn't want to acknowledge were happening here. Like the hotel's old ghosts were there too, cluttering up the rooms and stealing all the air.

"Is it hard?" He looked as surprised at the question as she was, and far more disgruntled. His strong hand tightened against the doorjamb before he dropped it to his side. He straightened.

"Being back in Montana."

"I didn't think it would be." Gracelyn felt the way she had when she'd stepped out of the car and found herself beneath that great, big, breathtaking sky. Small and awed, as if she was suspended in something sacred. Profound. But there was nothing here but Jonah Flint and that curious look in his dark gold eyes that she could feel everywhere. "Marietta is hundreds of miles away from where I'm from."

That hint of a smile on his mouth almost undid her, then. "That doesn't answer the question, darlin'."

"Ah." She smiled, and she didn't know why her eyes felt too bright, as if this was all deeply emotional. As if they knew each other. "There it is. *Darlin'.*"

"I did warn you of the danger."

"So you did."

And it felt as if maybe they weren't talking about endearments anymore.

Jonah's gaze was a brilliant thing, too bright and dark at once. And Gracelyn understood with the kind of perfect clarity that had once sent her running from the only home she'd ever known at eighteen that she never should have come here. She never should have come back to Montana, and she never, ever should have gone anywhere with him.

That nothing would ever be the same after this, least of all her.

"Your night is your own," he told her. And he was Jonah Flint, her boss, again. So abruptly and completely that it called even more attention to whatever had just happened between them. Gracelyn found she'd caught her breath. "I have some things to take care of, but I'll expect to see you for breakfast in the morning. I'm an early riser. Seven work for you?"

"Of course," she said, and tried to smile. "I'm not going to argue with the boss about start times."

"Not if you're smart," he agreed, without a hint of a smile in return, which only a truly insane person would feel like heat.

And then he was gone, closing her door gently—much too gently—behind him.

Leaving Gracelyn to stand there in the lengthening shadows of her bedroom, in this haunted place with her arms wrapped around her middle—the Montana she'd walked away from *right there* on the other side of her great big windows and Jonah Flint a cipher she shouldn't even *want* to puzzle out—thinking that as it turned out, she wasn't very smart at all.

Chapter Four

~

I T WAS REMARKABLY easy to fall into a routine, Gracelyn had learned at the hands of her deeply ill-qualified parents—even in the strangest of circumstances, for which her role as the uber-bitchy girlfriend of the great Jonah Flint certainly qualified.

"Not bitchy, necessarily," Jonah amended one evening as the four of them took a walk in the woods up in the hills above town. He smirked at her, while the other couple walked ahead. "Just perpetually unimpressed."

"I think I have that part down," Gracelyn muttered, glaring at him.

If only it were true. If only she could feel about Marietta the way she had about her own hometown. But instead, the town—and, God help her, the people—seemed to wedge its way further into her every minute she spent there.

Gracelyn woke at dawn every day and went for a long run, pushing herself further each time in the crisp, cool September mornings. She ran along the winding river that cut through town and then ambled along beyond it, or out the roads that led toward the foothills of the towering, soaring mountains in the distance. She ran until her legs felt like jelly and her breath sawed in and out of her chest, and yet it didn't work its usual magic. She didn't feel smoothed out and mellowed straight through when she was done, she only felt momentarily still inside.

And the trouble was that when she was still like that, there was no pretending she wasn't coming to love this place. The sky, the hills. The light. Montana itself. The compelling man who'd brought her here. The wilderness right there on the edge of town, instead of a long drive away. And she couldn't pretend there wasn't a huge part of her—that she hadn't known was there, or that she'd been ignoring for over ten years—that thrilled to it. All of it.

And yet despite that, Gracelyn knew those stolen moments at the end of each run were the closest to sane she was likely to get in the midst of this crazy situation.

This situation she'd happily signed up for, lest she forget.

Gracelyn hadn't forgotten. How could she, when she met Jonah in the living room of their suite at seven each morning, both of them showered and crisply professional, to discuss the day's plans over their breakfast?

To fall deeper and more completely under his spell, more like, which was about as far away from *smart* as she could get.

But she was ignoring that part. She had to. Because there was so much to do.

There were lunches with Chelsea and Jasper when Chelsea could steal away from her high school duties. There were hours spent trailing along behind the Flint brothers as they maneuvered around each other with gradually decreasing stiffness. There were a thousand opportunities each day to pretend that this was still just a job to her. There were dinners at local restaurants or in the loft Jasper and Chelsea shared above the microbrewery, rich with little moments that tugged at Gracelyn with far too much unwanted familiarity.

Or maybe—and much worse—that was longing she felt, and worse by the day. Pure and simple and terrifying.

"Being here must make you miss Montana a little," Chelsea

said on one of those nights, with the resolute cheerfulness she'd resorted to when she spoke to Gracelyn. That and her apparent failure to notice any digs were her weapons, and she used them well. She even smiled as she did it—leaving Gracelyn to reflect on the sad fact that under different circumstances, she'd probably *like* Chelsea Collier.

Or maybe she did like her. Maybe that was the trouble, because that certainly wasn't part of Jonah's plan.

"You mean the Montana of rugged mountains and cool, crisp, glacial lakes, I think," Gracelyn said then, with all of that longing churning around inside of her, making her feel reckless. "Good looking cowboys and prosperous ranches and the great blue yonder."

She and Jonah were sitting on their side of the dinner table as they all enjoyed an after-dinner whiskey. Jonah had his heavy, sculpted arm slung across the back of her chair, the very picture of the easy, relaxed couple they weren't. Gracelyn could see their cozy reflection in the antique mirror that took up most of the wall across from her, and it was so tempting to believe what she saw there. So tempting to sink into it, to pretend she didn't know better.

But she did.

She focused on Chelsea instead. "That Montana is not where I grew up."

"It's all the same Montana," Chelsea countered softly. Another potential bridge, as if she couldn't accept the possibility that Gracelyn wouldn't eventually cave and help her build one if she kept offering them, one after the next. "Isn't it?"

And Gracelyn shoved aside what she was supposed to be doing here. What games she was meant to be playing, night after night. She leaned forward and smiled at Chelsea, and it was a hard sort of smile that scraped at her as she aimed it across the table. It had more to do with the sudden heat she could feel prickling in her eyes than any agenda of Jonah's. And for some reason, in this open plan, artfully-arranged loft with the bold thrust of Copper Mountain framed in all the windows as another pink sunset cavorted over its peak, she didn't care the way she knew she should.

"I don't think it is," she said, and there was too much emotion in her voice. She felt Jonah go still beside her. "The Montana I come from is way out in the country, like any other rural place you can think of and a great many you'd probably prefer not to think of at all. Everyone is poor and that means everyone is desperate. There are more meth heads than First Families where I grew up, Chelsea. There's long and painful history anywhere you look, but no one's going to collect it and put it in a museum. We just try not to talk about it in polite company."

She knew her breath was too ragged, as if she was out running, and she could sense Jonah's movement beside her more than see it. She couldn't look away from Chelsea Collier's stricken blue gaze.

"People in *my* Montana don't know how to leave the place they were born, where they would go or what they would do, so they stay there and rot instead. It's not Marietta." Gracelyn let out a small, hollow laugh. "It's not a place you would stop your car if it had a flat, much less move in and build a future."

She started to say something else, but Jonah simply pulled her close with that arm on her chair and wrapped his hand right over her mouth, pressing his palm against her lips. She could taste the salt of his skin, and the heat of it, too, and the sudden contact was shocking. Erotic.

Their eyes met, a brief and electric warning, and she felt his dark gold, brooding gaze all the way down to the soles of her feet.

And she was certain he could feel the way she shivered,

then. She watched the gold in his gaze flare, too bright and too hot when there were eyes on them. Too wild and untamed, when this thing between them was supposed to be an act.

"And that," Jonah said, turning his attention back to the table, and even cracking that small smile of his that made Gracelyn's stomach flip over, "is why Gracelyn shouldn't drink whiskey. It makes her a little bit maudlin and whole lot feisty, every time."

Everyone laughed, even Gracelyn laughed. He pulled his hand back, running his fingers along the tender skin of her jaw and up toward her temple as he went, and she felt it everywhere. *Everywhere.* It lit her up, making her shift in her chair around the surge of near-painful need that came with it, and he wasn't even looking at her. He was concentrating on his brother. Of course he was.

It was the sexiest thing that had ever happened to her, and it wasn't even real.

Worse, it was dangerous, because Chelsea was still watching her. Gracelyn forced a smile, made a rueful sort of noise, and pushed her glass away from her with a hand she was pretty sure only she could tell was shaking.

"Sorry," she murmured. "He's not kidding. I really shouldn't drink whiskey."

They didn't speak of her outburst again.

As the days wore on, they talked about the upcoming rodeo and the cowboys already descending on the town, many of them getting into the usual sort of trouble at FlintWorks or the other bars in town—the historic Grey's Saloon on Main Street and the rougher Wolf Den further down Front Street. Gracelyn drifted in the sweet pull of the long, blue September afternoons when Jonah took his conference calls and kept tabs on his empire. She wandered past the particular quaintness of the storefronts in town, and admired the direct courtesy of the locals that could have bled into friendliness, if Gracelyn had let it. She lost herself in the contrast between the magnificent Graff Hotel, on one end of the same block that, way down on the other end, held the Wolf Den and a brand new, eclectic tattoo parlor. The way the sun filtered through the evergreens that lined the foothills and the cottonwoods down near the water; the way the river danced beneath its light. The way the great big sky folded itself over everything, so vast it hurt.

It was much too easy to be in Marietta, no matter what she might have told Chelsea. It was much too easy to relax into its pure Montana embrace and forget she wasn't going to stay. To punch in her grandmother Betty's number again and again on her cell phone each night when she was alone in her bed, but refuse to push SEND every time. To forget that none of this was real and none of it was hers—including and especially Jonah.

Because the *touching* was the worst part. Or the best part. Or the hardest part, she couldn't quite decide—but it was killing her.

Every morning they sat on separate couches in the gold and wood accented salon of a suite where the original owner had spent his first fortune on the local prostitutes, his second on a copper boom that had never quite materialized, and his third on the railway that ran behind the hotel, but had ultimately bankrupted him. All of which Gracelyn knew, because she did her best to look at anything but Jonah during their scrupulously polite breakfast hour.

Because the rest of the day, all she did was look at him. Touch him, smile at him. Sit on his lap when he tugged her there, snuggle into his side when she could. Do a thousand things that suggested the physical intimacy she was finding it harder and harder to remember was all for show.

On the last day of their first week in Marietta, she ran a

personal best, banging out seven hard miles on the coldest morning yet. She was filled with a kind of dark jubilation when she made it back to the hotel to see Jonah running toward her from the opposite direction, because she felt like she could handle anything in the world at that moment.

Even him.

And who cared that it had taken her long hours to fall asleep last night? She'd stared up at the canopy of stars she could see out her window, doing her best to forget about the way Jonah had slid his hand over the nape of her neck after another painful dinner, like a prelude to a deeply possessive kiss that had never come.

Or the way he'd wrapped his arm around her shoulders as they'd walked back to the Graff, holding her close against his side like he knew how wretched her role here made her feel— but maybe also so she could feel that same tension simmering in him that she knew was in her, too. That same tension they'd both ignored when the door to the suite had shut behind them, springing away from each other and heading for their rooms, as if even a second more in each other's company meant they'd explode.

This can't go on, Gracelyn had thought, lying there in the dark feeling scraped raw and hollow and scarred by all the things she wanted. *This is going to kill me.*

But she knew it wouldn't. That would be easy.

It took her a second to realize that the dark blonde, too-handsome man who stopped before her then, in athletic trousers and a green t-shirt and the wrong hair, wasn't Jonah at all.

"Good morning, Jasper," she said.

He grinned that lazy grin of his, but maybe because it was directed only at her this time, Gracelyn noticed that it didn't quite reach his eyes. She smiled brightly to cover the little lurch in her stomach.

"Walk with me," he said, in that voice that was so familiar, yet different. More drawl, less doom, and Gracelyn didn't know what it said about her that she liked Jonah's version better. "Let me buy you a coffee. I can't offer you any of that six-bucks-a-latte crap, but there's decent coffee shop around the corner."

"You're so much like your brother," she said, falling into step with him, wishing she wasn't quite so sweaty from her run, because this felt like she was facing the enemy defenseless. Which was probably why he was doing it. "Because I don't get the impression that was an invitation so much as an order."

Jasper's grin only widened. "Jonah gives the orders. He's the one who likes to rule the world. Me, I'm just a simple small town bartender."

"Meaning you take orders rather than give them, then?"

"Meaning I take the orders I feel like taking and otherwise concentrate on keeping the bad element out of my brand new brewery," he replied easily, and she thought that really, he was nothing like Jonah. That they were identical only in appearance—and that as beautiful as that appearance was, curiously, Jasper did nothing for her. She wasn't sure why that felt like a relief. "You'd be surprised at the kind of bad element that can turn up in a tiny Montana town way out in the middle of nowhere. Or maybe not, since you're from here."

"Not quite from here," Gracelyn amended as they walked. "Where I come from it was all bad element and a few prairie dogs, for local color. I'd be happy to tell you all about it if the coffee you're offering this morning is Irish, but you might not enjoy the conversation. I hear it's maudlin."

That time his laughter reached all the way to his eyes, and then he blinked, as if surprised. They turned down Main Street, which was fairly deserted so early in the morning. There were only a handful of pick up trucks and hardy four-wheel-drive wagons clustered outside the few restaurants and cafes that catered to the breakfast crowd, such as it was. It didn't take them long to reach the coffee shop Jasper indicated, or to place their order at the bustling counter inside, which offered many coffees and coffee drinks but at far more reasonable prices than six dollars.

Gracelyn glanced at her watch when Jasper sat down at a little table in the corner near the window and gestured for her to do the same.

"I don't have long," she said as she obediently took her seat and held her latte in its cardboard cup between her palms. "Jonah and I have a—" she almost forgot herself and said *meeting,* which was far too corporate for a girlfriend—"*date* for breakfast in ten minutes."

"Y'all seem pretty close," Jasper said. He was watching her a little too intently, and she was glad she'd had a week to work on her lack of reaction to him. She was glad she'd learned how to simply smile blandly back at him and give nothing away. Or so she hoped. "He says you've been together six months."

Gracelyn nodded, as if that was a simple fact that didn't require comment. She decided not to torture herself wondering how Jonah had arrived at that particular number. If it *meant something* beyond whatever it was he was trying to convey to his brother. That way lay only madness, she was sure of it.

Jasper studied her a moment or two more. "You understand that makes you his longest relationship, don't you? Ever."

It would make it hers, too, she reflected with a jolt of surprise. Had it actually happened.

"I'm sure Jonah would be thrilled to think we were sitting around discussing his personal life like this," she replied coolly, taking a sip of her latte. "Since he's so open that way."

Jasper settled back in his seat with his coffee cup in his hand. "I can't get a handle on you." He cracked that smile of his again, like he was being nice. She understood, on a very visceral level, that he wasn't. "Jonah's raved about your resume. And who can blame him? You're an impressive woman, Gracelyn. Not everyone can come from nothing and set themselves on a course to success the way you have. It's admirable."

Yet the look he was giving her was more assessing than admiring, she couldn't help but note.

"You and Jonah had amassed a major fortune or two by the time you were my age," Gracelyn countered, swirling her three dollar latte around in her own cup to bring the foam down. "I'm not any more admirable than anyone else for getting an academic scholarship. Many people do the same thing."

"Here's the thing," Jasper said, making no particular attempt to soften that segue, and grinning as he did it.

"There's a thing? And here I thought this was just a friendly chat."

"Believe me, Gracelyn." And that grin of his was as much a weapon as that Lone Star drawl was, she realized with a sudden start. He wasn't quite the dilettante Jonah claimed he was—and she very much doubted that she was the first person who'd underestimated him because he pretended to be so lazy and at his ease. She blinked, and tried to readjust—knowing all the while that he was watching her do it. "You'll be the first to know if I stop feeling friendly. I'm just the tiniest bit concerned."

About his soon-to-be-fiancée, she assumed, and braced herself for the slap down she richly deserved after a week of her little campaign.

"The same sort of concern that led to you leaving Dallas and not seeing Jonah for two years, I assume?"

She hadn't meant to say that, surely. But there it was.

Jasper's grin went hard, but he only took a pull from his coffee, then lowered the cup to the table. His gaze never left hers.

"Fair enough." He nodded toward the door. "It's coming on

seven. I'll walk with you."

"Thank you," she said dryly, "but that would probably feel more chivalrous if you weren't headed to almost the same place yourself."

"That's the thing about the Flints, Gracelyn," he said as they walked back outside and then headed back toward their little stretch of Front Street, the sun warming the crisp air around them as they moved. "We're nothing if not masters of the convenient."

"I'll keep that in mind," she said, and they both grinned. And it hit at her hard, then. That this wasn't actually her life. That she wasn't going to have any kind of friendship with this man. This wasn't the beginning of anything. He probably didn't like her very much, and why would he? She wasn't going to spend the rest of her life with his brother and make nice with his girlfriend and turn this all into some brightly animated set piece with dancing furniture and singing animals.

That was a Disney movie. That was something she would have said, a scant week ago, wasn't even something she wanted. This, by contrast, was reality. This was the job she kept forgetting to do.

"Thank you," she said, hoping she didn't sound as stiff and subdued as she felt, when they arrived at the old train depot. The Graff was barely half a block down, rising solid and faintly gleaming in the light of the new day. "I can walk the rest of the way to the hotel myself."

But Jasper stopped her with a look that was so like Jonah's, it made her ache all over again. It made everything that much worse.

"The thing is that my brother might look like a ringer for the next Wolf of Wall Street, but he's not," he said quietly. "And no matter how loud and fierce and ferocious his bark, that's not who he is. Not where it matters. Though between you and me, I think he might keel right over and die before he admits that."

Jasper's gaze was level on hers, quietly commanding, and Gracelyn found she couldn't look away. She felt caught. Terrified, again, and she couldn't have said why.

And then Jasper smiled again, and she knew why. It was because she was falling apart in every possible way, and she couldn't admit it. Couldn't show it. Couldn't do a single thing but let it happen.

Jasper's smile became far too knowing, then, and something too much like sad. "I don't want to think that he's with somebody who looks at him and can't see that, Gracelyn. I've been there before myself. I don't want that for him at all."

SHE WAS MUCH too quiet that night and Jonah didn't like it.

It was like an itch he couldn't quite reach. It sat there, beneath his skin, despite the way she played her role to the hilt. He let them into their suite with the old fashioned key and locked the door behind them, taking his time with it because he was a freaking coward and he knew it. God, did he know it.

Because if tonight was like every other night she would bolt off and barricade herself in her room by the time he made it into the salon, and he was well aware of that. He was counting on it.

But when he walked down the long, gleaming hallway, she was still there. She stood in the living room in the dark, with the moonlight from outside the big windows skimming over her figure. It made her seem like something more like a ghost.

Jonah didn't need any light to see her. She was burned into him, deeper by the day. Like she was inside of him.

He stood there, just inside the door, and watched her. Hungry. Needy.

Wary.

"I heard them talking about us tonight," she said softly, and she didn't turn when she said it.

His eyes adjusted to the darkness, and he could see more of her. She'd tucked her lusciously tight jeans into a pair of knee high boots tonight, and was wearing something flowy on top that made him think of the mountains in winter. Of cold nights and long snowfalls. And her hair was still tugged back into that always-sleek ponytail that made that itch in him expand, until he thought it might drive him wild. Right there where he stood.

He didn't dare answer her. He didn't know what he'd say. He only knew it would have nothing to do with his brother or the schoolteacher or the point he was trying to make here. He couldn't imagine, looking at her athletically trim body right there in front of him, gleaming in the moonlight and so tempting it actually hurt, that he could bring himself to care about either one of them, much less some *point*.

"They think we match." She let out a small, empty kind of sound. "Isn't that funny? They both laughed when they said it. Somehow I don't think it was a compliment."

She swung around then, and Jonah saw she had the whiskey bottle from the room's fully stocked bar in one hand. And a dangerous kind of glitter in her gaze that made his chest feel tight.

Tighter.

"We've been here an entire week. It feels like a year." She took a swig from the bottle and if he was any kind of a good man, Jonah couldn't possibly have found that as sexy as he did. Pure sex and danger in one sharp-mouthed, lethally-curvy package and God help him, he was losing his grip. "I was thinking I might take a day off from all this excitement and drive back out to the prairie tomorrow. Just to say hello, you know, and remember what it was like to *really* feel badly about myself. This is Little League in comparison."

He didn't think she had the slightest intention of digging up her roots, or maybe it was that he had no intention of letting her leave him, even for a day trip down memory lane. But he chose not to explore that thought any further. Not when she was right there in front of him, looking like a country song waiting to happen.

And Jonah had always loved a good country song.

"I thought you wouldn't stop a car there." He was still in the doorway, though he already knew he wasn't walking away from her. Not tonight. Not again. "Much less visit."

"*You* probably shouldn't stop one of *your* cars there," she corrected him. "*I* would be perfectly safe." She took another pull from the bottle and then wiped her mouth with the back of her hand. "Physically."

"Your job is here, Gracelyn. Right here in Marietta, not off in whatever little house on the damned prairie you grew up in."

With me, he thought, but didn't say. When had this happened? When had he become so fascinated by this woman he couldn't see anything else? It was another thought he didn't care to examine too closely just then.

Gracelyn only rolled her eyes at him. Only a deeply perverse man would feel that like a lick of her sharp tongue, right where it counted the most.

"Who knows? People are making a lot of money in eastern Montana these days. Maybe the Packards have taken up mining and come on up in the world like everyone else." She smiled then, slow and something like sweet, and Jonah thought it might have ripped him wide open. He could feel the scrape of it, deep and harsh. "Then again, more money only means better access to worse choices." Another one of those painful laughs. "Look at me. Look at this."

He was much too tense, Jonah realized. And there was a dark current running in him that he didn't entirely understand. He only knew he wanted his hands on her, and not in public this time. Not where he would have to stop or pretend anything or worry about who was watching them. And he was starting to think he would be willing to do or say just about anything to make that happen.

But that wasn't what they'd agreed. That wasn't why she was here—though it seemed he had to remind himself of that more and more often with every passing day.

Every second, more like.

"Didn't we decide that drinking whiskey wasn't a great idea?" he asked instead, and even he could hear that his voice was too harsh. That it filled the dark room and was too aggressive, too fierce.

"Maybe I want to be maudlin," she retorted, but she put the bottle down on the table nearest her and made no move to pick it up again. "Maybe maudlin is the appropriate response."

"Gracelyn." And he didn't know when that had happened, either. When her name had become the endearment, all by itself. When it had wrapped its way around him, into him, like a great tangle he had no hope of ever unraveling.

More alarming, he didn't want to know. He didn't care.

He wanted her. That was all. *He wanted.*

But she was frowning at him, the way she didn't do when they were in public. The way he was starting to crave, because he knew it was real. He wanted real.

"Why are we here, Jonah?" she asked then. "Why do I have to play the bad guy while you hang around pretending that you've suddenly become so nice and sweet and friendly, fooling absolutely no one?" She rubbed her hands over her face and dropped them again with a loud slap against the tops of her thighs. "If you don't want your brother to marry that perfectly nice woman who's never done a thing to you, why not just say so? That's what he did."

"He did? When did he do this?" Jonah didn't like that. She

muttered something he didn't hear, and he didn't like that, either. "Are you having clandestine meetings with my brother, Gracelyn? That can't end well." *For Jasper*, he didn't add, and didn't like that hot, possessive thing that streaked through him.

"I believe," she said with a quiet sort of dignity, "that he was trying to figure out my intentions toward you."

And everything seemed to tilt a bit, there with the moonlight dancing over her, making her gleam. Making his breath catch.

Making him *want* and *need* and *want* some more.

"And what did you tell him?"

Her smile was a twisted thing. "What could I tell him? My orders are to convince him we've been fake-dating for six months, not that we're on track to a fake wedding." She shrugged, though it struck him as defensive. Maybe that was wishful thinking. "I wouldn't want to fake-escalate our fake relationship. What if that made you fake-nervous? A man hates it, I hear, when he's just fake-boning but *she* thinks it's fake-something-more. All hell could break loose in our fake life!"

There was nothing fake about the way he felt about her, or the way he said her name. "Gracelyn."

"What you should probably know is that he didn't say any of the things he could have said," she threw at him, sounding as raw as he felt. "He didn't ask me why I was so relentlessly awful to Chelsea. He didn't wonder—out loud, anyway—why an obviously career-minded person like I've always been is supposedly sleeping with her boss. He didn't try to twist things around and come between you and me, though I can't imagine he thinks I'm any kind of positive influence in your life. Why on earth would he after the past week?" She shook her head at him.

And he was sure that was despair he saw then, etched all over her lovely face, making him crazy with the need to touch her. Soothe her. Save her. Just touch her, damn it. "He was *nice*, Jonah. A Flint through and through, sure. But nice."

"Yes," Jonah gritted out, furious or torn or *something* he didn't want to look at just then. "That's why he's the Good Twin. It's annoying."

"It's only annoying if you're an idiot," Gracelyn snapped back at him. "He loves you, Jonah. He was *concerned* about you. And meanwhile, all you want to do is destroy him."

And this time, it wasn't that the world seemed to shift beneath him. It shattered, and all that was left was Gracelyn and her luminous dark eyes and that way she was looking at him that he couldn't stand. He didn't care if everyone hated him, including his brother. But she couldn't.

She couldn't.

"Enough," he said, very carefully. Very quietly.

But she glared at him as if it had been a shout.

"You know what, Jonah? Our fake relationship sucks."

And he couldn't take the itch anymore, the unbearable *need* that moved in him and made him feel like howling at the moon.

He couldn't make sense of it, of this, of her. There was too much he didn't understand. Why he was gripping the doorframe as if he wanted to take it apart—or as if it was the only anchor he had, keeping him at a distance from her, keeping this as barely professional as it had been so far. Where she came from way out there on the Great Plains, or why she hated it so much she was still hiding from it all these years later. Why she was so driven, or why she looked at him sometimes with a light in her dark gaze that made the air feel perilous and beautiful around them. He refused to give that up.

Jonah wasn't the emotional one. He wasn't *emotional.*

He'd spent this whole week trying to convince himself that all these *feelings* were nothing more than leftover family stuff. Leftover Flint Brothers' stuff.

But he knew better here, now, all alone in the moonlight. It was her.

It was all her.

So he let go of the door frame. He cut the anchor and he started toward her, his pulse like a drumbeat. His eyes on her face. Her beautiful face, the one that haunted him asleep and awake, and he hadn't even kissed her yet.

It was long past time, he thought when he stopped in front of her. When she tilted her head back to look him in the eye. When she mouthed something that sounded like his name, her voice too insubstantial over the riot inside of him.

He didn't touch her. Not yet. He knew he wouldn't stop if he did.

"What if it's not fake any longer?" he asked, his voice like gravel. "What happens then?"

Chapter Five

E VERYTHING STOPPED.
The world. Her heart.

Gracelyn tipped her head back and fell into those dark gold eyes of his, and she was sure, then, that whatever happened in the next breath, in the next few moments, she wouldn't survive it. She couldn't possibly.

And she'd spent the whole of her life surviving anything that was thrown at her. She'd prided herself on her ability to do it. But she couldn't seem to care that Jonah Flint was the thing that was going to finally take her down. Instead, she welcomed it.

Though she didn't want to think about the ramifications of that, not here in the moody dark with nothing but moonlight and that sweet, bright heat between them.

"I told you," she said in a very precise, very prim voice that she hardly recognized as her own, and that couldn't disguise the playful heat beneath it. "I refuse to get involved with someone I work for. That's begging for trouble."

He was like something out of a dream, standing there before her with his gaze so bright and his mouth so hard, and she couldn't think of a single thing she'd ever wanted more than this. Than him.

Especially when his eyes gleamed a bright, brilliant shade of gold she'd never seen before, and that perfect mouth of his broke into a smile. Wide. Genuine. *Hers,* she understood. *All hers.* And yet it was etched with the same need that swirled through her, making her forget all the reasons this was a bad idea.

"You're fired," he told her softly, the way other men might have whispered words of love, of sex, of terrible need. "Does that help?"

He shifted closer, so much closer. She wished she wasn't wearing the western-style shawl she'd thought was so cute earlier this evening. She wished that when he leaned close, his chest brushed hers instead of the soft cashmere. She wished so many things, all of them carnal and wicked and comprising her own destruction in each act. And even though she knew it, all she wanted was this. Him.

Jonah. Here. Now.

"That strikes me as a solution that doesn't help me at all," she murmured.

She found it hard to breathe as his hands moved to her face, as his fingers brushed over her cheekbones and then moved to her hair. He cupped her head in one hard palm as he tugged on her ponytail and it took her a moment to realize he was pulling her hair out of its elastic.

Then he was raking his fingers through the length of it as it tumbled down to her shoulders, making a low sound she couldn't quite place. But then she did. If he'd been a cat, it would have been a purr.

"I have an in with the boss," he assured her, his mouth almost severe, but she knew it was the same stark need that moved in her. "I'm pretty confident he'll hire you again in the morning. Every morning."

"How sweet," Gracelyn whispered, and though she tried to keep that tartness in her voice, her expression, she melted into a smile instead. "It's like our own little corporate fairy tale."

Jonah's fingers sunk deep into her hair, pulling her head back as if he wanted better access, and Gracelyn's heart kicked at her, hard, as every other feeling in her body streaked into a brilliant fire and pooled between her legs.

"Once upon a time," he whispered, leaning in close, so she could taste the words against her lips. She brought her hands up to brace them against his chest, and felt the heat of him like a furnace. Like a roar. "There was a beautiful princess and a terrible ogre trapped in a hotel suite far, far away. And he had absolutely no intention of letting her go."

"This is already the best story I've ever heard."

"Then you better prepare yourself, darlin'," he told her, right there against her lips with the moon between them and too much Texas in his voice. It made her shudder with need. With rich longing. "Because I know how it ends."

And then Jonah bent his head that last little bit and finally, *finally*, took her mouth with his.

EVERYTHING SIMPLY *IGNITED*.

He didn't tease. He didn't play. He *took*—and Gracelyn loved it.

He was like gasoline poured on a dancing flame and oh, how she burned. They burst into a wildfire together. She couldn't get enough. She wanted to be closer. She *wanted*. And he simply held her head where he wanted it, angled his jaw, and claimed her.

As if she'd always been his. As if she'd never be anything but his.

As if this was only the beginning.

Jonah kissed her again and again. He tasted her deeply and carnally, stroking into her and driving her wild, until she realized she was making low, greedy little noises against his mouth.

He pulled back then, his hazel gaze a bright gleam in the dark, and she didn't know which one of them was breathing harder. He reached down and pulled her shawl up and over her head, making a sound of deep male approval when he saw the camisole she wore beneath it with no bra.

"You're going to kill me," he muttered, but Gracelyn was pretty sure she was the one dying.

He urged her back until she felt the windowsill behind her, and then he simply bent down and pulled one of her nipples deep into his mouth, camisole and all.

Gracelyn heard the sound, a high moan filled with sex and lust and overwhelming desire—and it was only when he increased the pressure and she heard it again that she realized she was the one making it.

Time seemed to blur and slow at the same time. Jonah's mouth was a torment and a joy. He teased her through the silken camisole, making her writhe against him, moving from one breast to the other. Up the length of her neck, then back again, before he stripped the flimsy garment from her and bared her to his view.

His smile then was a dark thing, edgy and irrevocably male, and it made her hips buck as if he'd pressed it deep into her.

Then he bent his head to the flesh he'd bared and he started all over again.

He used his teeth this time, his hands and his mouth and his remarkable voice, until Gracelyn was sobbing against him, begging for things she couldn't even name.

"Not yet, darlin'," he told her. "Not just yet."

And then, he pinched one nipple while he feasted on the other and just like that, he tossed her right over that edge. Into pure sensation.

Into joy.

When she could think again, or try, he'd lifted her into his arms and was striding through the darkened rooms of the suite. She hadn't been in his bedroom before and something about entering it now made her shudder all over again. He pressed his lips to her temple as he shouldered his way inside and then he set her down at the side of his bed.

She thought she should say something, that she should address the storms that still raced through her, that she should make it all funny somehow. More palatable, more easily dismissed. But there was something too powerful in the room with them, and she couldn't bring herself to break the hush that had fallen between them. She could feel the weight of it like a taut rope looped around the both of them, pulling them together, knitting them into one where they stood.

It was only a ghost, Gracelyn told herself. A hazard of an old hotel like this one. A trick of the moonlight, nothing more.

But she knew better.

And she couldn't handle the way he was looking at her. That bright, gold thing in his gaze that reminded her of sunlight, that transformed his face and made him almost too beautiful to look at directly. She felt something huge shift inside of her, then expand, and she was terrified she might do something terrible right there as he helped her step out of her boots and peel off her jeans—like burst into tears.

She didn't want that. God, but she didn't want that. If she didn't protect herself here, what would be left of her?

So when she was finally naked, when his hard, impatient hands had finally moved from kicking up flame and longing all over her skin to unbutton his own jeans, she slipped down onto her knees and knelt there before him.

Jonah let out a curse, somewhere up above her, but Gracelyn ignored it. She remembered their first day here, when he'd appeared in her doorway half dressed and had pulled his t-shirt on in front of her, giving her that stunning glimpse of the sheer male perfection of his body. She hadn't been able to do anything about it then, but tonight she could do as she liked, at last. She could kiss her way down that arrow of dark hair that dipped down toward the hardest part of him, reveling in his taste, his scent, the heat of his skin beneath the press of her lips. And she could pull him out when she found him, and measure his need in her hands.

But when she bent to take him in her mouth, he laughed, a dark sort of sound that moved in the room like magic. And then his hands were on her again. He pulled her to her feet and then tossed her backward onto the soft bed with an easy strength that made her stomach swoop down to her toes.

"Unless you want to rush straight to the happy ending, that's not happening," Jonah told her in a dark, strained sort of tone. It took her a moment to realize he wasn't talking about a fairy tale. He meant this act, this night, right here.

And Gracelyn sprawled across his soft coverlet, as he rid himself of the rest of his clothes and dealt with the condom, and wondered how the hell she was ever going to make it out of this in one piece.

But then he was right there, that magnificent body of his hot and hard and finally stretched out above her, and she stopped caring about *pieces*. She stopped caring about anything but the slide of skin against skin. Heat and lust, fire and need.

This. Him. *Jonah.*

And they rolled. They tangled.

She didn't know who was tasting who, or where. There was only the bliss of the touch, the rush of it, the sheer and intoxicating sensation, as if she'd been waiting for this forever. She was sure she had been.

But eventually, they were both stretched taut, strung out on their hunger. She found herself on top of him, her knees on either side of his hips. He sat up himself, his hands sinking deep into her hair again, his mouth the same slick joy and the same wild torment as it plundered hers.

Gracelyn knelt up, then reached down between them. He reared back slightly to watch her with narrow-eyed intensity as she lowered herself onto him, inch by perfect inch, until they both groaned at the slick fit.

His laughter was a breath against her neck. "You taking charge, darlin'?"

"Why not?" She didn't know when she'd started to like being called *darlin'*—she only knew she did. But then, there was very little she didn't like about this man. She teased them both with a roll of her hips, and Jonah's expression shifted; turned dangerous. "I don't work for you at the moment."

"No," he agreed, his voice a dark promise. "You don't."

His hands were streaks of fire down the length of her. He gripped her hips, and when he was holding her where he wanted her, she began to move.

It was a sleek dance. It was fire and longing.

It was perfect.

This time, when she shattered all around him, he rolled her beneath him and came over her, taking charge in a sleek twist. He set a new, wild rhythm as she shook around him that made her cry out and shake harder, until she was flung straight into another burst of light.

And he whispered her name like it was a mantra as he followed her into oblivion.

It can't last, she told herself when she woke later on to find herself curled into him, her face tucked into the crook of his neck like it fit there.

It couldn't. It wouldn't. She couldn't let herself start thinking about *fitting* with him.

He was *Jonah Flint* and when this strange Marietta interlude was over, he would go straight back to his three piece suits and his corporate retreats on the ranch he reportedly accessed only via helicopter. And she would still be the same old Custer County sow's ear, who'd spent her whole life trying to look as much like a silk purse as possible.

She would never see him again when they got back to Dallas. In the dark, in his bed and in his arms, she told herself she accepted it.

With her mouth, with her hands, with her body.

She accepted it, she reveled in it, and she vowed that she would steep herself in whatever time they had left. That she wouldn't worry about what came next or what they were doing here. That she would stop tearing herself apart about the things that wouldn't change.

They had a week left. Gracelyn promised herself she would use every last moment of it.

In the morning, later than usual thanks to the long, hot night they'd shared, she ran down a winding road headed into a sweet blue morning, crisp with possibilities she already knew came stamped with an expiration date.

But almost as if he knew how little time they had, too, and wanted every last second of it to be real, Jonah came with her.

"YOU MIGHT AS well just get to the point," Jasper said out of nowhere.

They stood in a relatively quiet spot near the bar in Flint-Works, sampling one of Jasper's new ales, while the early dinner crowd spread out at the tables and a local band played on the small stage.

Jasper's gaze was hard. "I'm proposing in two days and the suspense is killing me."

"What point is that?" Jonah asked carefully.

Yesterday, once Chelsea had finished with school, they'd all gone on a leisurely hike, deep into Copper Canyon and back. And now that he considered it, his brother's girlfriend had seemed unduly quiet at their dinner afterward in the Italian restaurant in town. Was it all finally coming to a head?

Jonah ignored the part of him that whispered he wasn't ready. That he wanted to live in these last few, bright days with Gracelyn forever—

"You've been my brother a long time," Jasper said in that lazy way of his that meant he was pissed. Really, truly pissed. "Give me a little bit of credit. You didn't come all the way here to take in a country rodeo and congratulate me over some kettle corn at the barrel racing finals. I'm not an idiot."

It was Thursday night and the entire town of Marietta was in a happy sort of uproar. The rodeo was in town at last, with a slate of events set to start the following night. That meant there was hardly a square foot of real estate within the town limits that wasn't decked out in banners or otherwise showing as much enthusiastic support for the annual festivities as possible. There was a real, live country singer coming in from Nashville on Saturday to add a little star power to the proceedings and if the singer in question wasn't one of Jonah's favorites—give him a Blake Shelton or a Landry Bell any day—Jake Kohl was certainly a big enough star to raise the profile of the whole enterprise.

And if Jonah hadn't spent the last few days in a delicious, delirious haze that had Gracelyn's name written all over it, he might have been a little more prepared for this moment with Jasper. After all, *this* was the reason he was here.

"Did you expect my support?" he asked coolly. "With or without kettle corn?"

"I don't care one way or the other," Jasper said. He didn't bother to throw out one of his big, bullshit grins, which told Jonah that exactly how angry he was. "And you can sulk about it all you want. You've gotten pretty good at that over the past couple of years."

"I assume that by 'sulking' you're referring to me picking up the pieces you left behind when you stormed off in a huff," Jonah replied, his own voice much too smooth, like that might cover the sting of Jasper's words. "You didn't walk out on a family dinner one night, Jasper. You walked out on a multi-million dollar business. I apologize if my reaction to having to sort out all the details was a little less happy-go-lucky than you'd like."

Something like guilt moved over his brother's face then, but Jonah felt no particular sense of victory at the sight. What the hell was the matter with him? He'd been so sure this long overdue conversation would have made him feel vindicated at the very least. Instead, he felt something a whole lot more like sad.

"Just call off your attack dog," Jasper gritted out after a moment, moving to let a group of laughing tourists surge past him. "Chelsea's had enough."

"Let me guess. In Jasper-speak, that means my girlfriend, is that right?"

Jasper let out a taut little bark of laughter.

"Your girlfriend," he repeated, like the words were in a foreign language, and then he shook his head. "You can't think that's serious, Jonah. She's basically just you in female form. All ice and spleen, and I've been dealing with that charming combination my whole life." His gaze was as hard as nails then. "No one can put up with it forever, Jonah. No one would *want* to put up with it. Not even you."

Funny how Jonah really didn't want to play this out any longer. But he pushed on anyway. "I don't know what you mean."

"You do." Jasper ran a hand through the hair he'd always insisted on keeping too long—to make sure they were different,

Jonah had always assumed, at a single glance. "I get it. We came from nothing, Dad was a dick, and we had too much to prove to him before he died like every other angry young man in the history of the world."

"Unlike most of them," Jonah pointed out crisply, "we proved it."

"There's more to life than making money," Jasper growled at him.

"Says the man who made enough of it to retire at thirty-five," Jonah retorted. He rolled his eyes. "You'll forgive me if I find your sudden one-eighty on that topic a little suspicious."

He took a long swig of the ale, and wasn't surprised to find his brother glaring at him when he lowered his pint glass. What did surprise him was the *way* Jasper was doing it. As if he pitied Jonah. Deeply.

Which Jonah didn't like much at all.

"There's more to life than money," Jasper said again, very deliberately, as if Jonah might have misheard him the first time. "And you can collect as much of it as you want. You can fill your life with snotty, passive-aggressive corporate girlfriends, who act more like one of your minions than any kind of partner. It's not going to feed the empty thing inside you."

Jonah let out a sigh. "Are you also a psychiatrist, in all your spare time? You wear a lot of hats up here in the hinterland, Jasper. You're bordering on unrecognizable."

"I'd tell you what would fill it, but you wouldn't believe me," Jasper said, his gaze hot and intent on Jonah's as if he hadn't even heard what Jonah had said. "You wouldn't know how to believe me. And that makes me sad for you, but I spent thirty-four years taking care of you, Jonah. I'm taking care of me now. And I'm taking care of Chelsea, who believe me, I'm marrying, whether you like it or not."

And there was that grin. Jasper's friendly shark's grin, that

Jonah had seen a great many times in his life, but never directed at him. He told himself it didn't make everything inside him freeze up. That it didn't matter if it did.

"Which is the point I'm making here," Jasper continued quietly. "If you sic your little Doberman girlfriend on Chelsea again—if Chelsea cries one more tear over something Gracelyn says or does—I'm not going to respect that you're my brother and she's your problem, the way I have been. I'm going to handle it myself. And I don't think either one of you is going to appreciate that."

Jonah had never wanted to punch his brother in the face as much as he did then, and the worst part was, he didn't know if it was because Jasper had insulted him or that he'd insulted Gracelyn. *Maybe both,* a small voice inside him suggested. And he knew, dimly, that it was revolutionary that he cared about anyone who wasn't himself or Jasper.

He felt his fingers curl into a fist—and then he had to check that urge and remind himself that this wasn't why he was here. That he'd spent a week and a half working to get to this point with his brother and there was no point wasting it on a bar brawl.

He thought of Gracelyn, lying naked in his bed this morning with all her thick, dark hair tumbling around her. He thought of that smile on her face as she'd laughed at the stories he'd told her and then haltingly shared her own. And he reminded himself that he could do anything. Even use her the way he'd always intended to use her when they'd come here, despite how gross that felt tonight.

Because he knew the truth, he assured himself. He knew what he felt, and that had nothing to do with what was said here. Unlike Jasper, he knew reality.

Unlike Jasper, Jonah had never known anything *but* reality.

"I don't understand," he said, keeping his voice perfectly

even, and it was the first time in his life he could remember it costing him. "Do you think I'm making a mistake with Gracelyn?"

Jasper let out a bark of laughter. "Of course not. Every man dreams of his only brother hooking up with a vicious, fanged creature, who likes to use other people as her chew toy. By all means, Jonah, keep it up. But when she tears you up and spits you out, and you can count on it, she will—don't say I didn't warn you."

There was a slight shift in the crowd behind Jasper then, and Jonah knew before he looked. *He knew.* He felt it deep in his bones, like fate. But he looked anyway, and there she was, a little bit early for the dinner they'd agreed to have here at FlintWorks tonight. His beautiful Gracelyn, who deserved so much better than this, standing right behind his brother and clearly waiting for Jonah to defend her.

He saw the very second she understood that he wasn't going to do that.

"Let me return the favor," he said to his brother instead, looking back at Jasper then and ignoring the furious, spiked thing that tore at him from the inside out. "You married Marlene in this same haste, if you'll recall. You didn't want to hear that trophy wives tend to look a little bit less like a prize when you want more from them than just standing around, looking pretty on a shelf somewhere. You made me promise never to let you act so foolishly again."

Jasper went very, very still.

"Don't compare Chelsea to Marlene, Jonah." He sounded conversational, casual even, but Jonah could see the murder in his eyes. "Don't ever do it again."

"The only comparing I'm doing is you to you," Jonah replied calmly. While other people might look at an obviously angry Jasper Flint and see a man to steer clear of, Jonah only saw his little brother. And it would be a bitterly cold day in hell before he'd let his little brother take him in a fight, no matter how big a man Jasper might think he was these days. "You walked away from more money than most people ever dream of making—certainly more money than *we* ever dreamed of making. You got divorced when your trophy wife cheated on you with the personal trainer you paid for. You relocated from a big city to a tiny little town in the middle of rural Montana. From a giant mansion in Preston Hollow to a studio apartment above a bar. You went from corporate America and oil fields to artisanal beer and the local rodeo fundraising committee. Now you want to marry a high school history teacher and what? Run for Mayor of Nowheresville?"

"I believe that position is currently filled," Jasper bit out. "But I'm not ruling it out. I like it here."

"They have names for this kind of thing," Jonah said gently. Kindly, even, though he doubted his brother would appreciate it at the moment. "You're a little early for it, but then, you always were quick on the draw. It's called a mid-life crisis, Jasper. Or sometimes even a downward spiral. Why the hell else would you wake up one morning and decide you needed to live out your life in downtown Mayberry?"

"This is not my crisis, it's yours." And Jasper's voice wasn't hot, or lazy, or even angry. It was as direct as the way he stared at Jonah then, like they were strangers to each other. Something cold seemed to sweep over Jonah, turning him to ice where he stood. "You're my brother. My twin. You know I love you. But I can't be all things to you. You have your girlfriend, I guess. And we have other family—"

Jonah was appalled then and didn't try to hide it. "They're not our family. Why would you mention them?"

"They're Mom's family. They're our sisters. More than that, they're coming here." Jasper glanced at the watch on his wrist, and then back at Jonah, and the look in his eyes was painful. It hurt. "They should be in town within the hour. Chelsea's a big fan of roots. Family in all its forms. And it turns out, so am I."

"I'm your family."

"You are," Jasper agreed quietly. "And it's the only reason I didn't kick your ass and rip that woman of yours in half. But I'm not playing this game with you any more. This is the future. This is *my* future, and you can either take part in it and support it or you can get the hell out of it." He lifted his hand when Jonah started to speak. "This isn't a debate, Jonah. You don't get a vote."

And by the time he'd recovered himself, Jasper had turned and walked away, disappearing into the heedless, happy crowd all around them while the band kicked into an old Bob Seger song and the world kept right on turning.

But worse, so had Gracelyn.

Chapter Six

~

THE SUN WAS still out, but the shadows were long when Jonah pushed his way out of the bar and onto the street. There were already too many people wandering around the town, he thought, and the rodeo hadn't even officially begun. Tourists snapping pictures. Locals taking in the festive atmosphere.

And he was like a stranger inside himself after that conversation—as if Jasper was a limb and he'd hacked himself off.

Jonah felt something like dizzy.

But there, walking quickly toward the hotel with her head down, between a couple of grinning cowboys and an overexcited brace of teenaged girls, was Gracelyn.

And Jonah couldn't process what Jasper had said to him. He couldn't seem to look at it straight, not any of it. The only thing he could see was the way Gracelyn had stood there looking at him in that crowd, an awful sort of bruised acceptance in her dark gaze, completely unlike the woman he'd come to know.

Earlier, he'd pulled her to him in the entryway of their suite when they'd been on their way out. He'd already had her in the shower that afternoon, long and soapy and sweet in ways he wasn't ready to acknowledge, but he couldn't seem to stop himself where she was concerned. She'd looped her arms around his neck and tilted her head back in that half-challenging, half-seductive manner of hers that made his pulse pound, thinking about it now. He'd wanted to taste that little smile of hers, trace it with his fingers, learn it with every sense he had.

He'd settled for a taste, picking her up and wrapping her legs around his waist. Then, when she was high against him and holding him tight, he'd walked with her. She'd laughed against his mouth. And when he'd toppled them both over the arm of the longer sofa and deep into the cushions there, her dark brown eyes had sparkled so bright, he'd felt it like fireworks in his own chest.

He still did.

And that had been before he'd lost himself deep inside of her and heard her sigh out his name like a song into his ear.

Jonah couldn't bear the thought that he'd ruined that, too.

He caught her outside the hotel's front door and moved her out of the flow of traffic, and he didn't care that the people around them did that double take when they saw him. He didn't care that this was a small town and his every move would no doubt be reported back to Jasper and discussed endlessly. He wouldn't have cared if there were tabloid reporters camped out to get a piece of him. He only cared about that look of stunned misery on Gracelyn's face and the way she refused to meet his gaze.

For the first time since he'd met her.

"You're going to have to look at me sooner or later," he said quietly.

He wanted to plant his hands on either side of her head, back her into the brick wall behind her and kiss her until she smiled again, but he didn't. He couldn't. Something in the way she stood there, like she'd been this fragile all along but he hadn't noticed it, stopped him where he stood only scant inches from her.

Jonah shoved his hands in his pockets and told himself to be patient when it was the last thing in the world he felt capable of doing. His heart was too big for his chest, suddenly, like a heart attack in the making—but he knew, somehow, that his condition wasn't medical. Not yet.

I'd tell you what would fill your heart, Jasper had told him, *but you wouldn't believe me.*

Jonah shoved that aside. And then Gracelyn looked at him, her dark eyes glassy and haunted, and that was a whole lot worse.

"I knew you had a plan," she said, very matter-of-factly. He hated it. Jonah wanted to throw back his head and howl like something wild. His hands bunched into fists, but she kept going. "I knew you were using me to execute it. I signed up for it! There's absolutely no reason I should feel like you betrayed me in there."

"But you do."

She nodded, short and convulsive. "I do."

"Gracelyn . . . "

She waited for a moment, as if maybe he could fix this somehow if he had the right words. But he'd never had the right words. He'd never needed words. His father hadn't heard a single thing anyone said, and Jasper had never needed them.

Or maybe he had, Jonah thought then—that possibility like a punch to his gut—and he'd never understood that until now.

But that didn't help him here. He wasn't sure anything could.

He reached over and slid his hand over her cheek, letting his thumb trace over that sulky mouth he knew, now, could drive him wild. He wanted to take some measure of comfort from the fact she leaned into his hand, just slightly, but that miserable thing in her eyes, stamped across her face, told him there was no comfort here.

"Do you know why I'm called Gracelyn?" she asked. Jonah blinked. Gracelyn smiled, but it was a hard quirk of her lovely mouth. Worse, she pulled her face away from his touch. "My mother was only a kid when she had me. Eighteen. She had also been high through what few high school classes she attended." Her smile sharpened at the look on his face. "Oh, don't worry. That was her harmless weed phase. She wouldn't upgrade to the hard stuff for a few more years yet."

"You don't have to do this."

It was a plea, and she ignored it.

"She wasn't much of a student," Gracelyn confided. "She thought that was the name of Elvis's magical mansion down in Memphis and she wanted me to be magical in the same way." She laughed, and the raw sound made him tense. "She knew exactly what my life was going to be like. She had it all planned. And she was disappointed when she figured out how the name was really spelled, but not as disappointed as she was when she discovered I was a whole other person with a set of my very own thoughts and opinions, and not very magical at all."

"I take it there's a message in that story?" he asked, feeling too tight, too on edge, *too much*.

"I've never told anyone that story," she said, too much emotion in her voice, but she didn't seem to notice it and he couldn't seem to do a thing to stop it. "And I've always, always hated Elvis. I'm no corporate attack dog, Jonah," she threw at him when he was very nearly tempted to laugh at the Elvis crack. "If this debacle has taught me anything, it's that I need to stop denying my roots."

More roots. Jonah was tired of all the damned *roots*.

"I own my past," he told her then, his voice too hot. Uncontrolled. "I know exactly where I come from. An angry man with very few skills and less money, and the woman who abandoned him and her two young sons in the bargain. What more do I need to know? There's a difference between acknowledging your roots while choosing to move on from them, and letting them choke you and trip you and drag you down into the dirt."

She stared at him, and he didn't know if he'd been talking to Jasper or to her. All he knew was that she was only a few inches away from him and it felt like miles.

"How would you know?" she asked quietly. "It sounded a lot like you have a whole branch of your family you've never even met."

He wanted to rage then. Howl again, and louder than before. He wanted to tear off the top of the world and make it tremble—or maybe that was just the way it felt inside him, then. And he could only think of one thing on the planet that might make him feel any better, and she was looking at him in a way he really, really didn't like.

"Come on," he said, his tone abrupt. But he couldn't seem to help that, either. "Let's go inside. This is pointless."

"Then I think you're missing the point," she said, very distinctly, her eyes trained on his. "Because you gave your brother a choice and he chose the woman he's going to marry."

He felt his jaw tense. "I came after you, not him."

Gracelyn made a scoffing sound. "Because you knew you could catch me. I'm a sure thing, aren't I?" She pulled in a breath, and everything was dangerous, everything hurt, and he couldn't look away. He couldn't stop this. He couldn't keep either one of them safe. "But I'm betting you knew that when you called me into your office, didn't you? I'm betting that's exactly what you were looking for. An ambitious little would-be Doberman with more desperation than sense."

Jonah actually took a step back. He was reeling and he thought if he touched her just then it would all tangle and knot and destroy him, and he had no idea if he'd survive that. He had no idea how he'd survive any of this.

"Stop," he said, but he didn't know if he was talking to her or to himself. There were volcanoes under Yellowstone National Park a mere hour or so south and he was sure he could feel them inside of him, boiling over, getting ready to blow. "You know. You know I—"

She stared at him. She waited. Jonah stared back at her, stricken.

He could hear the music from his brother's brewery. He could hear cars and pick ups passing by on the street behind him. He could hear the sounds of a town gearing up into its festive weekend all around them, weaving in and out of the last of the day's light. He could hear the shifting, lethal tectonics inside of him, the seismic disaster he was terribly afraid had already taken place.

And he didn't finish that sentence. He didn't know how.

He still didn't have the words.

Her delicate face crumpled slightly, just slightly, and then smoothed out again so fast he almost thought he'd imagined it. Almost—but the pit in his stomach told him otherwise. She swallowed, hard.

And when she met his gaze again, it scalded him alive.

"But this isn't really fair, is it?" Gracelyn asked softly. "You're not the only one pretending. You're not the only one hiding yourself away in work, because it hurts too much to feel. It's hypocritical to act like I'm not just as bad as you are."

"I'm not doing that." He could feel his hand, couldn't he? So tightly balled up into a fist it made his whole arm tremble. "You're not doing that. No one here is a hypocrite."

"I get it," she told him quietly. It felt like the end of everything. And Jonah had no words to describe how that beat at him. Or how *hurt* couldn't begin to cover all the ways it tore through him. "Sometimes an ogre is just a guy who doesn't know any better, and a princess is just a girl who should, and fairy tales are made up stories to make us feel better about how little sense it all makes."

"I have no idea what that means." He didn't want to know. He had the awful feeling that he already did.

Her smile then ripped into him. He thought maybe it broke him wide open, right there in the shadow of Marietta's grand hotel. He was surprised, on some level, that no one else seemed to hear it or see it or feel it, all that shattering right out there in the evening air.

But maybe that was because he was still standing there, acting as if he was still alive when the truth was, he doubted that too.

"How could you possibly have stood there and told your brother who I really am?" Gracelyn asked. "When the truth is, I don't even know?"

And that time, when she walked away from him, ducking around him and disappearing into the evening, Jonah didn't follow her.

Because he didn't know how to that either.

SHE'D KNOWN BETTER, of course.

They'd had a handful of perfect days, she'd let herself pretend—but she'd known it couldn't last. She'd *known*.

You didn't lose yourself, Gracelyn thought fiercely as she slammed her foot down hard on the gas pedal of the Range Rover she'd liberated from Jonah's driver. She pointed the luxurious SUV east on the Interstate. *You just lost track of it there for a minute.*

Because she'd known from that very first night that whatever happened with Jonah wasn't something that could survive the week, much less their inevitable return to reality. Hadn't she told herself exactly that? Right there in his bed?

So she had no explanation for why, despite all the things she'd told herself—all the things she'd chanted over and over again in her head, trying so hard to ward off any potential pain—she'd obviously convinced herself that when push came to shove, Jonah would choose her over this stupid plot of his.

Or that he would choose her at all.

At some point, Gracelyn reflected as she hurtled down I-90, she was going to have to face the fact that she was pretty much always wrong.

Always.

As a little girl, she'd been sure her parents would choose her over their assorted addictions. As a teenager, she'd thought her extended family would welcome it when she'd decided to throw the truth around, as she prepared to leave town in a cloud of her own righteous indignation. As an adult, she'd believed she could handle mixing her upward trajectory with a man she'd known full well, and at first sight, was going to pose a serious problem to her.

Wrong, wrong, wrong. She was always wrong.

Gracelyn drove too fast, and it didn't help. She drove as the sun finally dropped out of sight behind her, reflecting fire off of her mirror as it went. She had to grit her teeth to keep from turning back. She drove while her phone sat silent in the drink holder next to her, as Jonah, who hadn't come after her, failed to so much as shoot her a text. Which was its own message, wasn't it?

She drove in and out of what few radio stations existed out this way where there was precious little between the land and sky. She drove until the mountains were a memory and the stars were a tumult in the clear skies overhead. Past Big Timber and Billings and on toward the Dakotas.

She headed north when she hit Miles City—which looked a whole lot nicer than she remembered it, even if only in her headlights—and the further she got from the city, the further she drove herself straight back into the past.

There were lights on in the old bar and fewer boarded-up windows on the small collection of houses she passed when she finally got to her hometown. It was coming up on ten o'clock when she took the last turn down the old country road that had never had a name as far back as she could remember. She slowed way down to allow for its still-unpaved state, bumping her way over the same old ruts and remembering all the hundreds of times she'd done this before.

She remembered coming here as a small child and then later, living here after her grandmother Betty had liberated her from her parents. She remembered driving her granddad's pick up truck when she was well below the legal driving limit and she remembered taking this same road much too fast when she was finally a legitimate driver in her own right. Back when driving a car had felt as close as she'd ever thought she'd get to flying.

And she remembered, in stark detail, that bright blue June afternoon when she'd left in a cloud of dust and had promised herself she would never, ever return. Not as long as she was alive.

Which meant this worked out perfectly, because she was pretty sure she'd died on the side of Front Street in pretty little Marietta earlier this evening, and this apparition jolting its way home was a ghost.

The weathered farmhouse at the end of the long lane was exactly as she remembered it, with its different sections slapped together haphazardly over generations to form a lopsided, rambling L. She knew they'd have seen her coming from far off and still, she took her time getting out of the Range Rover. She stood beside it for a moment, breathing in the too familiar scents of a country evening out on the Plains. Growing things and prairie air. Dirt and gas and the dark itself.

She heard the mournful whisper of the wind through the trees and the rustle of the branches as it moved through them. She heard the dogs making a ruckus out back near the great old barn where she'd played a thousand games of make believe in her time. She heard a TV set blaring from the old living room, where her grandmother Betty liked to sit in the evenings with her feet up and her needlework in her lap.

And she still could have picked her way across this yard blind. There was a different truck fetched up near the door where the outside light shone. There was a brand new coat of paint peeling off the sides of the farmhouse right beside it. But she knew this place. She knew every last inch of it by heart.

Gracelyn didn't know how she'd managed to convince herself she'd forgotten it.

And there were so many things tilting and rolling inside of her then, like she'd strapped herself to a roller coaster and let it run wild. She couldn't tell whether she hated this place or she loved it, if she was happy she'd come back tonight or if she wished she'd kept right on pretending it had never existed . . . Hell, she didn't even know if any of her family still lived here these days, that's how long it had been.

But none of that changed the fact that it was home. That it would always be home, no matter that she never planned to live here again. Gracelyn let out a little sigh, and something inside her, some open, hurting thing she'd hardly known was there because it had always been there, started to heal. Just a little.

The screen door swung open as she reached the steps with a great, long squeak of its hinges that sounded like a familiar song to her ears, and Gracelyn stood there blinking as the light from inside poured over her face.

She knew the woman who stood there instantly, though she'd only been a seventeen year old smart-mouthed kid the last time they'd stood this close to each other. She wondered if she looked as changed and yet the same. As if the girl she'd known was superimposed over the woman who stood there before her in the farmhouse doorway, a familiar stranger with the same dark Packard eyes, the same body shape they shared with all their female relatives, and even the same damned nose they'd always blamed on their least favorite uncle.

"Hey Bex," Gracelyn said to her cousin, once her best friend in the all the world, closer to her than a sister could have been. "Is Grandma Betty around? I was in Montana and I wanted to say hi."

That was stupid, of course. A stupid thing to say. And far more stupid, she realized then, as her cousin stared back at her in obvious astonishment, was the fact that she'd been so busy escaping this place and staying far away from everything it represented to her that she'd never considered what her reception might be when—if—she returned.

It had never crossed her mind that the family she'd abandoned so ruthlessly might not be all that overjoyed to see her, after all this time had passed. After she'd deliberately and very obviously and *literally* left them in her dust.

Maybe Jasper had been right, after all, much as it shamed her to admit it. She was exactly like Jonah, ice and spleen, and an arrogant fool besides—

"You dumbass," Bex gritted out at her, and Gracelyn realized with a start that her cousin was choked up. That the glimmering thing Gracelyn could see in those eyes so much like her own was emotion, not fury. Love, not hate. "We've been waiting for you and waiting for you. For *ten years*, Gracelyn."

"I think I got a little lost," Gracelyn heard herself say, in the same kind of messed up voice and too much wet heat behind her eyes.

"That doesn't surprise me at all," Bex replied with a thick little laugh. "You always did have a piss-poor sense of direction."

And then she opened up her arms the same way she'd opened up that door, and Gracelyn walked right back into them.

At last.

Chapter Seven

JONAH MEANT TO leave.

First, he waited for Gracelyn to come back Thursday night, but she didn't—a fact it took him until almost three a.m. to accept. He woke up Friday morning and went for a run in the Graff's fitness center. It was like every other fitness center in every other hotel he ever traveled to, and no matter how high he jacked up the treadmill, he couldn't seem to outrun the heavy thing that pressed down hard on him, like stone.

He meant to leave, and so he took a series of calls, each quicker than the last. He suspected that might have had something to do with his viciously dark mood that he did very little to hide. And when his calls were done, he packed.

But Gracelyn hadn't taken her things when she'd left last night, and he stood in the doorway to her room imagining that if he stood there long enough, she might appear from the attached bathroom and everything would reset and go back to what it had been—

Which, of course, didn't happen.

And he had no real explanation for how he found himself outside on Marietta's Main Street. He should have been in a car headed for his plane back to Dallas. The afternoon tipped over into early evening and still he walked. And around him, the whole town—and what had to be the better part of the Paradise Valley region—poured out into the streets to enjoy the mild September weather and the rodeo fever.

Jonah told himself this was a research opportunity, nothing more. A chance to figure out what his brother could possibly be thinking. He wove his way around excited children and sloping, surly-eyed teens. He avoided the parents treating the sidewalk like date night and the boisterous crowd spilling out of Grey's Saloon. He looked in the windows of a bakery, a book store, an upscale chocolate shop with a very long line. He avoided his own reflection as if he was some kind of vampire. He eyed the imported cowboys askance, and he narrowly escaped the determined pursuit of more than one cute little cowgirl with a bit of a buzz on.

It was Friday night. Summer was over, but this was its last hurrah. The rodeo was in town and that obviously meant something here. And Jonah was made of stone.

He was on his second loop around the town, and he was definitely leaving this time, just as soon as he got back to his hotel down at the far end of Front Street. Then he looked up to see two older, white-haired ladies sitting on a wrought-iron bench outside a tattoo parlor that looked like it belonged in the middle of funky Austin, Texas, not set down here in Marietta.

The little old ladies looked so much like they belonged in an animated movie that Jonah almost looked around to make sure the street signs hadn't burst into interpretive dance while he wasn't looking. The two women smiled at him, in a placid sort of unison that made him straighten at once, his eyes narrowing as he took them in. The one on the left wore her snowy hair up in a bun and was draped in scarves, the one on the right had short white hair and a lot of bold jewelry instead, and they both wore knee-length skirts and very brightly-colored cowboy boots.

"That is not our Jasper Flint, Martha, as much as he might

look it," said the one on the left, making no particular effort to modify her volume. Almost as if she wanted Jonah to hear her. "You can tell by the hair. Or the lack of it."

"That and the ferocious scowl," the one who was clearly Martha replied tartly. Then sniffed. "Don't nudge me, Harriet. He obviously wants to look mean, or he wouldn't be walking around like that right out here on a public street on rodeo weekend, making all the women and children cower before him in fear."

She was the one who smiled the brightest when Jonah stopped in front of them.

"Evening ladies," he said, sounding more like Jasper than he had in more years than he could count. He ignored it—and the hitch inside him that went with it. "I couldn't help but overhear."

"That's undoubtedly because we were speaking *to* you, dear," Harriet murmured, her smile never dimming. "Hardly any point in saying it, otherwise."

"And I also couldn't help but notice that neither one of you is cowering." He eyed the shop behind them through its wide open front door. Rock music spun out from inside, mixed with that buzzing sound that he knew was the tattoo gun. "From me or, apparently, the prospect of getting a little ink."

"We don't cower any longer," Martha assured him. "We gave it up in our twenties. Possibly our thirties, now that I consider it. It all blends together, after a while."

"There are a few things that stand out, of course," observed Harriet, shifting her bright boots beneath her. "Ink, for example. I always wanted a tattoo. But Mother told me they were the work of the devil and the Merchant Marines, which, it must be said, she did seem to feel were more or less the same thing."

"It's so pleasant to welcome in the time of one's life when one can do as she pleases," Martha said, as if in agreement.

"I don't know either one of you," Jonah said, though he felt as if he did, which he would likely find bizarre the moment he walked away, "but I feel confident that you both did exactly as you pleased, no matter what time of your life it was."

Harriet smiled at him. "Didn't you?" She settled back against the bench and nodded at her friend, though her gaze never left Jonah. "Tell me, Martha, didn't we read an article not too long back about the Flint brothers?"

"We did indeed." Martha gifted Jonah with a benevolent smile. "It talked all about their unshakable bond. They claimed it was that identical twin connection, far more powerful than mere brotherhood. You know how close twins can be, Harriet. Why, Bitsy and Gert Framingham practically had telepathy back in college!"

"If not, sadly, any wit to go along with it," Harriet replied dryly. Her calm gaze seemed to pin Jonah to the ground where he stood. "But do you know what the wonderful thing is about unshakeable bonds?"

Jonah shook his head, unable, suddenly, to speak past the constriction in his throat. It hadn't been there a moment before, surely.

"They can take quite a bit of shaking, it turns out, before they start to crack," Martha said, very distinctly. "No matter how it might appear."

Jonah had no idea what he might have said to that, but a man around his own age, who looked vaguely familiar to him, appeared in the shop's open door. He rolled his eyes at the women.

"Enough," he said. "Leave the man alone." He shook his head as he looked at Jonah. "Ignore the Grans, please. They want you to think they're your magical fairy godmothers or something. When, in fact, they just live in a small town and listen to every single bit of gossip they can. That's how they know your business. They have zero shame."

"Hush, Griffin," Martha chided him, though she didn't sound at all chastened. "Or I won't let you give me my first tattoo."

"It's not her first," Harriet confided to him, or maybe to the whole street, her eyes sparkling. "She just doesn't want to shock you with the delicate placement of the one she already has. You grandchildren can be so excitable."

Griffin had a hand over his face and was groaning into it as Jonah walked away. And he was almost all the way to Flint-Works before he realized that, while the Grans might not have been magical the way they'd seemed back there for a moment, they'd still managed to make him smile.

A minor miracle, he was sure.

And maybe that was why, when he found himself at the microbrewery's door, he didn't keep walking. He didn't go on to the Graff, grab his stuff, and get the hell out of this place, the way he knew he should.

Instead, he manned up and went inside to find his brother.

And found him—after asking three different blue t-shirted bartenders, who gave him three different, if cheerful, answers—out behind the building, tossing garbage bags into the dumpster.

Jonah let the heavy door slam shut behind him and stood there for a minute. Copper Mountain hung there in the distance, looking brooding and mysterious in the gathering dark, and he knew his brother knew he was there. That if he'd been anyone else, Jasper would have turned around and faced him already.

"I swear to God," Jasper said after a moment or two inched by, brushing his hands on his cargo pants as he finally turned from the dumpster. "If this is round two of your bullshit, I'll throw you in there with the garbage."

"Tempting," Jonah said. He eyed his brother across the little stretch of concrete. "But you couldn't throw me anywhere with a phalanx of major league pitchers standing behind you offering pointers, and anyway, that's not why I'm here."

He hadn't thought this through, he knew. *They can take quite a bit of shaking before they start to crack*, the old woman had told him. He went with it.

"Then why are you?" Jasper's gaze was hard. "Wasn't the last week and a half enough to—"

"I don't want to end up like Dad," Jonah threw out there, baldly. He thought maybe they both froze, with the motion light on them and moths dive bombing it up above them. "He latched on to something he hated and he just . . . ran with it. And the next thing you know, that's the only thing he had left in him. And I think I'm headed that way. Fast."

Jasper looked as startled as he was. And, Jonah had never realized how much he depended on his brother to *not* be like him until that moment. To *not* hold grudges. To *not* brood and go dark and do all the things that Jonah did to make it through the day.

Or how terrified he was, straight down into his soul, that this would be the time Jasper decided to take a leaf out of Jonah's book instead.

"You're not Dad, Jonah." Jasper's voice was dark, but certain, and Jonah let out a breath he hadn't known he'd been holding. Jasper glared at him for a long moment, but something had changed. And his brother's voice was gruff, but not unkind, when he continued. "You're a dick, let's be clear, but you're not Dad."

He could have laughed then. Muttered his way around it and let it all slide into a thump on the back and another subject avoided, but he didn't. He met Jasper's gaze instead.

"I think it's a thin line," Jonah said quietly. "I think it's not as hard to cross it as we thought when we were kids. And I think I've been so pissed at you for leaving the company that I haven't seen straight in two years."

"I left the company. I couldn't leave *you* if I tried." Jasper scowled at him. "I see you every time I look in the mirror."

"But I like the business, Jasper," Jonah continued, not caring if his voice rose a little, if he got hot. "I like making money, because I'm good at it. It's like a jigsaw puzzle that I get to put together every day. I don't get bored. I don't wish I was doing something else." He shook his head. "I don't want to move to the farm down the road and raise llamas, or whatever the hell people do here."

"No one asked you to move anywhere."

"And I never asked you to tolerate my *ice and spleen.*" They glared at each other, and Jasper folded his arms over his chest while he did it, which made Jonah realize he had, too. "Your *aw, shucks,* lazy cowboy shtick lost its charm around about the sixth grade, in case you wondered."

"You must have me mistaken with someone else," Jasper retorted. "I'm a well-known, much-celebrated delight."

"And I'm a CEO," Jonah retorted. "Ice and spleen is in my job description."

"Fine," Jasper said.

"Fine," Jonah agreed.

And they eyed each other for a moment, across a whole lot more than just the back parking area of a converted train depot.

"I feel like this could have been an email I could have read at my leisure," Jasper muttered after a moment or two had passed, but the storm was gone. They were okay. Jonah could see it on his face. "I have a bar to run, if you're finished."

"I thought I'd buy you a beer," Jonah said gruffly, and Jasper grinned.

"Is that . . . ?" He dropped his arms as he started walking toward Jonah. "My lazy cowboy ears must be deceiving me. Is that your version of an apology?"

"I'm not going to apologize for looking out for you," Jonah retorted. But he relented when Jasper drew near. "But I'll admit my methods might have been a little bit over the top."

"Just a little."

"I thought I'd buy you a beer to celebrate the next chapter in your life," Jonah said, almost formally, and Jasper reached over and clapped him on the arm, because he was still the demonstrative, emotional one. Even now. Even after all of this. And Jonah was deeply, profoundly glad in a way that might have felt like joy, he thought. If he hadn't lost Gracelyn in this mess. "And to apologize if the fact that I'm happy for you both got lost in translation."

"I will accept that beer," Jasper said in the same tone of voice. "And I'll accept that apology, but Chelsea might take a while. She holds a mean grudge."

And they were twins, after all. They didn't have telepathy, but they'd been sharing an identical skin for more than thirty-six years. So Jonah knew, when they stood there for a moment, that things really were going to be okay between them, because Jasper never would have brought Chelsea into it again, if it wasn't. He knew that the way he knew his own name.

He knew it, because he didn't know what he'd do if Jasper started in about Dobermans again. He suspected it would explode this fragile little peace between them, and Jonah wasn't as much like his brother as he should be. As he wanted to be.

Maybe Jasper knew it too, because he didn't go there. He slung an arm over Jonah's shoulders instead, and steered them both back inside FlintWorks.

"I'm not worried," Jonah told him as the walked into the crowd. "She'll come around."

Jasper laughed. "She likes a little bit of charm, Jonah. Not really in your wheelhouse."

"She won't be able to help herself," Jonah said, and smiled

when Jasper raised his brows. "She finds you irresistible and I look just like you, only better."

THE RODEO MADNESS was at full pitch when Gracelyn drove back into Marietta that Saturday night. In the Range Rover she was mildly surprised Jonah—or his driver—hadn't reported as stolen.

"You don't *have* to go back," Bex had said, more than once over the course of the previous day. She'd called in sick and they'd sat out near the creek on the same rock they'd claimed as theirs when they were kids. And Gracelyn had shifted a great weight off of her that she hadn't realized she was carrying. That she'd *been* carrying for more than a decade. "To him or that company or even Texas. You can just quit and go on with your life."

"I don't want to be that person anymore," Gracelyn had replied, with her feet in the almost too cold water and her eyes on the endless, rolling plain she couldn't believe she'd convinced herself was ugly. Empty. It was neither. It was like Jonah—it took a little patience, and little perseverance, maybe. And then it was impossible not to see its beauty everywhere she looked. "You think that when you cut things off, you're setting yourself free. But you're not. You're just running."

"Depends how you do it," Bex had said. She'd become a teacher while Gracelyn was gone, fiercely determined to teach the kids who lived where they did that they didn't have to feel stuck the way Bex and Gracelyn always had. That there was a whole big world out there, just waiting for them. That anything they could imagine, they could do. That living here should be a choice, not a life sentence. That everything should. "Some things need a little judicious pruning, now and then."

"Maybe so," Gracelyn had agreed, knowing Bex was talking

about some of their relatives who still couldn't be helped or reached or saved. But those were choices too, weren't they? "But I'm tired of running away from the things I love. All it ever does is break your heart."

Grandma Betty had seen her off that afternoon. She'd clucked when Gracelyn had gone all teary and pulled her into a hard, long hug the way she had when Gracelyn had woken up with nightmares as a little girl.

"Next time you visit," she'd said, her mouth muffled against the side of Gracelyn's head, where she pressed a kiss, "I'll give you your presents. You can consider that a bribe to return, because it is one."

"Presents?" Gracelyn had echoed. "What presents?"

"It was your birthday and it was Christmas every year, whether you were here or not," Grandma Betty had said in that way of hers, as solid as the great oak tree in the front yard and as seemingly imperturbable. "We saved them for you."

"What if I'd never come back?" she'd whispered. She'd pulled away, stricken. "What if I never . . . ?"

Her grandmother had only smiled. She'd reached out to tuck the hair Gracelyn had left down out of its usual ponytail back behind her ears, the way she'd done almost every single day of Gracelyn's childhood.

"I knew you'd come back, love. I hoped it would be sooner, but I knew."

"I told you I wouldn't," Gracelyn had reminded her, not sure if she'd been explaining or apologizing. Maybe both. "I was so sure."

"You were eighteen and spitting mad," her grandmother had replied. Her face was far more weathered now, creased and thin, but she still looked at Gracelyn with all that fierce, full love. "And I loved you enough to let you go. There's only one way on earth to make sure the person you love returns to you, Gracelyn.

And that's let them come to it on their own, in their own time, if they can."

Maybe that was why she'd come back to Marietta to find Jonah. Though she realized, once she'd avoided the blocked off Main Street and parked the Range Rover, that she didn't expect him to be there. He was probably back in Dallas by now—he'd probably left for Texas moments after she'd commandeered his vehicle—and if he was, that meant he'd already gotten the letter of resignation she'd emailed him from her grandmother's kitchen table yesterday.

It was well and truly over, this thing between them. She told herself she accepted that and this time, she meant it.

But then she pushed open the door to the suite that she knew would be even more packed with ghosts than usual. And saw the lights were all on, as if someone was still staying there. Her stomach flipped over and her heart kicked up a gear as she walked down the little hall, deeper into the suite.

Jonah's laptop was open on the living room table, if dark, as if he'd just walked out. His bedroom door was ajar, which meant she didn't have to invade his privacy—who cared that she'd spent so much time in there earlier this week, things were different now—to see that his luggage was there as well, piled on the luggage rack near the far wall.

Jonah was still here.

For a moment, Gracelyn stood there, frozen into place, while her head spun and her stomach twisted all around itself, because she couldn't decide what that meant. Why would he still be here? Why wouldn't he have left as quickly as he could after that scene with Jasper, with her? Could it mean—

But reality thumped down on her, hard, and she remembered who she was dealing with.

He wasn't who he was by accident. He was Jonah Flint, renowned for his tenacity and his focus. Jonah, who never wavered, which was why he was so successful and so devastating. Jonah, who got exactly what he wanted, eventually, because he never, ever gave up.

She heard the sound of music, as if from a concert when she knew there was no concert hall in Marietta, and the cheering of a crowd to match. And she remembered, then. The big dance in the street, where Jasper no doubt still planned to propose to Chelsea. That had to be where Jonah was, probably planning one last move to call the engagement off before it began.

He'd do fine without her, she was certain—if he'd even noticed she was gone. He was Jonah Flint. He didn't need her.

But he couldn't survive without Jasper.

She'd seen his face at FlintWorks that night. She'd seen how lost he'd been. It had broken her heart even further; ground the shattered pieces down into dust.

Which meant that because she loved him—it was like a fever, she'd told Bex, swift and all-consuming and devastating besides, but that didn't make it any less true—she had to stop him before he ruined his relationship with his brother forever.

She could do that much for him, before she let him go.

And by the time she made it back down to the street, she was running.

Chapter Eight

MAIN STREET WAS like a pageant, out there beneath the stars.

Like a great, joyful parade, except no one was moving. They were swaying to the music. They were laughing, talking, eating. Gracelyn heard scraps of conversation as she wound her way through the clusters of people. A runaway horse at the rodeo earlier. Winners and losers of the different events. Salacious gossip about people Gracelyn didn't know, while the singer currently performing at the far end of the street sang a song about broken hearts and old pick up trucks that seemed to pierce right through her ribs as she walked, like a running cramp.

She couldn't find Jonah anywhere.

The crowd was huge and happy. As the singer flowed from one song into the next they cheered and danced, and Gracelyn had a fierce moment of pure jealousy when she saw a couple near her, their attention focused so fully on each other she thought they must hardly know where they were. As if it didn't matter if everyone else on Main Street saw them. As if everything between them was real.

That cramp between her ribs intensified.

The country singer ended his set and told the crowd he'd be back in five. There was another great cheer, and a surge of movement, as if half the people there decided this was a perfect moment to get another drink, grab something else to eat, or find the restroom. Gracelyn twisted out of the way of the stampede, which gave her a perfect view of the stage.

And the man who strode out onto it with a huge grin stamped over his face.

Jasper.

It was happening.

Gracelyn scanned the crowd in a panic, looking for another darkly blonde, ridiculously beautiful man, but he was nowhere to be seen. Her pulse rocketed through her veins, and she thought the adrenaline might send her leaping straight on to the stage—but of course, that would make it worse. That would make her even more of a Doberman.

And then Jasper started talking.

"A year ago," he said, his rich drawl rolling down the street, making the crowd shift around and gaze up at him, "I managed to get a pretty schoolteacher to dance with me thanks to the power of the microphone up here on this stage. I'm hoping that with a great opening act like Jake Kohl—" the crowd burst into cheers, though it wasn't clear if they were cheering Jasper or the country star—"I can embarrass Chelsea Crawford Collier, better and eternally known as Triple C, just a little bit more this time around."

Someone pushed Chelsea onto the stage. Gracelyn thought she looked radiant and mortified at once—though once Jasper's gaze locked onto hers, she didn't seem to see anything else.

And that was when Gracelyn saw Jonah. He had his back to her, his face to the stage, and Gracelyn didn't wait to see if he'd do something. She threw herself through the last of the crowd that separated them, her heart pounding like a drum.

Up on the stage, Jasper took Chelsea's hand in his. He made some joke or other that Gracelyn hardly heard, but had the crowd tossing suggestions at him, each more ribald than the last.

And as Gracelyn pushed around the last of the people in her path, Jasper sank to one knee, right up there on the stage, in front of the whole of Marietta.

"Chelsea," he said in that voice of his that was so much like Jonah's that it made Gracelyn ache all over, like the Flint brothers were a virus she'd never quite conquer, "I love you. Will you marry me? Make an honest man out of me? Allow me to pollute the historic Crawford family bloodline with my upstart Texan ways—and hopefully, if we're lucky someday, with a baby or two?"

The crowd went wild.

And Gracelyn threw herself forward and grabbed Jonah by the arm, before he did the same.

"You can't do it," she said fiercely over the sounds of the crowd around them. "You have to leave them alone. It doesn't matter if you think this is the worst idea in the history of the world, that he's making a terrible mistake. He's your brother and you love him, and that's what matters, Jonah. That's what you have to protect."

His hands came up and steadied her, holding on to her upper arms, and his gaze was too dark too read.

"None of this is worth anything, if you lose the people you love," she told him, and it took her a moment to realize that she wasn't just breathing heavily, as if she'd run for miles, but that tears were trickling down her face.

"I agree," Jonah gritted out, like he was in pain.

"Yes," Chelsea said into the microphone then, a huge smile in her voice, and Gracelyn bit her lip. "I'll marry you, Jasper. You lunatic."

"See?" Gracelyn said hurriedly, as Jonah only looked at her with that shadowed expression on his face she couldn't read. "It happened. It's done. Now we can just leave them to it, go back home, and pretend it never happened. Can't we?"

"Answer me two questions." He sounded the way he had the day she'd met him, so cold and formidable and out of reach it made her tremble. His hands tightened slightly against her arms. She told herself not to let that mean anything, because it didn't. Of course it didn't. "Why did you quit? And why are you crying?"

And Gracelyn knew that a smart woman wouldn't answer him honestly. A smart woman would think about her survival. She'd protect herself. Insulate herself from any further risk. Or scorn. Any conflict or unpleasantness that remained.

But she'd been doing that for a decade, and what had it gotten her?

She was alone. She'd broken her grandmother's heart and could only hope she had enough time left to make up for it. She'd hurt Bex, and the rest of her family, and for what? To isolate herself way off in Texas? To learn how to put making money above everything else?

Gracelyn liked living with a healthy bank account a whole lot more than she'd liked living without one. But surely, there was balance. Surely, she didn't have to choose between all or nothing, between being ground down by her family or total exile. Surely, there was another way.

But she couldn't imagine she was likely to find it if she kept running. If she kept hiding herself away from the important things. If she didn't face what she felt head on for once. She'd been wrong about so many things in her life. But she'd never figure out how to be right about something if she didn't keep trying. And that started here.

With him.

No matter what he felt about her.

"I can't work for you," she said, before she lost her courage and ran anyway. "And it's for the same reason I'm crying, I guess. I didn't mean to, Jonah. But I accidentally fell in love with you." He blinked, and she pushed on, doggedly. "And I know that's crazy. I know it doesn't make any sense. It's too soon and I hardly know you and you certainly don't want to hear that kind of thing. I know all that. You don't have to say anything. But it's true."

"Why?" She'd never heard his voice so harsh. "I'm the bad brother. Jasper is the obvious choice. He's charming. Friendly. Hilarious, apparently, and—"

"Not you," Gracelyn said simply. She followed an urge that she would have tamped down a few days ago, and moved toward him rather than away. She slid her hands up over his perfect chest, and felt his heart thud against his ribs. Then she kept going, until she was cradling his beautiful, dangerous face between her hands. "I like the dangerous one, Jonah. The shark. The wolf who walks down the center of Main Street, not the one hiding in sheepskin and a lazy smile. I like *you*."

He stared down at her, those hazel eyes so dark, so wild, she thought he must be furious. That he must hate her for saying these things, for putting him in this position mere seconds after the engagement he hadn't wanted had happened.

"I'm sorry," she began, pulling her hands back. "I don't mean—"

His hands slid up to hold hers fast, right there against his face.

"Don't," he said, his voice like gravel. "Don't you dare apologize. You have nothing to apologize for." His hands were warm over hers, and as she gazed up at him she realized that that thing in his eyes wasn't fury at all. "I'm the one who should be apologizing, Gracelyn. To Jasper, to Chelsea, but most of all to you."

She shuddered.

"I *want* you to love me," he told her, his voice as intent as the way he looked at her. "I want you to teach me how to love you back, the right way, because the jury is in, ddarlin', and I'm no good at it." She shook her head, frowning up at him, and he turned his head to press his mouth into her palm. "The only person I ever loved was my brother and I almost alienated him for good. I can promise I'll probably mess things up with you, too. You can count on it. And I get the impression you hold grudges the way I do."

"I did," she whispered, "but I'm starting a new chapter. I left the only people I ever loved ten years ago and vowed I'd never go back and when I did, Jonah, they treated me like they loved me just the same. Like they'd never loved me more." She felt the tears like trails of fire along her cheeks, and she didn't care. "So I'll be working from that model, going forward. If it helps."

"I'm not good with words," he told her then, as the music started and the night pressed close. But he was closer, and he was what mattered. "But I want to do this over from the start. I don't want you to work for me. I want you to *be* with me. I want a thousand things it's way too soon for."

"Much too soon," she agreed, but she shifted closer as she said it.

"Date me," he said, and his mouth crooked up into that smile of his that made her crazy. It made her believe anything was possible. It made her see it right there on his face. "Be my real girlfriend this time."

"That's the thing," she whispered against his mouth. "I think it's been real with you from the start. Like this really was magic, even then."

"That's you, Gracelyn." He moved his hands to push back her hair, and his dark gold eyes were soft on her face. "That's always been you."

And for the first time in her life, looking up at a man so

beautiful she thought he rivaled the Rocky Mountains all around them, she believed it.

"Once upon a time," Jonah said then, holding her so tight it should have hurt, it should have felt claustrophobic—but instead it felt like the Montana sky, so big and so vast that no matter how small she was beneath it, she felt cherished. Beloved. *His.* "There was a beautiful princess and a terrible ogre trapped in a hotel suite far, far away. And he had absolutely no intention of letting her go, ever again."

"She's not going anywhere," Gracelyn told him fiercely.

And like all good fairy tale endings, she sealed it with a kiss.

Chapter Nine

THE FOUR OF them met at Jasper's place north of Flathead Lake for New Year's that year.

Chelsea and Jasper drove up from Marietta and whatever family thing they did there for Christmas. Jonah didn't inquire too closely, as he didn't want to know if he involved those half-sisters he was still on the fence about, and Jasper, to his credit, didn't push. Jonah and Gracelyn took his helicopter from the prairie, where her grandmother had stuffed him so full of her cooking, he thought he might lapse into hibernation for the rest of the winter.

"You really do only come here by helicopter," Gracelyn teased him.

He smiled. He did a lot more of that these days.

"I like helicopters," he told her.

He liked her more. He liked that she'd gotten herself a brand new job at a completely different sort of company, and at a much higher level, too. He liked that she refused to move in with him because, she said, he'd only asked her to do it for his convenience, not because it was the right thing for them.

And he liked that she was right about that, too.

The more he got to know her, Gracelyn Baylee Packard of the country-fried name, who still wouldn't let him call her *baby,* the more he confirmed what he'd known from the start. She was his. She was meant to be his.

So they could take all the time in the world to get where they were going. He still knew how it was going to end.

The night before New Year's, they sat in Jonah's cozy den near the great, roaring fire while the snow came down outside.

Life didn't get better than this, Jonah thought. His brother and his brother's fiancée, his woman. And what he was fairly certain was joy, as present in the room as if it was another person there with them.

"I have something for you," Chelsea said to Gracelyn, and pulled out a small parcel.

"I thought we weren't exchanging gifts . . ."

Gracelyn looked at him, worried. He knew things had been polite between the two women, if not necessarily warm. *How could they be anything else?* Gracelyn had asked reasonably only the night before. *It doesn't matter why I was horrible to her. I was, and I have to accept the consequences, whatever they are.*

But she probably hadn't expected consequences the next day. And Jasper only shrugged when Jonah caught his eye, giving nothing away.

Gracelyn pulled off the wrapping paper carefully, then blinked down at the box in her hands. "Is it a bomb?"

"Of course not," Chelsea said serenely from Jasper's side. "I'm sitting much too close to you."

Gracelyn's grin flashed briefly. "Noted."

She opened the box and laughed, then pulled out an ornament. A little bit gaudy, Jonah thought, but that was probably the point.

"For your first Christmas together," Chelsea said sweetly. "To remember our first meeting forever."

Gracelyn held it in the air, letting it hang there and dance from her fingers in the firelight, the way her eyes did when he met them. And Jonah knew everything was going to work out exactly the way it should. That he and Gracelyn were forgiven, which he knew they'd both do their best to make sure they deserved.

Because Chelsea had given them their very own, miniaturized, ceramic rendition of a Doberman.

THE END

ABOUT THE AUTHORS

Rachael Johns is an English teacher by trade, a mum 24/7, a supermarket owner, a chronic arachnophobe, and a writer the rest of the time. She rarely sleeps and never irons. She writes contemporary romance and lives in rural Western Australia with her hyperactive husband, three mostly-gorgeous heroes-in-training, two fat cats, a cantankerous bird and a very naughty dog.

For more from Rachael, visit www.rachaeljohns.com.

When not writing **Alissa Callen** plays traffic controller to four children, three dogs, two horses and one renegade cow who really does believe the grass is greener on the other side of the fence. After a childhood spent chasing sheep on the family farm, she has always been drawn to remote areas and small towns, even when residing overseas. Once a teacher and a counsellor, she remains interested in the life journeys people take. Her books are characteristically heart-warming, emotional and character driven. She currently lives on a small slice of rural Australia.

For more from Alissa, visit www.alissacallen.com.

Melissa McClone has published over twenty-five novels with Harlequin and been nominated for Romance Writers of America's RITA award. She lives in the Pacific Northwest with her husband, three school-aged children, two spoiled Norwegian Elkhounds and cats who think they rule the house.

For more from Melissa, visit www.melissamcclone.com.

USA Today bestselling author **Megan Crane** writes women's fiction, chick lit, work-for-hire YA, and a lot of Harlequin Presents as Caitlin Crews. She also teaches creative writing classes both online at mediabistro.com and at UCLA Extension's prestigious Writers' Program, where she finally utilizes the MA and PhD in English Literature she received from the University of York in York, England. She currently lives in California, with her animator/comic-book artist husband and their menagerie of ridiculous animals.

For more from Megan, visit www.megancrane.com or www.caitlincrews.com.

Thank you for reading

REMEMBER ME, COWBOY!

If you enjoyed this book, you can find more from all our great
authors at TulePublishing.com,
or from your favorite online retailer.

TULE
PUBLISHING

37572780R00311

Made in the USA
Charleston, SC
13 January 2015

37572780R00311

Made in the USA
Charleston, SC
13 January 2015